Praise for *The*

Named as one of the Best Holiday Romances of 2021
Entertainment Weekly

WINNER for OUTSTANDING HOLIDAY FICTION
2022 The Independent Authors Network

WINNER for BEST ROMANCE
2022 Indie Reader Discovery Awards

"In this sweet modern romance, Middleton ably portrays the beauty of festive London, but she also depicts the heartbreaking pain of the grieving process...a charming story for music lovers and Anglophiles." — *Kirkus Reviews (Starred Review)*

"Heartrending and heartwarming, [*The Certainty of Chance*] is an undeniably endearing romance, perfect to read over the holidays."
 — *The BlueInk Review (Starred Review)*

"Destiny intervenes to stir up romance in this appealing and sensitive holiday affair...Middleton crafts [Madeleine and Julian's] relationship into a mutually supportive, sweet connection. Great for fans of Helen Hoang's *The Heart Principle*."
 — *Publishers Weekly's Booklife*

"Packed with charming details, *The Certainty of Chance* brings the gift of London at Christmas to readers. An absolute delight!"
 — *Melonie Johnson, author of Too Good to Be Real*

"The perfect, heartfelt holiday romance!"
 — *Kelly Siskind, author of New Orleans Rush*

"Is there anything better than London at Christmas time? Glittering, hopeful, and touching, this is the perfect holiday read, especially for those who dream of a Christmas with tea and scones."
 — *Teri Wilson, author of Once Upon a Royal Summer*

Praise for *Say Hello, Kiss Goodbye*

"This sultry, yet sweetly heartfelt romance is a winner. Leia and Tarquin's chemistry sizzles…the playful and racy banter is delightful. Great for fans of Candace Bushnell and Alexa Martin."
— *Publishers Weekly's Booklife (Editor's Pick)*

"As steamy as it is heartwarming…the two main characters are undeniably endearing. Romance fans will be grateful they picked up this novel." — *The BlueInk Review (Starred Review)*

"*Say Hello, Kiss Goodbye* offers well-drawn, multilayered characters and stand-out sex positive romance." — *Kirkus Reviews*

Praise for *Until the Last Star Fades*

WINNER for ROMANCE
2019 The Independent Author Network

WINNER – BEST CANADIAN AUTHOR
2019 Northern Hearts Awards, Toronto Romance Writers

"A delightful contemporary romance [with] a good mix of poignancy and sexy fun." — *Kirkus Reviews*

"Hot new material with Hollywood appeal."
— *The Hollywood Reporter*

"*Until the Last Star Fades* is an incredibly moving story of love, relationships, and celebrating the time you have with the important people in your life…Read this novel and your heart will thank you."
— *Hypable*

A Smile in a Whisper

Jacquelyn Middleton lives in Toronto with her
British husband and Japanese Spitz.

She's an award-winning author and journalist who loves nothing
better than researching her Orkney roots, cheering on her beloved
Maple Leafs, and singing (badly) in the car.

A Smile in a Whisper is her sixth novel.

Follow Jacquelyn:
Instagram @JaxMiddleton_Author
Facebook @JacquelynMiddletonAuthor
Twitter @JaxMiddleton,
or visit her webpage at www.JacquelynMiddleton.com

A Smile in a Whisper

A NOVEL

JACQUELYN MIDDLETON

KIRKWALL BOOKS

KIRKWALL BOOKS

USA – CANADA - UK

A Smile in a Whisper

ISBN: 978-1-9992753-4-1
Copyright © 2023 Jacquelyn Middleton
First Paperback Edition, August 2023

Cover design: ThinkTank
Loving Couple photography: Phil Chester
Orkney photography: Kendra Towns
Editing by C. Marie

This book is dedicated to all the beautiful souls
dealing with invisible illnesses
who often hear "You don't look sick"
from a society in dire need of manners and empathy.
I see you. I am you.

And to my amazing sister Heather.
Orkney is in our blood and in our hearts. Forever.
Love you always. X

DEAR READERS,

Welcome to *A Smile in a Whisper*. Evie and Nikolai's story is a standalone romance; however it takes place in the same 'world' as my previous novels. Evie appeared (very briefly) in *London, Can You Wait?* and *Say Hello, Kiss Goodbye*. Nick appeared in *Until the Last Star Fades* and *Say Hello, Kiss Goodbye*. Within these pages, you'll find laugh-out-loud moments and sexy stuff, but this book, like my others, is not a rom-com.

This story unfolds on the Orkney Islands, an archipelago of seventy islands off the northern coast of Scotland. The largest, most populated island is called the Mainland, so when you see the Mainland mentioned in *A Smile in a Whisper*, it's referring to Orkney, not the Scottish mainland where Edinburgh, Aberdeen, and Inverness are located. FYI, the archipelago is called Orkney or the Orkney Islands, but <u>never</u> the Orkneys.

Evie in *A Smile in a Whisper* lives with Crohn's disease, a chronic inflammatory bowel disease (IBD). There is currently no cure. The root cause is unknown; however, it's diagnosed when the immune system attacks healthy tissues in the gastrointestinal (GI) tract. The Crohn's disease rollercoaster is a ride I know well—several people close to me, including my husband, live with it. Sometimes it flares horribly, while other times it's under control and barely noticeable.

It's important to note—all cases of Crohn's are different. Physical symptoms, food intolerances, and medical treatments deviate from case to case (as does how the patient copes); therefore, the Crohn's depiction in *A Smile in a Whisper* is one example and is not indicative of what others may experience. If you have questions about Crohn's disease, please consult with your doctor or medical practitioner for up-to-date information and advice.

I realize some readers get pulled out of a story if they don't know how to pronounce a character's name, so for reference, Nikolai sounds like 'Nick-oh-lie', Nico is pronounced 'Nee-co', Evie is 'Evee', and Sunita is 'Sun-ee-ta'.

Content note: this novel contains coarse language, open- and closed-door sex scenes, Crohn's disease/chronic illness, panic attacks, hospital scenes, underage drinking, drug use, infidelity (parental backstory), and divorce (backstory). Some scenes may also contain Orcadian words, so there's a glossary at the back of the book to explain terms that might not be familiar to all readers.

Love music? You can find the playlist for *A Smile in a Whisper* (and playlists for ALL my books) under 'Extras' at www.JacquelynMiddleton.com.

MAP OF THE ORKNEY ISLANDS

ONE

"Make a wish and wish we are together
For always and forever endlessly."
'Smile When We Whisper', Torquil Campbell

EVIE

Then, Thursday, May 26, eighteen years ago

Evie Sutherland had never seen a squirrel, a train, or a McDonald's. Not that she minded. Island life in Orkney with its unlocked front doors and mysterious standing stones was safe yet otherworldly, an unsupervised playground of seashell-strewn beaches, patchwork farmer's fields, and archeological wonders. The tight-knit archipelago offered an unhurried childhood where Evie grew up content, never missing what she didn't have.

Until last night.

I need to talk to Sun! Adolescent angst gnawed deep in Evie's chest as white-capped waves surged across the Bay of Skaill. Her impatient gaze leapt past classmates, past the tour guide, and along Skara Brae's elevated footpath where her bestie, mouth agape and dark hair dancing in the wind, stared off into the treeless horizon. Obviously, thirteen-year-old Sunita Kumari wasn't smitten by the trials and tribulations of Neolithic life either.

"The stone houses of Skara Brae are older than Stonehenge, older than Egypt's pyramids!" The lanky tour guide multitasked, serving up fascinating facts while leaning defensively into another ferocious gust off the bay. "But the people who lived here were just like us! They wore jewelry, used dishes." He clawed at his patchy beard, his brittle fingernails bitten to the quick. "They even kept

1

keepsakes in their dressers! Pretty *cool*, right?"

Seizing the straps of her backpack, Evie braced herself against the cheek-numbing gale as several classmates gave in to molar-flashing yawns. Others glowered. Plenty of sneering side-eye was shared.

Their teacher stepped in, rallying her troops. "We have *amazing* bragging rights! Did you know this is one of Europe's oldest prehistoric villages?"

Know? You won't let us forget! With a furious sweep of her home-cut bangs, Evie glanced at her Swatch, a colorful 1980s hand-me-down from her mother, and bowled into Sunita, breaking her friend's daydream. "Suuun," she grumbled, ignoring the guide's nasal ramblings about the Neolithic box-beds on display below her glittery sneakers. "I neeed—"

"I know!" Sunita moaned through a mouthful of metal as their teacher indulged the guide with a banal question about Stone Age pillows. "She's seriously out of control. Honestly, who gives a surprise quiz on the bus? I swear, if she steals our break—"

"I'll bloody die." Evie finished Sunita's sentence as a chorus of teen rebelliousness flared around them.

"This place is *so* stupid," snarled a chubby blonde girl, the daughter of the local butcher. Her defiant fists stretched the pockets of her Kirkwall Grammar School hoodie. "I HATE living here."

Sunita nodded. "When I leave for uni, I'm *never* coming back."

A red-headed boy, cheeks sprinkled with freckles, sucked in a mouthful of air. "Where's the toilet? Like, not a shitty ancient one—a REAL one." Desperate, his eyes bulged.

Luckily, he knew Evie. Over the past eight months, she'd memorized the whereabouts of (almost) every public washroom around the Mainland, a habit more born out of necessity than nerdiness. "In there," she said, gesturing away from Skara Brae's excavated houses. "The visitor center—"

"CLASS! Shhh!" warned the teacher over her shoulder. A hush swept the students as the boy dashed off. "And where are *you* off to?" she demanded.

With the teacher distracted, the class resumed their brazen chatting. The girl in the hoodie elbowed a yawning friend. "So—did you watch?"

Evie leaned further into Sunita. "Did *you*?"

"Ohmygawd, *YES*!" She squealed behind a veil of hair whipping wildly in the wind.

A dirty laugh loud enough to rattle a barn vaulted from Evie's throat. Heads turned, both student and adult.

"CLASS!" the teacher barked. "How many times! BE QUIET!"

Evie and her friends flinched. "Sorry, Miss!" they mumbled in chastised unison before slipping into silence, their uncomfortable pause filled with the shrill cries of Arctic terns dive-bombing the churning surf.

"I don't know what's got into you today." The teacher checked her watch. "You've got fifteen minutes before we head back. Make it count. This *will* be on the exam." With a glare, she stormed off, apologizing profusely to the guide as they neared the visitor center.

Sunita steered Evie away for a private chat. "Who cares about this crap! Jake and Amanda actually did *it*!"

"I know!" Evie gasped, replaying the previous evening's episode of *Dalston Grove* in her head. The television drama about a rough school in northeast London featured an ensemble of teenage actors and gritty storylines and had quickly become the talk of schoolyards around the country. But it was 'Jake', sixteen-year-old actor Nikolai Balfour, who stole hearts and adorned bedroom walls from the Isle of Wight to Shetland.

For two years, Evie had been doodling amorous vignettes in her study notes: Nikolai picking her up in his car for a picnic, writing her a song on his guitar, snogging her face off in front of a crackling bonfire. However, kissing was as far as her swoony reveries ventured. While the idea of "doing it" with Nikolai—with any boy—was titillating, it was also terrifying, until Jake and Amanda's tender tryst heated up her television screen. Nikolai, the cute and dreamy pin-up you could bring home for your mum's Sunday roast, was now the smouldering, thrusting sex god responsible for setting

Evie's mind and panties ablaze with all manner of lascivious possibilities.

There was no going back.

"I can't stop thinking about him naked!" Evie squeezed her best friend's arm. "Whatcha reckon? Has he done it, like, for real?"

"Of course he has," replied Sunita. "It looked real."

"How would *you* know?" A soft lilt butted in.

Letting go of Sunita, Evie spun around. Fiona Groundwater, a student from the island of Eday, blinked back. Like most teens from Orkney's smaller islands, Fiona came to the Mainland for secondary school and lived in the halls of residence during the week. Then on Friday afternoons, she'd take the ferry back to her family on Eday, returning to residence on Sunday night. Eleven months into her time at Kirkwall Grammar and shy Fiona was still finding her feet. Her busy schedule of schoolwork, fiddle practice, and ferry sailings home didn't leave much time for socializing with her Mainland friends. She had, however, forged a bond with Evie through their shared appreciation of dogs, scrapbooking, and of course, *Dalston Grove*.

"And how would *you* know?" Sunita retorted. Her eyes flew down the footpath, ensuring their teacher was out of earshot. "You've done it?"

Fiona tugged a hair tie around her messy brown locks. "No, but you can't say it looked real when it didn't show...*you know*." Her elfin facial features widened. "It was just kissing."

"And hands. Lots of hands," said Evie, her cheeks warming despite the brisk wind. "I swear he grabbed her boob." The thought of Nikolai touching her non-existent breasts made Evie reel with dizziness.

"Alaia said it looked real," said Sunita, the only member of Evie's inner circle with a female sibling considerably older and wiser at the ripe ol' age of seventeen. "Their faces, you know? *That* was real. Nikolai knows *exactly* what to do."

"I wish I could've seen it at yours." For Evie, it was one thing crushing hard on Nikolai Balfour and turning her bedroom into a pin-up-plastered shrine, but quite another drooling over his fictional teenage sexploits in front of her entire family.

Sunita winced. "Your mum and dad still watching with you?"

"Yep. Sam, too."

"Eww. I'm *so* glad I don't have an older brother," said Sunita. "Talk about embarrassing."

Evie recoiled. "They went on about pregnancy and safe sex for, like, an *hour* afterward!" She lowered her voice as she shrugged off her backpack, her tiny roller skate and orca bag charms swinging wildly. "I'm not a kid! I know where babies come from."

Fiona's upturned nose scrunched as she plowed into her school bag. "My parents still refuse to have The Talk. It's so dumb. We live on a *farm* for god's sake!"

Evie and Sunita eyed each other and broke into giggles.

"Although, my cousin did get pregnant at fourteen." Fiona pulled out a rolled-up magazine. "She got shipped off to Inverness and everything."

Evie's jaw dropped. "Her parents sent her away? Like, forever?"

Either Fiona didn't hear the question or chose not to answer. "Have you seen this?" She uncurled the glossy pages.

TEMPT HIM! LOOK HOT NOW! GOSSIP EVERY MONTH — the magazine's cover lines orbited around the cheesy grin of the bleached blonde presenter from *Top of the Pops*.

The July issue of Flirty Girl*?* Evie's stomach flipped, remembering the bright, bold advertisement in the back of the previous issue: a special *Dalston Grove* pin-up "Not To Be Missed Next Month". It *had* to be a poster of Nikolai. The magazine's editors weren't stupid. Nikolai's full lips, high cheekbones, and furrowed brow guaranteed that tens of thousands of British teens would happily part with £2 to take Jake home with them—Evie included. She chewed the inside of her cheek. "Where'd you get that?"

"Stromness," said Fiona as the wind rifled through the pages, making them flip and crackle. "Mum and Dad came in, took me there for dinner. We popped into the newsagent for sweets after and there it was! Had to get it."

Sunita threw a concerned glance Evie's way. Every four weeks, the shop in the neighboring town of Stromness received a single copy—a copy that for the past two years was put aside for Evie then picked up by her dad when he drove home from his dental practice. Someone had messed up. Terribly.

Fiona flung open the center pages. "Look!" A crumpled mini poster of Nikolai smiled back.

Nooo! A lovesick pang wrenched Evie's heart. Adorable dimples teasing, Nikolai rocked his *Dalston Grove* uniform like Paris couture. His school tie was casually loosened and the sleeves of his white button-down were rolled up, showing off a serpent tattoo winding its way around his left forearm. With one hand, he nudged his thick brown hair from his sparkling eyes while the other, punctured by a staple, clutched the neck of his acoustic guitar. He really was the most beautiful boy Evie had ever seen.

She settled into a pouty sigh. "So gorgeous."

"Especially when he sings for Amanda," added Fiona.

"Awwwww," the two girls cooed.

Sunita laughed and shook her head. "You guys…"

"What?" Fiona looked up from the poster. "You *still* don't fancy him? Not even after last night?"

"Nope," replied Sunita. "Too pretty for me."

As she admired Fiona's prize, envy bubbled in Evie's chest. She pictured the empty space on her bedroom wall, cleared especially for this long-awaited "exclusive" portrait, the centerpiece of her extensive Nikolai collection. But now Fiona would be the one falling asleep with dreamy Nikolai watching over her, while Evie would be taunted by an eyeful of faded flowery wallpaper. The whole thing sucked.

"Well, I think he's perfect." Fiona hugged the poster against her burgeoning chest. "He's single, hot, talented—what more could you want?"

Nick all to myself! Evie gazed off into the endless horizon. *We'd feed squirrels in one of London's big parks, ride the Tube, go to a McDonald's—share a Big Mac! Then go back to his and kiss and have some sex.* She swallowed hard, forcing a friendly smile. "No one comes close, 'specially round here."

Fiona fussed with the glossy pages. "Well, *someone* does, obviously…"

No! Not Fi too! Evie prickled. Eight of her classmates, including Sunita, had boyfriends of the kissing-behind-the-school, gropey-hands-under-shirts variety, but with no prospects of her own, Evie's hopes of becoming one of the cool, mature girls were drifting out to sea along with the lapwings and their sweet "peee-ooo-weeep" birdsong.

"Seriously? *You've* got a boyfriend?" A skeptical tone tinged Sunita's query, but that was Sun, always wary, always questioning, a budding journalist if there ever was one.

Fiona giggled. "You kidding? My parents would kill me."

Evie squinted back. "So, what are you on about, then?"

"Oh?!" Fiona's stare oscillated between Sunita and Evie. "You really don't know?" The wind walloped again and snagged the magazine's centerfold, tearing the poster free from one of the staples. "Shoot!" Fiona grasped the picture, creasing Nikolai's arms and chest in the process.

She's ruining it. Evie gawped at the crinkled photo. "Know what?"

"His dad's mum lives here in Orkney."

Evie's pulse rocketed. "What? You mean the rumors are—"

"Ridiculous!" Sunita's scoff stepped on her best friend's bliss. "Those stories have been circulating for ages."

"'Cause they're *true!*" Fiona gripped the magazine tighter. "The Balfours have this *huge* house and a farm and loads of land. Their ancestors were lairds. Who do you think Balfour Castle is named after?"

"Wow." Evie knew of the castle and the village of Balfour on Shapinsay, the neighboring island, but had never visited. Until now, she had thought the Balfour name, which also branded Kirkwall's hospital, was nothing more than an amusing coincidence. And it wasn't like Nikolai spoke with a Scottish or an Orcadian accent.

"They don't own the castle anymore, though," said Fiona. "Their farm's in Stenness."

Evie froze. "His grandma lives here on the Mainland?!"

"Yep. We saw his mum in Stromness once," boasted Fiona.

Brows soaring behind her bangs, Evie skipped closer, the desire for more info—now!—catapulting her heart into her throat. "The queen from *Equinox Ten*?! Sam would die!" Her brother was a huge fan of Kiki Balfour's 1990s sci-fi series and owned all the DVDs, but Evie only paid attention when five-year-old Nikolai's character wandered on screen. "What was she like?"

Sunita gave Fiona a head-to-toe once-over. "For someone from Eday, you sure visit Stromness a lot."

"We went during the holidays, brought our collies and everything." Fiona turned to Evie. "We saw Mrs. Balfour on Alfred Street. Dad got her autograph."

"Holy crap! Was Nikolai with her? Did you talk to him?" The questions flew from Evie's tongue. "Was he tall?"

"He wasn't with her," said Fiona. "But she did say her boys visit their grandma quite ofte—"

"Oh MY GOD!" Evie squealed. "When?! We should *look* for them!" In a parish of one hundred and fifty people, it wouldn't prove too difficult.

Sunita's nose twitched like she'd caught a whiff of sour milk while Fiona brightened, all eager and inspired. "Yeah, definitely! We could—"

A sudden, searing gale roared in from the bay, twisting Fiona's face into a clenched wince. Evie closed her eyes and hugged her backpack. Sunita shielded her face with her arm as the curses and playful squeals of classmates peppered the brisk air.

"Shiiit!" Fiona cried.

Evie's eyes popped open. Fiona leapt off the ground, her arms stretched, reaching overhead as the precious poster cartwheeled in the wind, eluding her splayed fingers. Nikolai's face, contorting with comical contempt, rose higher and higher, flirting with the salty spray from the bay.

"Noooooo!" Dropping her cumbersome school bag, Fiona scrambled after the airborne pin-up. "Please! Somebody help!"

Envy wouldn't hold Evie back. THUMP! Her backpack hit the footpath. "I'm coming!" She swerved around several befuddled tourists and past her Kirkwall Grammar classmates, their mouths gummed up with chewy cola cubes as she clambered over the wire fence.

Sunita hung back. "Good luck!" She snickered, retrieving the discarded magazine and Evie's belongings.

"Arghh! Why don't we have trees?!" Fiona bellowed as Evie caught up, sprinting through the waving fields of grass leading to Skaill House, the haunted 17th-century manor overlooking Skara Brae.

"It's the salty winds," answered Evie, her words labored and a stitch pinching her side. "Trees struggle to survive here—"

"I *know* that!" Fiona blurted, hobbling over a rabbit hole. "I'm just saying, maybe their branches…" She wheezed. "…would catch him."

The poster frolicked and dipped, kissing the bristly brush.

"Grab him!" Fiona lunged, but another blustery surge snatched Nikolai, lifting him up, up, and away. Fighting for breath, she stumbled to a stop. "Ahh, it's no use." She prised an inhaler from her coat pocket.

Evie continued on, arms and legs pumping despite her exhaustion. Glancing over her shoulder, she sputtered quizzically. "Fi! *C'mon*—"

"No, Evie!" Fiona shook her canister of asthma medicine. "Forget it. Let him go. It's not meant to be."

Two

EVIE

Now, Wednesday, June 21

With a decision made, all Evie had to do was stick with it.

Skirting the short midday shadows thrown by the imposing red sandstone of St. Magnus Cathedral, she let out a determined huff and swept her long hair out of her face, a losing battle Evie knew well. The island gales didn't care about her fresh blowout. They didn't care about the bagpipers wearing kilts or the homemade crowns they stole from the heads of the town's schoolchildren. Blustery weather and the Orkney Islands were like tea and biscuits—a double act for better, for worse—and nothing, not the spritzy rain nor the rolling clouds would halt the annual June magic that was the St. Magnus Festival parade.

Great turnout so far. Evie unscrewed the cap on her water bottle, tossing back a quick gulp.

"Aw, there they are! My little bairns!" The chatty woman by her side beamed, her kind eyes crinkling with great-grandmotherly pride. "What about you, sweetie? Seen Fiona's eldest yet?"

"Ava should be along soon. Her class is in charge of flags this year." Evie searched the rabble of giggling children for her beloved goddaughter. "Can you believe it? She's nine now! Had her birthday two weeks ago."

"Such a cutie, and she worships *you*!" The woman, a regular in Marwick's, Evie's mother's café and shop across the road, rested a wrinkled hand on the arm of her raincoat. "Ahh, must make you feel broody, eh, love?"

Different day, same question. Evie adopted a polite grin and left the messy conga line of children behind. "I love Peedie, but bairns of my own?" She shook her head. "I don't think so." That would put an end to the prying questions, surely. Raising her water again, Evie downed a long, generous sip.

"A good man will change that!" The granny pulled out her phone. "I'll text you my son's number."

Evie sputtered. Never mind the baby question, this was worse— much worse. Fifty-plus, recently divorced from his second wife, and father to twins Evie babysat once upon a time, she knew this "good man" had a proclivity for shower dodging and a taste for road rage.

Wiping her mouth, Evie fought through her fluster. "Oh! That's"—she fastened the lid on her water as the phone in her jacket pocket vibrated against her thigh—"*really* sweet of you, but I—"

"Auntie Evieeeeeee!"

Rescued by Ava's bubbly salutation and her gap-toothed smile, Evie lit up and waved fervently. "Peedie, look at YOU!"

"Like my flag?" Ava hollered, poking the air with her wind-whipped pink and silver triangle, her red ringlets bouncing with each jubilant step. "I used *all* the glitter!"

"It's perfect!" Setting her water bottle on the ground, Evie grabbed her phone, ignored the elderly lady's text, and fired off a burst of photos for Fiona, who was at home nursing Ava's three-and-a-half-year-old sister Poppy through a nasty bout of chicken-pox. "Your mum's gonna be so proud!"

Ava skipped triumphantly and bobbed into her best friend, who nudged her back with a playful hip bump.

Just like Sun and me at that age. Evie's heart felt full. Toes tapping along to the stirring drone of the bagpipes, her eyes skated over Marwick's then far down Broad Street where she spotted him.

Square jaw, rakish brown hair, shoulders broad and muscular. And his height—yeah, Evie liked them tall.

"Ogling your dream man?" A familiar voice wafted from behind, stealing Evie's attention away from the twelve-foot-tall Viking puppet trundling along the parade route in the distance. "Handsome, emotionally stunted, a bit of a showoff?"

"Sunita!" Evie threw her arms around her oldest friend. Living in London and covering breaking entertainment news as a showbiz reporter for *The National Mail,* one of the UK's biggest selling newspapers, Sunita only made it home a few times a year. "I thought you were flying in tomorrow."

"And miss this spectacle? Never!" Grinning, Sunita withdrew from their hug. "The paper can do without me for an extra day."

Evie eyed her best friend's diamond-quilted Burberry barn jacket. "London's loss is Orkney's gain."

"This weather, though, blowin' a hoolie. Some things never change." Adjusting the designer purse on her shoulder, Sunita narrowed her eyes, scrutinizing the Orcadians parading past. "So, where's Ava and her glittery flag?"

"You just missed her."

"Damn!" Sunita tsked. "I brought her the biggest stick of grape-flavored rock I could find. Drove all over Brighton searching for it."

"Fi's gonna kill you."

"If Ava gets a cavity, your dad'll fix it." Sunita watched the children flubbing their choreography and snickered. "God, remember doing this? We were so rubbish."

Evie laughed. "The worst!"

"Best part was gorging ourselves on fudge afterward, then staying up all night with a—"

"Sickly tum!" Evie blurted as Sunita finished with "—massive sugar rush."

"Beneath the sun that never sets," Evie added. "So beautiful."

"Man, I miss the summer solstice. It's not the same down south," said Sunita. "Speaking of, you game for a late-nighter? Drinks and dinner, lots of goss?"

"Sure, if you don't mind waiting," said Evie. "We're open till nine and I'm closing."

"Why you? Where's your mum?"

"On a Hawaiian cruise to Australia."

"Get out! They actually went?" asked Sunita.

"Yep, last minute. Mum dragged her heels as per usual."

"That shop is like her third child."

"And just as problematic." Evie gave in to a big yawn. "Dad convinced her in the end, thank god. You only celebrate your thirty-fifth wedding anniversary once, right?"

"You must be rushed off your feet, though," said Sunita, "running the shop, dealing with genealogy clients."

"This is my first proper break in days." Evie returned her phone to her pocket. "I should get back soon, actually."

"Invasion of the cruise ships?"

Evie nodded. "And catering clients."

"How's that going?"

Relieved the misty rain had stopped, Evie pulled her gaze free from the swath of color and festive music. "Surprisingly well. In the past month, we've done two weddings, a funeral, and the renewable energy conference, and starting tomorrow, the catering truck's headed to Shapinsay for a TV shoot."

"Another travel show?"

"No, a historical romance—a series."

Sunita leaned in. "Ooh, Eves! That's *so* you! Can you tag along?"

She smiled wistfully, picturing the old receipts and torn-out pages from magazines on her bedside table, bursting with messy ideas and scribbled dialogue for her own historical romance. "Can't. I'll be in the shop."

"Ah, that sucks. No ogling hot actors for you, then."

"There aren't any. I checked."

"Of course you did!" said Sunita. "How long they here for?"

"Two months. They've filmed most of it down in London already."

"This is huge! Your mum's really going for it."

"She doesn't have much choice," said Evie. "The shop's roof is falling apart, and we don't have enough savings to replace it. One bad storm and the whole building could flood."

"Jesus, that bad?"

"Yeah, but hopefully this TV thing will answer our financial prayers. The broadcaster wants hot meals, vegan dishes, and a fully stocked craft table and is paying a shitload to get it. We *cannot* mess up."

"So who's cooking while your mum's away?" asked Sunita.

"Gemma Hourston."

"How'd you pry her away from The Odin? She's practically part of the furniture there."

"Her marriage collapsed."

Sunita's head drew back. "Noo! She's been married for, what? Twenty-five years?"

"Twenty-seven, but it's more like thirty-one if you count how long they've worked together in the hotel's kitchen."

"Poor Gemma. Thank god your mum's looking out for her…"

Evie nodded.

"…plus, you know…sparing the clients from your cooking."

She playfully smacked her friend's arm. "Sunita!"

"*Well!* My tastebuds are still scarred from your cough drop chicken disaster."

"So I went a little overboard with the lemon honey glaze." Evie shrugged. "Live and learn."

Sunita laughed. "For his sake, I hope Brodie's a good cook."

Glancing away, Evie followed a trio of boys carrying model boats. "Shame I'll never find out."

"What? *Why?* I thought your first date went well?"

"The second didn't. I was home in bed—alone—after one glass of wine."

"What the hell happened?"

"The usual," said Evie.

Sunita blinked in disbelief. "But *how*? He moved here two weeks ago. How'd he—"

"A co-worker."

"These bloody islands," Sunita growled.

"The oil terminal crew couldn't wait to tell Brodie what he was in for, dating me."

"The bastards!"

Evie waved her off. "It's okay. At least he had the balls to tell me. Better to know now than down the road, right?"

"Well, he's a dick." Sunita sneered into a scowl. "The problem isn't you, it's him—it's all of them."

"What can I say? Guys want spontaneity and hassle-free fun, not a burden."

"Stop it!" Sunita leaned in, gripping her friend's hand. "Listen to me, you are *not* a burden!"

If only Evie believed that. Her history of going out with guys who couldn't handle her Crohn's disease dated back to her first and only love, a boy from London who spent his summers on her island. Time and time again when she'd open up to someone new about her condition, the glimmer of attraction in their eyes would dim. "No one wants to date the sick girl."

"You're not sick all the time," Sunita reasoned. "Just occasionally."

"Doesn't matter. *Occasionally* is still a massive deal-breaker."

"Well, they're missing out, 'cause what's more spontaneous than a Crohn's flare?" Sunita rubbed Evie's shoulder.

She laughed. "I'm so glad you're back, even if it's just a flying visit." Evie side-hugged her friend and let go. "Perfect timing, too." Exhaling heavily, her grin muted. "I've made a decision."

"Holy shit! You're actually doing it?! You're growing out your fringe!"

Evie's jaw dropped in mock horror. "No!" She smoothed down her bangs, but the unrelenting wind just tousled them again. She budged closer to Sunita, hoping the granny with the troubled fifty-something son wasn't listening in. "I'm gonna say yes to Caleb."

Her no-nonsense mention of an old school acquaintance made Sunita's eyes bulge. "Wait, what did I miss? Is this one of those 'if we're not married in our thirties, we'll marry each other' situs? You know, I've always thought he had a thing for you."

"Hardly! It's just dinner tomorrow. A pub date, no wedding dress required."

"So we're recycling old boyfriends now?"

"He's not an old boyfriend, you know that," said Evie.

"You snogged him, though."

"Once. Like in 2009."

"The Auction Mart Valentine's dance," Sunita recollected.

"By mistake!"

Sunita scrunched her face.

"C'mon, Sun, *you* know what it's like here. The dating pool is shallow."

"Don't you mean it's bone dry?"

"I was being kind," said Evie. "Everyone our age is either related or has a nightmare ex or—"

"Some weird flex," Sunita interrupted, her expression souring. "Like that fellow in Orphir who's obsessed with cacti."

"Oh, *that* guy! Yeah…he was such a prick!"

A laughing snort escaped Sunita's nose. "Holy shit," she muttered flatly. "You and Caleb. Again. Sorta."

Watching another pocket of flag-waving children, Evie's smile faltered. "I thought you'd be happy for me."

"I am, but are you sure? It didn't go so well the first time. You kissed him once and then…nothing."

"I was sixteen, Sun. What did I know?"

"Well, for starters, you knew you loved Nick."

Evie shook her head. "Like I said, I was young and clueless." Looking away, she fixated on the lumbering puppet, his arrival imminent. "A lot's changed since then. *I've* changed. I know what's important now, what I want in a partner."

"And that's One-Kiss Caleb?"

Evie lifted her shoulders in a half-hearted shrug. "I've been too picky, chasing after some ideal that doesn't exist."

Sunita grimaced. "But Eves—"

"I'm lonely, Sun."

Sunita opened her mouth to answer, but Evie jumped in first.

"I want what you have with Micah—someone by my side who loves me with his entire soul, ready to take on the world." Evie fussed with her long hair as it tangled in the chilly wind. "I know being with Caleb sounds random, but he's a good guy. Just got a promotion, too. He's the new head teacher at Kirkwall Grammar."

"So you're saying he's going places."

"While staying put." Evie braced herself as the gusts roared along Broad Street again. "That's one thing we have in common: our fondness for Orkney."

"Well, I guess you could do a lot worse."

"Exactly." Evie paused for a beat then pulled out her phone. "You know what, why make him wait?" Her thumbs flew over the screen.

Evie: 8 tomorrow sounds great.

She hit send and watched the swaying Viking on approach, its team of handlers fighting the gusts. "He's pretty fun, eh?"

"He reminds me of the giant puppets they had in Liverpool a few years ago," said Sunita, watching one of the performers raise and lower the Viking's muscular arms. "Pretty awesome."

A gentle buzz in Evie's palm dipped her chin.

Caleb: Perfect! See you there.

She lingered over the screen. "All confirmed. Dinner at Inga's."

"Mmm, nice!" Sunita's smiley eyes skimmed right, watching the disintegrating grade school conga line before it veered onto Castle Street. "Do they still serve that amazing sea bass with chili butter?" She raised her voice over the marching band passing through.

"Yep. I'll probably stick with their mac 'n' cheese, something yummy but safe." Hair flying in front of her face, Evie typed an extra Looking forward to it x then hesitated, a knot of uncertainty tightening her chest. *No, too soon.* She tapped the screen, deleting the x, and hit send.

Sunita's roaming gaze narrowed. "Shhiit." Her curse stretched along with her wince. "That's not…"

"Not what?" Evie stuffed her phone in her jacket pocket and tracked Sunita's stern glare where she clocked six feet one inch of square-jawed handsomeness on the corner of Castle and Broad. A sharp inhale lodged in her throat.

The trendy aviator sunglasses, the impeccable suit—bespoke, of course—and his dimple-framed grin, widening as he burst into the infectious laugh Evie had loved once upon a time. By his side, sharing in the hilarity, was a well-dressed, dark-haired woman she didn't recognize.

But there was no mistaking *Nick*.

Her pulse pumped quick and heavy in her ears, drowning out the children's carefree laughter and the fading notes of the marching pipe band. Teenage memories fizzed and strobed in her mind: seawater glittering on his bare chest; his mouth hungrily claiming hers; secrets revealed and promises spoken.

Then thirteen years ago, he vanished and broke them.

Despite her swallowing hard, the lump in Evie's throat refused to budge. She couldn't look away, lost to Nick's flirty and familiar I-only-have-eyes-for-you body language and his adorable yet unsuccessful attempts to tame his wildly frolicking hair.

"Eves?" Sunita's caring arm rub went unnoticed.

Every breath, every thought was consumed by the tortuous mix of simmering loathing and suppressed longing swirling inside her.

"*Evie?*" Sunita tried again. "Why don't we—"

A goosebump-raising scream cut her off and jolted Evie as the Viking puppet, free of its tethers, lurched drunkenly toward the large glass windows of her mother's shop.

Evie's blood ran cold. "FUCK!" she shrieked and tore across the street.

THREE

EVIE

Then, Wednesday, August 3, eighteen years ago

"Okay, everyone, turn to page twenty-seven." Mr. Remington licked his finger then flicked through a well-thumbed clothbound book. "We'll start with 'Pleasant Valley Sunday' then follow up with 'Downtown'."

A cacophony of fed-up groans and muttered curses proliferated around the room.

Can't we sing something new? Evie sighed. She stopped twirling her ponytail and cracked open the 1960s songbook.

Every summer, she had hope. Hope for new songs, new instruments, a new instructor, but each summer that youthful optimism ran aground, her hope shattered like a lost ship tossed into the rocks on the Mainland's west coast.

And yet, Evie kept coming back, kept walking beneath the baronial town hall's twin bartizans and carved stone figures, through its timber-paneled doors and into the community center. When she was eight, music camp was a fun way to keep out of trouble while her parents worked. Five years on though, hanging at the beach, roller skating with friends, and afternoons at the cinema were more Evie than singing the golden oldies once beloved by her grandparents.

Slumping in her chair, she shared a sulk with the bespectacled boy across the aisle, a friend since preschool. He motioned toward the teacher, curled his fingers together in a loose fist, and crudely moved his hand back and forth.

Evie laughed into her hoodie sleeve and nodded, mouthing "He IS a wanker" as Mr. Remington did the moist, mucus-y, throat-clearing thing that earned him the nickname Mr. Phlegmington.

"So gross..." Evie shuddered, burying her nose in the musty songbook.

"Class, before we start, we have a new voice joining us."

YOU need a new voice. Shaking her head, Evie lowered the discolored pages and peered over the rows of heads in front of her. All chiseled jaw and long legs, a teenage boy in a baggy, short-sleeved turquoise shirt, artfully distressed skinny jeans, and a sheepish half-smile stood by Mr. Remington's side. His wary gaze peeked through his tumble of brown hair then fled to his gym bag's drawstrings entwined around his fingers.

Wait, WHAT?! Breath bottled in Evie's chest. She shot up straight, her stare fixed as she sought confirmation this wasn't just *any* new voice joining in.

"Everyone..." Mr. Remington sniffed.

OHMYGOD! Evie gulped. *Nikolai?!*

"...this is Nick."

A strangled squeak escaped Evie's throat, the noise lost in a sea of rising whispers.

"Now, where can I put you?" The instructor's eyes washed over the rows of stunned faces.

Beside me! Evie's heart pummeled her ribs. She plucked her backpack from the folding chair beside her, ignoring the twinge in her right side. *Oh god, wait till I tell Fiona! He'll be close enough I can reach out and—*

"There!" Mr. Remington slapped Nikolai on the back and pointed. "Fifth row, far side—off you go..." Hugging his Chelsea FC bag, the teen actor shuffled across the room.

Evie deflated. "Nooo!" she moaned quietly, dumping her belongings back on the chair. Her misery wasn't lessened by Nikolai's new neighbors: two comely sixteen-year-old girls from Stromness Academy.

Five songs and a dozen throat clearings later, most of the girls hadn't sung a single note, including Evie, who spent 'Happy Together' and 'Never My Love' ogling Nikolai as he stealthily signed autographs for the teens sat nearby.

"Well, *that* went well." Mr. Remington's tone rose sarcastically. "Let's move along to our harmonizing exercises. Same as last time, folks. Pair off with the person on your left." His fingerprint-dappled glasses slid down his long nose. "Oh, except you, Evie."

"What now?" she murmured, her head lolling sideways as she turned away from the boy across the aisle.

"I want you to work with Nick."

THUD!

Evie's songbook hit the floor along with her jaw.

"You know the ropes better than most," explained the instructor. "Please show our guest what to do."

Best. Day. EVER!

Nodding excitedly, Evie snatched the book from the floor and grabbed her bag. "Sure, I'll do the ropes—I mean, I'll show him the singing ropes…"

Stop talking! Be COOL.

As she hurried up the aisle, the manager of the community center poked his head around the doorjamb. "Alan, call for you in the office."

Mr. Remington sputtered. "Let's take a peedie break. Don't go too far."

Chair legs screeched as most of the kids bolted from the stuffy room, leaving dust particles dancing in a ribbon of sunshine spilling through the stained glass windows.

Nerves fizzing in her belly, Evie lingered behind the noisy exodus. *Remember, he's JUST a boy…like Sam's mates.* Clutching the songbook against her chest, she rounded the front row of empty seats, passing a flock of girls, including the two from Stromness, cluttering the doorway. Autographs in hand, they giggled and shamelessly eyeballed Nikolai, but he didn't engage any further, choosing instead to plow through whatever treasures lurked in his small gym bag.

With each step, Evie's pulse hammered harder. Who was she kidding? Nikolai was *nothing* like Sam's school friends. They were loud and sweary sixteen-year-olds, into tractors, *Gran Turismo 4*, and drinking pilfered booze behind the five-thousand-year-old Ring of Brodgar after the snap-happy tourists had called it a day. None were jaw-droppingly pretty or smooth with girls, familiar with red carpets and big paydays. *Dammit.* Evie stared. The nerve of him, being even more handsome than he was on TV. The silky softness of his boy band hair, his shoulders caressed by his turquoise top, his lips twisting in thought…the same lips that had kissed Amanda's barely visible baby bump during the previous week's season finale of *Dalston Grove*. A gasp escaped Evie's mouth as her brain scrambled for something, anything but *that* to talk about. She couldn't blow this first impression, her one and only chance to make him like her. This was it.

Her fangirl brain clicked into overdrive, locating squirreled-away nuggets of Nikolai trivia. He liked cars and photography and, and…fashion! *Vintage and designer, he's into clothes big time.* Tightness gripped Evie's chest as she glanced down. *And clearly, I'm not.* Of all the days to wear her faded S Club 7 t-shirt with her oversized hoodie and comfiest (and Crohn's friendliest) track pants. Nikolai wouldn't be caught dead in gray sweats, his taste more expensive, more hip. Evie didn't know the first thing about designer labels, and the far-from-trendy wool sweaters and touristy puffin t-shirts sold in her mother's shop did little to expand her sartorial education.

Think of something else. Tugging her hoodie closed over her slim frame, she mined her memory. His Japanese Spitz Ross? Table tennis? Playing piano, gooey cupcakes? Nikolai loved them all, but he gave dishonesty, cats eating birds *(gross)*, coconut, and forgetting birthdays all the thumbs-down (according to *Flirty Girl* magazine). His favorite color was yellow. Fave breakfast food: waffles. His first kiss was—

"Hey."

Evie's focus flew, crash-landing on her crush. All words, all discussion topics queued and ready to launch, dried up on her tongue.

"How are you?" Reeling in his splayed legs, Nikolai reunited his butt with the chair and sat up, a wisp of a crooked smile teasing his full lips.

Just like Jake. Evie squeezed the handle of her backpack, her knuckles whitening. "Um…" She swallowed, forcing out a breathless blurt. "I'm gonna leave this—"

"No, don't go. Stay. Talk to me."

Her backpack dropped on the chair beside him. "Sorry?"

"You know, talk? Save me from looking like a sad Billy No-Mates." A wide, mischievous grin awoke the famous dimples she wrote about in her journal. "I sorta feel on display here." Nikolai tilted his head, his eyes flitting across the whispering throng. "Like a three-headed sheep or something." He let out a cheeky laugh, and Evie's exhale snagged in her throat.

Is this real life? Am I dead?

Evie's doubts were certainly warranted, especially after the unshakable nightmare of the past year: searing abdominal pains, frightening weight loss, and panicked sprints to the loo, not to mention the occasional accident. Carrying baby wipes, toilet paper, and extra underwear and jeans in her backpack *just in case* was a secret she didn't dare share, but even on her worst days, one thing always made Evie smile—daydreaming about Nikolai—and like a thousand birthday wishes come true, he was right *here*, he was—

"Pretend you know me, Evie. *Please?*"

Saying her name.

Giddiness whooshed through every vein, every artery, completely evaporating Evie's cool faster than a hot car on a sunny day. "Oh, I *know* you! I watch you every week, own alll the DVDs and magazines. Your storyline this year with Amanda and the pregnancy and—well, it was *SO* awesome!"

The fizzy sparkle in Nikolai's eyes dimmed. "Oh. Cheers," he muttered, his smile collapsing along with his conversational skills. "*Great.*" He dove into his bag again.

Oh nooo. Evie chewed her bottom lip. *Too fangirly. WAY too fangirly!* Her heart panged. She needed a do-over. Fast.

He pulled out a ballpoint pen, its cap riddled with bite marks. "I guess you want an autograph, too, yeah?" A resigned sigh escaped his mouth as he looked up, his gaze listless.

Yes. Yes, she did, but not at the expense of a possible friendship. That is, if one was within reach. None of the girls holding autographs in the doorway had been invited to stick around. Was it their high-pitched swooning, their monosyllabic fawning over his looks that saw them kept at a distance? A sour taste rose in Evie's throat. She couldn't—no, *wouldn't* suffer the same fate. She'd stifle her giddiness and find common ground, something shared to spark a meaningful conversation...even if it killed her.

Shifting her backpack off the chair, Evie sat down, maintaining a respectful distance. "Thanks, but I, uh...I'm not really an autograph person." She lied. "When I said I *knew* you, I meant your *character* Jake, of course..."

His chin dipped in a cautious nod.

"I'm taking drama in school, and watching you play him is *so* inspiring. You make it look effortless—although I know it's not. Acting is hard!"

Nikolai's face softened. "Aw, that's kind of you to say. Thanks."

An embroidered name above the right breast pocket of his shirt caught her eye. *Louis? Cute!* She picked the frayed edge of the songbook. "No doubt you'll slay these moldy songs, too."

"Moldy?" He slid the pen back into his bag.

"From the '60s." She flipped the hardback, showing Nikolai the cover. "It's all Mr. Remington lets us sing."

"So what's his deal, anyway?"

"God, where do I start," said Evie. "He's gross, has no sense of humor, acts overly familiar, like him calling you Nick. Did it bug you?"

"Nah, Nikolai is a mouthful. When I was little, I hated it. Could never spell it. Writing my name, I was always like, 'Cheers, Mum!'"

Evie cracked a smile, delighted by this inside information.

His eyes drifted to the orca and roller skate bag charms hanging from her backpack then bounced back. "My middle name is even worse. Have you heard it?"

If this were a 'How Well Do You Know Nikolai Balfour?' trivia quiz, Evie could ace it in her sleep. What wasn't so easy, though, was figuring out whether mentioning the correct answer would forever slam the door on a possible friendship, never mind a romance.

He cocked an eyebrow, waiting.

Putting her drama lessons to the test, she adopted a blank expression and shrugged nonchalantly. "Is it…Louis?"

He glanced down. "Oh! No, I'm not sure who Louis is. This is a vintage bowling shirt, second-hand from Camden."

"Ah, okay." Evie played along.

"My middle name is Crispin. Nikolai *Crispin* Balfour. If that's not a name that'll get you beat up, what is?" His laugh, all open-mouthed exuberance, signaled it was okay for Evie to giggle, too. "I get called all sorts of ridic things, but to my friends I'm just Nico or Nick."

There's nothing 'just' about him. She clasped the silver *Evie* pendant hanging from a delicate chain around her neck. *I'd die if he let me be his friend.*

"You can call me Nick—if you want."

OH MY GOD—YES! Evie tussled with the fizzy impulse to full-on squeal 'I love you, I love you, I love YOU!' rising inside her. Instead, she nodded calmly. "Okay."

"Evie's a pretty name."

Her heart swelled as her mind plunged pushpins into the corners of his unexpected compliment, saving it for posterity and a squee later. "Thanks! I don't have a middle name, though. Mum and Dad couldn't agree on one," she babbled. "Maybe that's a good thing."

"Trust me, you had a lucky escape." His fingers looped through a yellow LIVESTRONG bracelet on his right wrist.

"There's a village here called Evie and a lovely beach." She rambled proudly, fondly remembering her former home on the north coast of the West Mainland. "It has an old stone fisherman's hut, wildflowers, lots of sand. My parents lived there when I was born." She smiled, drinking him in. His upper lip and chin were dotted with fine, dark stubble, and a tiny scar she'd never noticed before blighted the bridge of his nose.

With a hard blink, he pulled back slightly. "Erm..." He flitted between her eyes and hair, down to her t-shirt and old Swatch, and back up again.

"What's wrong?" Evie let go of her necklace and looked down. S Club 7's squeaky clean grins were shining through the unzipped opening of her hoodie. *Oh god.* Tugging it closed, she remembered swimming at Scapa Beach the day before. Mortification rushed through her. "Oh shit!" She sprang back in the chair and whisked a panicked hand through her ponytail. "There's seaweed in my hair?"

"No, it's fine, it's just..."

She froze mid-swipe.

Nick let go of his yellow charity bracelet. "You're kinda staring."

"I am?!"

He scrunched his nose. "A *little*, yeah."

Squirming, Evie broke eye contact. "I'm SO sorry. Didn't mean to. I've never met a famous person before. It's a bit...weird." She pulled her hoodie's cuffs over her hands and fixated on the floor, missing Nick's smile.

"Yeah, can be. Hey, don't worry about it." He motioned across the room. "So that's pretty wicked, eh?"

She peered up tentatively.

"That bloke..." Nick raised his chin toward the wall and a poster of a man scaling the red sandstone of the Old Man of Hoy, a towering sea stack jutting out of the Atlantic Ocean. "Way up high, climbing that thing like bloody Spider-Man."

Evie followed his gaze, the furrow between her brows easing. Nick's affection for outdoor pursuits had been mentioned in the latest issue of *TV Tales* magazine. She let out a buoyant breath, for what was Orkney but a remote paradise framed by endless sky, jagged cliffs, and open sea? Much of her childhood had been spent recklessly hopping stone dykes, leaping off barn roofs, and digging through rock pools, the wilds of the island providing an enviable back yard. And then when the long summer days drew in and she ambled home, Orkney accompanied Evie inside. Handpicked flowers in her grasp, sandy seashells in her pocket, the rich earth clinging to her shoes. Evie could talk about that stuff for hours.

Scratching his temple, Nick zeroed in on her necklace. "You were telling me about your name?"

Evie lit up. As someone with a long family history tied to the islands, Nick would appreciate this. "Oh right! It originates from an Old Norse word, efja. It means eddy."

"Eddie?" His voice rose playfully. "Like the guy's name?"

Evie laughed and twirled her hoodie's drawstring around her finger. "No, silly! It's an oceanography term. You know, science?"

"Uh, not if I can help it."

"Oh. Well, an eddy is a strong circular current—"

"Yeah, I *know* what an eddy is," Nick snapped. "I'm not that thick."

Whoa! Where did that come from? Someone's touchy.

Evie's stomach soured. "I didn't say you were," she replied cautiously. "*You* were the one who asked about my name…" As she wrenched the cord tighter, the tip of her finger throbbed, growing scarlet.

Nick's eyes darted to the whispering girls in the doorway.

"The parish is called Evie 'cause it overlooks the eddy in Aikerness Bay. My parents liked the name and its relevance to the island." She shook her head and glanced away, unwinding the hoodie string from her finger.

He bowed his head. "Look, I'm sorry. I didn't mean to be a dick." He toyed with something steel, black-dialed, and probably eye-wateringly expensive on his left wrist. "It's just…I'm used to people assuming all sorts of shit about me."

Evie studied the sixteen-year-old closely. The cool snake tattoo of Jake's wasn't winding around Nick's arm or anywhere else, and his left knee bounced feverishly, betraying the cocky, confident persona celebrated in glossy magazines and gossip websites. This version of Nick wasn't what Evie expected. And why so fidgety?

"It grates after a while. Most kids don't have *The National Mail* writing articles about them failing their science and math tests," he huffed. "And I only failed 'cause—" Catching Evie's sympathetic nod, he clammed up, his need to explain seemingly overruled by a surge of second thoughts.

A flush of guilt coursed through her. Assuming things about Nick was one of her and Fiona's favorite pastimes. "That's awful. No one should ever assume—or invade your privacy."

"Most journos think I'm public property because I'm on telly. Some of the stories they write are pretty twisted."

Evie always thought fame would be cool and exciting. Meeting fellow celebrities, going to glamorous parties. Any downside had never occurred to her. "So, being famous sucks?"

"Sometimes." Head down, Nick stuck his fingers inside the strap of his watch and dragged it around his wrist. "People can be weird. Some touch you without asking. Others follow you. But the perks are brill. Most fans are fun, and who doesn't love posing for photo shoots and appearing in magazines? It's a trip. I score loads of free stuff, too."

"And the best tables in restaurants?"

The corners of his mouth curled upward. "Sounds like a cliché, but yeah, it happens."

"So the good cancels out the bad then?"

The muscle in Nick's jaw tensed and his knee bounced faster. "Hmm, let's just say, if you'd asked me six months ago, I would've said yes."

What happened? Evie's brow gathered then released, her eyes widening.

Her curiosity didn't escape unseen. Within seconds, Nick's sullen demeanor lifted, replaced by an awkward laugh. "God, what am I like?" Leaning back, he rubbed his eyes without mercy. "Take *no* notice of me, okay? I'm freaking about my GCSE results and it's turning me into a total prat."

Her brother Sam was sweating his exam results, too. In the UK, all sixteen-year-olds were dreading the first week of August when marks were released and futures and opportunities were set in motion. "Makes sense." Evie nodded, giving him the benefit of the doubt.

Nick dropped his hands and blinked several times. Evie noticed a stray eyelash riding his thumb.

"Make a wish."

"Sorry?"

She pointed. "The eyelash on your hand. When you lose one, you're supposed to make a wish and blow it away."

"Guess it can't hurt, right?" Nick closed his eyes for a beat then blew the lash off his finger. "Some proper downtime would help, too. I reckon we visited your beach once. The flowers and stone hut you mentioned, I think I saw those."

"Oh yeah?! When?"

"Few years back. Me and my brothers were searching for cowrie shells for our grandmother."

"Ah, groatie buckies! Love those," said Evie. "Tough to find, though."

He laughed brightly. "Yeah. We saw a washed-up starfish and some gray seals, too."

"Selkies! They're awesome! So fat and floppy. I saw a pod of orcas there once."

"Cool!"

Dissolving into silence, Nick played with the strings of his gym bag. Evie devoured every second, her eyes as round as saucers. *I want to touch him so badly.* She glanced up. "So, why are you here in music camp hell? Don't you have somewhere better to be?"

"You'd think, but uh…" His tongue poked the outside corner of his mouth. "I'm being punished."

Evie snorted. "Aren't we all!"

"No, I'm serious. I got in shit for bunking off."

"From where?"

"Private singing lessons," said Nick. "My mum booked me in twice in London, and twice I went to the cinema with my mates instead."

Evie's brows rose. Private lessons? She should be so lucky.

"Mum wants me to be a triple threat—acting, dancing, singing."

"But you already sing on *Dalston Grove*," said Evie.

He leaned in conspiratorially, and his subtle scent, something clean and deliciously Nick, teased her nostrils. She inhaled deeply, dreamily. *He smells like happiness.*

"That's just it..." Nick scanned the room before continuing. "Every time I strum my guitar, a phone rings or someone walks in. I never sing a bloody note. Haven't you noticed?"

"No."

"Every *single* time." Nick scratched his jaw. "Listen, if we're paired up, you're gonna—" He pouted, his knee still jumpy as his eyes flitted to hers. "You have to promise you won't tell *anyone*."

"I won't!"

"I can't sing," he whispered. "Or play guitar."

"What?!" she squealed.

Nick's focus sprang to the huddle of kids in the doorway. "Shh!" He ducked his head. "It's embarrassing, all right? I totally suck."

"No, you don't."

Nick scrubbed a hand across his brow, messing his floppy fringe. "I *so* don't want to be here."

Evie's heart dipped. For the first time in a very long time, she didn't want to be anywhere else.

"And I can't even do a runner. Mum's assistant is waiting outside."

Evie gaped, horrified. "She's *spying* on you?" None of her friends, boys *or* girls were kept on such a short leash. "That's awful."

A peeved frown dipped his lips. "If I don't stick this out, Mum will make me stay in Orkney for the rest of the summer."

30

"And that's…bad?"

He avoided her gaze. "I don't like it here."

Nick's confession felt like a sharp kick to Evie's gut. Orkney wasn't the most happening of locations, but it was safe, postcard picturesque, and well, *home*. "But…what don't you like about it?" Her eyes washed over his Adam's apple as he swallowed.

"It's nothing but wind and water, birds and ruins."

"But you *like* the outdoors."

Nick met her questioning squint. "What makes you think that?"

"Dunno, read it somewhere?"

Nick's slow nod released a brief but good-natured laugh. "Ahh, right. Those magazine Q&A thingies. I don't fill them out. My PR people do."

"Oh?" Maybe she didn't 'know' Nick so well after all.

But perhaps that was okay. Scratch that, maybe it was *more* than okay, better even. They could build a friendship based on truth and honesty instead of misguided assumptions, magazine exposés, and island gossip. After all, isn't the best part of making new friends discovering what makes them tick? Finding out their joys and disappointments, what they love, what they hate?

Evie relished the opportunity.

She forged ahead with a curious smile. "So what *do* you like?"

"I like high streets and shops and—and conveniences." Stretching out his long legs, Nick's gaze dropped, settling on his shoes. His trainers were blindingly white, obviously fresh from the box and wallet-flinchingly expensive. "Being in Orkney is very…*inconvenient*."

Evie balked, letting out a croaky "Oh!" Maybe Nick was being a little bit *too* honest.

"You like it here?" he asked, his eyes shifting, landing on her mum's red, yellow, and green Swatch.

"I don't know anything different. I've never been anywhere. I was supposed to go to Inverness last fall for my brother's track and field meet but came down with something."

Evie left it at that. Nick didn't need to know she spent the October school holidays two hundred and fifty miles south in an Aberdeen hospital being fed liquid nourishment through a tube in her nose. Upon release, the feeding tube remained as she resumed normal activities and returned to school where curious classmates posed non-stop questions: "Why is the tube taped to your cheek?" "Does it hurt putting it in?" "When can you eat real food again?" Not all were supportive, though. A few bad apples, older kids mostly, teased her relentlessly with a demeaning nickname: Noodle Nose.

Twelve weeks later, Evie's inflamed intestines had healed and the tube was removed. She'd gained an inch in height and seven desperately needed pounds, and pasta and chicken were back on the menu. However, the remission was short-lived. Evie's Crohn's was slowly waking up again.

"I was excited about going, too," she continued. "Seeing Urquhart Castle, Loch Ness."

"Nessie the monster?" added Nick.

Nodding enviously, Evie tugged on her name pendant, her fingers pressing each individual letter.

"You'll get there one day," said Nick.

Music campers flooded back into the room, some carrying drinks and snacks from the vending machine while others straggled in, engrossed in the last throes of clandestine conversation.

"How'd your brother do at his competition?"

"He won two silvers," said Evie. "Beat his personal best for javelin, too."

"Javelin?"

She grinned. "I know! Cool, right? Sammy trains *so* hard, he deserves all the good things."

"Sammy?" Nick blinked, his expression quizzical. "Not Sam Sutherland?"

"Yeah? Why?" Evie let go of her necklace.

Barking out a laugh, Nick launched backward in his chair. "Bloody hell!" He plowed a hand through his hair. "I *know* him. Holy shit, I can't believe this! You're Sam's baby sister!"

Baby? Evie's hopefulness curdled in her stomach. "But how—"

"Right!" Mr. Remington swept into the room. "Everyone take a seat!" He slammed the creaky door behind him. "Turn to page sixty-seven and 'How Can I Be Sure'."

"Sammy, you could've told me!" Evie stalked her older brother around their cramped kitchen. "You *know* how much I like him and—"

"And what, Sprout?" Sam gleefully teased Evie with her childhood nickname as he tore into a packet of ginger biscuits. "I spill and you and your giggly friends hound him to death?" He scratched his messy nest of auburn hair. "No chance."

Face reddening, Evie snatched the packet from his grip.

"Rude!" Sam lunged forward, but Evie backed up, holding the biscuits beyond his reach.

"How long have you been mates? Tell me or I'll chuck these in the bin." She stomped on the trash can's foot pedal, popping open its squeaky metal mouth.

Letting out a laugh, Sam inched closer. "Like that would stop me eating them."

"Ew!" Evie snarled, ignoring the slam of the front door. "TELL ME!"

"Two years."

Her face fell. "What?! *How?*"

Sam swooped and plucked the cookies from her hand as Marianne Sutherland, a russet-haired force of nature, breezed into the kitchen and sliced through their squabble. "*Sam*"—she rolled up the sleeves of her flowery blouse—"what did your coach say about eating biscuits?" Running the taps, she pumped a blob of soap into her palm and flashed her son a knowing look. Reluctantly, he relinquished the partially devoured packet, leaving it on the counter beside two deflated crisp bags and Evie's book of word search puzzles.

"Sam?" Evie pressed.

"I know his cousins."

Her eyes widened. "He has *cousins* here?"

"A few. They attend Stromness Academy." Sam bent over and scooped up their cat, Turtle, her white fur dappled with splotches of fiery orange and midnight black. "We hang out, play football, talk about girls...you know, *guy* stuff." He pressed a gentle kiss between Turtle's ears. "Nico joins in when he's here. When's he not, we play video games online."

"You serious?" Her tone darkened. "You're one of Nick's best mates?!"

"Hey, don't get pissed at me." Sam stepped aside so their mother could dry her hands on the cat-print towel hanging from the fridge. "Nico swore me not to tell anyone."

"But I'm not *anyone*!" Evie hugged her belly. "I hope you're this good at keeping *my* secrets."

"I am! Jesus, Evie! I'm not an arse."

"Could've fooled me—"

"Okay, you two, enough!" Marianne exhaled heavily and hung up the towel.

"Well?" Evie glowered. "He's the one who lied."

"I didn't lie. I just didn't tell you." Scratching Turtle between the ears, Sam avoided Evie's gaze. "I also...may have helped with his grandma's sheep—"

"*May* have?!" Evie's voice rose as their mother pulled open the cutlery drawer.

"What? It'll look good on my vet school application. And before you freak out more, I didn't meet the grandmother or his brother, all right?"

"He has two, actually, Sam," Evie sassed. "*Two* brothers."

"Yeah, I met Rupert. We trimmed hooves together."

She tossed up her hands. "Honestly!"

Marianne gave her daughter an exasperated look then lifted the fogged lid of the slow cooker and poked inside with a fork. Several drips of condensation splattered on the countertop. "The Balfours have lived here for generations."

"You know them?" Evie slouched on the counter, the mouth-watering aroma of garlic-parmesan chicken teasing her nose.

"I've served the grandmother a few times."

"She shops at ours?!" Evie straightened up, incredulous. "MUM!"

"But they keep to themselves," said Marianne, lowering the glass lid. It kissed the slow cooker with a curt clink. "They're polite but private." She set the fork on a trivet.

Evie balled up the crisp bags, their crackly crinkle swiveling Turtle's ears. "Fiona said their ancestors were lairds."

"Who lost all their money. The current Balfours made their fortune drilling oil in the North Sea back in the 1980s." Marianne opened the fridge door and pulled out a package of leafy greens. "They sold the company when the grandfather died. One son now runs a distillery, the other owns a chain of sporting goods shops."

"That's Nick's dad. He owns Sports Now." Sam returned Turtle to her threadbare sushi toy on the tile floor. "I went in the Inverness one." He stole two biscuits while their mother cleaned the romaine lettuce under cold water.

Evie loved fresh salads, but unfortunately post-diagnosis, they no longer loved her back.

"It must be strange growing up on TV, always being on display," said Marianne, scrubbing the leaves. "Evie, I know you like this lad, but he comes here to be a regular kid, not to sign autographs."

"I don't want an autograph." She picked at a cat magnet stuck to the fridge.

"No, she wants *his body*..." Sam snickered between bites.

"Sammm!"

"I hate to break it to you, Sprout, but Nick wouldn't be interested. He dates *loads* of girls. He's practically fighting them off with a shitty stick."

Evie's stomach rolled. Where was this in *Flirty Girl* magazine? "That's not true. He's single. The magazines say so."

"But they would, wouldn't they?" reasoned Sam. "Think about it: if they mention Nick's got a girlfriend, you lot will lose interest. You'll stop buying them."

"I wouldn't!"

Sam handed her a biscuit. "Evie, look. You know I love you, I think you're awesome, but you didn't seriously—I mean, you're *only* thirteen. You don't even have boobs."

Evie gasped into an incredulous open-mouthed glare. "Thanks a lot!"

"Samuel!" Marianne warned, turning off the faucet.

Snapping the cookie in half, Evie fumed as she crunched, but despite his teasing, her brother wasn't wrong. She'd been mulling over the same thing. Nick probably did see her as too young, too inexperienced, unworldly. Sam's *"baby sister"*. Sure, she had been useful, singing loudly by Nick's side so he could silently mouth along and escape with his secret intact, and to his credit, he didn't take her efforts for granted. On the rush out, Nick treated Evie to her favorite chocolate bar (a Twirl) from the vending machine then thanked her gracefully before disappearing into a waiting Range Rover. But her hopes for anything more felt like they were vanishing quicker than the biscuits in her brother's hands.

She glanced down at her breasts, barely a bump in her t-shirt. Delayed puberty was a frustrating and embarrassing consequence of her Crohn's disease. "I'm tired of looking like a little kid. All my friends have boobs and periods."

Her face softening, Marianne left the lettuce on a paper towel and wiped her hands. "Honey, it won't always be this way." She wrapped her only daughter in a loving hug. "Trust me."

Evie pouted. "I'll never have a boyfriend."

"Yes you will." Marianne kissed Evie on the temple. "When you're older and ready, but in the meantime, stop worrying. Remember what the specialist said? Low stress—"

"I know, I know—" A sharp ache ripped through the lower

right of her abdomen, stealing her breath. "Ow!" She froze, her stomach gurgling loud enough for her mother to flinch.

"Are you in pain?" Marianne pulled back, her brows drawing in. "Evie, you promised—no more hiding symptoms."

Her mother's concern was valid. Months pre-diagnosis, Evie had kept quiet about seeing blood in the toilet and experiencing abdominal pains so brutal they felt like an army of alligators gnawing their way out.

"I'm not hiding anything. It's just a little pinchy today."

"Did you eat chocolate again?" Marianne touched her daughter's forehead. "You are a bit warm…"

"Yeah, 'cause she met Nikolai Balfour!" joked Sam. "Oooo, Sprout's got it BAD!"

Evie swatted him. "Shut up!"

FOUR

EVIE

Now, Wednesday, June 21

Swerving crying children, distraught puppeteers, and rubbernecking bagpipers stampeding for safety, Evie avoided the buckled doorway and climbed through the massive hole punched in the shop's façade. Heart lodged in her throat, she held her phone against her ear.

"Are there any injuries?" asked the emergency dispatcher.

"I-I'm not sure." Breaths frantic, Evie squinted into a dense cloud of dust and debris, the sickening crunch of shattered glass and splintered wood beneath her sensible flats. "I'll have to l—" A scratchy, tickling cough stole her words. "Sorry," her voice rasped. "It's tough to see." Ducking a dangling light fixture, she tripped over the puppet's severed arm and pain rocketed up her shin. "*Ou—ch!*"

"Evie, listen to me," the dispatcher instructed in her ear. "It'll be safer if you wait outside. Emergency services are on their way."

A guttural groan rose from within the shop. *Oh shit!* Nausea churned in Evie's belly. "Jamie?! Gemma?!" she hollered, trampling chunks of ceiling tile as she searched for the injured party. "Where ARE you?!"

"*Evie,* wait outside!"

Ignoring the dispatcher's plea, she bolted past an upended table, devoid of its usual puffin trays, toys, and mugs, and spotted a middle-aged woman slumped on the floor against the shop's ice cream cooler, her pink bob sporting flecks of white plaster.

"Gemma!" Evie scrambled over the puppet's enormous head and fell to her knees, spying a rivulet of fresh blood trickling down Gemma's temple. She swallowed hard. "Where does it hurt?"

Supporting her elbow, Gemma rocked back and forth. "My arm...my head," she yelped through clenched teeth. "It hurts pretty bad."

The shrill wail of sirens rose in the distance as Evie relayed the information to the dispatcher.

"Keep her calm and use something to stop the bleeding—a towel, a shirt," replied the calm voice. "The paramedics are almost there, but keep me on the line just in case."

"I will, thanks." Lowering her phone, Evie prised an otter-patterned apron from a wicker basket. "Gem, you're gonna be all right. Help's on the way."

"*Please.*" She writhed in agony. "Don't go."

"I'm staying right here." Evie bit her lip, hoping what she was about to say wouldn't amplify Gemma's distress. "There's a cut on your forehead. I'm gonna stop the bleeding, okay?"

"I feel dizzy. Everything's blurry."

Evie gently held the soft cotton against Gemma's scalp. "Do you remember what happened?"

"Something hit me, sent me flying."

Stupid puppet. Evie frowned at its handsome face, scarred from impact but still smiling. Managing her mum's shop, she knew the basics of first aid—what to do when someone was choking, what steps to take for CPR—but she had no clue how to handle a head injury.

Or a lazy shop assistant with a criminal record for joyriding.

"Gem, where's Jamie?"

"Smoke break," she gasped.

Of course. It was always something: a cigarette, an urgent text. Evie's sixteen-year-old cousin spent more time outside Marwick's than in, but on this occasion, his dubious work ethic may have spared him stitches or worse.

The rumble of emergency vehicles eased the tightness in her shoulders. Outside, puppet handlers, curious onlookers, Sunita—all stepped back to make space for the first responders while a batch of bent postcards, liberated during the Viking's invasion, frolicked on the wind.

Two firefighters loaded with equipment sidestepped the decimated doorway and evaluated the hole where the windows once shone, ensuring the building was stable before entering. On their steel-toed heels came a pair of paramedics bookending a stretcher. Evie recognized them but didn't dive into small talk.

"Hey, Evie" was all the first firefighter said on his way to inspect the café and kitchen in the back, which, from her vantage point, appeared unscathed. Thankfully.

As the medical team ran through a host of health checks with Gemma, Evie surveyed what fifteen minutes earlier had been a bustling shop. Scattered pieces of puppet—arms (twisted horrifically backward) and torso (half-stripped of his green robe)—rested precariously atop collapsed tables, smashed ceramics, and a rainbow of sweaters still brandishing their wooden hangers. The café and kitchen may have escaped damage, but much of the shop, along with the sales desk, were in ruins, not to mention all the destroyed merchandise. *First the roof and now this?* Her chest ached. *How are we gonna pay for everything? Does insurance even cover puppet crashes?*

The straps on the stretcher clicked and Evie circled back. "Will Gem be okay?"

The older of the two paramedics, an uncle of Sunita's, adjusted the plastic prongs feeding oxygen to Gemma's nose. "She's got a badly broken arm, a possible concussion, and a bad attitude."

Evie suppressed a giggle. Gemma's take-no-prisoners brashness was legendary and obviously unaffected by the disaster.

"Tell them, Evie," she urged, swatting him away. "They can't keep me overnight. I'm needed here."

Tomorrow! Shit! The accident had completely scrubbed the catering gig and everything else from Evie's mind.

"Gem, I told ya once, I told ya a thousand times. The docs will make that call, so behave." The younger paramedic hoisted his medical bag over his shoulder. "And looking at this place, I doubt Evie will be here tomorrow either."

No kidding. Mouth going dry, her pulse raced again as Gemma and the first responders began their careful trek through the shop. *'Cause I'll be burning soup in a catering truck while a starved TV crew bays for my blood.*

Defeated, she closed her eyes and dropped to her knees, cursing rampaging puppets and her lack of prowess in the kitchen. She could blame Crohn's disease and her limited diet all she wanted, but the facts spoke for themselves—her cooking know-how barely exceeded what she could stomach and as a result, her lifelong disinterest in learning beyond her safety net of eggs, white rice, and skinless potatoes was now biting her in the ass. Hard.

"Back off!" Sunita bossed. "You are NOT going in!"

Sun can't stand guard all night. Slouching against the puppet's decapitated head, Evie's eyes wearily popped open. *I'll have to find plywood, board up the shop...*

"I need to know how she is!"

Nick? Evie's heart plunged to her stomach. "For god's sake," she muttered under her breath. "Read the room!"

"You've got some cheek!" Sunita snapped, her aggravation surging. "Asking *now*? Thirteen years later?!"

Then again, why NOT now? Evie threw her hands up. At this point, she had nothing left to lose.

Brushing dust and crushed ceiling tile from her cropped pants, she adopted a neutral countenance, rose to her feet, and swung around, facing the boy who had once meant everything.

"Eves," Sunita cautioned, "I'm sorry, but he just *barged* past."

"It's fine." Evie's indifferent gaze collided with Nick's worried gape, and thirteen years of bitter hurt surged forward, pushing play on her long-held vow to stay strong if they ever spoke again. Given his familial ties to the island, it was inevitable there would be close calls and near misses through the years, and yet, Evie was still waiting for *the* perfect moment to prove to him that the distraught teen he'd ghosted ages ago had moved on and was no longer buried under the devastation of his cruel breakup. However, standing ankle-deep in splintered wood and smashed merchandise wasn't exactly how she'd imagined it. "*I'm* fine," she huffed, tucking strands of drywall-speckled hair behind her ear. "Everything's fine."

Unfortunately, the butterflies quivering in her belly didn't receive the memo.

Dammit.

Nick looked so *good* and even better close up. He was older, sure, but more striking like he'd grown into his sharp cheekbones and broad shoulders and finally gained the confidence and swagger physical attractiveness and excessive wealth often afford.

Evie lingered on his lips, the beautiful flirty mouth she'd loved to tease and kiss once upon a time…

For god's sake! She dragged her attention away and pawed the back of her neck. *Get a fucking grip!*

"Thank Christ you're all right." Nick's reply rode a relieved exhale. "When I saw the puppet tip, I—"

"Why are you here?" Evie blurted, her blank expression hijacked by the incredulous glare she could no longer tame. She hugged her waist, her icy glower unforgiving, giving him nothing.

With a hard blink, Nick withdrew, fixating on the crisp cuff of his sleeve, which he straightened needlessly. "I'm, uh…doing a favor for a friend."

"I'm surprised you still have any."

Sunita snickered, but Nick didn't flinch.

"He was desperate."

"Must've been," said Evie.

His intense gaze returned with a conciliatory grin. All fidgeting stopped. "It's really good to see you."

Just…don't! Looking downward, she imagined his face on a cracked piece of mug and slowly crushed it beneath her shoe. "Well, now that you have…you can go fuck yourself."

Unease flickered in his brown eyes. "Evie, I…" He paused for a beat.

She scowled, exasperated. "What do you *want*, Nick?!"

"To tell you I'll be here for a bit and we might bump into each other."

"Not if I can help it."

"I think it would help if we could be civil to one another," said Nick.

Evie shook her head. "We've gone this long—why change now?"

"I'm working here this summer. The *Tomlinson* TV series?"

The catering job. Shit! Evie felt sick.

"You're kidding?!" Sunita jumped in. "You're *acting*?"

"Producing. I'm one of the executive producers. I'll be on set daily, sharing my Orkney—"

Sunita burst out laughing. "Expertise? Yeah, *right*!"

Ignoring her, Nick continued. "I know our production manager hired the Marwick's catering team, so—"

"*So* your production will receive two meals a day and a craft services table of the highest quality six days a week." Evie whisked perspiration off her brow. "Now if you'll excuse me, I have a shop to secure."

FIVE

EVIE

Then, Monday, December 25, seventeen years ago

Stood out of harm's way on the packed steps of the cathedral, Evie swayed back and forth, studying the testosterone-fueled street battle below. Part football, part rugby, the Ba' was a centuries-old Christmas Day free-for-all with a homemade cork-filled leather ball (the ba') and a huge scrum consisting of two male teams (the Uppies and the Doonies). With no rules or referees, no timeouts or ticking clock, the game's aim was simple: the first team to score wins. However, doing so was anything but easy. The Uppies had to push through the Doonies and touch a specific wall in the southern part of town, while dunking the ba' in the harbor—in the opposite direction—was the Doonies' goal. Amidst the scrimmage, bones were occasionally broken and tempers often flared, but a code of non-violent conduct kept fisticuffs at bay. Besides, year-long bragging rights were up for grabs. Their appeal, along with the thrill of competition, made the bruises and aching muscles more than worth it, according to Evie's dad, Graham, a Ba' participant since the tender age of eight.

Burying her mitten-swamped hands under the armpits of her coat for warmth, Evie craned her neck, fervently combing the growing crowd of spectators for Nick. Always looking, always hoping, she always ended up disappointed.

"Seen him yet?" Sunita's voice petered out as she slouched free from her overstuffed backpack.

Rising up on her toes, Evie skimmed the fray below, not for Nick this time, but for Sunita's latest crush, a fifteen-year-old 'Uppie' she'd snogged at the Auction Mart's holiday dance. The boys'

Ba' for kids fifteen and under was the opening act for the men's afternoon game, and a sparse sprinkling of Christmas Day snow made their struggle extra slippery. A half-hour into the festivities, the boys hadn't budged beyond their starting point below the Mercat Cross. Evie shook her head. "You sure he's playing?"

"Definitely." Sunita blinked away from the horde of sweaty boys and lowered her backpack carefully between her trainers. "Look for a guy with reddish-brown hair in a wine-colored football top." Hunching over, she gave the zipper a commanding tug and its plastic teeth gave way.

"Needle—haystack," Evie muttered.

Locking arms around each other's shoulders, the pushy pack of teens shoved and shouted, propelling a steamy cloud of breath skyward into the damp air. The ba' itself hadn't been seen since it was first tossed up—then swallowed—by the fracas. Its disappearance, though, wasn't unusual. It often went missing—hidden under someone's shirt or stashed in a trash bin—until it could be spirited away undetected through the mass of bodies toward one of the goals.

"I can't tell them apart." Evie dismissed her search with a wave of her floppy, handknit mitt. "They're all squished against the town hall." She shifted as several spectators squeezed past, hunting for a better vantage point.

"Oh, Evie, Sunita—hi!" Mrs. Robson, a plump, gray-haired woman who worked in the post office, leaned in. "Happy Christmas."

"Happy Christmas," they replied in unison.

Evie's spidey sense pricked. She knew what was coming next.

"You been well, love? How's your bowel disease?"

Grateful for Mrs. Robson's concern, Evie smiled, but being appreciative didn't cancel out the annoyance of being known around town as "That peedie girl with Crohn's." Nothing seemed to displace the label, not winning the school's science fair, not volunteering with the family history society, not serving customers in her mother's shop. Crohn's was always front and center, what people remembered most about her. If she wasn't defined by her disease like her mother said, why did everyone keep bringing it up? She brushed her bangs from her eyes and reminded herself not to be snarky. "It's been okay. Behaving."

"Aye! Glad to hear it." Mrs. Robson patted Evie's arm. "Say hi to your parents for me." She grinned then weaved her way down the packed steps.

Evie searched the crowd again.

"So…" Plowing through her belongings, Sunita nudged aside crushed bags of Cheesy Wotsits and a dented box of Tunnock's marshmallow Snowballs, sustenance for the long haul. The Ba' could last eight minutes or eight hours. "Does your mum worry—ahh! There it is!" Sunita pulled out her phone, flipped it open, and sat back on her haunches, checking text messages.

Evie peered down at her friend's tiny screen, the ache of being fourteen and a half and still phoneless flaring. "Worry 'bout what? Sam and Dad playing?"

Sunita took a beat to answer. "No…her shop."

Looking across the road, Evie eyed the temporary planks of wood running horizontally across the shop's windows and green door, temporary barriers against rampaging elbows and flying shoulders. Marwick's shopfront wasn't the only one; all the shops in the town center wore similar gameday protection. "Not really. Mum says we haven't broken a window in thirty years." When she licked her shimmery lip gloss, one of Sunita's Christmas presents, strawberry sweetened her tongue. She gawked at her friend's screen again. "Who's that from?"

"Fiona." Sunita raised her voice over the shouts from the Ba'. "She's totally chuffed. Got the Justin Timberlake CD."

JT owned Fiona's heart today, but who would claim it tomorrow was anyone's guess. Fickle Fi swapped heartthrobs as frequently as her underwear. Nick lasted barely two months before being replaced by a revolving door of actors, singers, and reality show contestants. Evie risked whiplash trying to keep up.

"Oh!" Sunita exclaimed. "She says, 'Thank Eves for my choker. Lovin' it!'"

"Knew she would," said Evie. "Fi's wanted it for ages." *Yeah, like me and a freakin' phone.* Picking at her bobbly mittens riddled with dropped stitches, she frowned, the dread of slipping further and further into teenage social oblivion weighing all too heavy.

"EVIEEE!"

Oh gawd. Squirming, Evie shifted her gaze down the street, away from the Ba', away from the beckoning voice.

"Wait! Is that—?" Sunita shot up onto her feet, her arms cradling a large plastic bottle of cola. Eyes darting, she scoured the sea of faces until she landed on her target. "It *is*! Evie, look! Stuart's over there, crossing the Kirk Green."

Acting oblivious, she glanced over. "Where?" Her tone dripped with disinterest.

"With the Flett twins." Sunita pointed. "See? He's looking this way."

A stocky eighteen-year-old with a stern brow and a buzzcut waved amidst the maze of rapt spectators. Proudly wearing his Scotland rugby top, old jeans, and steel-toed boots, Stuart obviously wasn't headed to his stepmother's Christmas lunch.

Evie raised her mitt politely, her brief acknowledgment unleashing another enthusiastic wave.

"Aw! Look at him!" Sunita giggled, bumping Evie with her elbow. "He *so* likes you!"

She turned away, hoping the University of Strathclyde freshman home for the holidays wouldn't come over. "I like him too, but not in *that* way." Eyes darting back, the former boys Ba' winner was gone, headed to the Uppie men's pre-game meetup. Not having her own phone held one advantage: Stuart Moodie couldn't bombard her with flirty texts.

Sunita tsked. "Why not? You moan constantly about wanting a boyfriend, and he'd be perfect. Older, fit, smart—he's studying mechanical engineering for fuck's sake! He's a parent's wet dream!"

Evie cringed into her scarf. "Then they can snog him."

"Ahh, Eves, you've gotta stop comparing Stuart and all the guys we know to Nikolai," said Sunita.

"I'm not!"

"You are! It's like you're waiting for something that'll *never* happen."

Evie shrank deeper into her scarf and pitched forward, evading Sunita's disapproving wince by scrutinizing a water stain on her knockoff Uggs.

"It's been a year and a half since music camp, and nothing—no Nikolai sightings, no conversations." Sunita scoffed through her braces. "And I'm sorry, but a stupid Twirl wrapper is *not* a token of true love..." She trailed off, watching the boys jockey for position, the ba' still concealed.

"It's not stupid." Evie punted the sandstone step with the rounded toe of her boot. "It reminds me of our time together." Parting with the chocolate wrapper wasn't up for discussion—not now, not ever, and as for the rest of Sunita's rant, Evie couldn't muster even a flimsy defense. Nick *had* vanished, at least around Orkney. Sam wasn't forthcoming with any information—were they even still friends?—and all island gossip about him had dried up, too.

Until a few days ago.

A taxi driver eating in her mother's café casually mentioned he'd driven the boys in from the airport for a Christmas celebration with their grandmother. Evie didn't dare blab the exciting news to Sunita, knowing full well how she'd react.

"Listen, I know Nikolai's like your ideal *everything*"—Sunita ducked her head, but Evie stubbornly refused to meet her beckoning brown eyes—"but what are *you* to Nikolai?"

Her words stung like a sharp, wet-handed cheek slap of reality, their blistering vibrations wrenching the remaining optimism from Evie's heart. It was one thing asking herself that pathetic question (and Evie had—many times), but quite another hearing it in the Orcadian lilt of her oldest, most trusted friend.

I hate when Sun's right.

Evie was fully committed...and not just emotionally.

Since meeting Nick, the musings in her journal had taken a one-way ticket to horny town, but her writing wasn't the only safe haven where her X-rated daydreams drew breath. Under her duvet, Evie fantasized of deep, open-mouthed kisses, Nick's hands on her breasts, and his hard length pressing hot and thick against her panties. Gasping, she'd slide in, pretending her touch was his, her inexperienced fingers exploring and teasing, making her delightfully dizzy and surprisingly wet until the most intense pleasure ripped through her, its breath-snatching waves slamming her deep into her pillows. The delicious, delirious haze of this once-secret release was unrivaled, the best EVER, until the next time, and the next.

Evie's hormones were calling the shots. Untangling herself from everything Nick would involve more than removing a few posters from her bedroom walls.

A blur of tears prickled. She raised her chin and blinked furiously, staring ahead as the bundle of boys lurched toward St. Magnus Lane, the dark alley carved between the town hall and an appliances shop.

"Oh, *Eves*." Looping her puffy parka sleeve around Evie's shoulders, Sunita tugged her close. Her sudden shift sloshed the fizzy cola inside the large bottle. "I didn't mean to make you cry." Sunita offered a sad smile. "I'm just looking out for you, you know that, right? I hate seeing you disappointed."

"I know," Evie mumbled, swiping away a rogue tear. "And you're right—I'm nothing more than a silly fan."

"One of thousands, unfortunately." Sunita agreed a little too enthusiastically.

"I feel so stupid thinking he'd like me." Evie sniffed as an epiphany elbowed its way into her thoughts. *Face it: Stuart is the best you'll ever get.* Her stomach sank.

"But at least you met him, right?" said Sunita. "How many fans can say that? No wonder you're smitten like a kitten. And I get it. I do…" She hesitated.

"*But…?*"

"Celeb crushes aren't real life. Eves, at some point you have to move on."

Yep. Evie knew that was coming. "I *am*!"

Sunita's brows arched. "Are you? 'Cause I swear the *Dalston Grove* Christmas special made you worse."

"The way it *ended*, though…" Shaking her head mournfully, Evie let out a forceful exhale. "Jake and the baby moving to Wales…he's gone. Forever."

"Characters get written out of TV shows all the time." Sunita dropped her arm from Evie's shoulder, her tone beyond fed up.

"They *have* to bring him back," said Evie. What would she do without her weekly fix of Nick?

"I guess there's always a chance. Unlike whatserface— Amanda." Sunita unscrewed the red cap from her cola. "She got on my tits most of the time, but even *I* think killing her off during childbirth was a tad harsh."

Evie paled. "I'm never, ever having kids."

"And on that bombshell, cheer up, would ya? Things aren't so bad. It's Chrimbo and you've got a REAL eighteen-year-old dying to snog your knickers off—"

"Ugh, don't!" Evie recoiled as the older woman standing next to Sunita, a history teacher from their school, shot them some judgmental side-eye.

Unperturbed, Sunita foisted the open bottle into Evie's mittens. "And *I've* got some holiday spirit!"

Evie snickered. "Fizzy pop."

Leaning in, Sunita hid behind her hand. "It's a quarter vodka," she whispered through an impish smirk.

"How'd you—"

"Alaia."

Evie's brows scrunched as she spotted the cathedral's minister stood behind them. "But—?"

"Don't worry," Sunita insisted. "She didn't steal it from my parents' cupboard."

Underage drinking—especially *public* underage drinking— wasn't really Evie's thing, nor were carbonated beverages, but under the circumstances…

She cautiously sniffed the potion, inhaling an eye-watering

brew of sweet cola and something reminiscent of rubbing alcohol.

"Go on," urged Sunita. "It won't bite."

Upon Evie swigging a mouthful, a searing burn hit her tongue and cascaded down her throat. *Holy shit!* Her eyes watered as the liquid heat blazed through her. "Sunita!" she croaked, coughing into the crook of her elbow as the adults in their spectator cocoon stared. "You sure that's"—cough cough—"*only* a quarter?" Evie blanched.

"My bad!" Sunita giggled as she pried the boozy concoction from Evie's grip. "If this doesn't make you feel better, it'll definitely help you forget." She took a careful sip and crinkled her nose, hugging the precious bottle against her parka.

"Did you see the photos in *The Mail* last week?" Evie's shoulders sagged. "Nick walking his dog Ross around London—with Bree Wilson-Jones?" His blonde *Dalston Grove* co-star Bree played baby mama Amanda to Nick's baby daddy Jake. "There were photos of them leaving a club holding hands, too. Sun, I think they're together."

Sunita offered the bottle to Evie again. "Don't dwell. Drink."

Slowly lifting the Coke and cheap vodka to her lips, she took a small mouthful, its fizzy burn painfully pleasant this time. Evie blinked lazily and cradled the bottle as she spied an auburn-haired cutie in the crush. Her eyes sharpened. "Sun! Is that your guy?" Gesturing ahead, Evie's thumb poked through the dropped stitches in her mitten. "In the wine-colored football top?"

"No, that's my brother," said the posh English accent to her left. "That's Tarquin."

NICK?! Evie's heart exploded into a million glittery stars of confetti.

Six

EVIE

Now, Thursday, June 22

Eyeing the ferry arriving from Kirkwall, Evie murmured a "Thank god" and set down her wooden spoon, leaving behind three slow cookers of simmering chili and Gemma's well-thumbed copy of *The Cookery Year*. She scrambled to the catering truck's passenger-side door and slid it open, her impatient wave quickly acknowledged by a disembarking Sunita. Evie's frantic greeting, however, didn't dissuade a pair of black-and-white oyster catchers flying cheekily close. "Nice try"—she snickered, wiping her hands on her tomato sauce-spattered apron—"but crab isn't on the menu today."

She squinted ahead, delighting in the sun's shimmery dance across the Sound's choppy waves and the colorful lobster creels stacked quayside, but her appreciation stopped short of the imposing stone castle bearing *his* surname. She could ignore its majestic towers and Victorian turrets (all seven of them) until the Highland cows came home, but there was no disputing Balfour Castle's charms or why the production chose the estate on the island of Shapinsay for their first day of filming in Orkney.

Ignoring Nick, though, wouldn't be as easy.

He had shown up briefly during the morning rush, deep in conversation with the director, but he kept a healthy distance, his appetite for confrontation considerably less than it had been in Marwick's the day prior. The dark-haired woman Evie saw with him before the puppet crash (his assistant, maybe?) collected his breakfast (a black coffee and an egg and bacon burrito), and together they disappeared up the long winding road to the castle, sparing Evie an awkward run-in while frantically feeding a continuous flock of ravenous actors and crew.

Three hours later, her hands had stopped shaking, but her stomach and forehead remained knotted.

"One mealtime down, only seventy-something to go," she mumbled, returning to the binder housing Gemma's production-approved meal plans, meals Evie had never made, let alone for a group as large as the one filming at the castle.

One meal plan read later, Sunita barged through the truck's doorway along with a bulging assortment of Tesco bags. "Mmm!" Her grocery haul rebounded off the knees of her dark jeans. "Smells good!"

Rubbing the elastic edge of her hairnet with the heel of her hand, Evie quirked a brow. "Don't sound so surprised."

"Chili?"

"Yep, served with chunky bread and a spinach salad topped with apple and a vinaigrette dressing."

Sunita lifted her chin toward *The Cookery Year* and the multitude of sticky tabs protruding from its pages like a neon fringe. "Someone was swotting up on recipes last night."

"And this morning." Evie brushed chili seasoning off the thigh of her yoga pants. "I feel like the walking dead."

"Well, you don't look it."

Evie smirked. "Yet."

Sunita parked her shopping on the floor with a *thump*. "Hey, did you hear Mrs. Robson from the post office died? I saw a notice on the ferry."

"Yeah. Hers was the funeral we catered."

"Aww, she was lovely. I still have the *Lord of the Rings* stamps she gave me."

"You got commemorative stamps." Bending over, Evie rifled through the groceries. "I got embarrassing questions."

Sunita chuckled. "Gotta love old people."

"And I love *you*"—holding up a frozen butternut squash lasagne, Evie smiled—"for saving my ass. I'll pay you back ASAP."

"No rush. I bought ten of 'em just in case." Sunita pointed to the bags. "Oh, and there's fresh parsley in there, too. Sprinkle some on top and *bam*—homemade lasagne. The vegetarians will be none the wiser."

"Fingers crossed." Evie wedged the boxes of lasagne into the small freezer, a complicated game of frozen food Tetris if there ever was one. "I'm so mad at myself for screwing up."

"Eves, you're not the first person to botch a recipe, especially one for over thirty people."

"I know, but I pray they don't question why they're getting veggie lasagne instead of the scheduled veggie chili."

"So Gemma's definitely out of commission, then?" Sunita reached past the steamed-up slow cookers and stole a carrot stick.

"For at least a month. She's on bedrest. Not for the broken arm or concussion but for brain bruising."

Sunita grimaced as she munched.

"It could bleed so—best to be cautious." Evie scooped up the empty bags and stood, leaving the fresh parsley on the counter. "I told her not to worry about work or anything else, but like she'll listen…"

"What about the shop? How long will you be shut?"

"A few days. The builders are doing their best, but even if they finish tomorrow, we'd still be unable to reopen till next week. With shorter hours, too."

Sunita nodded. "I was gonna say. All your staff are either here or in sick bay."

"Fi said she'll cover. Poppy's chicken pox should be gone by then."

"Did she know Nick was coming?"

"I didn't ask," said Evie. "We didn't talk long last night. She was in the middle of making dinner for the kids."

"And he still hasn't spoken to you this morning?"

"Which is how I like it." Evie began folding the bags. "So! Gimme the goss! How's London, how's work? Are you sick of *Hook-up Holiday* yet?" She giggled. "I counted all the articles you've written this season—one hundred and sixty-nine."

"Rather fitting…"

Evie laughed again. "I read every single one. I'm so proud of you, Sun!"

"Thanks." Sunita looked out the truck's concession window. "I'm glad it's over. I loathe the damn thing. Made it hard to be impartial."

"Well, I thought you were. That's the sign of a true journalist." Evie grinned. "And how's Micah?"

"He's good. Busy. Lots of tourists." Sunita's gaze swung back. "You know what it's like, owning a shop—"

A buzz from Evie's phone, propped up against the window, claimed both of their attention.

Sam: Still think we should tell Mum. It's HER shop, Sprout. Not yours. Yet

Rolling her eyes, she continued folding the bags.

"I take it that's your brother?" Sunita picked up a Granny Smith apple from the cutting board.

"Sam thinks all this is too much for me."

"Well, it *is* a lot, Eves."

She shot Sunita a dirty look. "Not you, too."

"Hey, all I'm saying is this would be a lot for *anyone*."

Evie winced. "I'm sorry. I didn't mean to bite your head off. It's just—Sam's been really overbearing."

"Protective older brother syndrome strikes again." Sunita twirled the apple by its stem. "Does he know Nick's here?"

"I may have mentioned it." Evie stuffed the bags in a drawer. "I have to nail this, Sun. I can't go down in flames in front of Nick— of all people."

"You won't! We'll make sure of it."

"*We?*"

"You didn't think I'd abandon you in your time of need, did you?"

"But this is your holiday," said Evie. "You've worked damn

hard for this week off."

"Yeah and I'd be spending most of it with you anyway, right?" Sunita glanced around the narrow galley kitchen on wheels.

Evie knew sweating over its burners and griddle weren't part of Sunita's original holiday plans but couldn't have loved her more for offering. "You'll have to take an online food safety course. Takes a few hours."

"I'll do it tonight."

"You'll have to wear a hairnet."

"Awesome, 'cause yours is so fetching!"

Evie smiled. "Ah, Sun, I love ya. Thank you." A buzz came from the window again. "God, what *now*, Sam?" Her glare darted to the screen.

Caleb: See you at 8?

Oh shit. Totally forgot. Evie grabbed her phone, her shoulders caving. "Looks like One-Kiss Caleb will remain that way for the foreseeable."

"He canceled?"

"No, but I have to." She typed a quick reply.

Evie: In catering hell at the castle. Sorry! Another time?

"I have to buy groceries tonight then organize tomorrow's meals"—she hit send—"and make sure today's screwup doesn't happen again."

"I can help," offered Sunita. "Enlist Jamie and we could do it all in half the time." She peered out the concession window. "Where is the little delinquent, anyway?"

Evie left her phone on the counter. "Good question. I sent him up to the castle to restock the craft table over an hour ago. He hasn't answered my texts either."

"Well, why don't you walk up there, bring him back?"

"You *know* why." Stepping away, she opened the fridge and

removed bags of freshly washed spinach and baby greens.

"Eves, you can't avoid he-who-cannot-be-named forever. Besides, don't you wanna see a historical romance being filmed?"

"Of course I do, but—"

"Then go! I'll hold down the fort." Sunita snapped the stem off the apple. "I'll even make your salad."

He could be lurking anywhere.

Wandering the halls of Balfour Castle, Evie was too preoccupied with skirting Nick and searching for Jamie to absorb any of its Victorian beauty or the television magic unfolding around her. The castle's paintings and priceless sculptures collected around Europe, its exquisite plant-filled sunroom, and the elaborately dressed actors swishing past—all overlooked.

Voices and light spilled out of a nearby room. Evie paused in its doorway, standing behind a tattooed makeup artist, his blotting powder and fluffy brush at the ready.

"And...action!"

With those two words, the castle's drawing room came alive with an amorous couple in colorful Victorian evening dress twirling and dancing to...well, nothing.

Where's the music? Evie rose onto her tiptoes for a better look. *How do they dance without it?*

The choreographer stood off to the side counting out the beats while a boom operator holding a microphone aloft and a Steadicam operator strapped into a vest with the camera closely followed every box step, whisk, and spin of the characters.

"CUT!" shouted the director from the far corner, his command halting the actors mid-twirl. "That reverse turn was too fast again."

The male lead pointed angrily at his muttonchop sideburns. "That's 'cause my earpiece isn't working. I can't hear the music *at all.*"

His female partner twitched her long nose. "It would be easier if you played it out loud."

"It would," agreed the director, nudging his wire-framed eyeglasses, "but then the mics won't pick up your lines."

Aha! That's why it's silent! Evie blinked, thrilled to be privy to this production secret. She admired the room, taking in its gilded neo-Jacobean plaster ceilings and silk wallpaper in an elegant shade of sage. *So stunning.* Her mind wandered, imagining sitting down to an indulgent high tea with scones and crustless sandwiches while savoring the unforgettable sea view.

"Sound crew, could we get a replacement, please?" The director pulled off his headphones and stepped back from his camera monitor. "And in the meantime, let's take five."

Both actors and a camera assistant bolted from the room. Evie jumped back from the doorjamb, allowing access to the dining room across the hall where the craft table's granola bars, fresh fruit, candy, and drinks could be enjoyed freely. From the abundance of food Evie had seen upon arrival, it was obvious Jamie had followed her instructions, but his whereabouts were anyone's guess. Keeping clear of crew traffic, she edged along a wall painted a rich clover green and found a quiet spot tucked beside a rack of costumes. She began texting.

Evie: J, you still at the castle?

A few feet away, a pair of crew members darkened the dining room doorway and were joined by a tall male in black trousers and a silky black dress shirt stippled with white polka dots.

Evie could recognize Nick's flair for fashion anywhere.

Great. She hit send and bowed her head, pretending to type additional texts, hoping she'd remain inconspicuous while spying from afar.

"We'll definitely reap the benefits." Nick popped a strawberry in his mouth.

A doe-eyed woman in overalls flipped pages on a clipboard. "Is there room in the budget?"

Tearing into a muffin, a brawny fellow wearing cargo pants shrugged. "Doubt it. Special effects ain't cheap."

Nick swallowed. "We'll make room. Trust me, CGI Highland cattle will save us *loads* of aggro. They'll behave the way we want and we could create as many as we like, fill the entire pasture so the laird's fold looks exactly like it's supposed to. And it would save us time shooting and editing, trying to make three measly cows look like hundreds."

"But how will we pay for it?" asked muffin dude.

"Well…" Whisking a hand over his chin, Nick narrowed his eyes like he was calculating something in his head. "If we reduce our fog and rain machine usage, scrap the extras flying up from Glasgow, and dip into contingency, I reckon we'd free up the necessary finances."

Nick? Adept at budgets? Evie stared, amazed at how far he'd come from the child actor whose dubious math skills were cruelly mentioned in *The Mail*.

"So, local extras instead?" asked the woman.

"Yeah." Nick chewed his bottom lip. "What's the downside? They'll be cheaper, won't need accommodation. Put the word out today and we'll get plenty signed up in the next forty-eight hours. *And* if we go over our original quota, even better. The more locals involved, the more support for the project. If they feel part of everything, they won't complain as much when we close their roads and take over their beaches."

Evie folded her arms across her chest. *You wanna bet?*

"They'll need costume fittings," the woman replied. "Wardrobe will have to work overtime."

"That's fine. We'll cover it." Nick turned to leave. "If wardrobe needs more hands on deck, my sister-in-law Leia could help. She's a fashion designer."

Presumptuous dick. Leaning into the costumes, Evie shook her head, knowing how busy Tarquin's wife was with work and their toddler. *Maybe ask her first?*

"Nick, before you go," the clipboard woman called out, halting his progress, "you need to sign off on additional catering. More extras, more food."

Evie gulped.

"Sure. Let the caterer know ASAP. If anything else comes up, I'll be at the Old Kirk with the second unit." With an affable nod, he broke away and headed in Evie's direction.

Shiiit! Burying her nose in her phone, she sucked in a breath as the mahogany floorboards creaked.

A shadow darkened the screen. "Evie?"

Feigning surprise, she peeked up, finding Nick's head cocked to the side, his gaze probing, sweeping her hairnet-free braid. She lowered her phone. "Hey."

"Enjoying the shoot?"

Is he insinuating that I'm bunking off? Evie seethed for a beat then reminded herself to be polite and professional, to represent her mother's business to the best of her ability, vegetarian chili foul-ups aside. "I was checking the craft table, ensuring everything is satisfactory."

"Typical."

Evie bristled. "I beg your pardon?"

Nick scraped a hand through his hair. "It's just that Marwick's used to pride itself on customer service and satisfaction. It's great to see some things haven't changed."

Unlike me, you mean? If Nick was hoping Evie would welcome him back with open arms and a forgiving heart, he was fooling himself. *And what's with the half dig, half compliment?* She drew in a slow inhale through her nose, refusing to acknowledge his words.

He looked past her briefly. "Listen, I hate to spring this on you last minute, but there's been a change to our catering needs. Starting Saturday, we'll require additional food, both meals and crafty table. I hope that's not a problem?"

Evie could feel her credit card flinch. The catering outlay was already substantial, and the broadcaster wouldn't be reimbursing

Marwick's for another three weeks. Add on the spiraling costs to repair the shop's puppet damage and leaky roof, and Evie was battling a financial riptide without a life preserver.

"Nope, no problem."

"Terrific!" Nick nodded excessively then added "The production crew will be in touch" before continuing on his way.

Terrific. Watching him meet up with his assistant at the end of the hall, Evie's boldness melted into a puddle of despair. *I can barely manage now.* Her phone buzzed in her palm. *This better be you, Jamie.* She glanced down.

Caleb: Can I help? I've been told I make a mean chicken and rice soup

Seven

EVIE

Then, Monday, December 25, seventeen years ago

Evie's breathing stuttered, but the same couldn't be said for her mind, which launched into action mode.

You've rehearsed this a hundred times: no staring, no swooning, and no stupid fangirl questions!

Swallowing hard, she hugged Sunita's boozy bottle and swung toward Nick. Hair perfectly disheveled, lips slightly parted, shining eyes trained on *her…*

"Hi Evie." Deeper than she remembered and a little husky, Nick's voice wound around her like a warm, velvety hug. "Happy Christmas."

Sunita blinked upward. *"Great,"* she muttered.

Tingling waves flooded Evie's chest, washing away her somber attitude. Forget a phone under the tree; her perfect present came wrapped in a black, single-breasted cashmere coat. "Hey! Happy Christmas!" She beamed as each ecstatic thump of her heart chipped away at her long-practiced cool.

"It's great to find a friendly face!" said Nick.

Sunita, ever the pragmatist to Evie's lovestruck fangirl, offered an icy nod. "I'm Sunita, Evie's best mate."

Jeez, Sun! She bit back her inner cringe.

Dimples deepening, apparently Nick wasn't bothered by Sunita's aloof welcome. "Lovely to meet you. How's your Christmas been so far?"

"Great!" Evie jumped in. *Better than great—now.* She beamed. "You?"

"Same, yeah," said Nick. "Presents, home bakes, board

games—what's not to love?"

"Ooh, I *love* games," said Evie. "What's your favorite?"

"All of 'em! I'm a game geek. But if forced to pick, I'd choose Snakes and Ladders, and Kerplunk. Oh, and Jenga. What about you?"

"Mouse Trap. Always."

"A classic, nice!" Nick's eyes detoured to the large bottle in Evie's grasp as he tucked his phone away in a pocket. "Is it okay if I join your party?"

Sunita stiffened.

He could be with anyone, but he chose US! Evie bounced. "Of course!" She passed him the effervescent concoction. "But I should warn you, it contains—"

"Booze? Great!" Nick took a long pull on the bottle then shuddered through his swallow. "Whoa!" His face scrunched. "That's got a kick!"

Evie laughed, dragging her gaze down Nick's frame. *He's taller!* Towering above with legs that went on forever, he had to be at least six glorious feet now. His chest and shoulders also seemed broader, more filled out, making Evie blush over what else of Nick's might've matured.

While he worked through his wince, she tugged off her mittens and squirreled the embarrassing knitting project in her pockets.

"Cheers, Evie." Nick licked his lips and handed back the bottle.

"Say the word if you want more." Evie glanced happily at Sunita. Jutting out her chin, she was uncharacteristically quiet. Not a good sign.

"Music to my ears." Nick leaned into Evie. "Like your accent."

"My *what*?"

"Your accent," Nick repeated as Sunita did a double take. "It's *way* cool."

A laugh burst from Evie. "Are you drunk?!"

"No, really! It's fab and sing-songy, kinda like Welsh," said Nick. "I never really thought about it before, being around my gran and dad, but now that I'm learning dialects for my acting CV, I've realized how tough the Orcadian accent is to master."

"Shouldn't it come naturally?" Sunita asked as Evie downed a small mouthful of vodka and Coke. "You know...being half-Orcadian?"

"Hmm, not sure." Breaking eye contact, Nick studied the heaving swarm. "Gran reckons it's the cadence. It's similar to Norwegian. I can't quite grasp it."

"We have Norwegian ancestry. Loads of Orcadians do. You probably do, too." Evie followed his stare. Red-cheeked boys on the outside of the pack leaned in at a precarious forty-five-degree angle, exerting pressure on the center. "If you're looking for Sam, he's playing after this." She twisted the cap closed on the bottle. "In the men's game."

"Yeah, he said."

Her gaze snapped back. "You spoke with him?"

Sunita pried her bottle from Evie's hands.

Nodding, Nick pawed through his floppy hair, which was longer and more chaotic than on *Dalston Grove*. "Yeah, he rang me a few days ago."

Sam has Nick's PHONE number? Evie bristled as she fought through her surprise. *Freaking Sam, he could've told me Nick was coming!*

"I've never actually been to the Ba', so Sam dared me to show up. Now the cheeky beggar owes me a pint!" The actor laughed, his joy deep and throaty, and Evie melted, her annoyance seeping away. Nick was here—with *her*. Nothing else mattered.

Eyes narrowing, Sunita's probing gaze lingered.

"Actually..." Nick rooted around in his pocket and whipped out his phone. "Could you take a photo of me? Prove I turned up?"

"Absolutely." Evie nodded, inwardly cursing the classmates who claimed she lied about hanging with Nick during music camp. A single photo would've silenced all the doubters.

Nick slid the color screen on his phone, revealing a full keyboard.

"Holy!" Evie gasped as he placed the device in her hand. "Now *that* is cool."

"Let's see?" Sunita hovered over her shoulder.

"It's the latest model," said Nick proudly. "It can play video *and* has an MP3 player. I'll show you."

After a brief lesson, Evie was snapping pictures like a pro: Nick with the cathedral's red sandstone brick looming behind him, Nick pointing at the Ba' scrum. With each click, the yearning for a phone of her own ballooned, as did the temptation to snoop through Nick's photos. What other memories lurked inside? Family celebrations, exotic holidays, famous friends—Bree? He hadn't mentioned her. Not once. Maybe they weren't together after all? A swell of hopefulness brimmed in her chest.

She handed back his phone.

"Oh, come on. I need one of us, too," said Nick.

Of us! Evie sucked in a breath.

"It's the ultimate proof I was here."

Sure is! Beaming widely, she fought the urge to run a victory lap around the churchyard.

Turning to the middle-aged woman stood on their left, Nick adopted his most charming grin. "Excuse me? Could you take a photo of us three, please?"

An obliging nod and a few instructions later, Nick crouched into Evie. "You ready? One-two-three—SMILE!"

Like he had to ask. Cheeks lifting, Evie figured her grin could probably be seen from space.

Nick couldn't wait to show off the result. "Aw, check it! Coolest kids in Orkney."

Eyes twinkling, mouth open wide as he held two fingers up in a peace sign, Nick looked cheeky and undeniably hot while Evie...well, the dark circles under her eyes and faded lip gloss weren't the most attractive, but who'd be gawking at her anyway? Sunita, meanwhile, the other half of the Evie sandwich, stared back blankly, but Nick was right. Collectively, they looked pretty darn cool.

Evie bloomed into a wistful smile. *I'd love a copy.* Wishing was the best she could do. Nick couldn't text the photo to her non-existent mobile.

"The reception here is dodgy as fuck." He pocketed his phone. "I'll email the pictures to Sam when I'm back at Gran's."

"Brilliant!" Evie glowed, envisioning their photo taped to her bedroom wall. She'd force Sam to print it out. After all, he owed her BIG for keeping Nick's Ba' arrival secret.

"So! Sam said your family are Doonies. Mine too." Nick pointed to the boy wearing the claret and blue football shirt in the melee below. "You've already seen Tarq, he's fourteen. My other brother Rupert is sixteen, so he's playing in the men's game for the first time. He wears glasses and is a slighter build, so Sam said he'd keep an eye on him."

"He will." Evie gave Nick another appreciative once-over: tartan cashmere scarf, black trousers, and the shiniest top-stitched, brown leather shoes she'd ever seen. The seventeen-year-old looked fit for an audience with the queen, not an Orcadian brawl. She met Nick's eyes. "Why aren't you playing?"

"Erm…" He sucked in his bottom lip and chewed it for a moment. "Well, I *would* if I was allowed."

"Allowed?" said Evie. "Everyone's allowed—*well*, if you're a guy."

"No, it's my mum," said Nick. "She's quite strict about me playing sports. In case I get hurt."

"But it's okay for your younger brothers?" Sunita huffed. "Someone's the favorite."

"No, I'm not. It's just…work." Nick clarified. "If I broke an arm or cut my face—"

"What?!" Sunita howled. "That's so privileged. And *weird*."

Evie threw Sunita a peeved look, but his explanation didn't make sense to her either. "I thought you played football with Sam?"

"Sometimes, yeah. What Mum doesn't know won't hurt her."

"You sure?" Sunita hunched over and crammed the bottle in her backpack. "People talk here."

"Not to my mum they don't," said Nick, keeping an eye on the surging horde of determined adolescents. "People here think she's a bit...much."

Sunita straightened up. "Yeah, well, we're not impressed by bigsy behavior or showbiz shite." Harsh but true. The more ego or pretense, the less likely Orcadians would be awestruck.

However, the last thing Evie needed was for Sunita to sour this special moment with Nick by criticizing his famous mother.

Sliding her boot sideways into Sunita's trainers, Evie delivered a subtle *Quit it!* tap and plastered on a breezy grin for Nick's bene-fit. "So no more *Dalston Grove*, eh?"

Sunita rolled her eyes and started a conversation with the wom-an in front of her who owned the fish and chip shop by the harbor.

"Do you miss it?" asked Evie.

"Yeah, I'm feeling a bit adrift. Our cast was super tight. Like family, you know? A part of me feels envious, watching them carry on without me." Diving into his coat pocket, Nick unearthed a packet of candy and unrolled the torn opening, offering the sweets—white bottle-shaped gummies.

Milk Bottles were never Evie's favorite, but she helped herself anyway. "Oh, I love these! Thanks." She popped several of the jelly candies into her mouth and chewed, their sickly-sweet flavor bring-ing back unwelcome schoolyard memories of scraped knees and playing kiss-chase.

"But I'm looking forward to a new challenge, something that'll stretch me as an actor." Sounding wiser than his years, Nick bit a Milk Bottle in half and examined the remaining piece. "Seven years is a long time to play one character."

"I guess, yeah. So you a triple threat yet?" she asked cheekily.

A blank look crossed his face as he chewed. "Sorry, what?"

He's forgotten our chat? Evie's heart dipped. "The singing? You said before? At music camp—"

"*Oh* right. I'm working on it, taking vocal lessons with this West End bloke. Andrew Lloyd Webber recommended him."

Evie's eyes bulged. "You *know* him?"

"My mum does." He held out the bag of candy again.

Fingers slipping inside, Evie rescued another squishy sweet. "Nice for some! You'll be the Phantom in no time."

"Nah, I'd rather play Judas. Now *that's* a role."

"What, like in *Jesus Christ Superstar*?" she asked.

Nick lit up, clearly delighted Evie was familiar with the musical. "You've seen it?"

"You kidding? I've seen nothing, but my mum's obsessed with anything Andrew Lloyd Webber, especially *Cats*. When I was five, she dressed me up as Bombalurina with stick-on whiskers and red fur."

Nick laughed. "Now *that* I'd love to see."

"No freakin' way! I'd rather eat those photos than let you near them." She shook her head. "I can't believe it. *You*...into musicals. You're the first boy I've met who likes them."

"Well, you do live in Orkney."

"True." She giggled and ate the Milk Bottle. "What are your favorites—besides *Jesus Christ Superstar*?"

"That's easy: *Rent, Miss Saigon,* and *Spamalot*. Film-wise, I'd pick *West Side Story* and *Grease 2*."

"*Grease 2*?!" Evie gawped. "Isn't it supposed to be crap?"

Nick stepped back. "Give over! It's *waaay* better than *Grease*."

"That's impossible. Nothing can touch 'Hopelessly Devoted to You'."

"*Grease 2* can! The songs, the choreography—there's even a big dance number in a bowling alley."

"So?"

"Evie, bowling is the most amazing sport ever!"

She wouldn't know. Orkney didn't have a bowling alley. "Didn't you say that about table tennis?"

He made a noise in his throat. "Don't believe everything you read. Same goes for reviews. *Grease 2* is brilliant. That's a fact."

"Hmm, well, guess I should watch it, then."

Her promise unlocked Nick's smile, reaching his eyes. "Defo! It's magic, Evie. Really." He scratched his neck. "What are your faves?"

"*Xanadu* and *Starlight Express*."

Nick's head jerked back. "Really?!"

"I recorded *Xanadu* off the TV. My mum's got the *Starlight Express* cast album."

"Well, your picks are certainly unique!"

"Hey, I like what I like." Something, however, didn't add up for Evie. "So, if you love musicals and want to star in one, why'd you skip singing lessons ages ago?"

He gave his bag of candy a terse shake. "Good question." Squinting into silence, he stared at the hazy cloud of adolescent breath hanging over the Ba'.

Like he's gonna confide in you *again.* Evie berated herself. The first time at music camp was a fluke, like finding a groatie buckie on Scapa Beach. She looked sidelong at Sunita, who was gossiping with a cluster of new arrivals, five classmates all wearing jingle bell-dotted antlers.

"The truth is…"

Evie glanced back, and Nick stooped, bringing his lips near her ear.

"…it terrifies me," he murmured, his face pinching. "Singing live on stage." His volume dropped further, bordering on a whisper. "You know, in front of people."

"But you act in front of people," Evie responded quietly.

"That's different. Although, that makes me break out in hives, too, sometimes."

"Then why do it?"

As she pressed, Nick straightened up and surveyed the crowd like he was wary of eavesdroppers. "It's what I'm meant to do."

"Says who?"

"Me mum."

"You don't have any say?" she asked.

"Of course I do. It's just, I started *so* young, right? What say does a five-year-old have? But nowadays it's not like she forces me." An awkward half-laugh split his fleeting grin. "Much." His brows bounced as he dove back into his packet of Milk Bottles.

The playful admission, tacked on for comedic affect, didn't sit well with Evie. There was a hint of truth, a red flag in his throwaway chuckle. She couldn't let it unfurl without saying something. "But if you don't enjoy it—"

"I do—a lot. I love it," he volleyed back like a polished tennis pro guarding the net. "Going on set, being someone else, telling stories—how many kids get to do that? I'm extremely fortunate."

Was this another PR-practiced fake answer? Tilting her head, Evie served up her challenge. "Fortunate doing something that makes you feel uncomfortable?" She cleared her throat. "Maybe I'm missing something, but itchy hives don't sound like a laugh riot."

"But those angsty feels mean I care." He rocked forward with a subtle shrug. "I want to do a good job, build a solid career, make my mum proud…"

Evie couldn't argue with that. She wanted all those things, too.

"…so I have to do everything I can *not* to screw up. I can't be shit."

"You won't be! I mean, you're not! You're super talented." Evie smiled. "You're doing what you love."

"You can, too," said Nick, popping a candy in his mouth. "Whatcha fancy doing?"

Genealogy, writing—you. A blush heated her cheeks. "Too many things." She stuffed her hands in her coat's pockets. If he knew where her future was really headed, it would be bye-bye Nick-endorsed cool, hello boring island girl. Evie cleared her throat, eager to change the subject to something safe and road-tested. "I was in a school musical once."

"Really?" His voice rose mid-chew. "Which one?"

"*Bye Bye Birdie?*" Evie snickered. "See, even our school musicals are ancient."

"What role did you play?" He offered his candy again.

Evie shook her head. "Kim." She paused, hoping Nick didn't suss she'd basically played herself—a lovestruck teen mooning over her famous crush.

70

"Ahh, the girl who wins a contest to kiss Birdie." Nick sucked on his bottom lip then let it go.

Bugger. He knew.

"Have you seen the film?" asked Nick.

Her eyes widened. "There's a film?"

"My mum has the DVD. I'll lend it to you...with *Grease 2*." Nick laughed deeply. "This is fun. I rarely get to talk about musicals without being teased. My friends Zach and Kyle are ruthless about it."

"Well, they're assholes," said Evie.

He let out another adorable but brief laugh.

"At least your Mum enjoys them."

"But she gets all technical, talking about how the singer projected their voice or why a scene was staged a certain way. Every discussion turns into a teaching opportunity. It sucks the fun out of it." Nick folded down the bag of candy and placed it in his coat pocket. "But you're a fan. Like me."

He glanced back to the Ba', but his words lingered. Kind and inclusive, they swirled around Evie, hugging her tight. She was the keeper of Nick's secrets and dreams and sincerest hopes for the future...and maybe one day—hopefully—she'd be part of them, too.

Admiring his hair cavorting in the breeze, she settled in, unabashedly adoring his long dark lashes and mesmerizing grin.

His eyes popped wide. "JESUS!"

Evie threw a look toward Broad Street. Thrust up in the air, two teens flipped head over ass, sending spectators scrambling for safety. People pitched backward, others froze, too gobsmacked to move—but not Nick. He seized Evie's shoulder and yanked her close as the boys landed with a guttural "OOF!"

She squealed, her cheek brushing the softness of Nick's cashmere coat. "My god!" Her heart galloped faster, wilder, out of control, the distressing spectacle conspiring with his firm embrace. She peered up from his chest, but Nick's attention was elsewhere.

"Bollocks!" His throat bobbed as shouts of encouragement filled the air and the game raged on. "We need, we need to *DO* something!" As his glare roamed, Nick's fingers curled, clutching Evie's coat.

"They'll be okay, see?" She motioned to a blonde woman rushing forward with a large backpack and two middle-aged males in tow. "That's Dr. Drever. She'll take care of them."

Rising slowly, the boys ignored their fresh scrapes and bruised egos and waved off the doctor's efforts. They flashed two thumbs up, then plunged into the ruckus again, eliciting a roar of applause that reverberated between the cathedral and the row of shops.

Relief and joy ballooned in Evie's chest. She closed her eyes briefly, blissfully lost in Nick's impromptu hug, his clench strong and sure and beyond romantic.

"That was AWESOME!" Sunita joined the Ba' ovation, clapping her approval. Her eyes skated over Nick, who stared back, incredulous.

"Bloody hell! They practically fell on their *heads*." His voice rose higher than usual. "That could've been my brother..." He trailed off and released Evie, the warmth and weight of his embrace dearly missed.

"You okay?" She leaned in, fighting a shiver.

"Yeah." He looked down at her, a flicker of a smile playing with his mouth, then quickly disappearing. "Sorry. I-I didn't mean to grab you like that."

Grab away! I loved it! Evie grinned. "Nick—"

"The crowd surged and"—he dragged a frantic hand through his hair—"instinct kicked in."

Protected by Nikolai Balfour. Evie now had a new scenario to add to her daydream repertoire, only this one was better.

This one was real.

She gave his arm a sneaky squeeze. "Nick, *seriously*, it was sweet. Thank you for looking out for me."

But her gratitude didn't seem to soothe his regret. Stashing his hands in his coat's pockets, Nick's pained gaze swooped to Sunita's glower. "But still...it won't happen again."

Evie's heart buckled.

"I'm headed back to London tomorrow."

"So soon?" Another pang rippled through her chest.

"Yeah, things to do, people to see."

Like Bree? Evie's lips pressed as her jealousy flared. "No rest for the wickedly popular?"

"Or the recently unemployed," said Nick. "Mum scheduled back-to-back meetings with some casting people on the 27th. Tarq and Rupes are staying for the New Year's Day Ba'." His sunny disposition darkened as a muffled ringtone erupted from his pocket. "But after today, I wish they weren't."

Evie twisted Sunita's way, expecting a terse eyeroll, but her best friend closed the distance with a sympathetic stroke of her arm.

Green Day's 'Boulevard of Broken Dreams' died abruptly in Nick's palm. "*Fuuck*, another dropped call?" Scowling, he rubbed his brow with furious intent. "This place—it's doing my head in."

A sour taste rose in Evie's throat. Nick's hate-on for all things Orkney wasn't budging, but didn't she count for something? Didn't their friendship?

"E-vie!" Sunita danced. "Gotta text for ya!"

"Forgot your phone?" Nick looked up from his.

"Yeah, the second time in as many days!" Evie shook her head self-deprecatingly then swung toward Sunita. "What's Fi want?"

"It's Stuart!"

Kill me now. Evie shot Nick a harried glance as he toyed with his phone. Would he think Stuart was her boyfriend? *Fuck no.* She cleared her throat. "It's probably nothing. Tell me later?" The effervescence in her voice drained away.

"He's asking you out!" Sunita flashed a full-on metallic smile.

Squinting at the phone's tiny screen, Evie hoped Sunita was, well...being Sunita, playing the I-know-how-badly-you-want-a-boyfriend card for the millionth time.

Stuart: 4 Evie: Will u go 2 xmas film w/me tmrw?

He texted like a ten-year-old. Evie scrunched her face. "I think

I'm busy."

Orkney only had one cinema screen at the Pickaquoy Centre (aka "the Picky"), so there was no mistaking the movie. "I thought you wanted to see *The Holiday*," Sunita prodded.

"The Cameron Diaz film?" Nick blinked Evie's way. "It's brilliant!"

He liked rom-coms? She did a double take. "You've seen it?"

Nick pressed his phone against his ear. "Bree and I went last week. You should definitely go"—eyes darting away, his grin brightened—"Hey, gorgeous! Happy Christmas!" Pausing for a moment, he laughed, and a puff of breath escaped into the air. "*Yeah*, sorry 'bout that. Reception here is shit." He turned away for privacy. "So how's London, Bree? Missing me?"

There it was. Definitive proof. Not from her brother, a gossip site, or a magazine, but straight from Nick. He had a girlfriend—a beautiful, famous one—whom he took to the cinema while Evie was alone, writing raunchy Nick fic in her bedroom, waiting…and for what?

Sunita whispered in her ear. "Stuart's nice, Eves. It's not fair to leave him hanging. Give the guy a break, yeah?"

She let out a long, mournful sigh. Oh, how she hated when Sunita was right.

EIGHT

EVIE

Now, Friday, June 23

Sunshine glowed around the edges of the blackout curtains as Evie, mid-yawn, shoved another book back onto its shelf. "It's gotta be here somewhere."

"You said that twenty minutes ago." Sunita skated her finger along a succession of colorful spines. "Kudos to your mum and all, turning your old bedroom into a library, but she should've asked *my* mum for tips on how to organize it. She's got her cookbooks mixed in with her novels and gardening books. It's every librarian's nightmare."

"Then your mum's had a lucky escape, right?"

Sunita sighed and pulled out an autobiography shelved between two travel guides.

"Good thing it's only six a.m.," said Evie.

Sunita yawned. "What's so good about it?"

Evie moved to another shelf. "We've got plenty of time. Our ferry doesn't leave for another hour."

"Why don't we look online? There will be tons of recipes for oven-baked chicken parmesan."

"Because I need Mum's *actual* cookbook," explained Evie. "I saw her change the recipe. She left handwritten notes in the margins."

Disbelief flamed in Sunita's eyes. "She *what*?"

Her continuous questions and complaints were beginning to grate. "Yes, Sunita, Mum wrote inside the book!" Evie scraped her bangs off her forehead. "I know it's a huge no-no and your mum would freak, but it's *Mum's* book, not yours or the library's. She

75

can write in it all she wants, okay? And I have to find it so I won't screw up again. It's the recipe she used for a retirement bash last year." Heavy footfall pounded up the stairs, but Evie didn't stir. "It has accurate ingredient measurements for a party of forty."

A breathless Fiona popped around the doorjamb. "Reporting for duty!"

"Fi!" Sunita leapt across the cozy room, enveloping the third member of their friendship trinity in a cheek-squishing hug. "God, I've missed you! How's the fam?"

"They're great!" Fiona grinned over Sunita's shoulder. "The doctor cleared Poppy yesterday for nursery, so here I am, ready to pitch in." Easing back from their embrace, she locked eyes with Evie. "Still no luck?"

She mournfully shook her head and plopped down on the carpet, searching anew along the bottom shelf of the bookcase neighboring her former closet.

"At this rate, we'll have the whole house torn apart." Sunita picked up a small step stool as Fiona kneeled down and began reading spines.

"Your mum sure loves her books and magazines," she said.

Yawning, Evie blinked. "What can I say? Like daughter, like mother."

Sunita placed the stool inside Evie's closet and stepped up, shifting a clear bag of cardigans on the top shelf followed by the lid of a cardboard storage box.

Evie glanced up from the floor. "Oh Sun, don't bother up there. It's just clothes and junk."

Holding up an old copy of *Flirty Girl*, Sunita smiled. "Like this gem?"

"Oh wow!" Fiona laughed. "You still have those?"

Sunita tossed the magazine down to Evie, its ragged cover graced with what had passed for teenage sophistication eighteen years prior: Amanda from *Dalston Grove* adorned in a bohemian peasant blouse and floppy hat from Topshop. "Mum must've packed them when I moved out." She flipped through its pages, pausing to revisit a dog-eared article entitled "Undatable: Are You Unlucky in Love?"

Sunita dug through the box. "I'll never forget that school trip to Skara Brae. You were so pissed."

"I wasn't *pissed*," she protested.

Fiona hauled a thick cookbook off a shelf. "What happened?"

"You bought Evie's copy of *Flirty Girl*," said Sunita. "The one with Nick's poster?"

"I did?" Fiona's tone was high and dripping with uncertainty.

"The newsagent always put it aside for her dad to pick up."

Brow creasing, Fiona lowered the heavy book to the floor. "Eves, why didn't you say something?"

She flicked the page. "And stomp on your excitement? No way."

"I don't remember any of this," said Fiona. A notoriously crap liar, Evie knew she was telling the truth. "The one thing I *do* remember was getting my period for the first time and having to ask the teacher for a pad."

"Oh, I remember that!" said Sunita. "I was so embarrassed for you."

"I was envious." Evie pored over another page.

Fiona's lips quirked. "Careful what you wish for, right?!"

"God, yeah. Truer words have never been spoken."

Grinning, Fiona dismantled another stack of books as Sunita, high up in the closet, tugged the corner of an old duffel, releasing something rectangular wrapped in turquoise fabric. "Oh shit!" she gawped, gathering the torn bag in her arms as Evie was struck on the head.

Her shoulders hiked protectively up to her ears. "Oww!" She grimaced, glaring at the culprits scattered around her: *Bye Bye Birdie*, *West Side Story*, *Grease 2*—Nick's DVDs—lying beside his crumpled bowling shirt. Post-split, he didn't ask for his stuff back, and Evie didn't have the heart to trash it either.

She knew she ought to. What was the point of hanging on to it? Like the old Twirl wrapper and the Ba' photo and every other doomed souvenir from their relationship, their mere existence was an agonizing reminder of her teenage foolishness and the boy she had loved and inexplicably lost.

Fresh from their split, Evie hid it all away and told herself tales to facilitate moving on: *Nick's a selfish dick, he HATES Orkney and you don't want to be with someone like that*, and the most sob-soaked tale of all—*Nick's not the empathetic, trustworthy boy you thought he was.*

With repetition and time and countless balled-up tissues saturated with tears, the words took root, growing into full-fledged stories, which shielded Evie from the harsh reality of her pain. She believed each one with every beat of her bruised heart, but to finish the job and ditch the mementos of their relationship? That was a step too far, a move toward permanently erasing something that was once beautiful and life-changing...*and real*.

Well, at least Evie thought it was.

"Babe, you okay?" Sunita hopped off the stool and kneeled down, gently resting her hand on Evie's back. "I'm sorry. How's the head?"

She dragged the shirt toward her, keeping the embroidered *Louis* hidden. "If I wasn't awake before, I am now!" Her playful smile wavered as she held up *Grease 2*.

Scrutinizing the film titles, Sunita snickered. "No wonder you buried those away. Eves, your teenage taste was in your ass!"

"Don't I know it." She hastily rounded up the DVDs.

"Hey, if you wanna get rid, I'm doing a drop-off at the charity shop this afternoon," said Fiona.

"Oh! Thanks, Fi...but Mum might have stuff to donate, too." Cramming the belongings into the nearest bookshelf, Evie flashed a grin. "Best to wait."

On the cusp of giving up, Evie exhumed the tea-stained cookbook from a pile of photo albums under the desk. With minutes to spare, she and Sunita waved Fiona farewell, picked up their chicken from the butcher, and raced through the morning fog to the Shapinsay ferry, ensuring that their hot breakfast of eggs, sausages, and hash-browns was cooked and served on time. Nick, however, didn't show or send his PA for the second meal in a row, leaving Evie wondering, *Were yesterday's breakie burritos that bad?*

Prepping for lunch with her mum's notes by her side, she fell into a pounding rhythm with Sunita, their mallets flattening a seemingly endless supply of chicken breasts.

"Fi said she's dying to see inside the castle," said Sunita, pausing for a well-deserved sip of coffee. "She might sign up the girls, too."

"She better act fast," said Evie. "I overheard the production manager say they've got thirty extras so far."

"I don't doubt it. I saw a notice on the ferry and in the window of the newsagent. They're *everywhere*. Got a mention on the radio, too."

Glancing out the window, Evie spied her brother in his blue veterinarian scrubs walking up the drive toward the truck and the castle's gatehouse. "Sam's here?" She shared a quizzical look with Sunita and slid open the glass.

He waved. "Hey, Sprout! My morning surgery got canceled, so I thought I'd come over, check on Mr. Rendall's bull." He patted the backpack dangling from his arm. "I brought sandwiches. Wanna bite before I head back on the ferry?"

"She does, yep! *Please* make her eat something." Leaving her coffee on the counter, Sunita walked over to the sink and began washing her hands.

Evie pummeled the last chicken breast, taking out her frustrations. "I don't have time."

"You don't have time to faint either," said Sunita. "We're not serving lunch till two." She peeked at her watch. "You have over an h—"

"Fine. I'll eat."

"Good!" Sunita tore off a piece of paper towel.

After washing her hands, Evie picked up a cola for Sam and a water for herself and joined him at one of the picnic tables dotted around the truck. He popped open a plastic container and handed her a sandwich.

Evie snooped between the bread, spotting purple jelly. A hit of nostalgia buzzed through her. "Woohoo, PB and J! Thanks, Sam! I haven't had this in ages." She bit into the spongy white bread, and sweet grape and salty peanut butter greeted her tongue. "*Mmm—memories!*"

"What's this *ages* business? It's one of your comfort meals." Sam wolfed a corner of his ham and cheese.

Chewing blissfully, Evie grinned into a swallow. "*Was* one. I've grown up. My tastes have changed."

"You say that," he mumbled through his mouthful, "but I saw you tear into a pack of Snowballs last week."

"Shh! You're blowing my cover. I'm supposed to be a connoisseur of the culinary arts, don'tcha know." With a laugh, she licked grape jelly off her bottom lip. "How's the Rendalls' bull?"

"Better. His eye is finally healing. How are you?" Sam took another substantial bite of his sandwich, leaving little behind.

"Hanging in." She nibbled the crust. "Praying I don't poison anyone."

"It's not too late to call Mum."

Evie lowered her sandwich. "Would you stop?! This is the first time she's been away in literally decades. I want her to enjoy herself. I'd like the chance to make her proud, too, show her I can cope. She's always so hands-on."

"I know, but you look shattered, and Mum wouldn't want you stressed—"

"I'm not!" *Much.*

"When's your next infusion?" asked Sam. Evie's current treatment for Crohn's was an intravenous medication administered at the hospital as an outpatient every eight weeks. The meds worked well, keeping most of her symptoms at bay, but exhaustion wasn't one of them.

"July 29. After work."

"Evie, you're running yourself into th—"

"I'll be fine!" She tucked into her sandwich, feeling her brother's gaze lingering.

They both fell silent, eating their lunches while a band of gulls harassed a fisherman on the pier. As the sun poked through the clouds, spilling its shimmer across the waves and the approaching ferry, Evie smiled, hoping the weather would hold out.

"I thought I'd see joyriding Jamie about," said Sam, stowing his empty sandwich container in his bag. "I hope he's not hiding in the truck's loo having a sneaky smoke."

"No, he's around back," said Evie. "Probably having a sneaky smoke while setting up the tea and coffee station."

"Has he been giving you much lip?"

"No. He goes walkabout more than I'd like, but at least it's on foot and not in a stolen car."

Her brother cleared his throat. "And what about Nick? You spoken to him?"

"Briefly." Evie lifted her bottle of water. "Just work stuff." She downed a sip.

"He didn't say anything else?"

"No. Why would he?" She snapped the bottle's sports cap closed. "Assholes don't apologize, Sam. Haven't you learned that by now?"

He nodded slowly as a stream of actors neared the truck, most glued to their phones. "Sprout, you sure you're all right?"

Evie contemplated the remaining half of her sandwich. "I will be."

Sunita rested two baking sheets filled with hot chicken parmesan on the counter and stole a glimpse outside at the hungry crowd. "You're popular today."

Tossing a substantial green salad, Evie looked out the window, her gaze narrowing. She set down the tongs. "What's he...?" Wiping her hands on her apron, she rushed outside.

Dressed in a flannel jacket and faded jeans and hefting a bulging backpack the size of a small child, Caleb's blue eyes lit up with his wide smile. "Hiya! I had the day off, so I thought I'd make myself useful." The kiddie wagon trundling behind him drew confused glances from the waiting crew. "Looks like I made it in the nick of time, too." He let go of the handle and scratched his dark blond beard as he shifted toward two large steel pots, their lids secured with cling wrap and several strategically placed elastics.

Evie grinned back. "Is this your famous soup?"

"Enough to feed at least twenty. They just need reheating."

She laid her hand on her chest. "Caleb, really, this is so kind of you."

He shrugged off his backpack, leaving it on the ground. "It's what we do here, right?" Bending slightly, he lifted one of the heavy containers. "Pitch in, help one another. I'll bring 'em inside?"

"Sure. Thanks." Leading the way, Evie hopped up into the truck. "On the stove would be great." She raised her brows as she squeezed past Sunita. "Caleb brought us soup."

"Ooh, I know what I'm having." Holding her oven mitts close, Sunita leaned into the counter, gifting Caleb sufficient room to pass.

"Well, I figured it's been rather chilly this week, and what you don't use today, you can serve tomorrow." Setting the pot on a vacant burner, Caleb gestured toward the open door. "One down, one to go." He hurried back outside.

With Caleb clear of earshot, Sunita gave Evie a smug grin. "I don't like to sound like a broken record, *but*..."

Evie rolled her eyes then looked out the window as Sunita removed the taut elastics stretching from handle to handle on the pot.

"...but if this isn't proof he has a thing for y—"

"Sun!" Evie trod on her foot.

"Ow—what?!"

"He's back," she murmured as Caleb swept through the doorway.

"Now you're all set." Edging past her, he placed the second pot on the stove. Sunita removed its elastics and plastic wrap and lifted the lid for a cheeky sniff.

"Will you stay for lunch?" Evie switched on the two burners. "We have plenty."

"I'd love to, but I'm meeting the scouts on the far side of the island. We're camping this weekend."

"You're a scout leader?" She raised her voice over Sunita's handwashing. "I didn't know that."

"Yeah, I loved it so much as a bairn, I thought I'd give back," said Caleb. "And who can say no to sleeping under the stars on a summer's evening?"

Not me. Evie smiled.

"Granted, with the solstice, we probably won't spot any." He wiped his brow as Sunita lowered a ladle into one of the soups, giving it a vigorous stir. "Well, I should make a move…"

Evie accompanied him to the door and touched his arm, his muscles firm beneath her fingers. "Thanks so much."

"Anytime!" Caleb turned back. "And no pressure returning the pots or rescheduling our date. I know things are hectic."

"I'll text you soon."

"Looking forward to it." Collecting his wagon and backpack, Caleb headed toward his SUV.

In his absence, the truck fell silent. Briefly.

"*Who can say no to sleeping under the stars*," Sunita teased, grabbing compostable paper plates and bowls. "He wants to *do* you. Outside."

Evie fought back a delighted grin. "At least someone does!" Maybe One-Kiss Caleb would lose that unfortunate nickname soon after all. She tossed the salad, ensuring every buried tomato was glistening with olive oil. Stuck in a sexual drought the past four years, the thought of steamy sex left her breathless. "Isn't he love-ly?"

"Yeah." Sunita motioned to the window. "He's also chatting with Nick."

Alarm bells rang between Evie's ears as her past and present collided. She pitched sideways, stealing a look. "He's *here*?" Not only had Nick skipped breakfast, he had also skipped the previous day's lunch.

"Yup. Middle of the queue."

True to form, he was immaculately dressed in a dark suit that probably cost more than Evie's monthly rent. "I was hoping he'd been called away."

Sunita began filling plates with chicken. "Want me to serve him?"

Caleb did that guy-patting-another-guy-on-the-back thing and strolled off, leaving Nick immersed in his phone.

Evie pulled her gaze away and gave the salad one last flip. "No, better not. I have to learn to leave my emotions at the door and deal with him."

"It'll get easier."

She pressed her lips together.

"It will," said Sunita kindly. "I promise."

Evie slid open the concession window and greeted the first crew members in line with a welcoming smile and a buoyant, "Hi! What can I get you? Chicken parmesan with salad or chicken and rice soup—or both?"

Plate after plate, bowl after bowl, Evie and Sunita were in constant motion, dishing up meals and placing them into eager hands, the chorus of thank-yous upon receipt making their harried efforts worthwhile. The lead actors, however, had requested lunch in their trailers, so Sunita loaded up a tray with everything on offer and set off with Jamie to serve the VIPs.

Returning to the window, Evie received an all-business "Hello" from Nick.

"Hi," she replied, dampening any emotion in her voice. "Chicken parmesan or chicken and rice soup?"

"Chicken parm. Cheers." He rocked back on his heels and looked away.

Yeah, sure. Evie picked up a plate. *Don't ask about my health and open up* that *can of worms.*

Adding salad along with a paper-wrapped, compostable fork, Evie approached the window, realizing she'd forgotten his knife. "Oh, hang on one sec…"

Eyes on his chicken parmesan, she reached sideways and…plunged into a bubbling cauldron of scalding liquid.

The soooup!

Squinching, Evie yanked her hand free from the scorching hell, and in the process, tipped Nick's food down the front of his designer suit. He shouted—something—but Evie was consumed by her searing nightmare, spitting out a shrill "Shiiit!" as the chaotic *OH GOD, OH GOD!* screaming in her head snagged, halted by hitched breaths and the escalating throb pulsing through her fingers.

She buckled forward, the swell of nausea sloshing in her stomach as she whimpered, cradling her blistering hand. All thoughts of slopped food and hungry clients evaporated like the billowing steam escaping the pots on the stove.

"How bad is it?" asked Nick, suddenly by her side. "Let me see."

"I-I'm fine," Evie stammered, her watery wince locked on the red splotch blighting her hand.

"Come with me."

Body stiffening, Evie's stare darted, her gathering tears blurring the splodge of cheese and splattered tomato sauce soiling his suit. "No!"

"Just to the sink," said Nick. "To cool the burn. Water will reduce pain and swelling."

The sizzling agony wobbled her knees and weakened her resolve. As much as Evie hated being reliant on Nick, she'd do just about anything to stop her hand feeling like a pancake left too long on the griddle. "Okay." She sniffed, shuffling to the back of the truck.

Running the taps, Nick stuck his fingers in the water, testing the temperature. "It might sting at first."

Evie cautiously placed her hand under the stream, its coolness prompting a flood of stabbing tingles through her skin. She sucked in a breath.

"You're doing great," said Nick. "Now, hold it there for a few minutes, okay?"

Evie withdrew her hand. "I have to serve lunch."

"The crew can wait. This can't," he answered confidently and widened his eyes like he was urging her to obey. "Evie, you've got to trust me."

I can't. She balked, another piercing throb pulsing through her hand and her heart. Swallowing hard, hot tears rolled down her cheeks. *Not now. Not ever again.*

"Honestly, this *will* soothe the burn."

The ache intensified. "Oww!" She gritted her teeth.

Nick's expression grew flustered. "Evie, *please.* Don't fight me on this. I'm trying to help."

Begrudgingly, she complied as he removed his phone from a trouser pocket and began texting. She wiped away the teary evidence on her face with her other hand. "Who are you messaging?"

"Our on-set medic. While we wait for her, I'll serve the crew."

Putting his phone away, Nick washed his hands then stepped up to the counter, passing two plates of chicken and salad through the window to the next people in line.

Evie craned her neck. "You need a hairnet. The box is—"

"Got it." Without protest, Nick pulled the elastic and plastic cap over his hair, squashing his pride and joy.

He's actually wearing it!

Washing his hands once more, he resumed serving. "The soup? No, we're all out. Sorry." He leaned closer to the window and his colleague waiting outside. "Between you and me," his volume lowered, "the chicky parm is better anyway."

Evie slipped into a pout, simultaneously annoyed and bewildered by his kindness. *And I've ruined his suit.* The sting of guilt prickled.

Several served meals later, Nick joined her at the sink, checking on the red, blistering blotch marring her right hand. "How's it feel?"

"Sore but numb, too—the water…" Fixating on his damaged suit, she cleared her throat. "If the dry cleaners is closed in Kirkwall when you get back, dab a mixture of dish detergent and white vinegar on the stain. Let it sit for twenty minutes then rinse with cool water. But don't saturate it. That'll make it worse. If that's possible," she mumbled.

A surprised glint arose in his eyes. Nick opened his mouth to say something—

"Oh my GOD!" Sunita and her serving trays clattered through the door. "What happened?!" Mid-double take, her lip curled at Nick and his hairnet. "What's *he* doing here?!"

"I burned my hand. I was serving him when it happened."

Notoriously grossed out by blood and gore, Sunita peeked over Evie's shoulder. "You okay? Looks painful."

"I'll live."

Nick leaned in. "So the bloke who brought the soup…"

Evie snuck a sidelong glance at his razor-sharp cheekbones and chiseled jawline, worthy of a Norse god. A breath caught in her throat.

"…he's a member of your catering team?"

"No. A friend."

"Yeah!" exclaimed Sunita, stowing the trays under the counter. "One with benefits."

His lips pressed into a straight line.

If her hand hadn't been throbbing, Evie would've laughed and pounded Sunita's palm with an exuberant high-five. "Why?" she asked innocently. "You know him?"

"No. He asked for a selfie. His sister is a *Dalston* fan."

"Jeez, that must suck, huh?" Sunita jumped in without a whiff of sympathy. "Peaking in your teens, being reminded of it constantly…"

Nick looked like he'd been slapped but didn't take the bait.

"*Sun.*" Evie shot her best friend a *knock it off* glare as the truck groaned with the medic's arrival. Nick may have broken her heart thirteen years ago, but he was currently a client, one deserving respect and professionalism. Her mother wouldn't have it any other way.

"Sorry to interrupt." Tugging on a pair of examination gloves, the medic's focus flitted from Nick and Sunita to Evie.

"No, of course." Nick backed up and Sunita followed, making space. "Thanks for coming quickly."

The medic nodded. "Evie, can I see your hand? How does it feel?"

"Tight and stingy"—she pulled away from the running taps— "but not as bad as before."

"That's the cool water." The medic carefully examined the burn. "It slows inflammation, soothes the pain. Someone was on the ball."

"Too right," said Sunita. "Evie knows her first aid inside out."

She shook her head. "Not this time. I froze, I…" *Failed.*

"That's normal," said the medic as Nick removed his jacket. "It's our body's way of protecting itself. It prevents us from making a rash decision that could cause further harm." She surveyed the counter. "Do you have cling wrap?"

Evie nodded. "Sun, can you…?"

Sunita placed the box in the medic's open palm. "What's it for?"

"To wrap the burn." She tore free a sizeable piece. "It'll prevent infection until Evie's seen at the hospital."

Eyes popping wide, Evie braced as the thin layer of transparent plastic covered the angry burn, its sticky graze triggering a piercing throb through her hand and down her fingers. She gulped as a second layer swaddled her skin. "I guess it's a good thing." Her voice quivered. "That we're done cooking for the day."

Nick tugged off his hairnet. "Well, uh…you're in great hands now. I'll just…" He tilted his head toward the door and met Sunita's judgmental stare. "Excuse me," he nodded, inching past with his suit jacket flopped over his forearm.

"Nick?" Evie called after him, poring over the broad shoulders and firm butt of the man who'd once owned her heart.

He slowed but didn't turn around. "Yeah?"

"Thank you."

Glancing back, he offered a tight-lipped smile and exited the truck.

NINE

NICK

Then, Tuesday, August 7, sixteen years ago

"Dad said we've got thirty minutes." Nick slammed the passenger door of his grandmother's Range Rover as Tarquin hopped on his skateboard and pushed off. "Tarq, seriously! No fucking around." His stomach rolled, dreading the scolding they'd receive from Richard Balfour if they returned late.

Tossing his russet locks from his eyes, Rupert licked a trickling river of melting ice cream from his cone and pocketed the car keys. "You do realize you're wasting your breath, right?" The middle Balfour brother nudged his black, thick-rimmed eyeglasses up his freckled nose and shared an exasperated look with Nick.

Leather shoes gleaming beneath his dress trousers, Tarquin stomped on the tail of his board and scraped his other foot forward, gaining air for a few precious moments until his wheels touched down on the sidewalk with a loud *clack*.

SQUAWWK! A gull screamed and flapped furiously, abandoning several flattened fries in the middle of the road.

"Shiiit!" Nick's heart kicked against his ribs as he ducked the agitated bird, praying it wouldn't soil his pink button-down, navy silk tie, or dark gray trousers. Running a hand through his hair, he checked his appearance in the flower shop's window. "Honestly, Tarq!" he snarled over his shoulder. "Can you quit it?"

Unfazed, his fifteen-year-old brother ignored him and dug in, picking up speed on his board. With a bend of his knees, Tarquin leapt again, landing a shaky kickflip, but his wavering balance catapulted the board's nose upward, chucking him off. "Bollocks! Fuck! Arse!" he hollered, tumbling into the street.

Nick fussed with his hair, ruffling it into the right amount of messy. "You never learn."

Watching his board trundle off without him, Tarquin sulked. "You're such a twat, Nico." He looked back. "Always obsessing about your stupid hair. It's windy here—get over it!" He shook his head. "And I *do* learn, unlike you, constantly blethering on like I broke Gran's gift on purpose. It was, still is, and always will be an *accident*."

"Mum's gonna kill ya if come back filthy," said Rupert, swerving around him.

"Rubbish! Like she'd even notice." Tarquin brushed a grimy fry off his tie and rose to his feet. "She doesn't care."

"Well, you should. For Gran's sake." Nick abandoned his hair-styling and peered beyond his reflection. Buckets of tiger lilies fresh off the ferry mingled with jolly sunflowers and a buoyant balloon or two. *Problem solved!* He grinned, checking his watch. They could snap up a showstopping bouquet and be headed back to their grandmother's with time to spare. "Whatcha reckon? These look nice."

When no answer came, he glanced down Broad Street. Mid-frown, Tarquin was inspecting his scraped palms while Rupert chucked his ice cream in a bin and veered into Marwick's.

"Like he'll find anything better in there." Nick followed begrudgingly. "It's a shop for tourists, isn't it?"

"Snobbishness, thy name is Nikolai." Tarquin hopped on his board and attempted another ollie, landing it with barely a wobble. "While I'm a skating god!" He fist-pumped the air. "YES!"

"Skating wanker, more like," murmured Nick, his narrowed eyes skirting over the stoneware mugs greeting him inside the shop. "And I'm *not* a snob. I'm…discerning." His fingers raced along a shelf of fragrant candles and Ring of Brodgar-themed coasters. While charming, the items were hardly an eighteen-year-old boy's nirvana, nor were they special enough for their doting grandma's seventieth birthday. But the delicate Murano glass vase he and his brothers brought back from their family's month-long sojourn in

Venice, now *that* was special—until it became a heap of smashed shards after one of Tarquin's boardslides gone horribly wrong. With a five-course, celebrity chef-created birthday celebration two hours away, Nick and his brothers were running out of time and choices. Something—*anything*—would have to do.

Rupert examined a black sweater with embroidered sheep circling the collar as Tarquin tramped in with his skateboard. Flicking a hand through his blond-tipped faux hawk, he lurched toward a throw pillow featuring a black and white photograph of Orkney's famous Twatt road sign. "Hey, Nico!" He snickered. "Found your Christmas present. Even has your name on it!"

"Dickhead," Nick retorted sharply and skulked deeper into the shop. Passing a pair of French-speaking seniors passionately discussing the "*chutney de tomates fumées*" and a pregnant woman with her dawdling toddler, Nick spied an impressive display of silver necklaces gracing the back wall. *Now this is more like it.* Pausing beside an ajar door affixed with a 'Stockroom - Employees Only' sign, his scrutinizing gaze landed on a delicate leaf-shaped pendant dangling from a silver chain.

A girlish giggle wafted around the doorjamb. "Did your wrist hurt?"

"A little. It took *forever*." A familiar laugh, easy and quick, punctuated the reply. "I thought I was doing it wrong…"

Nick's ears pricked as he liberated the necklace from its hook. *Sounds like Evie?* Sam's sister always seemed slightly besotted in his presence, but in a sweet, non-abrasive way. Like her brother, she was discreet and trustworthy, never clingy or intense. A nice, normal kid. *I should say hi.*

"…but then he grunted and fisted my hair," said Evie.

What? A knot cinched in Nick's stomach. *Someone hurt her?*

"And?!" The other girl's pitch rose. "My god, Eves, did Stuart, *you know*—?"

"Come? Yep. Alll over his rugby top." She dissolved into giggles.

Little Evie? Nick's jaw fell slack. *But she's only—and she's wanking off some bloke?!* When he stepped back, the floorboards complained beneath his size tens.

"Shit! Fiona?!" Evie's voice trembled. "I-is someone *there*?"

Bugger. Nick's cheeks began to burn. He had to get out of there. NOW.

Abandoning the necklace, he swerved the pregnant shopper and hunched behind a tall display jampacked with puffin souvenirs—t-shirts, pillows, tote bags—and plotted his escape. A few more large steps and he'd—

CREAK! The temperamental floor near the jewelry voiced its displeasure again, followed by an abrupt door slam. Like a starter pistol firing, the loud bang launched Nick's already elevated pulse on a reckless sprint. *They're headed this way!* A dash across the shop wouldn't go unnoticed now.

Nick wasn't going anywhere.

He quickly grabbed the first item within sight, a cellophane bag of beige stones, and acted his heart out, playing a shopper engrossed in his prospective purchase. *What is this?* His eyes bore into the cheery cartoon puffins on the label…*Tammie Norrie Poo?*…then jogged to his watch. *Half-four already?* Unease flooded his chest. *Bollocks. Dad is gonna freak.*

"H-hello?" Evie's salutation quivered on the opposite side of the display. "May I help you?"

She works in this place? Nick peeked between the two headless mannequins. He could see Evie's retro Swatch and the customer's pregnant belly, but everything else was compromised by the mannequins' billowing puffin partywear.

"Sorry, love," said the mother, picking up her chubby tot. "Can you speak up? I'm a bit hard of hearin'."

"Oh! *So* sorry," Evie's voice was giddy with relief. "I mumble sometimes. My mum's always on me about it. What can I help you with?"

Nick let out a quiet exhale. "Safe as houses." He straightened up and stole a quick look around the mannequins.

His jaw dropped.

Eight months had a lot to answer for.

Evie had always been cute, but *this* Evie seemed so much *more.* Taller, prettier—delightfully desirable. Smiling confidently as she shared the merits of the shop's whiskey tumblers, she bestowed the customer with her full attention, listening closely and answering questions with patience and professionalism. Then the woman's toddler babbled something and playful Evie emerged again, her brown eyes sparkling as she laughed and smoothed her hair, untethered from her usual ponytail.

Following her hand, Nick's rapt gaze skated down her shiny tresses, their soft sweep against her décolletage coaxing his curiosity along the straps of her daisy print dress to where the cotton hugged the curve of her breasts. His eyes widened as a curse caught in his throat. *Sam's little sister ain't so little anymore.*

The instrumental strum of Green Day wrenched him away from Evie's allure. Jamming his hand into his trouser pocket, he wrestled his phone free, zeroing in on the caller ID.

Dad

Shit! Nick's pulse skyrocketed as he struggled to concoct an excuse that might thwart World War III.

"I'd know that ringtone anywhere! Nice tan, by the way."

Nick looked up, his dread of the bollocking he'd receive once he hit accept tempered by Evie's welcome presence. "*Oh!* Hey!"

Head tilted, she smiled, all friendly and familiar. "Need to get that?"

Need? Yes. Want? No. He squeezed the phone. Pissed off was Richard Balfour's default setting, and while his father's blistering character assassinations were nothing new to Nick, the last thing he wanted was an audience. Notoriously loud and habitually cruel, his father's phone rants could easily be overheard. Talk about a mortifying overshare, one to be avoided at all costs, even if it meant he'd pay significantly later for dodging his dad's call.

"It can wait." Turning his phone off, Nick slipped it in his pocket, silently apologizing for the explosion of expletives that in three...two...one—would be tormenting the innocent ears of his grandma's sheep and cows, and probably those of the flown-in celebrity chef, too. "So! You're working here this summer?"

"This summer and every summer after. It's my mum's shop and café, so..." Evie's voice rose with unabashed glee. "I heard you were back. It's great to see you!" Her eyes traveled, sweeping across his chest and shoulders before springing back to his face. "Love your shirt. The color suits you. Guys never wear pink here."

Nick matched her grin. "Ah cheers! It's a favorite." He gestured toward her, eager to reciprocate. "You look great, too! Your dress is beautiful. Really lovely." *And kinda hot.*

"Thanks!" She clasped a fistful of skirt and playfully swished it back and forth. "It's from London. I ordered it online." Raising a hand, she shielded the side of her mouth. "Don't tell Mum. Or Sam."

Nick laughed. "So how are things? How's your summer been?"

"Not bad. Working loads, seeing friends—the usual, you know?"

Yep, he knew. Too much, actually. A sickening drop churned his stomach. *This bloke—I hope he isn't forcing her into stuff before she's ready.*

"Oh! And you'll appreciate this!" She bounced. "Guess who played Cordelia in *King Lear* during the St. Magnus Festival?"

"Evie, that's fantastic! Congratulations! I bet you were amazing."

"Thanks. Remembering lines was hard, but I had so much fun! The cast party was epic, too." A naughty laugh launched from her throat as she twirled her necklace around a finger. "How's your summer been?"

"Good, yeah. Busy." He nodded, the pleasure of bumping into Evie tangling with the fear of his father's reprisal. Out of the corner of his eye, he spotted Rupert pushing up his glasses and chatting enthusiastically with another shopgirl. Wide-eyed and glowing, she held a ceramic pitcher dotted with Highland cows against her chest while mentioning something about fiddle practice. Nick glanced back, subtly sweeping Evie from head to toe. *All grown up. SO pretty.* He grinned, determined to keep his focus above her breasts. "I did some modeling, went on a few auditions."

"Awesome!" said Evie. "You know, I heard a rumor…"

Oh god. Nick swallowed. "Which one?"

"About a *Star Wars* thing? You playing a young Han Solo?"

Relief raced through him. "Oh, *that* rumor! Yeah, maybe. I read for it, but so did everyone else with a pulse."

"I can totally see you wielding a light saber."

Nick laughed. "Yeah, much to Tarquin's annoyance. He's a huge fan. He's worried I'll ruin it."

"Brothers, eh?!" Evie smiled. "Well, I think you'd be great. You'll be back on our screens in no time."

"Yeah," Nick fibbed, the less said about the worrisome lack of callbacks the better. He cleared his throat. "We just got back from Greece and Italy. Went snorkeling, sailing."

Evie's bemused grin dropped to the packet of beige ovals in Nick's hand. "And obviously worked up an appetite for our yogurt-covered raisins."

That's what these are? His gaze dipped. "Ah, no—sadly. I'm allergic."

"To yogurt?"

"Raisins." He returned the Tammy Norrie Poo to the puffin display.

"I'm not a raisin fan either," said Evie. "When we were peedie, Sam forced me to eat them. I'd cry 'cause they looked like shriveled bugs."

Nick cringed. "Yes! Like some Bushtucker Trial on *I'm a Celebrity…Get Me Out of Here.*"

Evie burst into laughter. "Ooh, I would pay good money to see you on that!"

"Well, if my career flops, I'll get my agent to make that happen, but in the meantime I need some last-minute birthday gifts for Gran."

"It's her birthday? Aw! What would she fancy? A jumper, a food hamper, jewelry?"

"Jewelry?" Nick widened his eyes, acting as if the thought had never occurred to him. "Uh, do you have necklaces?" He gave himself an imaginary pat on the back. *Playing a blinder, kid.*

"Yeah! Right over here…" Evie waved him toward a familiar corner. "They're all handcrafted by Orcadian artists. We have pendants with Viking graffiti, flowers, seabirds. Mum's always on the lookout for new designers. She's meeting one right now in Finstown." She scooped up the necklace he'd discarded earlier and draped it over its hook as a chorus of baaing sheep rose from the far side of the shop.

Nick's eyes darted. *Dad's calling Rupes?* His heart began pummeling beneath his button-down. *Fuuck. I'm in for it.* Fiddling with his cuffs, he rejoined their conversation, flashing Evie a nonchalant grin. "That one's pretty."

"Yeah, it's special," said Evie proudly, displaying the pendant against her palm. The single leaf in sage enamel glistened next to a tiny, elegant moonstone. "In Scottish folklore, the Rowan tree and its berries symbolize life, renewal, and protection from harm."

Nick would need protection from his dad if he didn't hurry up and haul ass back to the farm. "Yeah, I'll take it." He nodded, the thumping in his chest quickening his breath.

"Great!" Evie slid the necklace off the hook. "I'll giftwrap it for you."

"That would be magic. Cheers, Evie."

Zigzagging indecisive shoppers and merchandise-crowded tables, Nick's shallow inhales and sharp exhales flew fast and tight. *What's with this breathy business?* He slipped a hand underneath his tie and rubbed his breastbone, berating himself. *Gran's gift is sorted. Chill, dude.*

"…for a while?" The tail end of Evie's question pricked his ears.

"Uh, I'm sorry?" Nick blinked as they detoured around the edge of the café and a traditional straw-backed Orkney chair. "I didn't catch that—"

"Nailed it!" Tarquin bounded into his brother's path, arms full of fragrant soaps, a puffin rubber duck, and his skateboard. "Gran will LOVE these bath smellies." He smiled, rousing the famous Balfour family dimples.

Beads of perspiration tickled between Nick's shoulder blades. *Christ, when did it get so hot in here?* Swallowing thickly, he wedged a finger inside the stiff collar of his shirt, giving it a tug away from his neck. "Evie, this is Tarquin."

"Hi." She nodded in greeting as the youngest Balfour released a friendly "Hey!" and launched into his favorite cheesy chat-up line, but Nick's attention spun elsewhere, analyzing every warning, every possible sign. *It's not, is it?*

Frantic pulse? *Check.* Non-stop sweats? *Check.* Shallow breaths? *Check.*

His throat cinched tight, impeding another swallow. *Oh god!* A whoosh of fear shot through him as his thoughts swirled down a twisty spiral, chased by the dragon of dread.

Not now. Not here!

Digging into the knot of his tie, he yanked it loose as his desperation for control consumed every passing second, every jagged breath. He had to stop the worst from happening. He just had to!

Something stabbed his ribs, disrupting the dominos of dark thoughts tumbling through his mind. He blinked, finding Tarquin's elbows flying as he bobbed his plastic puffin up and down through the air.

"Tarq," Nick gasped. "What's with the rubber duck?" He asked it, not out of interest, but self-preservation. Keeping up appearances, pretending all was well was paramount so no one, not his brothers nor Evie, not the customers browsing jams and jumpers—*no one*—would detect this epic unraveling.

"Puffy ducky's mine," said Tarquin as they approached the sales desk. "Isn't he brilliant?"

Nick didn't answer or take the piss. The internal storm of impending doom was sweeping him out to sea again.

I KNOW this means something. As he blotted sweat from his upper lip, tingling pins and needles flooded his fingers. *Heart attack, stroke, suffocating death!*

Each second stretched into a torturous minute, every word spoken a drawn-out, buzzy soliloquy. A foggy flash of Rupert's wallet. The scuff of a shopping bag sliding across the counter. Evie and her friend laughing with Tarquin. Business as usual for everyone but Nick.

Leaning forward, he slapped a steadying hand on top of a glossy magazine flipped open on the counter. *What if this ends up in The Mail?* He sniffed and glanced sidelong at his brothers, joking and carrying on, completely oblivious to the uncontrollable panic surging inside him. *Everyone will find out. It'll kill my career.*

"You sure that cow jug isn't for you, Rupes?" Tarquin taunted. "I swear, the thought of becoming a farmer gives you a raging boner."

"Shut up!" Rupert dove into a salty verbal exchange, trading not-so-brotherly putdowns.

Make it stop. Knees watery, Nick closed his eyes. *This is it. I'm dying. In bleedin' Orkney.*

A soft hand touched his.

He looked up wearily, his vision blurred.

"Nick? You all right?" Evie's whispered question echoed, joining the ringing torment filling his ears.

I have to get outta here. As he pulled away, the magazine lifted with his sweaty hand. "I-I'm good." He choked, barely pushing the words out as he peeled away the page and dropped the magazine on the counter.

Mid-sibling spat, Tarquin did a double take. "Blimey!" He scanned the colorful spread. "Not THAT rubbish."

"What's rubbish?" asked Rupert.

Me. Nick sniffed, rubbing his nose with the back of his hand. *Dad's right.* His woozy gaze straggled over the article. Full color photos sat below white capitalized letters shouting something about AT HOME and EXCLUSIVE. Chasing breaths, a picture of his mother blurred, then focused, then blurred again. *I'm a no-talent waste of space.*

"The *Cheer* magazine article," spat Tarquin. "Remember, Rupes? Mum fake baking cookies, us in bloody polo gear—"

"It's out?" Nudging his glasses, Rupert snuck a peek at the pages. "Ohh, man!" He cringed. "It'll be hard to live this down."

Tell me about it. A circus of bright lights and distorted chatter swirled and churned as Nick grasped the edge of the sales desk.

When he pried his eyes open, a cracked slab of cement stared back.

"Where…?" Nick's pulse pounded in his ears. Something tightened around his arm.

"It's gonna be okay." The words, calm and reassuring, hung somewhere up above.

Nick's fuzzy gaze meandered…across the toes of his leather oxfords…up the hems of his trousers jutting forward in crisp triangular points. The same fabric hung like curtains beside his cheeks while something silky and navy dangled, kissing his chin. *What IS…my tie?* He blinked sharply as snippets of murky memories—staggering through a doorway, landing hard on his butt, a muffled voice—flickered through his mind like the most miserable vacation slideshow imaginable, culminating in one final recollection: a lurch forward and the silent stillness of everything going dark…

SHIIIT!

A surge of embarrassment ripped through him. "I-I have to—" Swatting his tie away from his mouth, Nick threw his head back, his vision a rattled swirl of two-story buildings and cloud-mottled sky until his spine collided with an unforgiving bench.

"*Careful,*" the voice urged.

Too late.

Stars speckled Nick's groggy gawp as a swell of dizziness

swirled the puffy clouds like a merry-go-round of cotton balls. His right hand scrambled up his tie, clutching its decimated knot for stability. *Stop the ride, I want off!* Heavy with exhaustion, his eyelids bowed, followed by his chin…slowly…meeting his chest.

"You're safe here." A hand gathered his fingers in a protective embrace. "I'm not going anywhere."

Comforting and warm with the perfect amount of squeeze. Who was this angel?

As the lightheaded whirl of his pounding headrush subsided, Nick opened his eyes again. His glassy gaze crawled left, off his lap and across a cotton meadow of whimsical white and yellow flowers.

Evie? Sinking dread rolled through him as he peered up slowly. *She witnessed every pathetic second.* His ears burned. *Fuck.*

"How you feeling?" She leaned in, concern softening her squint.

"Tired, headachy," he croaked, his tongue like sandpaper. Glancing around the small, stone-walled yard, he saw two green recycling bins, a rogue traffic cone, and a sand-filled bucket peppered with cigarette butts kept them company. A back door, which Nick assumed belonged to her mum's shop, remained closed and free of onlookers. Thankfully. He swallowed languidly, an embarrassing but necessary question bubbling up. "Did I pass out?"

"Only for a few seconds," said Evie. "You were pale and wobbly just before. I told you to put your head between your knees, just in case."

"So that's why I was…"

Evie nodded. "Bent over."

"Less distance to fall."

"But you didn't. I held your shoulders."

A shaky breath left his lungs. "Thank you. You saved me from a bloody nose…and a lot of questions." Grateful, Nick grinned sheepishly. "What happens in Orkney, stays in Orkney, right?"

Her forehead creased. "Sorry?"

"Like the tourism slogan for Vegas."

She stared back blankly.

Dumbass! Like she'd know. Nick muted his smile, worried his flippant reference made Evie feel dense. "It's from an advertisement. It means whatever happens there goes no further. No one will hear about it."

"Ohh. Yeah, I won't tell a soul. Cross my heart. Not even Sam." Her thumb stroked his hand slowly, back and forth. "Do you remember coming out here?"

The gentle brush of skin against skin pulled Nick's focus down toward the bench, her touch merciful and surprisingly calming. "Um…sorta?" He blinked, his thoughts fuzzy yet overwhelmed by her unexpected compassion. *Is this for real?* Clearing his throat, he looked up.

Her eyes widened. "Oh! *Sorry.*" She pulled her hand away. "I didn't mean to be so…"

"Kind?" Untethered, Nick craved her closeness again, the familiar ache of loneliness swelling in his chest. "It was nice, actually. Comforting."

A sweet smile stretched her lips.

"Did I look…*weird?*" Nick whispered, seeking reassurance. "Before—in the shop with everyone?"

"No. A bit sweaty, but who doesn't sometimes."

He rocked back in relief, letting out an exhale. "Thank fuck."

"But you went quiet suddenly and, I dunno, you seemed not quite right."

"That's when you leapt into action?" Nick murmured. "Shepherding this saddo outside?"

She tipped sideways, gently bumping his shoulder. "You're not a saddo. You're a devoted grandson, though. That's how I got you out here, to see something for your gran's garden."

"Smart."

Evie shrugged. "I figured some air and a private spot to sit might help."

"It did—*it does*," said Nick. "Thank you."

"Good." As silence settled between them, Evie turned away, grabbing her denim jacket from the far end of the bench.

Knew it. This was too good to be true. Bowing his head, the bench's wooden slats creaked beside him. *She can't escape fast enough.*

"Want some water?"

Lifting his chin, Nick found Evie still seated, offering a bottle. It must've been concealed beneath her jacket. She hadn't made a run for it—yet.

"Yes. Please."

Cracking the lid, Nick took a shaky swig. Boring ol' water never tasted so good. A pressing question followed his swallow. "Where are my brothers?"

"Sampling our new fudge with Fiona. Should keep 'em busy for a while." Evie opened her mouth and closed it again like she was choosing her words with utmost care. "So my mum, she uh, has this *thing*." Pulling at her necklace, she continued, "Her heart races. Sometimes she can't breathe and feels faint."

Where's she going with this? Stay on script. Agree to nothing. Nick downed another sip and stifled a watery burp. "Your poor mum. That must be scary."

"Yeah, but it's nothing to be ashamed about."

Easier said than done. Nick flexed his grip on the bottle, which answered back with a plastic crackle.

"Has this happened before?" she asked, tucking her hair behind her ear.

So many times.

On the Tube, eating caramel-covered popcorn at the cinema with Bree, sat cozy at home watching *EastEnders*. Occasionally sparked by stress, but often random and unpredictable, Nick's history of panic attacks wasn't something he wanted to shout from the crowstep gables of Orkney's rooftops or anywhere else for that matter.

A simple, well-rehearsed fib would immediately snuff out Evie's questions. It had worked brilliantly before in other places with other people...

Lowering the half-empty bottle, he caught Evie's earnest gaze.

Dammit.

She'd witnessed his struggle for breath, heard the quiver in his voice, felt the sweat soaking the back of his shirt. Was she so familiar with her mum's symptoms that she'd refuse to buy the lie Nick hoped to sell?

Truth be told, he was too weary and exhausted to even make that pitch.

Nick rested the water bottle beside his thigh and braced himself for the inevitable fallout. It was one thing admitting he couldn't sing, but quite another divulging something so tied up with ugly stigma he'd kept it locked away within himself for the past eight years.

He swallowed hard. "It's happened a few times."

Evie didn't recoil or appear alarmed. Calmness emanated from her. Nick could feel it, comforting and unwavering.

"But your brothers? They didn't seem—"

"They don't know." Nick cut to the chase. "I've never told them. Neither has Mum."

"But *she* knows?"

"She was there the first time. It happened on the *Dalston* set. I was ten."

"God, so young." She rubbed her stomach. "You must've been terrified."

"I was absolutely bricking it. The palpitations, my throat closing up…I swore I was a goner." Nick sniffed. "Then the paramedics arrived and carted me off to A&E. One EKG, two blood tests, and several autographs later, they diagnosed me with a panic disorder."

Evie nodded but didn't interrupt, letting Nick continue.

"Mum flipped. She practically flew through the bleedin' ceiling tiles."

"How come?"

"If word got out, I'd be kissing my career goodbye faster than you can say Equity card." A shiver crept up his spine. "So Mum went into protection mode, told the docs they were wrong, and marched me out of there before treatment options were discussed."

Evie reared back. "Protection? Of what—your career? But what about your health? I'd say that's more important than—?" She stopped short, the rest apparently too distasteful for her to verbalize.

Yep. Welcome to my life. Nick's mouth went dry. "No, no. It's not like that. Of course she cares more about me than my career." He averted Evie's disapproving gape and picked at the hem of his pink button-down, wrinkled and untucked from his trousers. "But she also knows how the business works. The truth is, *nobody* wants to book a kid with mental issues."

"*Nick!* I'm sure that's not true."

He looked up. "No, it is! It happened to this girl I know. The director spotted her ADHD medication and axed her straight after. She hasn't booked a role since." Shaking his head, he fussed with his shirt's buttons. "We couldn't risk it, so Mum told the *Dalston* bosses my"—he made air quotes with his fingers—"'*episode*' was a life-threatening reaction to shellfish."

Evie's jaw dropped. "She lied about your health?!"

"It was only a little lie."

She shook her head. "Little lies have a way of becoming big messes!"

"Yeah, I guess. The producers banned prawn cocktail crisps from the craft services table. Then that snowballed into the catering company removing fish cakes, fish fingers, and cod and chips from their menu in case they made me ill. My poor castmates paid the price. They *hated* me. For months."

"Jeez, I'd probably hate you, too." Evie reached over, collecting his hand. "For all of five minutes."

Her touch roused Nick's smile.

"*But* if *I* was sick and my mum didn't get me the treatment I needed...I wouldn't call that protective," said Evie. "I'd call it neglect."

A pang of truth wrenched Nick's heart. Touchy-feely his mother was not. He couldn't remember the last time she hugged him, let alone asked how he was feeling. "It's not, though. Mum did what was best *for me*. Acting is the best medicine. I'd be lost without it."

"But you can't give your all to acting if you're not feeling well, right?" she countered, facing him.

Nick scratched his temple. "Evie, look, I appreciate your concern, really I do, but it's okay. *I'm* okay. The attacks don't happen often, and when they do, I act like everything's fine and no one notices." He glanced down, studying her slender fingers wrapped firmly around his, her nails painted a pale lilac. "But then again…" Nick blinked up, meeting her eyes. "You're not like other people."

She bit her bottom lip and smiled shyly behind her hair, a glimpse of the old Evie shining through.

A flutter took flight in Nick's chest. *I can't believe she's still here.* Evie had been nothing but kind and protective. *Imagine that!* He squeezed her hand. "I can't thank you enough for helping me. God knows what might've happened if you hadn't."

"It's nothing, really." A blush rose on her cheeks.

"No, it's *something*. I've been dealing with this on my own for yonks. It's nice to finally talk about it."

Evie leaned closer. "You don't with Bree? What about Kyle and Zach? Your parents?"

"I haven't told my friends. Dad thinks only wimps have them. Mum refuses to discuss it."

The moment his answer left his lips… *Shit, that sounded worse aloud.* Nick cringed inwardly, and Evie's reaction—her wide-eyed stare—confirmed his suspicion.

He let out a carefree laugh, determined to course-correct and alleviate Evie's concern. "But it's a good thing, keeping quiet. This way, the press are none the wiser and my mates can't take the piss. Trust me, I already get enough stick playing Jake!"

"But hiding it won't help you," said Evie.

Gazing down at their entwined hands, Nick slapped on a confident grin. "Ahh, but here's the thing—there's loads online: info, tips for coping, all without going to get professional help. It's all good."

Evie sat silent for a moment, then disentangled her fingers from Nick's. She held out her palm. "Gimme your phone."

"Why?"

The dawn of a smile brightened her face. "You should have my number in case you ever need to talk."

A lightness filled Nick's chest. *"Really?"*

"Yeah." She paused, the glimmer in her eyes dimming. "Unless you don't want—"

"No. Evie, I do!" Nick let out a relieved laugh. Stretching his legs, he dug in his trouser pocket and pulled out his phone. "I really appreciate this. Seriously." He opened his contacts and placed the phone in her hand. "You're a total legend."

"And I mean it, okay? Call or text anytime, night or day."

"You might regret saying that." Nick grinned, captivated by her benevolence. He inched closer, watching her type in her number as the beachy scent of her hair—or maybe it was her perfume?—teased him.

But sat so close, there was something else about Evie, too. Something jarring.

Why didn't I notice before?

Partially hidden by concealer, faint blueish shadows ringed her eyes. If she was sad or exhausted, she hadn't let on, but this glimpse of vulnerable Evie gnawed at Nick and wouldn't quit. *Is it stuff at home? School?* He frowned. Whatever it was, his dad could sit the fuck down and wait. He couldn't rush off to his grandmother's party without offering Evie the same kindness and selflessness she'd so graciously shown him.

Sometimes all you needed was someone who would listen, who wouldn't judge when you were hurting. Someone who knew the pain and loneliness of carrying a heavy secret.

Falling apart in front of her, revealing his most devastating flaw…a newfound trust had been forged, a special intimacy stretching beyond their shared love of musicals and board games. Nick felt it, but did Evie?

If only she'd open up.

Hopefully, what he was about to say would come out breezy and encouraging. "So, come on then. We've done me." Nick half-laughed. "What about you?"

Evie looked up from his phone. "Me?"

He leaned into her shoulder and stayed there. "Yeah, you! You say everything's been ace, but I get the feeling more's been happening than you're letting on."

Her expression softened.

"I know how lonely it can be, dealing with stuff on my own." Nick smiled. "If there's anything, you know…getting you down? You can talk to me. I won't judge."

She swallowed hard, her gaze holding Nick's as she opened her mouth.

"Eves?" Peeking sheepishly around the edge of the back door, her friend waved tentatively. "Sorry to interrupt."

Shoot. Nearly had her. Nick sat back as Evie cleared her throat.

"Hey, Fiona." She handed Nick his phone. "What's up? How'd the fudge tasting go?"

"Raves all around." Fiona gave in to a coy grin. "Rupert especially."

"No surprise there," said Nick. "That one could eat for England *and* Scotland."

"Mum will be thrilled by that review." Evie trailed a hand over her belly. "We never know what we're getting with a new supplier."

"Oh and one other thing…" Wincing, Fiona gestured reluctantly behind her. "Stuart arrived five minutes ago."

Hand job bloke? Nick looked Evie's way, but she skirted his eyes.

"Oh shit! I lost track of time."

"I'll tell him you're on your way." Fiona eased the door closed.

Flustered, Evie snatched her denim jacket and stood, forcing her left arm down its rumpled sleeve. "He, uh, hates when I'm late."

"But five minutes is nothing." Nick rose to his feet and held up the shoulder of Evie's coat, helping her slip her right arm inside.

She pulled her hair free from the stiff collar. "Thanks."

"If he's pissed, blame me." Nick tightened the knot of his tie, the desire to shield Evie from prospective fallout paramount. "It's my fault, not yours."

Evie removed her phone from her jacket pocket and peered up at him, her big brown eyes wistful but torn like she wasn't ready to say goodbye. At least not like this. "It's no one's fault. Sometimes stuff just...happens."

She swallowed hard and licked her lips...and something inside Nick shifted, sending his pulse on a heated sprint. *Stuff like this?* His gaze lingered on her mouth, wet and pouty and irresistibly mesmerizing, the urge to kiss her, to hold her close, all-consuming.

"Evie..." Nick whispered as he reached out, slowly tucking her hair behind her ear.

She sucked in a breath. "Yeah?" A spark of a smile teased her cheeks.

"*S-O-S!*"

The rousing chorus made them both jolt. Evie's eyes fell first, followed by Nick's. Alight in her palm, the name STUART beckoned on her phone as Rihanna sang urgently.

"I-I gotta go." Stepping back, Evie accepted the call and spun toward the door, phone pressed to her ear. "I'm sorry! I'm coming!"

"I'll text you!" said Nick.

Evie didn't glance back.

TEN

EVIE

Now, Saturday, June 24

"Remember when we were small and we'd try to write with our non-dominant hand?" Evie dumped another cup of rolled oats into a pot of boiling water. "It's like that." She held up her right hand swaddled in gauze. "Only this time I can't swap back."

Dressed in a high-necked, floor-skimming, Victorian-era nightgown, Fiona tucked an escaped curl back inside her cotton nightcap. "How long does it have to stay bandaged?"

"A week or two. Depends how quickly the blistering goes away." Evie turned the burner down to a medium-low heat.

"Good thing Nick was around." Fiona picked up her tea. "It could've been much worse."

Evie added a large pinch of salt. "Yeah..."

"How's it been working together?"

"Bizarre." Plunging a spoon into the pot, Evie gave the dancing oats a stir. "The Nick I used to know was always taking directions, not giving them. He's making financial decisions for the entire production. What's up with *that*?"

"The guy who used to throw money around like confetti." Fiona snickered above her cup. "God, remember how he'd show up with the latest phone, the trendiest clothes? I don't think he ever wore the same thing twice."

Except his pink button-down...and the bowling shirt. Evie stifled a melancholy sigh. *Nick loved those.*

"He stopped in to see Ava and Poppy last night," said Fiona. "Stayed for dinner. He couldn't believe how big they've grown."

"Did Ava remember him?"

"Barely. Tarquin will be happy." Fiona grinned. "He's still her favorite uncle by a country mile."

Sprinkling cinnamon and nutmeg into the oaty mix, Evie tossed her bangs out of her eyes. "It's wild to think Nick hasn't been back for three and a half years—basically Poppy's entire existence."

"Yep. At least he graced us with his presence at her baptism," said Fiona. "But even then, he couldn't hightail it back to New York fast enough."

The last time we saw each other. Evie gave the oatmeal a determined swirl.

In the thirteen years since their split, Evie had only set eyes on Nick twice: Fiona and Rupert's wedding ceremony ten years ago and Poppy's baptism, his habit of missing most family gatherings and special occasions in Orkney making it easy for Evie to avoid him. However, with his schedule cleared for his second niece's christening, Fiona had given her best friend a heads-up and Evie braced for impact. She prepared a highlight reel of brag-worthy talking points (her successful career, busy social life, a stylish flat), got a fresh manicure, and splashed out on a new dress. Evie's life may have been far from perfect, but it was still pretty sweet and would be even sweeter once Nick knew how incredibly well she was doing...without him.

But on the actual day, Evie's resolve had withered. Spotting Nick, tie loosened and beer in hand, crossing the party and headed in her direction, she bolted, robbing herself of the satisfaction of finding closure on her own terms.

And now, three and a half years later, swirling a wooden spoon through a large batch of oatmeal, she was back at that starting line again wanting to speak her piece and prove to Nick that she had not only survived since their split but had flourished.

But how to go about it?

Nick was her boss for the next two months, and a sharp-tongued "You were shitty for dumping me 'cause I had Crohn's" speech could put a reference and future catering business with the BBC and other visiting broadcasters in jeopardy. She was at Nick's mercy however she sliced it. Maybe putting her need for closure on the back burner was for the best?

Evie gave the oatmeal a succession of laborious stirs, feeling another nagging question bubbling up, the same one raised by Sunita two days earlier.

"Fi, did you know Nick was working this shoot?"

She set down her tea. "Oh god no. We were as surprised as you. Nick's been keeping things on the down low lately."

Lately my ass. Evie bit her tongue. *Try always.*

"Guilt does strange things to people, I guess," Fiona concluded.

"I'm sorry I've made things awkward with him."

"Any awkwardness is on *him*, not you, Eves," said Fiona. "*And* you did nothing wrong."

Except have Crohn's. Grateful for Fiona's loving loyalty, Evie smiled warmly, but with Nick's unexpected return, angst percolated in her chest again. She dragged the spoon through the oats as Jamie popped his head around the doorjamb, his dark hair sticking out from beneath his beloved New York Yankees cap.

"The tea and coffee station's done." He rubbed his sleepy eyes. "What's next?"

"Cutlery and napkins. Oh, and the oatmeal toppings: honey, banana, berries—you know, all the things we prepped earlier?"

"Got it." Jamie rummaged through the cupboard, grabbing a box of cutlery, and left as quickly as he had arrived.

Evie glanced back at Fiona. "So you excited about being an extra?"

"I am! Barely slept last night. You should come up to the castle on your break. We're filming in the library and apparently, there's a secret passage hidden behind the bookshelves."

"Maybe I should ask the builders to add one to the shop. Might come in handy the next time Nick pops in."

Fiona adjusted the chin straps dangling from her nightcap. "Eves, don't get mad, but…I think you two should talk."

Exhausted from her pain medication and a late night of baking, Evie didn't have it in her to get into the whole *He's my boss* argument, so she gave in, albeit evasively.

"Talk about what?" She churned the goopy oats. "His marriage? The subsequent divorce? The salacious sex scandal? There's *so much* to unpack."

Evie didn't know all the gory details, but she knew the gist of what Nick had been up to during the intervening years. Social media and the island gossip mill made sure of it, which raised the delicate question: which was worse—knowing or not knowing?

"You have every right to stick the knife in," said Fiona, "but I don't believe Nick's a bad guy."

"Well, he ain't a saint! Clearly."

"Has he made poor decisions? Yes, loads of 'em, but who hasn't?"

Holding up her gauze-covered hand, Evie grimaced. "Guilty as charged."

"Then speak to him," urged Fiona. "Get it all off your chest. I know you want to."

"I do, but—" Pausing, she fussed with the spoon.

"But...what? You wait another thirteen years?" Fiona blinked. "Evie, there will never be a perfect time and you'll never be one hundred percent ready. Bottling up what you really want to say isn't good for you—or your Crohn's."

"You sound like Sam."

Fiona's eyes widened. "He wants you to talk to Nick, too, right?"

"No! He thinks revisiting the worst time of my life will cause *more* stress, not less." Evie banged the spoon on the edge of the pot, dislodging a gluey blob of oats. "And ultimately, what will it get me? A bunch of silly excuses? A half-assed apology?" She huffed. "He was a crappy, immature boyfriend—end of. I'll do this job, be a pleasure to work with, then move on."

"While keeping his DVDs and bowling shirt?"

She dodged Fiona's stare.

"Eves, I know they're Nick's. You hate *Grease 2*."

I wouldn't say hate. Evie cleared her throat. "I meant to toss them but got busy and forgot."

Fiona's expression relaxed. "Forgot or—" Jamie tramped back in, and she paused abruptly.

"I gaffer-taped the napkin and cutlery boxes to the table in case the winds pick up." He tugged his hoodie, clearly pleased with himself.

"Smart call!" Evie smiled, hoping some positive reinforcement might spur her cousin on to further good deeds.

Diving into the fridge, he loaded up a tray with the oatmeal toppings. "I'll keep lids on till we're ready to serve."

"Perfect, thanks." As Jamie left, Evie looked at Fiona fiddling with her costume. She dipped the spoon into the pot, the oatmeal's consistency as thick as the atmosphere between them. Perhaps a change of subject might clear the air.

But Fiona leapt first.

"Whether you admit it or not, I think Nick still means a lot to you. It'll give you some peace if you can find a way to be friends."

Or dig up old unwanted feelings. Evie's eyes skated across the Ring of Brodgar postcard—a thank you note from Gemma—taped to the truck wall. "Some things aren't meant to last, Fi. Flowers wilt, the sun sets, relationships run their course…"

Fiona's stare wasn't budging, so Evie threw her a breezy "Fine, I'll think about it" and her friend relaxed into a satisfied grin while adjusting her Victorian nightcap.

"I can't wait to see Tarq's costume."

"Tarquin's an extra?" Evie moved a stack of serving bowls closer to the oatmeal.

"Was supposed to be Leia, but Nick put her to work altering costumes."

"Who's looking after Luke?"

"Rupes." Fiona chuckled. "Here's hoping he'll find three kids, a dog, and a barn full of animals too much and will stop asking when we can have another baby."

Evie smiled. "Did you hear back about the dig?" The summer archeological excavation at the Ness of Brodgar, a substantial Neolithic find of stone buildings dating back five thousand years, was recruiting volunteers. Fiona was hoping to dust off her degree and put it to good use.

She nodded. "I haven't told Rupert. Didn't feel like the right time with Poppy being unwell."

"Starts soon, right?" Evie spied the crew and extras congregating outside as well as Sunita walking up the path, swinging bags of shopping.

"Beginning of July," replied Fiona. "I have to tell him soon."

Sunita rounded the doorjamb. "Bon matin, mes amis!" She held up her bags. "I come bearing croissants, blueberry scones, and carrot muffins."

"*More* muffins?" asked Fiona. "Eves baked some last night."

"I did, but my pain meds made me sleepy. I got woken up by the smoke alarm and two charred muffin pans. All my hard work, binned." She returned to the pot and gave it a churn. "Sun, can you arrange the baking on the table outside? We'll need labels, too. You know, the usual contains nuts, eggs, wheat…"

Sunita dipped into a playful curtsey. "Already done, my lady. Wrote them up on the ferry." She collected several serving trays and shared a smile with Fiona.

"Guess I better join the extras."

"Fi, our very own star!" Sunita joked.

"Wanna bet Nick leaves us on the cutting room floor?" Fiona waved farewell and followed Sunita out of the truck.

While Sunita manned the tables outside, Evie got to work scooping oatmeal into bowls and serving the breakfast onslaught. Three days in and most of the faces waiting outside the window were now familiar, but the one she knew best didn't appear. With only two crew left to feed, she looked up, spotting Jamie galloping toward the truck.

"Eeevie!" he hollered, waving furiously.

If Jamie was jonesing for another smoke break, she was the last person he should hound for a light.

Ducking inside, his chest rose and fell, scrambling for breath.

"Someone's having an allergic reaction!"

Evie's stomach flipped. "You serious?!"

Chewing his thumb, Jamie nodded anxiously. "I called 999, but..."

She yanked open a drawer and grabbed an epinephrine pen. "Let's go."

Running through the maze of tables, they cut through a huddle of concerned crew. Sunita was sat on a picnic table bench with Nick, her arm draped around his quaking shoulders. Lips swelling, he clutched at his throat.

"Muffins..." His was voice raspy, his gaze fixed. "Raisins..."

Oh my god! Shaking, Evie held the EpiPen straight up in her good hand, its blue cap pointing toward the sky. "Jamie, I need you to remove the safety cap for me. Pull upward, like straight up."

Snapping it free, Jamie stuffed his fists into his hoodie's pockets. "Oh man." Her young cousin gulped. "He's *blue.*"

Without hesitation, Evie positioned the autoinjector parallel to the ground and swung its orange end toward Nick's outer thigh, plunging hard into muscle.

ELEVEN

"When you take the time to think of one you love
It makes you wise and strong.
Love makes us wise and strong"
'Smile When We Whisper', Torquil Campbell

EVIE

Then, Wednesday, August 8, sixteen years ago

Was last night for real? Or is my brain making stuff up again?
Morning rain pelted the windows as Evie lowered herself gingerly
onto the sofa, her splayed fingers rubbing her bloated belly.

Deflating into the cushions and a handknit throw, she loosely
retied the drawstring on her pajama bottoms. *I helped with his panic
attack. He felt grateful—that's all! He's not into you. Stop torturing
yourself thinking otherwise.*

A blood-curdling shriek exploded across the room.

"Sprout?" Calling out over his shoulder, Sam clicked the mouse
of the family's computer, blasting a snarling pack of rampaging
zombies into oblivion. "What was that? Loo trip number four?"

"No. Six." Evie groaned, another cramp rippling through her
abdomen. "Please don't tell Mum." Afraid to eat, she nudged her
untouched plate of dry toast across the coffee table with her bare
toe.

"You're your own worst enemy, you know that?" said Sam.
"Totally in denial."

About Nick? Evie shot him a glassy stare. "What are you on
about?"

"Last night, eating whatever," said Sam. "You're not like everyone else, kiddo. You have to be careful."

"I only had a little salsa."

117

"And look how that turned out," said Sam, the spluttering growls from the computer game intensifying. "Were you boozing, too?"

Ducking her brother's scrutiny, Evie's pulse quickened. She opened her book of word search puzzles and leafed through the pages. "*No.*"

"Wanna try that again?" Slaying another ghoul, Sam jerked as its teeth flew toward the screen. "I can always tell when you're lying. Your voice dips."

Shoot. She pinched her lips together. "Fine! I had two ciders in the park." Her gaze diverted downward. "And a shot at the pub," she mumbled, flipping the page.

"*A shot*?!" Sam tsked. "Oh, Evie—"

"Oh, Evie, *what?*" she seethed, her mood growing spikier by the second. "I can't have fun? I have to stay home? Be the *only* one of my friends who can't drink or have a boyfriend?" A tingly burn prickled the back of her nose.

Sam kept his big brother cool. "I'm not saying that."

Evie's chin trembled as she returned to her puzzle book, the page blurring. "Sounds like it."

"I'm *saying* you need to listen to your body. You've felt dodge all week and still went out."

"You really have no idea." Tears spilled through her lashes. "You've always been popular, Sammy. You've never had to worry about fitting in or being left behind."

Sam's throat bobbed. "I wouldn't say never." Pausing his game, he nudged his breakfast sandwich aside and swiveled around. His face looked pained.

Usually when Evie felt unwell, she'd retreat, cancel plans, and stay home, but...

"I *had* to go out last night. If I didn't, it would've been the fourth time in three weeks that I canceled on Stuart. He'd probably never ask again 'cause dating me is such a freakin' headache." Evie wiped her cheeks. "I'm tired of feeling crap. All I want is to be like everyone else. Is that too much to ask?"

"No." Sam leaned forward, resting his elbows on his knees. "But if you were like everyone else, you wouldn't be Evie."

She flinched. "Ew. *Don't* make me barf—"

"Hear me out," begged Sam. "I've seen you in action—helping new students, being kind to Mum's elderly regulars. You're always empathetic, always make people feel seen. That might not seem important or cool now, but trust me, being caring and compassionate matters…more than you know. The right friends will appreciate that. They won't see you as a headache. They'll see you as someone wonderful, someone they want to be with no matter what." He smiled broadly. "So, don't sell yourself short. Being different can be a great thing."

Not when you're fifteen and worried about where the nearest loo is. Blinking quickly, Evie tried desperately to stifle a further swell of tears. She shrugged a bony shoulder. "I get what you're saying, but it's hard to agree when I feel this rotten. No one understands what I'm going through."

"You could always call that girl you met in Aberdeen," said Sam.

"And be ignored? Uh, no thanks. I had enough of her snootiness in hospital. Worst roommate ever. Obviously, having Crohn's doesn't automatically make you a nice person."

Sam scratched his dark ginger stubble. "I'd trade places with you in a heartbeat. It breaks me, seeing you like this. It's not fair."

Her heart dipped. Impressive exams results in hand, Sam would be leaving for veterinary school in Bristol next month. For all the teasing and big brother posturing, he really was a sweetheart. Evie would miss him terribly. "Thanks. I know I don't say it a lot and we get on each other's nerves most of the time, but you know I *love* you, right?"

"I love you, too, Sprout. And don't worry. I won't tell Mum."

A flood of relief filled Evie's chest. "Really? Oh, Sammy—!"

"*But*"—he held up a finger—"on one condition: promise you'll play it safe next time? Have one drink and order something safe to eat, something you've had before with no problems."

"Oh, trust me, I'm *never* touching a corn chip again." She swiped a few lingering tears away from her eyes. "I don't care if they're Stuart's favorite."

"He didn't stop you from tucking in?" asked Sam.

Evie bit the inside of her cheek. "Uh…"

Her brother's brows knitted together. "He doesn't *know*?"

"No, he does. He just doesn't know all the gory details. And…he thinks I'm still in remission."

Sam scoffed. "Evie, if he's gonna be your boyfriend, you gotta tell him when you're in a flare. He can't be there for you if he doesn't know."

He'll look at me differently. Evie fretted. "But what if he's repulsed?"

"If he is, he's an arse and doesn't deserve you." Sam paused for a beat. "Is he pressuring you for sex?"

"Noo!" Her cheeks burned hot. "Yuck, I can't *believe* you asked me that!" Her shrill reply propelled Sam back to his game.

Evie touched her lips, still tender from the previous night's make-out session. Four dates in and Stuart definitely fancied her judging by his eager hands and demanding kisses, which, while wonderfully flirty, tasted like stale cigarettes. He'd begged for a blow job ("Everyone does it, babe") behind the pub, but Evie resisted, not ready to *go there* quite yet, especially in an outdoor space reeking of spilled beer and rotting scallops. "No worries," he said, but his immediate offer to take her home suggested otherwise. If her uncomfortable feelings about a blow job soured Stuart's evening, how would he deal with a sudden bout of nausea, excessive gas, or worse, this morning's diarrhea emergency?

The thought made her shiver. *Would ANY guy feel comfortable with all that? Would Nick?* Evie swept her hair away from her face. *I mean, he's great. He knows what living with an invisible health issue is like, but…unlike me, he's not bolting to the bathroom hoping he'll make it in time.*

Evie could write a book about it. The embarrassment, the loneliness of being the only one in her social circle with a life-disrupting affliction. But at least she could confide in her parents and Sam, and more recently, Sunita and Fiona, whereas Nick had no one. Well, he had *her*—now—but whether he'd actually ring was anyone's guess. Guys were weird like that. She'd seen it firsthand with Sam. She'd confide in him, but vice versa? Rarer than a Starbucks coffee in Orkney.

If Nick didn't call, Evie had to hope his parents weren't as uncaring as he made them sound. He had to talk to someone. Talking always helped. Their conversation the previous night was proof of that.

"Sam?" She wriggled on the couch. "Have you met Nick's parents?"

The growling creatures on the monitor froze and the room fell quiet again, apart from the rain's patter on the windows. "*Shit!*" Sam swirled the mouse around in circles on its mat. "Bloody internet's cut out *again*." He exhaled heavily. "Why? They came into the shop?"

"No, Nick did. With his brothers."

"I met his mum once." The game shuddered alive again, unleashing a spine-chilling scream. Evie jolted as Sam continued his massacre—and the conversation. "Once was one time too many."

"How come? You love her on *Equinox Ten*."

"She's great on TV. In person, she's a bit plastic—a total diva." Eyes locked on the screen, Sam clicked the mouse nonstop with one hand while absently reaching for his breakfast roll with the other.

"But isn't being a diva a good thing sometimes?" asked Evie. "Taking control, knowing what you want?"

"Not in her case. She's stuck up and humorless and really hard on Nico. She heard he lost out on some film role and tore a strip off him in front of all of us." Bloody limbs and eyeballs flew as Sam annihilated another zombie village while feasting on his ketchup-drenched bacon sandwich.

All that gore and he isn't bothered? He'll make a great veterinary surgeon one day.

A muted beep sounded beneath Evie's puzzles. "Finally!" she

exclaimed, shifting the book. Sunita was volunteering for the first time at the local newspaper and promised an update during her midmorning break. *1 New Msg* sat in the tiny window of her pink flip phone. She prized it open and selected the unread text.

Nick: You're the BEST

What?! Heart soaring, the events from sixteen hours earlier pranced through Evie's head: Nick admiring her dress, his fingers laced between hers...his vulnerability, sharing his biggest secret, revealed to her and her alone.

She swooned, reliving his hand tucking her hair behind her ear and the lingering look in his eyes. His gaze was intense and familiar—like her own. The enduring ache of wanting more...

It's not all in my head! He likes me!

Her phone beeped again.

Nick: Gran LOVED her necklace! That's all down to YOU, my brilliant friend! Thank you thank you thank you.

Friend? Evie wilted. *What the fuck am I doing? Nick's never gonna fancy me. Why would he? He has Bree.*

She stared woefully at Sam's zombie slaughter for a good five minutes, then went to work, pressing the 9 key three times, the 2 key once, followed by the 9 key three more times to spell out **Yay**, then moved on to the next word and the next, pushing buttons multiple times until her message was ready. She hit send.

Evie: Yay! How was the party?

His response arrived promptly. The joys of having a fancy phone with a proper keyboard.

Nick: Dad ruined it

How? Her eyes widened.

Evie: Deets pls

Within seconds, she received…

Nick: How long ya got?

Evie paused. Texting would take forever and unlike most teens, Evie didn't have instant messaging via MySpace or Bebo. Internet services in Orkney were basic at best, and teamed with her parents' strict rules about going online, web-based profiles and messaging tools weren't part of Evie's social arsenal. The fact that she had her own phone was a miracle in itself.

But one option remained.

Pressing keys as fast as she could, she replied before any second thoughts swooped and stole her nerve.

Evie: CALL ME?

Biting her nails, she relocated to her bedroom upstairs for privacy. Recently redecorated and painted a calming sage green, there was nary a poster of Nick in sight, but his Ba' photo held pride of place, smiling from Evie's bookshelf alongside nostalgic souvenirs from her young life: candy-colored My Little Pony toys, schoolgirl snaps with Sunita and Fiona, octopush ribbons, and an old birthday card from her beloved granny, dearly missed ten years and counting.

Evie waited five agonizing minutes…then another five, plus fifteen more. She hugged her plush orca. Threadbare and missing an eye, only Evie saw her whale's true beauty. *Where'd Nick go?* She contemplated texting again, but an urgent twinge in her abdomen sent her scrambling phoneless to the bathroom.

Fifteen minutes later, she decamped to the kitchen table and traded her message-free phone for the sad, forgotten banana in a bowl of apples. She peeled away its squishy, mottled skin, hoping the fruit's bland, stomach-soothing magic would curb future sprints to the toilet. "Maybe Bree called him," she mumbled through a yawn. "Or maybe Nick doesn't want to talk to me." Taking a modest bite, she looked out the window, the negative talk in her head surrendering to the monotonous drum of rain pummeling the trampoline in their back garden.

Three bites in, her phone beeped. Evie dove toward the tiny screen.

Stuart: How r u?

She smiled weakly. Typical Stuart, a man of few words. Nasty nachos and blow job anguish aside, their night out watching the Euro 2008 qualifiers had brought much-needed levity to her difficult week. He wasn't Nick. He'd *never* be Nick, but he was local and available…and interested. Her thumbs hovered over the keypad. Maybe Stuart would be fine with the severity of her condition if given the chance?

Evie started texting but didn't get far.

Nick: Soz! Can't ring you. Dad's hovering—foul mood again. I know you & Sam don't have IM, so what's your email addy?

Eyes widening, a burst of adrenaline whisked Evie's pulse on a familiar joyride. A half-eaten banana and five minutes of frustrating key pressing later and…

Evie: rollergirl92@orknet.co.uk

…was winging its way to Nick's phone.

Dumping the fruit in the bin, she padded into the living room, figuring she'd beg Sam for time on the computer, but he was nowhere to be found. Only his crumb-filled plate and warm seat remained. Evie logged into her email, dragged her cursor past spam messages for prescription drugs and bogus lotteries, and clicked on Nick's much-anticipated message.

From: Nico B. <saxyboy@yahoo.co.uk>
To: Evie Sutherland <rollergirl92@orknet.co.uk>
Date: Sent today at 10:32
Subject: And you thought Dalston G had drama

Sorry, Dad's gone full dictator, won't let us make calls.

Balfour family functions always end in someone losing their shit. This time it was my dad, all shouty and red-faced during dinner. He blew up in front of Gran's guests including the head dude from Formula One racing and the artistic director of the National Theatre (I'd sooo like to perform there one day). Even worse, Muggins here was Dad's target.

First, he threw a wobbler because I ignored his calls at the shop and got us back late. Okay, I own that. It was my fault, but did he have to belittle me publicly? He said I was "neither use nor ornament." You should've seen the theatre bloke's face fall. Pretty humiliating. Then someone mentioned uni and Dad went full-on meltdown, ranting that I'd thrown back everything he'd ever done for me by having the audacity to even THINK I could take a gap year. He shouted so loud, the pastry chef, who'd flown in from Paris, dropped his croquembouche in the kitchen. And just like that, we had no birthday dessert for Gran.

Aren't you glad you asked?

So, following up on our interrupted convo: how are you—really? And how was your boyfriend yesterday? Not cross with you, I hope.

Nick and his questions! She'd *almost* talked about her Crohn's with him behind the shop but now? Not happening. She couldn't bear it if he felt sorry for her. She didn't want to be stigmatized or seen as sickly. Ever. And as for that second question, well, it could *definitely* wait. Evie had too many questions of her own.

She typed quickly.

From: Evie Sutherland <rollergirl92@orknet.co.uk>
To: Nico B. <saxyboy@yahoo.co.uk>
Subject: Re: And you thought Dalston G had drama

Nick, I'm GOBSMACKED and SOOO sorry! Neither use nor ornament? I CAN'T BELIEVE he said that in front of those people. I would've been in tears if it was me. What did you do? What did your mum and gran do? Why does your dad have it in for you like that? Also, what's a croquembouche? :P

Waiting for Nick's email response, Evie texted Stuart back.

Evie: I'm good. Tired. You?

Pushing all those number buttons took *way* too long. Sharing her Crohn's 'truth' would have to wait until they were face to face again.

A few minutes after she hit send on Stuart's text, Nick's reply popped up in her inbox.

From: Nico B. <saxyboy@yahoo.co.uk>
To: Evie Sutherland <rollergirl92@orknet.co.uk>
Date: Sent today at 11:02
Subject: Re: And you thought Dalston G had drama

I said nothing and stared at my plate, hoping I wouldn't have a panic attack (I didn't, thank fuck). Tarquin played with his phone. Rupert ate his weight in filet mignon. Can't say I blame them. Mum missed the entire thing. She left after canapés to fly back to London. She had an early call time on set this morning.

But Gran looked mortified and told Dad to sit the hell down. He did the opposite, tossed his napkin on the table and stormed out. My uncle followed, trying to talk him down. The guests all made their excuses, wished Gran well, and left straight after the entrée. Only Tarq, Rupes, our cousins, and aunt remained. I got wasted on champers. Seemed like a good idea at the time, but today my head's banging.

My dad's furious because I want to take a gap year for auditions before uni. He says my future has already been decided. He wants me to attend Cambridge for business this autumn, then once I have a shitload of impressive letters after my name, I'll carry on his legacy as king and pope of Sports Now. Parental expectations—I'm sick of both of them!

Evie rubbed her belly. *Wow, this feels sorta familiar.* She read on.

I want to continue acting. Mum's on my side, but that means they fight all the bloody time.

I'm freaking because Dad knows people at Cambridge. He says he can still get me in for the fall semester. But if I could just get booked for another series or a film, maybe he'd stop harassing me and recruit Rupert instead? Evie, pray for me, cross everything! I need this gap year! I can't quit acting cold turkey!

A croquembouche is a tower of profiteroles stuck together with loads of ganache. It's proper yum! Translated into English it means *crunch in the mouth*. Weird, eh? Glad my A-level in French is good for something.

What's with your e-addy? You roller skate? I would guess yes if your fave musicals are anything to go by.

No more mentions of Stuart, no more begging to know what was "going on." Evie breathed easier. She appreciated his concern and would tell him about her Crohn's one day. If she had to.

From: Evie Sutherland <rollergirl92@orknet.co.uk>
To: Nico B. <saxyboy@yahoo.co.uk>
Subject: Re: And you thought Dalston G had drama

I'd LOVE to try champagne! Hopefully your head's not too bad. I'm glad you didn't have a panic attack.

Your dad's expectations are excessive (I'm sorry!). I can kinda relate. I'm supposed to help run my mum's shop after I graduate from uni. Then when she retires, it'll be all mine. OOH, THE POWER! The shop's been in my mother's family for generations, so it's not a surprise or anything.

Roller skating...IS MY LIFE!

Evie paused. *Used to be* would more honest. Since her diagnosis, her favorite physical activities—roller skating, bouncing on the trampoline, octopush—were put on a temporary hold whenever her Crohn's flared, replaced by genealogy, word search puzzles, and creative writing. She resumed typing.

I can also eat loads of Rice Krispie squares and not gain weight, wiggle my ears, and fold a fitted sheet.

Oh, I meant to ask—did you know my best friend Fiona has been texting your Rupert? They exchanged numbers yesterday.

And what's up with YOUR address? SAXYBOY? Is that a typo or what? Someone thinks highly of themselves. LOL

Hitting send, her mood lifted. As she waited for Nick's response, she checked her phone. Still no reply from Stuart.

From: Nico B. <saxyboy@yahoo.co.uk>
To: Evie Sutherland <rollergirl92@orknet.co.uk>
Date: Sent today at 11:32
Subject: Re: And you thought Dalston G had drama

But do you <u>want</u> to run your mum's shop? Doesn't your heart's desire matter? There's a big world out there just waiting to be conquered by the one and only (roller skating) Evie Sutherland. And when you do, I'll bring the champagne and we'll say, "Fock eht! Life's too short to live someone else's dream!"

Hmm. Mystery solved. I was wondering who Rupes was texting. Thanks for the dinner table ammunition!

I must say, I'm très impressed by your talents, Evie, but I'll have you know I can play a recorder with my nose (yes, really!), ride a unicycle, and do an awesome cartwheel. Maybe I should add these to the special skills section of my acting CV? Whatcha reckon?
Re my email addy, I played jazz saxophone in school. Badly.

Don't judge.

You didn't answer my other questions. How are *you*? How were things with Stewart when you left?

Nick spelt Stuart's name wrong. Evie bit her lip. Discussing Stuart with him was unsettling. She felt disloyal—to both of them.

From: Evie Sutherland <rollergirl92@orknet.co.uk>
To: Nico B. <saxyboy@yahoo.co.uk>
Subject: Re: And you thought Dalston G had drama

Stuart was a bit miffed (he reserved a pool table at the pub), but he got over it. I didn't tell him about *you know what*, of course. What happens behind Marwick's, stays behind Marwick's, I promise.

I'm okay, thanks. Tired but fine. Been working way too hard.

Me, judge you for playing sax? NEVER. Sax is cool, unlike that recorder thing with your nose, which leads me to the million-pound question: how on Earth did YOU, Recorder Dude, become a teen pin-up?

Evie wasn't sure if Nick was still featured in *Flirty Girl*. She had moved on, her monthly order replaced with the more sophisticated *Bella Faith* magazine, which served up the hottest fashion trends and relationship advice. Gobbling up every page, every tip, Evie mimicked Bree's look of camisoles, mini vests, and bubble hemmed dresses, striving to be more mature, more Nick's type of girl, but unfortunately, her new favorite read couldn't help her answer his trickiest question.

I LOVE our shop and all the fun things we sell. I meet people from all over and kinda feel like an Orkney ambassador, helping them find a piece of the islands to take home with them. Is it my heart's desire? Not sure. I have NO IDEA what that might be. Is that bad?

Clicking send, Evie hoped Nick wouldn't be disappointed by her response. He seemed so ambitious and worldly. She, on the other hand, had grown up believing her future was Marwick's. But what if Nick was right…what if it *wasn't*? She gazed out the window, lost in the novelty of *what-ifs* as rain throttled their front garden.

The computer chimed with an incoming email.

From: Nico B. <saxyboy@yahoo.co.uk>
To: Evie Sutherland <rollergirl92@orknet.co.uk>
Date: Sent today at 11:59
Subject: Re: And you thought Dalston G had drama

Not bad, nope. I reckon some people <u>never</u> know their heart's desire and that's A-OK. If anything, NOT knowing opens you up to all sorts of activities and interests. Why be dull like me and pick just one?

Seeing you in action at the shop yesterday, I was dead impressed. Dealing with the public is hard and you're a natural. You're so friendly and knowledgeable. And if you love it, that's awesome—in a way, you'll never 'work' a day in your life!

Me a pin-up? I have <u>no</u> idea why fans like me. It's super flattering, but I think if they really knew me, they'd go off me. I'm <u>nothing</u> like Jake. Most people seem disappointed when they figure that one out.

But I hope you won't be. ;)

Dad wandered past again shouting, "Pack. Now!" We're leaving for London later, so I better crack on.

I'm glad you're all right, but if you're ever not, I'm always around, yeah? Even if YOU DO LOVE YOUR CAPITALS A BIT TOO MUCH! Ha!

Thanks for being here, Evie. Chat soon, okay? xo

Evie laughed at the screen, enchanted by Nick's xo and his promise to be in touch. "You could *never* disappoint me," she said aloud.

"Who?" Sam called from the hallway. "Me?"

Another giggle tickled her throat. "Yeah, you. Who else?"

TWELVE

EVIE

Now, Monday, June 26

For years Evie had journaled about how, if given the golden oppor-tunity, she would enact her revenge on Nick for his brazen careless-ness with her teenage heart. Taking scissors to his precious ward-robe, cutting his gorgeous hair with Rupert's sheep shears, smash-ing the keys on his piano—all brilliant payback ideas—but throwing him into a potentially life-threatening allergic reaction? *That* was never scribbled on any page, and the mere thought of Saturday's catastrophe left her tearfully shaken and drowning in old feelings.

Even on Sunday, the shoot's first day off, when Fiona called to report that Nick was out of danger and had been discharged from the hospital, Evie still couldn't eat or read or sleep, her mind spiral-ing.

If only she had taken a moment to check the package's ingredi-ent list for potential allergens *before* sending Sunita out with the breakfast treats.

If only.

The carrot (and hidden raisin) muffin episode may have been an unfortunate accident, but the messy mistake was Evie's—and Evie's alone. Now she had to wait and see if the big-bucks broadcaster would name Marwick's in a costly and potentially business-crushing lawsuit.

And to see if Nick would forgive her.

Her heart ached with the thought that he wouldn't. Nick had been so gentle and caring when she burned her hand. He didn't have to be, not when she had been so prickly, so...unforgiving.

But my reasons are still valid. Aren't they?

Even so, in light of Nick's terrifying brush with anaphylaxis, Evie couldn't pretend any longer. She still had feelings for him…conflicted, messy, unrequited feelings she needed to douse before they blazed out of control and suffocated her again.

Dread soured her entire weekend, rousing sinister cramps in her belly, which carried through to Monday morning. She tried her best to ignore them as she drove the fourteen miles to Stromness, grateful that today's shoot didn't involve a half-hour ferry trip to another island and an extra sixty minutes tacked on to an already long stressful day.

Parking the truck around half six on Ferry Road, a narrow street hugging the harbor, Evie kept her fears and discomfort hidden, and her hands—well, her good one—busy. Sunita pitched in as per usual, cooking scrambled egg and sausage sandwiches for the breakfast rush while Evie stuck to her tried-and-true oatmeal, praying her one and only chance to make her mother proud wouldn't land her in court and tarnish their reputation.

As meals were handed out, a knock on the door reverberated through the truck's metal shell and Evie's chest.

They're here. She swallowed hard, scoping out the closed-off street and chatty crew beyond the window. "That's probably for me."

Sunita gave her a sympathetic smile then handed a breakfast sandwich to a sweatsuit-swaddled actress, her boned bodice and sloping bustle still waiting on a hanger in the wardrobe trailer.

Evie smoothed her freshly laundered apron, fighting the pesky static that made the creases cling to her tunic and tummy-friendly leggings. She held a breath in and slowly let it escape, releasing the latch on the door.

When she slid it open, Nick—and only Nick—was revealed like some wannabe boyfriend on one of those TV dating shows she used to watch with her mum. Instead of a bouquet of roses, he gripped a takeout coffee in front of his leather jacket and slim-fit charcoal trousers, obviously giving the fresh pots Evie had made for the crew a wide berth. He glanced up with a brooding squint, a hot rebel with a cause decked out in Prada.

Evie's heart skipped an ill-advised beat.

"Was it how you imagined?" he asked flatly, a muffled buzzing escaping from inside his jacket.

She blinked and stepped down from the truck. "Excuse me?"

"Stabbing me with a sharp object." His wince dissolved into a wry grin. "Don't tell me you haven't thought about it…"

This moment was neither the time nor place to go *there*. Instead, Evie plunged headfirst into groveling mode. "Nick, I am SO sorry! I should've checked the muffins—"

"No, *I* should've. My allergy is uncommon. I never leave it to chance." His pocket whirred again. "But I was mid-phone call and someone texted and I was careless"—he shrugged—"and paid the price for being a hungry, impatient twat."

"But you wouldn't have had I checked."

"It was a fluke. Don't worry about it; I'm not." Nick waved his hand in front of his mouth. "See? Completely fine. No hives, no swelling—"

"Nick?" His assistant swept around the front of the truck, her heart-shaped face bare except for a tint of mascara and a lick of lip gloss. Her shiny dark hair was wind-gust-ready in a low, neat ponytail, and her cropped, black leather motocross jacket, which kissed the top of her high-waisted black jeans, mimicked Nick's outfit to a T.

Fashionable and sophisticated—exactly Nick's type. Evie's head-to-toe perusal leapt up from the woman's western-style ankle boots. *I was delusional for ever thinking he and I would work.*

His assistant squeezed his arm, silver rings gracing every manicured finger. "You need to pick up! Wardrobe has been trying to reach you *for ages*"—she held up her phone—"and now they're calling me." Her accent sounded similar to the American tourists who visited Marwick's.

Nick flashed an uncomfortable smile as the woman let go of his arm. "This is Ashley, assistant extraordinaire."

"Hi." Evie nodded. Ashley stared back, her sour gaze pinging to the hairnet on her head.

"And this is Evie," said Nick, "head of catering and…"

Her stomach tensed. *The girl I left behind.*

"…an old friend."

The polite way of putting it.

"Aw." Ashley wrinkled her nose. "That's nice." If her tone was anything to go by, "nice" was something contemptible.

Evie had met Ashley's type before: outsiders who poked fun at islanders and wrote them off as backward and unsophisticated, in-bred and boring, assuming (wrongly) that they led meaningless, insignificant lives and didn't have a clue about anything happening beyond their shores.

People like Ashley couldn't be more wrong.

For a moment, Evie felt sorry for her narrow, uneducated opinion, but then Ashley threw a dismissive smirk toward two twenty-somethings hauling in their morning's catch on their boat, and a bolt of revulsion ripped through her.

"Ash, I'll meet you by the picnic tables, okay?" Nick motioned across the closed street, toward the seating area in front of the bronze statue of Dr. John Rae, an Orcadian-born surgeon and Arctic explorer. "I'll ring wardrobe shortly." Stealing a sip of coffee, he faced Evie again.

"*Right…*" Ashley retreated a few steps but lingered on the periphery, eyes on her phone.

Nick resumed their conversation. "So, like I said, I'm fine. Please don't be hard on yourself. If anything, your quick thinking saved me."

"Uh, hello?!" Ashley twisted her lips, begging to differ. "Nick, you saw my email?"

Closing his eyes for a beat, he dipped his chin. "Ash, would you *please* drop it? Things are done differently over here. We don't ring the lawyers every time there's a minor hiccup."

Lawyers…? Evie swallowed hard.

"Now please, call wardrobe and find out what they need." Nick's pointed stare hopped across to the picnic tables, delivering a simple, non-verbal request.

Letting out a defeated huff, Ashley wandered toward the statue.

Nick rubbed his forehead. "Sorry about that."

An apology, but not the one Evie's heart yearned for. She looked down and adjusted her apron. "Thank you for not taking this any further."

"Never crossed *my* mind." He smiled warmly, his focus dipping to the hand she held against her abdomen. "How's the injury?"

"Much better."

"Good. Well, I better see what wardrobe wants. Last time they wanted to discuss knickerbockers."

"Sounds right up your alley," said Evie.

"Whoa, I'm not that much of a fashion victim, am I?" With a grin, he raised his hand in farewell and set off across the road.

Evie stepped up into the truck, finding Sunita hovering around the doorjamb.

"Sorry!" She cringed. "Journo habit."

"It's fine. It's good to have a witness."

"Nick taking the blame"—Sunita blew out her lips—"I didn't see *that* coming."

"Me neither. I thought I was done for." Evie inched past. "And what's up with that Ashley? You can tell she hates it here."

"Her loss." Sunita adjusted her hairnet. "Evie, if it's fine with you, I'd like to help a bit longer."

She moved the empty oatmeal pot to the sink. "You're actually enjoying this?"

"*Yeah.* And I'm owed loads of time, so…I booked off through August."

Eyes widening, Evie abandoned the taps. "I'd love if you stayed on!" Throwing her arms around Sunita's shoulders, she rocked back and forth. "Thank you!"

Sunita lifted her chin. "*Oh*, before I forget…"

Evie let go.

"…you got a text."

Evie picked her phone up from the counter and opened her

messages. "It's Caleb. He heard about my hand. Feels terrible."

"He shouldn't. Sounds like an excuse to text you."

"*And* to ask me out for dinner tonight at The Odin," added Evie. "His treat."

"Go!" said Sunita. "If anyone deserves to be spoiled, it's you."

Sipping still water from her wine glass, Evie glanced across the table. Caleb's flannel jacket and faded jeans from the previous week had been replaced with a white dress shirt, unbuttoned casually at the collar, and black trousers. *Rugged on his day off, refined for our date. Don't go all ideal man on me, One-Kiss Caleb.* She smiled. "How's the salmon?"

"Delicious." He swirled a potato through the lemon herb sauce with his fork. "How's the macaroni and cheese?"

"Heavenly." Evie set down her glass, noticing the server on the approach with Caleb's second pale ale. "The best thing about everyone knowing I have Crohn's is I never get funny looks when ordering from the kids' menu." She dove her fork into the cheesy bowl of pasta joy.

"How's it been lately?" Caleb nodded with a "Thanks" as the server removed his empty glass and replaced it with a freshly poured pint.

"Pretty good. Just the odd twinge saying, 'Hey, remember me?'" Evie rarely shared further details unless she had to. Caleb seemed fine with her Crohn's—*Is my luck actually changing?!*—so she happily moved on to something else. "How was camping?"

"Fantastic! We almost lost one of the tents to the wind, though. Now the scouts understand why it's important to secure those suckers."

Evie chuckled softly, more out of politeness than hilarity. Caleb wouldn't be challenging any famous comedians with his humor, but he was easygoing and humble, and his love of outdoor pursuits was a huge turn-on along with the toned arms and firm pecs lurking beneath his form-fitting button-down. She grinned, a forkful of macaroni, breadcrumbs, and Orkney cheddar cheese lingering in front of her lips. "Did you go hiking or rock pooling?" She nibbled her pasta.

"A bit of both. The highlight was probably Burroughston Broch. The kids loved climbing all over it. I tried to give them a bit of a history lesson, but it flew over their heads."

Like Fi, Sun, and I at Skara Brae all those years ago. Evie nodded. "And how's school? End of term is...?"

"Two days away." His gaze leapt upward. "Hallelujah! At times, I thought it was never gonna end."

"Juggling your old classes with head teacher duties must be tough."

"Yeah, it's been a steep learning curve. Don't get me wrong, I love the job and the kids, but I'm more than ready for some Caleb time."

"Which is...what?"

"Fishing on Harray Loch. It's my favorite thing, relaxing on the water, waiting for a taut line to wake me from my reverie."

"I used to go with my dad when I was peedie. I loved it." Evie smiled, the memories precious. "But then again, I might've been more interested in the sweets he packed than hooking a squiggling trout."

"Are you squeamish?"

"Not at all. We had all sorts of pets growing up: a frog, fish, guinea pigs, plus the usual cats and dogs. I wanted a lizard, but Mum said no."

"All those animals, great training for your brother."

The server reappeared with a carafe and topped up Evie's water. "Thank you." She looked up, catching Nick and Ashley toting glasses of wine as they were seated at a table in the far corner. A pink-cheeked server followed, two half-eaten meals held aloft in her hands.

Popular place tonight.

"Sorry about the noise in the bar," said the server, setting Nick and Ashley's plates in front of them. "If you need anything else, please don't hesitate—"

"Evie?"

Her thoughts skipped back to Caleb. "Mmhmm?"

"I was just saying you should come fishing with me sometime. I'll bring sweets."

"Well, that seals it." She grinned, setting down her fork. "Count me in."

Caleb matched her smile and returned to his meal. As he sliced off a sizeable chunk of his pan-fried salmon, Evie surrendered to the gravitational pull across the room, stealing another look.

Ashley gestured Nick toward her plate, and he helped himself to a bite-sized piece of beef.

Oh?! They're dating? A pang of nostalgic yearning gnawed in Evie's chest as Nick offered Ashley his fish. *Yeah, she's much more deserving of his cultured tastes and gorgeous hair.* Chewing quickly, Ashley's eyes roamed the room, and Evie flew back to her mac 'n' cheese, berating herself for being so nosy…and jealous.

"I think it's great, you fishing with your dad as a lass," said Caleb. "You have a goddaughter, don't you?"

"Yeah, Ava—Fiona and Rupert Balfour's oldest. She wants to be a firefighter when she grows up, although I'd put good money on her changing her mind again. So far, she's wanted to be a figure skater and a fashion designer."

Caleb's grin grew. "Both exceptional choices. Do you spend much time with her?"

"She sleeps over twice a month. We watch films, play board games."

"Ava must love that." He paused for a moment. "I know it's not ideal first date talk, but…I'd love a houseful of kids."

Shiiit. Evie deflated inside. *Finally find a nice, normal guy and he wants his own rugby team?*

"That said, I'd gladly settle for two. Let's face it, I'm *not* getting any younger." Caleb laughed.

Her attention strayed again. Nick had drawn his chair closer to Ashley's, their conversation peppered with knowing looks and sly smiles. Breaking into a laugh, Nick surveyed the restaurant, his sweeping glance tangling with Evie's.

Her heart stuttered as she blinked away, extricating herself from their mutual gape. Hand scrambling for her fork, she knocked it onto the carpeted floor. She grimaced with a flustered "*Sorry*" then peered underneath. "I'm such a—"

"Let me." Caleb shifted his chair and ducked, rescuing the fallen fork. On his return, he stole a clean one from the empty neighboring table and tossed a look over his shoulder. "Oh, it's that actor." Wide-eyed, Caleb smiled as he turned and handed Evie the clean cutlery.

"Thanks." Her curiosity jogged back. Nick's assessing stare was burning a hole in the back of Caleb's head.

"I got a selfie with him the other day," said Caleb, noticeably starstruck. "Nice guy. I think he used to spend summers here."

Evie nodded as Caleb swiveled again and waved subtly. Nick raised his glass in greeting, his focus snapping to Evie. She promptly reunited with her dinner.

"My sister was thrilled." Still grinning, Caleb relinquished the dirty fork to the edge of their table. "Apparently, he's around all summer." He picked up his beer and settled in for a substantial guzzle.

Careening beyond Caleb, Evie's gaze collided with Ashley's. She whispered something in Nick's ear with a self-satisfied smile.

Temptation simmered inside Evie. If Nick was gawking, why not put on a show? She could hold Caleb's hand across the table, howl with laughter like he was the most amusing guy *ever*, or share a slow kiss like the heroines in her favorite historical romances.

But Evie wasn't a fictional character and this moment wasn't a scene on an e-reader. Caleb was *truly* into her, and to take advantage of his kindness and genuine feelings and use them as a battering ram to vengefully knock Nick off his perch didn't sit well. A heart wasn't a toy, especially when it belonged to someone who fancied you more than you fancied them, who wanted kids when you didn't.

"Sorry to sidetrack the conversation. We were talking about children..." Caleb took a sip of ale.

Evie painted on a grin. "Yeah. Kids are...great."

A glimmer of reverence shone in his eyes. A scout leader and teacher, Caleb couldn't wait to read bedtime stories and go fishing with his own brood.

Unlike Evie.

Ruggedly handsome with a sweetness belying his mountain man demeanor, Caleb was the perfect Orkney boyfriend—for someone else.

A dart of disappointment plunged into Evie's chest. She couldn't lead Caleb on in front of Nick or anyone else. They weren't on the same path, and the sooner he knew...

"I bet you'll make a great mum someday."

No, no, no. Smiling tightly, she played with the napkin on her lap and leaned over her mac 'n' cheese. "That's lovely of you to say, but...actually, I don't want kids."

A wave of surprise crashed through Caleb's baby blues. "You don't?"

She shook her head slowly. "I love Ava and her sister, but being a mum myself has never been a dream of mine."

"Yeah, but lots of people say that, though." Caleb edged closer. "I bet you'll change your mind."

"Will you?" Evie volleyed back with a soft grin, hoping her pleasant countenance would dim any perceived harshness in her reply. She wasn't being snarky or judgmental. She just wanted Caleb to understand they were both entitled to their decisions and neither one was wrong.

Caleb eased back into his chair. He opened his mouth but said nothing.

"I'm sorry. You're a great guy, but I can't pretend to be someone I'm not."

Disappointment lingered in his eyes. "I appreciate your honesty."

"We could still be friends, though," said Evie.

Caleb nodded. "I'd like that."

Thirteen

Evie

Then, Saturday, August 9, fifteen years ago

The snap of fire-ravaged driftwood spit amber sparks into the dusky sky above Inganess Beach, its temporary inhabitants in various degrees of undress and intoxication. The arrival of exam results was a reason to blow off steam, and while Evie still had two more years of revising, stressing, and testing before heading to university, she relished the opportunity to spend the last gasp of summer with friends.

"We've so earned this." Sitting on a sand-speckled blanket bathed in the distant glow of the crackling bonfire, she tossed back the dregs of the cider she'd been nursing, its warm liquid tart on her tongue.

"Too bad it's your last week of freedom," said Stuart, munching crisps as Sunita made out with her boyfriend.

Evie lowered the empty can and stared out into the bay where the rusted hulk of *The Juniata*, an abandoned WWII blockship, sat amid the choppy waves. "Summer can't be over already!" She grimaced into a groan as several classmates splashed and squealed in the chilly water. "I've done nothing but work and worry..."

Her gaze meandered to the bubble-gum pinks dappling the sleepy sky, the palette similar to a certain someone's favorite shirt.

...and chat with Nick.

True to his word twelve months earlier, Nick was regularly in touch. He'd share audition woes and family tales, and whenever Evie's exam stress robbed her of food or sleep, he'd commiserate and send study fuel—decadent biscuits—all the way from ritzy Fortnum & Mason in London. Evie, in turn, was the reassuring voice at the end of Nick's phone, offering calm support until his panic attacks subsided, giving way to their usual banter about musicals and school, the joys of genealogy and roller skating (Evie), and the merits of *Grease 2* and bowling (Nick).

Sometimes flirty but always respectful, Nick's growing bond with Evie was unlike anything she'd ever experienced. No longer starry-eyed, she viewed him as a trusted confidante, one who made her feel seen and heard, and yet, her most guarded secret remained hidden. Evie didn't want the shadow of Crohn's to follow her into this blossoming friendship—at least not yet. The time would surely come when she had to open up, but for now she was reveling in the delight of being known for her wacky taste in musicals instead of her disease.

A tug of her gray cardigan and a "…don't you think?" made her retreat from the cotton candy sky.

"Think what?" she asked.

"Summer hasn't been all work," said Stuart. "The snogs, blow jobs—we've barely come up for air." Discarding the crisps, he tilted closer. "Come here."

Evie complied and met his lips, salty and slightly parted.

"Snoggin's the BESST!" Slurring into a giggle, Sunita untangled herself from Puggie, a chubby, fellow part-timer at the pharmacy with a wispy moustache and dark curls. "It cures all." She lurched forward, scoring a lager standing up in the sand.

Evie broke her kiss with Stuart as Sunita wrenched back the can's ring pull.

"But snogging doesn't fix shitty exam results." Puggie's eyes dimmed.

"Oh, *baby*." Sunita pouted.

"There's only one thing for it, beuy," said Stuart, scratching his bristly hair. "More booze."

"YES!" Arms outstretched, Sunita thrust her beer into Evie's hand and draped herself around Puggie, pulling him downward for another sloppy kiss.

Laughing, Stuart plucked his car keys from his jacket pocket. "Evie, more cider?"

"Uh…" She diverted her eyes away from Sunita's ravenous mauling of Puggie and spied Sam and his friends down the beach tossing driftwood on the fire. "I…think I'm good." She anchored Sunita's beer in the sand and smiled. "Thanks, though."

Stuart pushed himself up. "No worries," he grunted. "Won't be long." Plodding across the sand, he swerved a cluster of plastered teens shouting nonsense and waving sizzling sparklers, their defiant gestures carving *fuck* into the impending darkness.

Fuck, indeed. Evie slowly released a breath, but the knot in her chest wouldn't unravel. Stuart was leaving in a few weeks for his third year of university in Glasgow. Evie had discovered the previous autumn that distance did little to make her heart grow fonder. If anything, it rebelled.

How are we gonna make this work? She glanced down the beach, ignoring the beer-fueled kisses across the blanket. The farther Stuart walked, the dimmer he became until he disappeared completely into the falling shadows.

Her mind detoured, leaping south, wondering what Nick was up to in France.

"OH, BEHAVE!" Puggie's nasal Austin Powers impression snapped Evie back. Prising himself free from Sunita, he flashed his girlfriend a flirty leer and heaved his unbuttoned shirt closed over his doughy stomach.

Sunita grabbed his leg as he stood up. "Bein'badissomuchfun!" All mushy consonants and flat vowels, her words ran together like a boozy, verbal stampede.

Evie laughed, but even a moment of hilarity couldn't suppress the envy squeezing her core. Drinking with the goal of getting "off her tits," as Sunita would say, was a luxury she could ill afford. Evie's last piss-up with Stuart had been a month earlier, and while she paid dearly for it afterward with stomach cramps, she still hated being stuck on the sidelines, especially when all her friends were letting loose and pushing boundaries. Crohn's was stealing invaluable coming-of-age experiences, and the ache of missing out sometimes hurt more than her symptoms.

"Dude! Wait up!" Running barefoot, Puggie hobbled through the curly doddies and prickly roadside brush where Stuart's chariot, a dented 1998 Vauxhall Corsa, came alive with a caterwaul of rattles, its only functioning headlight a beacon in the growing darkness.

Sunita wriggled closer. "Sooo!" She sprang with a hiccup. "Tell me, tell me! How was last night? What'd you end up gettin' Stu, anyway? Cologne or the rugby DVD?"

"Neither." Evie looked at *The Juniata* as the swimmers sprinted past, swearing through chattering teeth. "I gave him a monogrammed flask and..." She arched her brows.

Sunita's jaw dropped. "NOOO!" she screeched. "Evie Sutherland, you—!"

"Shhh!" Evie spotted her brother by the bonfire with the girl he was dating, both craning their necks in her direction as the Fletts strummed their out-of-tune guitars. "I don't want Sam to know."

Eyes wide, Sunita mouthed, "You fucked him! Finally!"

"I did!" She laughed giddily, still buzzing with the relief of it.

"Happy twentieth birthday, Stuart!" Sunita slurred into a perfect smile, her braces long gone. "So, gimme the goss! Where'd it happen?"

"The old camper in his mum's garden."

"Better than his shitbox car," said Sunita.

Barely. Evie nodded, the camper's ancient stench of mildew and weed still a stomach-churning memory.

"You were careful, right?" Sunita plucked her beer from the sand. "Used the condoms I gave you ages ago?"

"Yes, Mum," Evie joked as her friend took another sip. Buying condoms herself would've set off alarm bells from Kirkwall to Yesnaby, but having a best friend who worked part-time in the pharmacy? Priceless.

"And? Was it everything you'd hoped?"

Hello, loaded question. Evie had built it up in her head for so long, how could anything compare to her hyper-horny imagination? And there was that one unrealistic wish—that her first time would've been with Nick. While irrational and ridiculous, she'd never given up hope.

Or told Sunita.

"Not exactly." Evie shifted, tucking her legs beneath her bum. "It was over pretty fast. And hurt at first. I'm glad you warned me."

"But after that?"

"Good, I guess? Stu wanted to do it again."

"Guys *always* think it's amazing even when it's not," said Sunita, a seasoned veteran of three brief sexual relationships. "They're just happy getting laid."

Doubt rolled in Evie's stomach. "Shit. So I *was* crap?"

Sunita snorted. "Yeah, right! The amount of steamy novels you read?"

Raucous laughter erupted down the beach. The bonfire clique was pleased about something, not that it mattered to Evie. Head down, she budged closer to Sunita, determined to keep her conversation out of the ears of the spliff-smoking swimmers sat nearby.

"But…" Evie whispered, a gentle breeze rustling her bangs. "I didn't come. Stuart did. Both times."

"Of course *he* did. Guys can be so selfish sometimes."

Evie's shoulders buckled. "*Great.*"

"Hey, it's no biggie," said Sunita. "Show him what you like. You'll be popping orgasms in no time!"

"Yeah, but he won't, you know…go down on me."

"Have you asked him?"

Evie nodded.

"Then tell him no more blowies till he does," said Sunita. "And get proper protection, too."

"The pill?"

"Get an IUD fitted. You might forget the pill. And keep using condoms. You *do not* want an STI. Whatsherface from the Picky caught one and it was gross! All itchy and discharge-y. Totally put me off my rice pudding during break."

Evie scrunched her face and hefted up her blouse's neckline. "You'll go to the free clinic with me?" She tugged her cardigan closed over her top.

"Yep." Sunita's eyes dipped, following Evie's frantic fingers. "Whataya doing?"

"Hiding Stu's love bite. It's big and ugly and on my boob."

They sat quietly for a moment, the boisterous shouts of Sam's friends and the off-key warbling of several classmates butchering "Shut Up and Let Me Go" echoing around the bay.

Sunita pulled in her knees, bunching the blanket as she moved. "Did last night change anything?"

Evie winced.

Sunita's face soured. "Bugger."

"Sun, what do I *do*?" Evie pleaded. "It's been a year now and—"

"You still don't love him."

Sunita was blunt at the best of times, but her alcohol-soaked honesty felt like permission to unpack everything.

Slouching into herself, Evie's chin dropped. "I feel *awful*. He's been great, you know? Texting every day, picking me up after work…"

"He's cool about your Crohn's, too."

"Pretty much." Evie's gaze pinged upward, scraping the citrusy sky. Lucky for her and Stuart, her Crohn's had been relatively quiet since December. "But our dates are *soo* boring. They're always the same: beers in the park before the pub, watching snooker in the pub, then messing around in his car *after* the pub."

"And messing around is bad? Eves, he's crazy for you."

"I like him, too, but—" She blew out her lips. "I dunno."

Sunita bumped Evie's shoulder. "C'mon. Don't do a Fiona on me."

"Huh?"

"Be all shy and annoyingly private."

"I thought I'd fall hard once we'd—I mean, I *am* attracted to him. I *like* having a boyfriend…"

"Well, that's good," said Sunita, her lazy reply drowned out by a car's clattering engine on the road behind them. "So what's the problem?"

A weighty exhale escaped Evie's mouth. "Maybe I'm expecting too much."

Sunita chuckled. "Sounds like you."

"It's nice to feel wanted and liked—"

"And fucked senseless. It's what you've been dreaming of for ages!"

"I know, but..." Evie played for time, adjusting her Swatch as *I wish he was more like Nick* flashed like a Piccadilly Circus billboard in her head. "He barely talks."

"*Talks?*" Sunita swiveled her empty beer can into the sand.

"Yeah—and I don't mean post-blow job ramblings about windfarms and solar panels."

"What's wrong with you? That's hot!" A giggle flew through Sunita's lips, fanning Evie's smoldering frustration.

"It's so *not*." She snatched the silver *Evie*, pulling the charm to the front of her neck. "It's great he's passionate about his course, but sometimes it feels like he knows nothing about me." She sighed, exasperated. "He never asks about my hobbies, where I might go for uni. He just assumes I'll follow him to Strathclyde in two years."

"Hmm, so what you're saying is"—Sunita touched Evie's knee—"Mr. Moodie isn't the most chatty?"

Finally, she gets it. "If we never talk, I'll never know him. Not properly. Sun, how can I fall in love with someone I don't even know?"

"But if you're screwing, who needs talk?"

"*Honestly?*" Evie addressed the heavens. "Why do I bother?"

Lifting her hand, Sunita's amused glint dimmed. "Look, it's not your fault if the feelings aren't there."

Torn, Evie met her eyes. "So I should break it off?"

"Oh no. It's still early days."

"It's been a year, Sun—*a year*. I don't know what to do. I always thought I'd love my first boyfriend."

"Who says you won't? Give it more time, especially now you're banging each other."

Evie shot her a sidelong glance. "Nicely put…" She let out a mournful sigh and surrendered to a troublesome thought that wouldn't quit. "Maybe I should've waited."

"And be the last virgin in our class? Eves, you did yourself a favor. People were beginning to talk."

"*What? Who* was?"

Ignoring Evie's question, Sunita leaned in. "Good boyfriends are hard to find, and Stu *adores* you. Plus, he's old enough to buy us booze"—she rammed her point home with an annoying finger poke—"so no binning him just yet!"

Is this as good as it's gonna get? Evie's shoulders sank along with her heart. Maybe Sunita was right. Maybe love would bloom if she stopped being so picky. *I'm gonna try.*

"At least wait till you orgasm with him." Sunita smirked. "I promise, coming will change *everything*."

"Well…this looks intense." Nick's voice wafted over their heads.

Evie sucked in a breath.

"What'd I miss?" he asked.

Oh god, what'd he hear? A flush crept across her cheeks as she yanked up the neckline of her top. "Uhh…" Painting on a tight smile, Evie turned around.

Nick looked as gorgeous as always, but also older, more sculpted, his to-die-for cheekbones more high-flying runway model than adolescent heartthrob. Nineteen looked great on him.

Gulping back a captivated gasp, Evie's grin burst wide open. "You're here!" she cooed, her effusive glee earning a frown from Sunita.

"Surprise!" Hiding something bulbous and heavy under his turquoise bowling shirt, which finally fit him properly, Nick rocked back on his heels, his buzzy smile matching her joy. "I know yesterday's text said otherwise, but we managed to escape Mum and Dad's bickering after all."

Evie leaned into Sunita. "Nick and his brothers were in France for two months."

She refused to look over her shoulder. "Yeah, Fi said."

"I knew celebrations were in order, so I called a taxi and..." Nick hitched his shirt up, gifting Evie a fleeting glimpse of abs as he revealed his strangely shaped 'baby bump'—a large bottle swaddled in a handkerchief. "I brought champagne!"

"Coool!" Her eyes swept the embroidered Louis on his vintage bowling shirt. *I still love that!*

"Champagne? At a bonfire?" asked Sunita.

"Better believe it," said Nick, peeling away the foil covering the cork. "Evie's always wanted to try it."

"Always?" Sunita raised a sardonic brow. "*Really.*"

Evie nodded. "I really wanted some for my sixteenth." She let out a giggle. "Guess I should've told someone."

"Your birthday was the 29th of April, right?" Nick crouched down, joining the girls on the blanket.

"Yes!" She beamed, engrossed by the ceremony unfolding in front of her.

He tossed his head, flicking his hair away from his eyes. "Well, how 'bout we celebrate EVERYTHING now, eh?! Birthdays, your exam results, my newfound freedom..."

Joy effervesced in Evie's belly. "Nick! Does this mean—?"

"Yeppers!" Pointing the champagne away from everyone, Nick held the handkerchief over the neck and cork and rotated the bottle slowly until it released a muffled *POP.*

"Woohoo!" Evie clapped, amazed nary a drop was sacrificed.

"In English, please?" asked Sunita.

Nick handed the open bottle to Evie first, its weight dropping her hands into her lap. "My dad backed off. I don't have to join Sports Now or take over when he retires."

"Nick!" Evie squealed. "I'm SO happy for you!" Fighting the urge to wrap him in a tight, congratulatory hug, she hoisted the heavy bottle up, pressing the glass opening to her lips. Chilled bubbles, citrusy and fizzy, danced on her tongue and tickled all the way down her throat. *So decadent!* Evie fought back a giggle. *And so not Orkney!* The unexpected thrill of sitting on the sand, bathed in the ripe pinks of a late summer sunset with Nick and his champagne was almost too much. She snuck another sip.

"You like?" He stuffed the handkerchief in his back pocket. "If you don't, that's fine. You don't have to drink—"

"No, I love it!"

"It's nice, isn't it? It's a 1996 vintage, found it in my gran's wine room."

"She has a *room*?" gaped Evie.

"As big as my bedroom, yeah."

"When'd you find out about Sports Now?" Evie offered the champagne to Sunita, who shook her head.

"About an hour ago. Dad rang. Something must've changed his mind this afternoon." Nick shrugged casually into a dimple-flexing grin. "But hey, who cares about details? It's a win. I'll shut up and gladly take it."

"What about Cambridge?" Evie fidgeted with her top again.

"That's off the table, too, but he held firm on uni. *So!* Guess who's headed to the University of Salford next month?"

"Salford?" asked Evie. "Where's that?"

"Greater Manchester," said Nick.

"Wow! How'd you get in? Acceptances already went out."

"How'd you think?" Sunita sloppily rubbed her thumb over the tip of her index and middle fingers, hinting at a cash transaction.

He bought his way in? Evie cocked a brow. *No way.*

"I applied months ago—on a whim." Nick pulled out his phone and paused, his expression pensive. "Mind you, I never thought I'd actually *go*."

Evie's eyes locked on his phone's fruity logo. *What?!* Her mouth fell slack. *Nick's got one of those Apple iPhone thingies?!*

Sunita waggled her head back and forth. "Blah, blah, blah! Does he always talk this much about himself?"

Evie ignored her. She also parked her curiosity about Nick's phone despite dying to ask if he'd lined up for it. Temptation twitched inside her, but unleashing it might catapult another snide remark from Sunita about Nick's wealth. "So, you'll study drama?"

she asked instead.

"No, television and radio production." Nick checked something on his phone then tucked it away. "I figured I should learn what goes on *behind* the scenes. Can't hurt, right? If anything, it'll be backup in case acting doesn't pan out."

"Like you *have* to work," said Sunita.

Nick raked a hand through his hair. "I don't have to. I *want* to."

"Hey, it's always smart to have a plan B," said Evie, playing peacemaker as she pressed the bottle into Nick's hands.

"Exactly! This way, I can earn a degree and audition on the side. It's all good. I just hope the industry doesn't forget me before I graduate." He downed a generous swig of champagne.

"So, in other words"—a hiccup jolted Sunita midsentence—"you didn't land any parts during your gap year."

"No. Not for want of trying, though." Nick passed the champagne back to Evie. "Work's been scarce since *Dalston*. Seems I'm either too young or too old, too tall or too Jake."

"I hate that," said Evie as Sunita dragged her purse closer and plowed inside. "Being judged for things you have zero control over."

"And while we're on the topic," said Nick, "I didn't book the young Han Solo role."

Evie pouted. "Nooo. I'm so sor—"

"Dammit!" Sunita wailed, sloppily chucking her bag on the blanket. "I *knew* I forgot something…"

"Like what?" Evie motioned toward her backpack. "Maybe I have what you need."

"Oh yeah? I'm looking for…the world's tiniest violin?!"

Evie's jaw fell. "Sunita!" Hugging the champagne, she turned to Nick. "*Sorry.* Ignore her. She's—"

"Calling out Nick's bullshit," said Sunita.

Drawing back, Evie narrowed her gaze. "You're what?!"

"Sunita, have I done something to piss you off?" asked Nick.

"Yes, Nick—yes, you have—but where to start!" she bellowed. "You can't fool me, Mr. *TV Tales* Hunk of the Year. Evie and everyone else might be charmed, but I know what you actor types are *really* like."

"And what is that exactly?" he batted back calmly.

"Self-obsessed, two-timing *users* who don't give a toss who they hurt."

"He's nothing like that!" said Evie as the sun finally surrendered to the sea. "I should know. We talk all the time."

"I KNOW!" Sunita's sneering glance rolled over his bowling shirt. "And I really take issue, *Louis*, when you message Eves for months, stringing her along, then you show up with your pricey plonk and your come-to-bed eyes and make her doubt her choices."

Nick snickered. "Come-to-bed eyes? That's a first!"

"I don't doubt my choices," said Evie.

"Nice try, Pinocchio!" Sunita snorted. "Should I remind you of what you said earlier—"

"Sun, *don't*!" Evie snarled through clenched teeth, her intense stare a silent warning. What she had shared about Stuart was private and not up for public debate. Ever.

"Deny, deny, deny, but every time Hurricane Nikolai whirls into town, *I'm* left dealing with the bloody wreckage." Waving a finger, her scowl vaulted to Nick. "She doesn't need YOU messin' up her head."

"He's not!" Evie hissed.

Nick raised his palms in surrender. "Hey, I would *never*."

"She's got a boyfriend, you know, one who could beat your ass like"—Sunita tried to snap her rubbery fingers twice and failed—"well, like that!"

"Stuart isn't a secret, Sun. Nick knows—and he's with Bree."

"Yeah, Evie and I are just mates," said Nick, his focus vaulting above the girls' heads. "She's said it herself. There's *nothing* going on—"

"Evie, you all right?" asked Sam.

Her mouth ran dry. *Shit.* No 'Sprout', no light-heartedness in his voice. Sam's blunt intrusion meant one thing—his protective big brother mode was in full, cringe-worthy effect. *Oh god, kill me now.*

Looking over her shoulder, Evie caught Sam's pointed gaze sliding toward Nick. This nonsense had to end. Now.

She flashed a cheery smile. "Hey, Sammy! We're just discussing—"

"How Nick's stroking his ego with YOUR sister," blurted Sunita. "He's such a fake."

Nausea swelled in Evie's belly. She ducked her chin, wishing she could toss the blanket over her head and vanish. Or better yet, run into the bay and drown.

"You're talking bollocks, Sunita, and you know it!" said Nick.

Evie leaned toward him. "I'm *so* sorry."

Sam eyed the bottle in front of her. "Who brought champagne?"

"I did, mate." Nick peered up, his voice unruffled. "To toast Evie's exam success. She's worked damn hard and I thought, you know…she deserves something celebratory."

Brows drawn and lips in a straight line…Evie knew that look. Sam wasn't impressed. "Nico, you know I love ya like a brother, but—"

"But?!" Nick interrupted. "There shouldn't be any *but*, Sam. My intentions were honorable. I wasn't trying to get her drunk, I swear."

"Well, you *would* say that, wouldn't you?" Sunita slurred.

"Sunita, look I'm sorry—but you know absolutely *nothing* about me!" Nick exhaled hard and turned toward Evie's brother. "Unlike Sam. Mate, you know I'd never hurt your sister—or any girl for that matter. I'm not that bloke."

"But vintage champagne?" Sam gestured toward the bottle. "C'mon, Nick, it's a bit over the top. And Evie's only—"

"*Hello?!* I'm still here! Can you gimme *some* credit?!" Mortified, she threw her arms up in the air. "I've had like two sips and one can of cider, which Stuart gave me. I'm nowhere near pissed and can prove it." Evie raised her chin, goading Sam for a challenge. "Go on, ask me: What's twelve times eleven? What's the capital of Canada?"

Her brother swatted away a bug. "I'm not gonna sober-quiz

you."

"Well?" Evie squinted as headlight beams swung across the beach, temporarily illuminating their argument for all to see. "Stop being a buzzkill."

"I'm trying to *look out* for you." Sam's eyes bored into hers with the unspoken *You can't drink like everyone else*, a reminder Evie didn't need or want. She'd always be different, even when her Crohn's was in check, even when she was being sensible.

"I swear," said Sunita. "If you dump Stuart for champagne boy—"

"I'm not dumping anyone!" Fury coiled in Evie's belly, but the damage had been done. It was all too much: Sam's questioning, Sunita's drunken meddling, but it was Nick's presence...watching everyone treat her like a silly, irresponsible child that set her fuse alight.

"I'm sixteen *fucking* years old!" Evie yelled as car doors thumped in the distance. "I can make my own decisions! I don't need you or Sam telling me what I can and cannot do!"

"Whoa!" Sunita sat back, allowing Evie's rant to float away on the breeze, past their friends whispering on the sand.

Sam looked down the beach. "Evie, you need to—"

"Calm down?! "Don't you dare!"

Nick swallowed hard, his stare hovering over the horizon. "This is my fault. I didn't mean to cause any aggro." He reclaimed the champagne and stood. "I should go."

Sunita waved him off dismissively. *"Yeah, buh-bye!"*

"No, wait!" Evie pleaded. "You've done nothing wrong." Brushing sand off her jeans, she scrambled to her feet as Fiona wandered over, her hand cozy in Rupert's.

"Hey?" Fiona's narrowed scrutiny ping-ponged between Evie and Sunita. "What's...going on?"

"You okay, Nico?" Rupert's attention dawdled on Sam.

Sunita huffed. "God, just what we need—more Balfour boys."

"Rupes, I know you just got here, but could you give me a lift back?" asked Nick.

Nearby naughty laughter and the slam of car doors accompanied his younger brother's awkward pause. "Uh..." Rupert nudged up his glasses as his wide-eyed blinks dashed between his brother and Fiona, who nodded warily. "I guess?"

"Nick." Evie stepped closer. "Don't go."

Meeting her sad gape once more, he gave her a resigned grin. "No, really, I shouldn't have gatecrashed. Congrats on your results. I'm honestly chuffed for you."

Evie's heart sank. "I'm so sorry."

Nick squeezed her arm. "It's okay. We'll talk soon, yeah? I'll message ya," he whispered then walked away with Rupert, who hounded him with non-stop questions.

"Happy now?" Evie glared at Sunita and Sam, oblivious to Stuart and Puggie's approach, their rowdy banter skidding into silence as they tramped past the Balfours. Humiliation blazed through her. "Now he'll want nothing to do with me, thanks to you!" Impending tears stung her nose.

Fiona picked at the strap of her tote bag. "Should I even ask?"

Evie did a double take and spotted the boys, their arms crowded with heavy paper bags. Stuart flashed her a tense smile.

"Hey, cheer up!" Puggie shouted triumphantly as he dropped to his knees. "Reinforcements have arrived!" He emptied their haul on the blanket: lager, cider, coolers.

"Give us one!" Sunita claimed a neon-hued alcopop. "We all need a drink after *that* drama."

Sam cleared his throat.

"I know, Sammy! I know!" Chin trembling, Evie couldn't look at him as he strode off, the swell of hot tears threatening her lashes. She plopped down on the blanket and stared into the distance, cursing big brothers who stick their noses in where they're not wanted.

Fiona sat by her side, eyes brimming with unspoken curiosity. "Eves, can I get you anything? Some water, crisps? I brought homemade toffee." She dipped into her bag and pulled out a clean tissue.

"Thanks." Evie sniffed. "How 'bout a new best friend? Got one in there, too?"

Fiona's gaze hopped across the blanket.

"*Eves*," Sunita pleaded. "I was just looking out f—"

"Don't talk to me." Evie wiped her nose.

Puggie nudged Sunita.

"Ask me later," she muttered, then glugged her alcopop.

Stuart picked up a can of lager. "Evie, come walk?"

Swallowing her hurt, she nodded.

Leaving behind the bonfire's crackle and the Flett twins' torturous guitar playing, Evie ambled stiffly by Stuart's side, her mind a firestorm of uncertainty about Nick and Sunita and how—no, IF she could forgive her best friend. Sunita drunkenly tearing into her and Nick was one thing, but it was quite another threatening to spill her most intimate secrets in front of half of Kirkwall Grammar. The only saving grace—Stuart missed most of it, although this being Orkney, he'd get caught up quickly.

CLICK-CRACK! He bent back the ring pull on his lager.

Evie glanced sidelong as his Adam's apple bobbed with a swallow, then another and another as he greedily guzzled the amber liquid.

She couldn't leave it to chance. Stuart needed to hear about Nick's innocence and about Sam and Sunita's meddling from her. Left to spread on the island's grapevine, gossip had a habit of becoming rancid and damaging. She inhaled deeply. No time like the present.

Fishing for Stuart's free hand, she weaved her fingers between his. "Sun and I had a fight."

He lowered the can and stifled a burp. "I gathered."

Studying his cropped haircut, buzzed to oblivion on the sides with only a short layer of length on top, Evie waited for something more, but nothing came. Typical Stuart. If words were currency, he'd have accrued a fortune. She tried again. "Want to know what happened?"

"Not really. You'll work it out." He quaffed another prolonged sip.

"Right." Evie sighed. Their conversation was drying up faster than the seaweed strewn on the beach. She blinked downward, the cool sand shifting beneath her bare feet.

"Unlike this," he mumbled. "*This* isn't working."

A rift tore through her chest. "*What?*" She stopped and looked up, but Stuart skirted her bewildered gawp and dropped her hand.

"I wanna break up."

Evie froze. "You?! But…last night, you—we…"

His hardened gaze fled to his beer can. "What do you want me to say?"

All the anger and frustration swirling in Evie's belly surged to the surface, stinging her nose and breaching her lashes. "Th-that you didn't *use* me!" She shivered.

"As if," he scoffed under his breath.

She lunged forward, her shove dislodging the beer from his grip. "You asshole! I shouldn't have wasted my virginity on YOU!"

Stuart grimaced over his shoulder. Evie's blurry squint followed.

Down the beach, Sunita, Puggie, her brother—everyone—rubbernecked, their curious whispers bathed in the bonfire's golden flicker.

They all know. Even Sam. Evie gasped, wishing the sand would swallow her whole.

Turning back, Stuart lowered his voice. "Sorry you feel that way, but the timing isn't intentional."

Tears spilled down Evie's cheeks. "Isn't it?" Her voice cracked as Stuart mumbled something about "wanting different things," but his excuses were lost amid the rumble of the tide and Evie's careening thoughts.

Stupid girl. You should've waited.

FOURTEEN

NICK

Now, Wednesday, June 28

Salty gusts and a pelting horizontal deluge on the Mainland had postponed outdoor filming at the Standing Stones of Stenness, arguably Britain's oldest henge monument. They would've normally pushed through, erecting a canopy over the actors and dressing the crew in rain attire, but this storm was an unrelenting beast and the risk of injury from fallen equipment or electrical shock was too much of a gamble. Best to be safe and behind schedule than sorry and in litigation.

Nick grasped the unexpected day off for some much-needed self-care, driving his rental car out to Inganess Beach where he could be alone with the choppy waves and his turbulent thoughts. He had joined the *Tomlinson* production in the hopes he and Evie could find a path back to friendship—for everyone's benefit—but so far the terse words they'd shared over catered meals and burnt hands, while better than nothing, were doing more harm than good, acting as stand-ins for what they both really wanted to say.

Is it too late, though? Have we left it too long?

He stared through his rain-spattered windshield at *The Juniata*, remembering the last time they were together on this beach and how he hated himself for walking away, leaving Evie near tears.

After an hour mulling things over, rereading her old texts, and listening with only one AirPod to a playlist of musicals she'd created years earlier, he drove off toward the center of Kirkwall hoping to find a replacement pair. Construction meant he had to park farther than he would've liked, but like a true Londoner, he always packed an umbrella in his messenger bag. However, what works in

London doesn't always translate to Orkney, and within minutes, the soggy gales had decapitated his umbrella and waterlogged his leather jacket. With each hurried step, Nick's drenched socks rubbed mercilessly against the heel of his stiff (and probably ruined) leather Oxfords.

"What the hell am I doing?" he muttered, flinching through the stingy attack of burgeoning blisters as the cold, prickly rain pecked his face. *You won't find AirPods here.*

Slowing to a walk, Nick glanced back the way he'd come, spotting his sacrificed umbrella poking out from a garbage bin. He had a choice: sprint back to the car and create an even greater bloodbath inside his socks or find somewhere dry and hospitable to wait out the worst of the downpour. It had to be somewhere he could loiter without being conspicuous or hassled to buy something, which ruled out the women's clothing store, the appliance place, and the community center on the stretch of Broad Street ahead.

St. Magnus Cathedral, a port in many a storm for generations, towered to his left, but the hearse and line of cars hugging its curb eliminated it as an option.

That leaves Marwick's. Unease bubbled in his hungry belly as he approached the reopened shop, the repaired façade painted its usual dark green. *If you're lucky, Evie and her mum won't be in.* Sweeping his drenched hair from his forehead, Nick pulled open the door and locked eyes with Fiona.

"Nick?" She handed a Twatt pillow to a happy customer, her gaze flying over her shoulder toward the heart of the shop. "Uh"— licking her lips, she turned back—"Evie's working the kitchen. I'm not sure if—"

"Fi, it's fine. I'm only here for a quick brew and a place to wait out the rain."

"Gotcha." Fiona pointed at the single row of tables along the left wall behind the sales desk. All five were occupied spare one. "Grab a pew and I'll send Jamie over to take your order."

"Thanks." Leaving his sister-in-law, Nick meandered around the merchandise tables, recognizing Evie's handwriting on every price tag and sign. He passed two wagging golden retrievers keeping their soup-slurping owners company and claimed the last and only seat available, a traditional Orkney chair handmade from coiled oat straw and driftwood. A design dating back hundreds of years, the chair's short legs and floppy cushion played second fiddle to its high back and rounded hood, which jutted out over Nick's head as he sat down. Before the days of central heating, the hood would've protected the chair's occupant from chilly drafts. For Nick, however, the chair offered an unexpected perk. With its tall back facing the kitchen, he could sit with Evie being none the wiser.

Jamie loped around the edge of the big chair. Cap pulled low, he looked up from his pad of notepaper, his eyes widening. "*Oh*. It's you."

"It's me."

"Erm"—he spun sideways, staring off into space—"I don't *think* we have raisins in our stuff, but I can check—"

"No!" Nick leaned forward. "I'll have a café latte, please."

"Nothing else?" If that was Jamie's upselling technique, it needed plenty of work.

Nick's stomach answered for him with a low and lengthy how-could-you-skip-breakfast snarl. He tugged the laminated menu free from beneath a pair of salt and pepper shakers and eyeballed the list of offerings. "Ham and cheese on brown?"

"Comes with salad." Jamie scratched the order on his pad and turned on his heel without further word.

Smoothing his wet hair, Nick craned his neck, checking out the store. The damage from the week before had been all but erased, the only tell-tale sign being a fresh lick of paint. Everything else was exactly as he remembered from the last time he'd been here with Evie thirteen years ago.

It's mad to think I've only seen Evie twice since we split.

Poppy's baptism and Fiona and Rupert's marriage ceremony— two occasions peppered with unshakeable regret and guilt, the wedding especially. Fiona had been four months pregnant with Ava and was a vision in white silk and lace walking up the aisle with her proud father and Sunita and Evie in tow. So absorbed in her shared maid-of-honor duties, Evie hadn't noticed Nick in the second pew with his girlfriend of two months, Olympia 'Pia' Castellanos, a glamorous art gallery owner he'd met in Berlin. He had debated whether to bring her along, but when Tarquin informed him that Evie had started seeing someone, he booked two last-minute plane tickets instead of one and flew north hoping they would clear the air and be friends again.

He couldn't have been more wrong.

Evie was single, dating no one, and apparently hoping for an honest conversation and a possible reconciliation. Upon spotting Pia clutching his hand outside the cathedral, she dissolved into tears and vanished with Sam. Nick didn't see either of them for the rest of the day.

Glancing around her family's café, his once raging appetite curdled with remorse. "This was a mistake," he murmured, pushing the chair back and rising to his feet.

"One ham and cheese on br—" Peering up from the plate, Evie met his eyes. "*Oh?!* You're leaving?" Her voice dropped along with her expression.

The slightly parted rosebud lips, the contemplative brown eyes, the gentle curves teasing beneath her off-the-shoulder gray sweater and black drawstring pants—Nick still fancied Evie like it was yesterday. Even the matronly apron, ugly hairnet, and her long-held (and fully justified) hostility couldn't stifle his longing. *Winding back the clock will be impossible, though.* He rubbed his chin, his two-day stubble coarse like sandpaper against his fingers. *What I did was stupid and unforgivable. I don't deserve her.*

Evie lifted the sandwich. "Gimme a sec. I'll wrap this for you."

But Nick couldn't leave now, not when she seemed disheartened for some reason. "No, it's fine. I was just getting comfortable." He sat down again. "Wet jeans…"

Her gaze flitted down his jacket, the leather still sporting flecks of rain. "Ugh, the worst." She set down his plate, her demeanor softening. "This is on the house, a thank you for being so understanding about the raisin mishap."

But she already thanked me two days ago. Nick grinned. "Cheers, Evie. That's really sweet of you."

"Enjoy." Dipping her chin, Evie walked away, but Nick had more to say.

"Wait…"

She peeled back. "Oh right! Your café latte—"

"Take a break and join me?"

Stopping midstride, Evie blinked several times as the dog owners two tables away stood up, followed by the elderly couple sat beside them, pulling on their coats. She tucked a loose tendril under her hairnet and turned their way, smiling. "Thank you. Please come again." Her grin, however, faltered as she swiveled back toward Nick, her brow furrowed.

"I know that face."

Meeting his eyes again, she skimmed her perspiring forehead with the heel of her hand. "What face?"

"That one. The one you make when you're shattered. You've earned a break, Evie."

Her wince slackened as Jamie brought over Nick's latte. "That's kind of you to say, but…"

Her cousin skulked away with his tray.

"…I have those tables to clear and—"

As the words popped through her lips, Jamie began collecting the dirty cutlery and dishes.

Nick fought back a smirk. "Looks like you're free after all."

"I have food to prepare."

"For who?" Nick eyed the empty tables. *Make this about business and she'll stay.* "Hey, if someone new arrives, by all means go, but in the meantime can I borrow you for a minute? We need to discuss"—he clocked the remnants of smoked salmon, egg, and pastry on the plates Jamie was carting away—"quiche."

Her brows knit together. "Quiche? We already confirmed all meals with your production manager."

Nick's focus dropped to her fingers picking the gauze on her right hand. "But maybe we could add some local alternatives? I've been sat here for ten minutes, and three of your five tables were all eating smoked salmon quiche. If that's not a good review, what is?"

"I guess, yeah."

Nick jumped up and fetched a vacant chair for her.

Evie sat gingerly on the edge like she might flee at any moment.

"So here's the thing. After a long week of shooting, Saturday arrives and people are wilting energy-wise. If we could get an extra protein boost, something hearty and comforting like quiche, I reckon it would help kickstart the day."

She nodded thoughtfully. "Do you have a preference? Smoked salmon or traditional quiche Lorraine—eggs, bacon, Swiss cheese?"

"No, let's do salmon. It's more Orkney." Nick wondered how she'd react to what he was about to say next. "I had the salmon the other night at The Odin."

Evie cleared her throat. "Oh really?"

Like she didn't notice. "I forgot how good the seafood is here."

The corners of her mouth quirked as she leaned in. "You still avoiding shellfish?"

Nick smiled slowly. "In public, yes."

A faint grin met her cheeks then disappeared.

"It was nice seeing you out. You seemed…happy with soup bloke."

"I'm not."

"Happy?"

"With Caleb. I don't date much."

She's single? A surge of selfish glee arose in Nick's chest, but it was quickly overtaken by a twinge of sadness. He had meant what he'd said, hoping she was happy, but learning she was alone crushed his heart a little. If anyone deserved love, it was Evie.

"I'm too busy, actually," she added quickly.

Nick nodded and shifted closer, unsure if she was telling the truth. "I can understand that. I don't date a lot these days either. I'm mostly in the office."

Brow creasing, she opened her mouth like she was about to say something—

"Eves!" Fiona cut her off as she ambled past with a young mum and two little kids cuddling puffins as tall as they were. "We need to order more toys."

Whatever Evie was about to say was gone, replaced by shop talk. "We can't keep those in stock."

Nick lifted his cup, watching the puffin parade make its way to the biscuit shelves. "Glad to see Tammie Norries are still hot sellers."

"You always reminded me of a puffin," said Evie.

Nick snickered above his coffee and glanced back with affection. "Because I'm cute and loved by the masses?" He took a tentative sip.

She snorted. "Conceited, much?"

He licked milky foam off his lip and laughed. Evie's gaze slipped then quickly leapt upward again.

"I'm kidding! In my case it's more like *forgotten* by the masses." Nick traded his cup for his ham and cheese. "So how exactly am I puffin-esque?"

"You'd return every summer and vanish every August. You were always flying away."

I guess I deserve that. An enduring ache throbbed in Nick's chest. "Well, if I was a puffin then you were a swan."

Evie shot him a bewildered glare.

"What?! Swans are lovely and regal—"

"And nasty!" Her eyes followed his sandwich to his mouth. "At least the ones at Stenness Loch are. I'd like to think I'm more...a watery pleep."

Nick chewed quickly. "What is *that*?"

"A redshank, a wading bird that stays in Orkney and never strays far."

Motioning toward her with his free hand, Nick set down his lunch. "But this redshank was an outlier. You flew the coop to London, right?"

Evie looked down. "I guess you know all about that."

"I don't." He held up his right hand, palm facing out and his thumb holding down his little finger. "Scout's honor."

"You weren't *a scout*."

Nick lowered his hand. "No, but you rarely post on social media and Rupes and Fi never told me what you were up to. I'd ask, but…" He picked the crust of his sandwich. "Did you stay a while? Did you work?" *Did you look for me?*

"I had jobs with the Churchill War Rooms and Buckingham Palace's gift shop, but my favorite was with a bakery/café in Notting Hill. They even promoted me to manager."

"Smart people."

A glimmer sparkled in her eyes. "Most nights I'd bring biscuits home for Sunita. We didn't have much money, so we'd eat them for dinner then go out dancing. Get lads to buy us drinks. Sometimes a cheeky McDonald's, too. At the time I thought we were totally basic and uncool, but in retrospect, we didn't do too badly for two nerds from a small island." She paused for a moment, a hint of a grin retreating like the sun behind an encroaching cloud. "Anyway…"

More than anything, Nick wanted to ask about her Crohn's, but coming from him, it was a loaded question. Bringing it up in her workplace wasn't really the proper way to go about it either.

Evie swept her hand over her apron, brushing away nothing Nick could see. "I should get back to the kitchen."

As much as he would've loved to visit longer, the fact that they'd chatted for ten minutes was a major win. He nodded. "Thanks for lunch and the company."

Evie eased her chair back and stood. "See you tomorrow." She glanced over her shoulder, adding, "Hopefully."

Smiling, Nick rose to his feet and pulled out his wallet. "Definitely." He left several ten-pound notes on the table and looked back toward the kitchen, catching Evie's lingering gawk, which dissolved upon detection. His grin widened. *Maybe there's still something between us after all.*

Ducking his head, he swerved several customers and checked his texts before the dreaded sprint to his car. As he opened Ashley's latest message, he rounded a tall sweater display and slammed straight into a freckly wall of muscle.

Sam? Nick's stomach dropped. *Fuck!*

Fifteen

NICK

Then, Thursday, August 6, fourteen years ago

Twelve months of longing and questions. *So many questions.* They swirled and taunted Nick as he meandered through the heaving Kirkwall house party, the pong of teenage boy and cannabis hanging in the haze.

Should I do another loop? See if she's in the next room?

As he turned a corner, a crew of boisterous males began hollering "CHUG, CHUG, CHUG!" while draining can after can of beer into a large funnel, the beer bong's plastic tubing snaking between the lips of a glassy-eyed teenager kneeling below. The kid glugged, keen to impress, until his gag reflex kicked in and beer gushed like a geyser from his mouth.

Despite jerking away from the boozy human fountain, Nick's efforts were in vain. A sizable amber stain crept across his pale blue linen shirt. "*Shiiit!*" He tugged at the material. *This was a huge mistake.*

One hour and two beers earlier, Nick had been hopeful—hopeful he'd see Evie for the first time since the bonfire twelve agonizing months ago. Fiona and Rupert had sworn she was headed to this party, a birthday bash for a girl from her octopush team, but as the night wore on and the house filled with familiar tunes and not-so-familiar faces, his fizzy optimism began to go flat. Evie had obviously chosen to socialize elsewhere, not that Nick could blame her.

The heavy thump-thump of a techno track rattled his chest. *I'm getting too old for this shit.*

Storming around the kitchen doorjamb, Nick spied a disheveled brunette in a sweaty tangle of frantic hands and eager mouths. *Fuuck!* His stomach plunged as he stumbled backward. *It's not...?*

When she glanced up from her bedraggled suitor, the woman's bloodshot blue eyes and nose piercing calmed his fears.

"Carry on," he mumbled as a flock of teen girls perusing food on the counter disbanded, leaving behind a lone straggler in an ivory baby doll top, black cardigan, and skinny jeans, her attention glued to an old flip phone.

The wispy chestnut curtain sweeping her forehead, the vintage Swatch, the silver necklace with her name in flowy script—unmistakeably Evie. Savoring the view, butterflies frolicked in Nick's stomach as he figured out what to say. What *do* you say after twelve months with little to no contact?

Evie looked up and did a double take. "*Nick?!*" Her eyes dipped, drifting over the beer stain on his shirt before reuniting with his face.

"*Hey*, hi!" Nick flapped his hand in an awkward wave and regretted it instantly. He stuffed both hands into his pockets.

Evie cocked her head. "Never thought I'd see you here."

"That makes two of us," Nick blurted, desperate for a safe conversation starter. He scanned the mishmash of food piled precariously on the counter. Crisp-riddled dips, two picked-over (and cigarette-garnished) pizzas, and a platter of soggy, upended tacos. "I'm here for research—for *Hell's Kitchen!*" He flashed a wry smile, gauging her reaction. "Looks like the chef here needs an intervention from Gordon bloody Ramsey..."

A tentative grin played on her lips. "Yeah. Not exactly *cordon bleu*, is it."

Nick let out a laugh. *Good icebreaker. Keep her talking.* "I thought Sam might be here."

With Evie's shake of her head, they tipped into a tongue-tied silence.

Say something, so she'll stay. Nick leaned on the old standby. "Can I get you a drink?"

"I'm good. Thanks." Pulling on the strap of her small crossbody bag, she locked her eyes on the stain on his shirt.

"Oh, this? Beer bong dude sprayed me. I need something to…" Nick yanked open the fridge. "Apparently, sparkling water works."

Pressing her lips together, Evie stuffed her phone into her back pocket. "Not for beer." She browsed the counter. "But *this* should." She claimed a bottle of green dish detergent and a fistful of paper towels.

"I'm glad you know what you're doing." Nick closed the fridge as Evie set down her supplies and filled a clean glass with water. "I love this shirt. Cost a bomb."

Evie's face fell. "No pressure then." She cleared her throat and motioned with her hand. "You'll uh, have to take it off for me to—"

"Of course." Plucking each button open, he whipped the long-sleeved shirt off his shoulders and down his arms, giving the cuffs a final tug over both wrists. For Nick, getting undressed in front of people was no big deal. His love scenes on *Dalston Grove* meant he was often shirtless (and sometimes jeans-less) in front of the crew, spending hours wrapped around Bree with only his boxers and her underwear (and sometimes a strategically placed pillow) between them. No one minded, no one stared. Nick's body wasn't as ripped as some of his acting contemporaries, but he was still pleasantly firm and toned. None of the girls he'd dated had complained.

Neither did Evie.

Mouth open and brows raised, she gawked at his chest and six-pack in training, then her eyes dipped below his belly button, following the wispy trail of dark hair until it disappeared beneath the elastic band of his boxers. A sly smile bloomed.

She likes! Nick folded the shirt into a bundle, keeping the stain visible on top. "Let's get this party started!" He glanced over again, but Evie was preoccupied, lost somewhere between the waistband and crotch of his jeans. "*Evie?*"

Jolting, she looked up. "*Ohh.* Yep! Yes!" She waved the crumpled paper towel. "I was just—you—" Shaking her head, she clamped her eyes shut. "*Never mind.*"

Stifling a laugh, Nick handed over his shirt.

After several minutes, Evie held up her work in progress. The beer stain had morphed into a large, apple-scented wet patch. Only time would tell if her attempted rescue was a success.

Threading his arms through the sleeves, Nick erupted into a grateful grin. "Cheers, Evie. I'd still be faffing about if it weren't for you." His fingers flew down the placket, fastening one button after another.

"All in a day's work for laundromat lass." Evie disposed of the paper towels in the bin and squirted a blob of soap into her palm.

"I thought you worked in your mum's shop?"

A blur of green hair and dungarees barged around the kitchen doorjamb, a crowded tray of colorful cupcakes in her grasp. Discovering Nick, the teen did a double take as she passed.

Evie smiled at the girl. "Depends on the day." She washed her hands, the bubbles dripping onto the lopsided pyramid of dirty dishes. "In summer, I'm at Marwick's all day Monday through Wednesday, then again on Saturday. Thursdays I'm in the laundromat, and on Fridays I answer phones at my dad's dental practice. In between, I do genealogy for tourists at the library."

"You have *four* part-time summer jobs?" A growl escaped from Nick's belly. He eyed the girl, dithering over where to park her cupcakes. "When do you have fun?"

"I suppose in between all of that..." With a smirk, Evie shut off the taps and ripped a piece of paper towel from the roll. "I'm saving for uni." She dried her hands. "My parents will pay half, but there's still a large amount I'll need to cover. Every penny counts."

Evie's working her cute butt off 24/7 while I travel, shop, and attend uni—all on my bloated actor's salary and family's dime. Nick swallowed thickly, the shame of privilege creeping in.

The teen baker abandoned her tray on the stove. "Help yourself, 'kay?"

"Thanks, Becca." Evie tossed the used paper towel in the trash as the girl careened around the doorjamb and rejoined the rowdy celebrations.

Nick's gaze darted. Half the cupcake creations boasted blue

frosting and multi-colored sprinkles, while their neighbors were crowned with sticky chocolate ganache and thick ribbons of golden caramel. Immaculate in execution, the fairy cakes (along with his rumbling stomach) begged his taste buds for a closer inspection. He motioned to Evie, who was removing a bottle of apple juice from her bag. "Want one? You've earned it."

She unscrewed the cap. "No thanks, but you go for it."

"I will! I'm *so* flippin' hungry even those gross pizzas are starting to look appealing." Liberating a sprinkle bomb from the platter, he tore the bottom off the cake and pressed it on top, squishing the generous swirl of blue frosting.

Evie's brows met quizzically as Nick took a substantial bite of his improvised cupcake sandwich, the sugary sweetness a welcome hit of happiness on his tongue.

"You just—that's new," she exclaimed.

Covering his closed lips with his hand, Nick chewed for a moment until his mouthful was manageable, then answered. "It's the best way to eat it. I get icing with every bite *and* avoid a blue moustache. It's win-win." Taking a smaller second bite, he closed his eyes and chewed quickly.

"Good?" She sipped her juice.

"Mmhmm." He nodded into a swallow and blissfully blinked, finding Evie studying him, her expression unreadable. "I never turn down a cupcake."

"So some things they write about you *are* true, then…like that bit about you hating to forget birthdays." She lowered her bottle and exhaled heavily. "Nick, I'm *so* sorry."

She's sorry? Small talk had officially ended. He looked at the last chunk of cupcake, ready to grovel if need be. "Evie—"

"No, hear me out." She swept her bangs away from her eyes. "I'm sorry I didn't ring you after the bonfire." Her index finger stroked uneasily, back and forth, across the juice's label. "I should've, but I was so upset with Sunita and Sam, and my breakup. It was a lot to process all at once. I needed time. I could barely speak to Fi about it, let alone you."

Nick ditched the last of his cupcake on the messy counter.

"Fi came round the next morning, sat with me while I bawled my eyes out. She told me to text you, but I was embarrassed. I wasn't ready. But weeks later when I was, it felt like I'd left it too late." Evie gazed down at her drink. "You were off at uni, meeting exciting people, learning amazing things. You'd moved on. You didn't need Sam's little sister bothering you from the middle of nowhere." Screwing the cap on her juice, she tentatively looked up. "Then April 29th arrived and there was an e-card in my inbox from SaxyBoy. I couldn't believe it! You remembered! And I *loved* the roller-skating rabbit. Thank you."

So she DID open it. Nick muted a smile. He had texted Fiona asking how Evie was doing several times, but Rupert's girlfriend was also Evie's best friend and, loyal to a fault, didn't divulge much. "Was it a happy seventeenth?"

"No, 'cause I was torn up about what to do. I really wanted to write you back. I almost sent you a Facebook friend request, too."

A grain of hope swelled in Nick's chest. "What stopped you?"

"Me, being stupid." She blinked, her face pained. "I don't ignore people. I'm not a rude person—"

"I know you're not—"

"That's why I rang you."

Adrenaline whooshed through him as he met her eyes. "You—when?"

"Three days later," she said softly, discarding her juice on the counter. "But your number was out of service."

Bugger. Nick frowned. "Some fans got hold of it. I had to get a new one."

"Which I didn't have…"

"But I texted it to Sam. I told him to let anyone—" Nick caught Evie's subtle headshake. "He didn't pass it on?"

"He's swamped with vet school. We're lucky if we hear from him once a week."

Nick nodded. He hadn't heard from Sam in months.

"I would've asked him for it, but"—Evie glanced downward

and hooked her fingers into the hem of her top—"I was afraid." Her gaze circled back, avoiding Nick.

"Of what?"

"Of finding out you didn't give it to me on purpose." Eyes glinting with tears, Evie's stare fled to the floor. "Of finding out…you didn't want to be friends anymore."

Her pained honesty pierced Nick's heart, sending regret swirling through his veins. "Evie, no," he whispered, the desire to soothe her pain with a hug or a touch of his hand an unrelenting ache. "That's not true at all. I missed you!"

"So why didn't you ring *me*?" Her voice cracked.

There was that. Nick pawed the back of his neck and took a deep breath. The reasons behind his hesitance to reconnect were complicated. Like Evie, fear played a part, as did busyness—his first year of university with its essays, seminars, and hands-on productions was overwhelming. And then there was his mother Kiki. When Nick called home in May suggesting a quick weekend jaunt to Orkney, Kiki scolded him and Rupert for making friends with "that backward Kirkwall lot," a disdainful phrase he'd never share with Evie. But meeting her perplexed gape, he knew he couldn't dance around the truth any longer. Best to dive in, come what may.

"I should've, but I-I thought maybe…I…" So much for diving. His aimless ramble felt more like a painful belly flop.

Evie tilted her head. "I, what?"

"Maybe I was to blame. Maybe my presence at the bonfire had something to do with Stuart's actions that night. Evie, I felt guilty about it. I still do."

"About him *dumping* me?" Evie shook her head. "Nick, you shouldn't. Our split had nothing to do with you."

"But walking past me and Rupes, he shot me daggers."

"That's just his face," explained Evie. "Fiona says he's got angry eyes—you know, like the tattie in *Toy Story*?"

A ghost of a smile bent her lips, followed by an abrupt giggle, and twelve months of worry and regret lifted from Nick's shoulders. Sharing a grin, he let out a laugh. "I am *so* relieved. God, what are we like?"

"Well, clearly we're idiots." Evie mock-frowned and scooped up a sprinkle-topped cupcake. "Peace offering? Never again, okay? We'll never go another year without talking."

"It's a deal." Nick gladly accepted Evie's gift as a blonde girl charged into the kitchen, her palm glued to her mouth. Lunging between them, she retched into the dish-cluttered sink.

Evie gagged. "*Oh god.*" She grabbed her juice and slapped a hand over her nose.

Nick cringed. "Get out of here?"

Nodding, Evie led the way. "YES!"

Strolling past the pebble-dash houses of suburban Kirkwall, Nick gazed up into the star-peppered sky. Catching up with Evie, his stomach satiated by the most glorious cupcakes—in Orkney!—the night had taken an euphoric detour from the raging dumpster fire a half-hour earlier.

"And that's the other one I love—the old Sinclair house." Evie pointed across the street where a small community church had been converted into a private dwelling.

"That's cool." Nick marveled, looking over his shoulder. "It's freakishly quiet here. We haven't seen a single soul since we left."

"I like it." Evie tugged her cardigan tighter. "It feels like I have the island to myself."

"Do you feel safe? Walking alone after dark?"

She nodded. "It's hard to get away with shit here. Everyone knows everyone else, pretty much." Nick peered behind them again, and Evie giggled. "Don't worry. Paparazzi won't leap out from behind the wheelie bins. No one will see your Smurfy blue tongue. Not like before!"

"Before?"

"*The Mail* photos?" Evie added. "Last spring?"

Mining his memory, snippets of a rowdy Salford pub lock-in featuring numerous blue drinks swam through Nick's head along with an intrusive exposé that appeared online the following morning. "Ohh, *right*. Yeah, my uni mates thought being papped was hilarious."

"Was it easy…making new friends?"

"Not at first. But eventually they saw me as boring ol' Nick and not some privileged tosser from telly—*well*, paparazzi ambushes aside."

"Sounds like you're having a great time."

"I am, strangely enough! Going in, I thought uni would stifle me, but it's been grand. I'm learning loads, meeting interesting people, livin' like a typical twenty-year-old—and fucking *loving* it. I'm an all-new Nick!"

"That's great!" Fiddling with her necklace, Evie gestured to the road bending off to the left. "My house is down here."

"Brilliant." A chilled buzz flowed through his veins. Two beers wouldn't usually affect him like this, but with a busy week of travel, stress, and little sleep, everything felt a little fuzzier around the edges. Nice, but definitely fuzzy.

Nick cleared his throat. "How are things with Sunita?"

"Much better. She rang me the morning after the bonfire, hungover and mortified. She must've apologized, like, twenty times. Still, it took me a while to forgive her. My dad says being slow to forgive is a Sutherland family trait." Evie shrugged and reached into her bag. "Who knew?" Her hand exited with her bottle of juice. "But I missed Sun, so I invited her for chips after class one day and we made up for good. I've never seen Fi happier."

"Good. I'm glad," said Nick.

"Yeah. We cleared the air about a lot of things—including you." She unfastened the lid of her juice. "Sun thinks you're okay now."

"You think?"

"She's not a bad person, Nick. She's just overly protective. We both got picked on when we were younger. It was one of the things that brought us together, looking out for each other and standing up to bullies." Evie sipped her drink.

"But I'm hardly a schoolyard bully," said Nick.

"I know, but when it comes to guys I like—" Evie halted mid-sentence, her abrupt silence unintentionally highlighting '*guys I like*'.

A wave of hopeful curiosity crashed inside Nick, but Evie wasn't forthcoming. Skirting his eyes, her lips waffled, closing and opening twice until she expelled a hurried "She interrogates people," which she punctuated with a shaky swig of juice and an apparent attempt to change the subject. "Seen any musicals lately?" She chased the question with another drawn-out sip.

But Nick wasn't having it. "So, you *like* me?"

Swallowing, Evie lowered the bottle. "*Nick.*"

"What?"

"I'm not doing this." Her voice rose.

Nick threw his hands up. "Doing what?" he asked, playfully aware of being an annoying tease.

"Honestly!" Evie twisted the cap open and closed on her juice. "Someone's starved for attention."

She's so cute when she's flustered. Nick laughed. "*You like me*," he sang back.

"Would I be friends with you if I didn't?"

"Okay, but this *like*, is it—"

"Nikolai Crispin Balfour!" Evie pointed her juice at him. "Keep going and you'll be wearing this!" She bit her lip like she was quashing a grin.

"Yeah, I saw how you gawked. You want me shirtless again—admit it!" Nick bounced his brows as Evie stared back, her mouth agape.

"Okay. *Fine*." A pinkish hue brightened her cheeks. "Yes. Yes, I would. I mean, who doesn't appreciate—" She halted, slipping into an eye-scrunched headshake. "GOD! Shut up, Evie!" Blinking, she dropped the juice in her bag. "*Please* don't tell Bree I said that.

Shit, I haven't even met her and I'm…" Evie dissolved into a mumble and fussed with her purse's zipper.

Fretting over nothing. Nick scratched his jaw. "Listen, Evie—"

"How is she?" Smiling tightly, Evie looked up. "Bree?"

"She's good." They ambled around the corner, a red, rectangular post box imbedded in its stone wall. "Last I heard."

Evie gasped. "You…you broke up?"

"If you could call it that. The truth is, we were never really together."

Her expression wavered between gobsmacked and elated. "Oh! Nick, I'm *so* sorry. Long distance sucks, doesn't it?"

"Yeah, but Bree and I weren't *together*-together. We weren't a real couple. The whole thing was fake."

Confusion clouded Evie's gaze. "Fake? But I saw—"

"Stories? Photos?" Nick interjected. "Heading to the cinema, hanging at Wimbledon, walking Ross?"

"Holding hands, cuddling, *kissing*!" Evie added.

"All acting, all the time." Nick peeked over a bushy hedge as they strolled past, the house behind it cloaked in darkness. "We'd go out and the *Dalston* PR team would ring up the papers, tell them where to find us."

"But…why go to all the trouble?"

"Money and exposure. If people thought Bree and I were a real-life couple, more might tune in. The more people tuning in, the higher the ratings. The higher the ratings, the higher the advertising revenue. Everyone benefits."

Evie hugged her waist. "By lying to everyone."

"It wasn't done maliciously. Fake relationships happen all the time in our industry. Bree and I weren't the first, and we definitely won't be the last."

"How long were you…?"

"A year and a half. It started when I was sixteen, just before Jake and Amanda slept together, and ended when the *Dalston* Christmas special aired."

Easing into a squint, Evie's lips puckered like she was trying to figure something out. "So, it ended around the time of your Ba' visit?"

"Give or take a week, yeah. It wasn't a big ask. Bree and I were—*are*—good mates. We hung out a lot, weren't dating anyone. Neither of us could think of a downside."

"But you had to put your private life on hold," said Evie. "That's massive."

"To be honest it wasn't *completely* on hold. We could date if we wanted." Approaching a pair of forgotten recycling bins, both Nick and Evie swerved. "Provided we kept all activities behind closed doors and had the person sign an airtight non-disclosure agreement. Bree tried it for a while but eventually gave up. Was a total hassle."

"So, you've never had a real relationship, then?"

Brows knotting briefly, he flashed a smile. "I'm twenty years old, Evie. What do you think?"

"Well, if it was before Bree, before you were sixteen..." Chin dropping, Evie leaned in. "My god, how *old* were you?"

I don't want to talk about this. Nick looked away, studying the stone wall running in front of the house across the street. "Old enough."

Wide-eyed, she nodded slowly like she was mulling over Nick's confession, then asked, "And after Bree?"

"There's been a few. Here and there."

Evie's brows jumped. "*Here?* In Orkney?"

"No, not literally here," said Nick. "At uni."

"So during the last twelve months..."

Is she jealous? Nick searched her face.

Suddenly, Evie became captivated by her shoes. "I'm just curious. Everyone brags about uni being a boozy sex fest."

"It can be."

"And was—*is*—it? For you?"

Nick plowed his hand through his hair, not sure how much to divulge. "Depends, really. Most of my hookups were one-off drunken snogs."

"*Most?* But not all?"

"Hayley wasn't," said Nick. "She was a third-year drama major. A friend of a friend."

Looking up, Evie's face pinched. "Ooh, an older woman. Niiice," she hissed.

"So?" Nick glanced over. "*Whatshisface* was older, wasn't he? Sam said he was."

"You were discussing my love life with Sam?"

Dammit. Nick bristled, annoyed at himself for drinking on an empty stomach and relaxing a little *too* much into this conversation. Every question, every answer was tied to an emotional landmine. "No, we weren't *discussing* it. Your ex just—I don't know, came up one day. Sam mentioned he was older, had one more year of uni left." He paused. "Sam also said you were seeing someone new."

Evie shot him a quizzical look. "*No.* I kissed someone at the Auction Mart Valentine's dance, but that was a sad, drunken mistake." Her lips pursed like she was fighting a smile. "So it was recent then, this *non*-discussion with Sam."

"Evie, I hadn't heard from you and I wanted to make sure you were okay. Breakups are hard."

"Yeah, well, *real* breakups are."

"I know. I've been there." He stole a glimpse down Viking Place.

"Been?" Evie pressed. "Past tense?"

"Yes, grammar girl. Past tense. Hayley and I are no longer together."

"Together-together?" Her voice jumped higher.

Nick laughed. "Nope-nope. She ended it in June."

"*She* did?"

"Yep. Hayley moved back to New York and texted me before takeoff."

Evie halted in her tracks. "She broke up with you…from the plane?! That's so—"

"Hayley." Nick turned around. "Spontaneous to a fault."

Mouth open, Evie didn't look like she was buying it. "There's spontaneous and then there's cruel." They both resumed walking. "You're better off rid."

"Yeah..." Nick flashed a resigned grin.

Evie blinked several times. "Oh god. You're missing her, aren't you? And I dissed her!"

"No, it's not like that. Hayley was like Times Square: fun and flashy, but a bit *too* much. And completely exhausting. Loved raisins, too, the heathen." Nick's smirk met Evie's smile. "What about you? Missing Angry Eyes all these months?"

She snort-laughed. "Hardly."

"Good. He didn't deserve you."

"Did Sam say something?" She picked at her nail polish.

"No, but if Stuart couldn't see you as the smart, caring person you are, he can fuck right off."

Evie grinned demurely. "Aw, nice to know you care."

"I do! A lot, actually..." His gaze lingered. "Evie, I'm really sorry. I should've called you. Just to hear your voice would've—" He let out an unsteady breath.

"Oh, Nick," she said quietly. "You had *more*? Were they bad?"

He dropped his chin to his chest. "I abandoned Hayley at her sister's wedding."

"What happened?"

"We were sat at the head table. The attack came on quick, felt like seconds. I barely had time to drop my fork before legging it to the loo."

"That must've been scary, being alone."

"Ahh, but I wasn't," said Nick. "She ran after me."

Evie's eyes widened. "*Oh*. Hayley knew?"

"No. I blamed the meal for my hasty exit, thinking she'd leave me to it, but nope. I had no choice; I had to kneel and pretend I was gonna puke. She couldn't disappear fast enough."

Approaching another road, Evie gestured to their right. "We turn here. How'd you feel after?"

Nick followed her lead and peeled around the corner. "Wobbly, sweaty, out of it—the worst wedding date ever. Hayley called a cab and sent me home with an empty champagne bucket in case I was sick. Definitely not my finest moment."

"But it wasn't your fault."

"True, but something had to give. Come the Monday, I rang a therapist. It's been almost three months now and we're making progress. Slowly." The medication Nick had been prescribed was helping, too, but he conveniently left that part out. Seeing a psychologist was a big enough reveal for one day.

"You did the right thing." She squeezed his arm. *"Really."*

Same old Evie: empathetic, supportive, discreet. "You reckon?" He did a double take. "It's not...you know, a bit crap? Being weak?"

"No! Asking for help is a total power move. I'm so proud of you!"

Her effusive praise, kind and reassuring in its sincerity, felt like coming home. "Ah, cheers, Evie. You're the only person I've told. Not everyone understands like you do."

She looked up, meeting him. "Your secrets will always be safe with me."

Nick broke into a slow grin. "You know, I've missed this. Us talking..."

Her smile crinkled her eyes. "Same." She ran a hand through her long hair and paused like she was building up to something. "Would you like to go to the County Show with me this Saturday?"

The granddaddy of Orkney's annual agricultural fairs—beloved by farm-friendly Rupert, spurned by city-loving Nick. Farmers from every corner of the archipelago would descend on Kirkwall's Bignold Park with their cattle, horses, and sheep.

"They have rides and games, motorcycles—a beer garden," Evie added quickly, like she was verbally polishing the rustic event into something exciting and enticing for Nick's more sophisticated tastes. "Awesome food vans, too. Their waffles and candy floss are to die for."

"Death by carbs *and* sugar? You know me well." He nodded enthusiastically. "I'd love to go. Sounds great."

"Great!" Evie gestured toward a modest two-story house at the end of the road, its grassy front enclosed by a thigh-high stone wall. "So, this is me." All five of its front-facing windows stared back, quiet and dark.

Gravel crunched under their shoes as they walked up the driveway past a blue SUV. "This is nice," said Nick politely, taking in the beige pebble-dash exterior and the welcoming pots of flowers flanking the front door. Most of the homes in Kirkwall were unremarkable design-wise, built more for warmth and functionality than a spread in *Better Homes and Gardens*.

"We moved here eight years ago," said Evie. "It's close to everything, which is awesome. Mum likes the garden. She puts a lot of love into it—not that you can tell. Sam must've forgotten to leave the front light on."

"Your parents aren't home?"

"No, they're visiting my uncle in Norseman Village."

"Don't they mind you having guys over when they're not here?" asked Nick.

"I don't know." Pushing the unlocked front door open, Evie smiled over her shoulder. "You're the first."

Twenty minutes later, surrounded by an open box of marshmallow Snowballs, torn bags of locally baked biscuits, bottles of cola, and their discarded shoes, Nick and Evie lay on their backs, staring up at the stars from the polypropylene comfort of the Sutherlands' trampoline.

"The sky's so glittery here." Nick tucked his arms behind his head. "I love astronomy, but I rarely see stars in London."

"I come out most nights to decompress," said Evie, finishing a Snowball, its coconut sprinkles speckling her top. "Sometimes I see the Merry Dancers, too."

Nick had never been so lucky. The luminous greens and shimmery whites of the aurora borealis didn't usually come out to play during summer when he was on the island. "So, it's been busy, eh? Loads of tourists?"

"You mean cruise ship hell?" said Evie. "Everyone wants their genealogy researched, and for a place with few trees, there are a ton of the *family* variety here."

A low growl erupted from Nick's belly. Obviously, the cupcakes hadn't done the trick. He eased onto his side and chose another biscuit over Evie's coconut monstrosities, hoping a change in position would stifle further racket. "Rupert's big into ours." He bit the shortbread cookie. Buttery, crumbly, melt-in-your-mouth perfection, just how he liked them. "Our ancestors kept detailed records."

"The lairds?" Licking sticky marshmallow off her fingers, Evie rolled sideways and shifted up on her elbow, facing him. "How's it feel having your last name on *everything* here?"

"Ha! Says the girl who shares a name with the village down the way." His gaze hopped along the string of clear lights stretching between her house and the garden shed, a twinkly smile in the crisp darkness.

"It's hardly the same thing!" said Evie. "A village and parish don't equal the cool factor of a castle in the family! Or a hospital."

"I guess, but it's not like I personally had anything to do with it. The Balfours of yesteryear were mavericks. Shame the current crop are such a bleedin' disappointment." He blinked at the shortbread in his hand, rustling up the courage to share something he hadn't told anyone yet. "My parents are getting divorced."

"Oh no." Evie's hand landed gently on his arm. "Oh Nick…"

"Nobody's surprised. They've always bickered and fought." He took in Evie's pained expression, her non-judgmental concern a green light to keep going. "Mum even left us a few times."

"Where'd she go?"

"Into the arms of sympathetic male friends," said Nick.

Evie's eyes seemed to grow twice their size.

186

"I've had *loads* of different 'uncles' over the years buying me toys and trainers, basically kissing ass to stay in her good books. When I was nine, one treated me to a ride on his helicopter."

"Just you? Not your brothers?"

"Yeah." Nick paused, knowing how much the next truth would unsettle Evie. "Mum plays favorites."

Evie's brows rose and disappeared behind her bangs. She opened her mouth and closed it twice.

"I'm not proud of it. I've *definitely* never encouraged it." Nick's throat tightened. "I love my brothers—" His voice cracked as he glanced down, hoping Evie didn't notice the tears gathering in his eyes. *Whoa. Where's this emotion coming from?* He swallowed thickly and tried again. "But I worry, you know? Has her favoritism made them hate me?"

Evie rubbed his arm. "Have they said something?"

"We don't talk about it." He sniffed. "But sometimes they leave me out of things or tease me incessantly. I guess it's their way of getting their own back."

"Nick, they should be angry with your mum, not you."

"I know, but I can't blame them. I've told Mum to treat us the same, but there's no telling her. Kiki does what Kiki wants."

"Is your dad any better?"

"He's just as bad, maybe worse," said Nick. "Not about playing favorites 'cause I am *not* his favorite. Actually, to be fair, I don't reckon he has one. He resents us equally. But where cheating is concerned, he's voracious. I can't tell you the number of times I've gone downstairs for waffles and met some woman wearing little more than a horrified grin."

"*Shiit.*"

"Yeah. Gran says my parents have affairs like other people have hot dinners."

"Your gran knows?"

Nick nodded. "So, yeah—we might have landmarks named after us here, but the current Balfours are dysfunctional as fuck."

"God, I can't even imagine what I'd do if…"

"Your parents don't fight?" asked Nick.

"They disagree sometimes, argue, but it never escalates."

"You're lucky." Nick frowned. "It grinds away at you."

Sitting up, Evie clutched his hand. "C'mon."

"Where?"

"I hate seeing you sad." She eased up onto her feet, her fingers still clasped around Nick's. "Bouncing always cheers me up."

"Bouncing?"

"Don't knock it till you try it, Balfour." Evie tugged his hand.

My brain is SO fuzzy. His eyes swept the army of snack packages. "What about the biscuits?"

"Excuses! Don't worry about 'em." She banished the rolling bottles of cola from the trampoline with a flick of her bare foot. "Hey, did you notice? The beer stain's gone."

Nick looked down at his shirt, dry and blotch-free. "So it is! You're a savior, Evie." He kneeled and awkwardly rose to his feet. "Although, this…this might kill me."

"You'll be fine. Just think, you can add trampolining skills to your acting CV." She held his hand tight. "On three, okay?" she instructed. "One. Two. Three!"

They both leapt into the air then met the taut surface again, their first bounce leading to countless more. Jumping and rebounding, their irregular rhythm shimmied the packages of biscuits across the trampoline.

"Let's go higher!" Evie begged as Nick slowed down.

"I might have to let go of your hand. Our height difference is fucking us up."

She laughed and released her grip. "You have become *freakishly* tall!"

Nudging the biscuits out of danger, Nick couldn't remember the last time he'd been on a trampoline, but like Evie had promised, each leap loosened the familial anguish knotted around his heart. "You were right. Can't be sad doing this."

Evie contorted her shoulders, pulling her cardigan down her arms as she jumped. "I love bouncing. It's my happy place." Arms free, she flung her sweater onto an obliging lawn chair.

"Well, in that case, you'll hereby be known as Tigger," said Nick with a flex of his dimples.

"LOVE IT!" Evie howled.

Nick bounced harder and faster, gaining air with each exuberant spring. "Okay, Tigs, check this." Bending his knees deeply, he vaulted higher and threw his arms up as he somersaulted backward...his feet arcing through the star-speckled sky.

"Oh my god!"

Evie's squeal teased Nick's ears, but her alarm was unwarranted. He landed his backflip like an Olympic athlete.

"What the hell?" She gawped.

"Gymnastics. Mum thought it would help with strength and movement, especially on stage. It's important to be flexible."

A strangled giggle escaped from Evie. "I can do this." Midjump, she threw her legs straight out in front of her and landed on the trampoline butt-first before rebounding back up on her feet.

"Nice!" Nick's gaze glided past the thin spaghetti straps of Evie's top and lingered on her breasts, bouncing beneath the flimsy material. "I could watch you do this all day." He zeroed in on her peaked nipples.

Evie laughed, leaping higher and higher. "Boys!" She pointed at her face with both index fingers. "Oi, Nick! My eyes? UP HERE—!" Her words snapped as she landed on the sliding Snowball package and propelled shoulder-first into Nick.

"Ooof!" Breath punched from his lungs, he buckled, collapsing with Evie in a laughing, wheezing heap on the trampoline. Her nose landed in his crotch.

They both froze.

"Oh my god!" She squealed through giggles, pushing herself up.

Nick roared with rumbly laughter. "Hey! At least buy a bloke dinner first." A dog barked next door, startled by their youthful exuberance.

Straightening her top, Evie wouldn't look at him. "I'm sorry!"

Longing panged in Nick's chest. "I'm not." He swallowed, boldness taking over as he sat up. "But I *am* sorry I didn't kiss you."

Evie's flustered shirt-pulling ceased. She blinked up, her posture stiffening as her cheeks grew pink. "Kiss—when?"

"Two years ago, behind your mum's shop. I might've been mistaken, but I swore you wanted me to…"

Eyes and shoulders softening, her throat bobbed.

"And the thing is, I still do." Nick let out a shuddering breath. "Evie, I need to know. Am I too late—?"

She lunged and crushed Nick's mouth with hers.

Soft and warm and marshmallow-sweet, her kiss was a heady dream come true. Nick's hands dove into her hair, grasping, twirling, holding her close as goosebumps prickled his arms. He let out a gasp and Evie shifted, the tip of her tongue teasing the seam of his lips. Nick couldn't hold back anymore. Tilting his head, he caressed her jaw and pulled her bottom lip into his mouth, sucking hard. A heated moan escaped Evie's throat and Nick let go, taking their kiss deeper as her hand swept under his shirt, her splayed touch exploring, climbing, desperate for more. She wasn't the only one. A tingling ache grew hot and hard beneath his zipper. *I want her so badly, but…* He eased back, conscious of going too far, too fast.

"You all right?" Evie whispered, her mouth pink and deliciously swollen. She didn't wait for his answer and kissed him again.

Nick's eyes flittered closed, but his blissful stupor was short-lived, shattered by a flash of two blinding lights.

Sixteen

EVIE

Now, Thursday, July 20

Weeks into filming, Evie and Nick's working relationship had found its groove. While they only saw each other once or twice each day, their interactions were cordial and brief, leaving no hints for onlookers of their tumultuous past. Evie had also fallen into a rhythm with Sunita. Now a proven catering team, they still ran into the occasional foodie hiccup, but most were minor and, thankfully, didn't threaten any lives.

Waving goodbye to the Mainland, the shoot had moved thirty-eight miles north to the island of Sanday where, after a particularly hectic Thursday, Evie was contemplating a solo stroll to clear her head.

Sunita, however, had other ideas.

"Eves, stay in! Live large with me." Sipping her canned gin and tonic, she sank back into the pillows on her bed, one of two singles in the B&B bedroom they were sharing.

"I will. I just need some me time first, you know? Dealing with people all day—"

"*Demanding* fuckwits, you mean," Sunita corrected.

Evie zipped up her khaki jacket, its nipped-in waist and feminine silhouette defying its wind- and water-proof sensibility. "I won't be long—" Her pocket buzzed.

"That better not be work-related." Sunita tossed back her G&T as Evie awoke her phone.

"It's Gemma. She's still having vertigo and headaches. Doc says they need to operate on her arm again."

Sunita shivered. "Ouch!"

"She feels like she's letting us down. Lemme just…" Evie typed a quick text and hit send.

Evie: We're okay! All that matters is you getting better. Let me know how the op goes & when you feel up for a visit. x

Ignoring the insistent itch of her healed burn, she put her phone away. "You'll be okay till I get back?"

"With booze and a *Lord of the Rings* marathon on telly?" Sunita winked. "Couldn't be happier."

Leaving the B&B, Evie took a short detour and double-checked that the catering truck was still plugged into the electrical mains at the island's motorhome facilities (she couldn't risk a fridge full of food spoiling) then set off down a narrow road toward Roos Wick Bay.

Passing grazing cows on her left and endless green fields on her right hemmed in by dry stone dykes, Evie pushed forward into the bracing wind, allowing its salty persistence to disperse the stress of the day along with wispy strands from her messy bun. The treeless horizon stretching out in all directions would occasionally be interrupted by a farmhouse or an electrical pole, subtle reminders she wasn't alone.

As she met the end of the road, she rounded a stone croft house and found sand and Nick, hair fluttering in the breeze, snapping a photo. Evie tensed as he lowered his phone.

"Of all the beaches in all the towns in the world, you walk onto…" He paused, his face doing the endearing scrunched-nose thing that still stole her breath. "What's this one called?"

"Roos Wick." She gave him a once-over. Nick didn't took too windblown or tired, and his designer nylon jacket, dark jeans, and red-laced hiking boots were spotless. "How'd you get here?"

"Drove. My rental is parked at that croft over there."

Evie would've fainted if he had walked.

"I haven't been sleeping." His gaze leapt, tracking a passing lapwing. "Too much time staring at spreadsheets in the production trailer, I reckon."

"Fresh air should help."

"Hope so. I've never been to Sanday before. It's beautiful."

"You'll probably see more of Orkney this summer than you have your entire life," said Evie.

"Feels that way, yeah." Nick pocketed his phone. "I thought I had this place all to myself, but"—he pointed several feet away to three chubby seals basking on their sides in the late-day sun. Another surfaced in the water, its large puppy dog eyes and long whiskers judging from afar.

"Well"—Evie smiled—"enjoy your new friends." She headed in the opposite direction.

"Hey, want company?"

No—yes. I dunno. She sucked back a groan and slowly turned. "Afraid of getting lost?"

"Yup."

"C'mon."

Nick grinned and matched her pace. "I'll give you a lift after."

"You're at the hotel?"

"In Kettletoft, yeah. You're there, too, right?"

"No. The B&B down the road."

"Ahh." Nick scratched his head. "How are you feeling these days?"

He's actually going there? She looked downward, discomfort coiling inside her. "All right. More good days than bad."

"That's great. I'm happy to hear it."

And...? She glanced up at him, and Nick flashed her a tight smile then blinked ahead, plunging into silence. *What, that's it?!*

Did he completely bottle it? Or was that all he cared to say?

Either way, Evie felt miffed. *Well, this rivals my breakup beach stroll with Stuart for awkwardness.* She racked her brain for something innocuous to talk about, something like...work! "So, early call time tomorrow."

"Yes!" Nick replied quickly. "Need to get everything wrapped so we can catch the last ferry. Gotta keep this beast on schedule—or else."

"How is it, working behind the scenes?"

"Fan-bloody-tastic. Being in control, there's nothing like it."

"You don't miss acting?"

"No, but I did in the beginning." He swerved a blob of seaweed. "My identity was so tied up in being an actor, I didn't recognize myself. But therapy helped me realize acting was a job and not a personality type. It's also made a huge difference with my panic disorder."

She grinned up at him. "I'm glad."

"Thanks. Even so, I was still shit scared working behind the cameras, especially when I didn't earn my first job on merit."

Ages back, Fiona had told Evie about his mother pulling strings, working her contacts to land Nick a plum gig.

"But I worked my arse off. Found my feet eventually and land-ed in New York as the BBC's VP of TV Sales and Co-Productions."

Evie plowed her hands into her coat's pockets. "That's more than finding your feet, Nick."

He smiled. "Yeah, New York was immense: the restaurants, the clubs, the shopping—I couldn't get enough. And the job was in-credible. I was even in the running for the senior VP position. Would've bagged it, too, if things hadn't blown up."

The sex scandal four years ago. Evie knew it well, having read and re-read (several times) the tabloid kiss-and-tell entitled 'Lairds Stunner Bree Nicked with Stripper', which temporarily foisted him back into the headlines again. Nick and former co-star Bree, who was starring as the female lead in the popular *Lairds and Liars* se-ries at the time, were at a television festival in Banff, Alberta where they hooked up with a TV exec from Glasgow, a former topless dancer. Months later when the woman lost her broadcasting job, she sold her story *and* the sex tape of her racy, booze-fueled night with the two former *Dalston Grove* stars to the highest bidder—*The Na-tional Mail*. The exposé was like a wrench to Evie's heart, leaving her wondering if she had ever known Nick at all.

He sighed wistfully. "I learned the hard way. Now I no longer fish off the company dock or mix business with pleasure, no matter how tempting."

Playing back what she'd witnessed at The Odin a few weeks previously, Evie squinted at the sand. *So he's not dating Ashley then?*

He winced into a self-depreciating grin. "It's amazing how seeing pixelated screengrabs of your junk at the local newsstand can change you. And the fallout dragged on for *months*. Whispers behind my back, snide jokes in the break room, and then the final slap—they packaged me out. Losing a job I loved, and for such a stupid reason. I was gutted."

"What did you do?"

"Returned to London, disappeared to Greece for a bit. Tried to get my shit together. I started ringing old colleagues, hoping someone somewhere still believed in me. It took a while, but last year a friend from uni invited me to join his production company as an executive producer. He wanted to build a reliable, hardworking team, and I was 'sign me up!' Around that time, Ashley moved to London with her new husband and I hired her again as my assistant."

"Again?"

"Yeah, she worked with me in New York."

"Is she still married?" asked Evie.

"Yep. Quite happily, too. Why'd you ask?"

Evie swooped, collecting a piece of pink sea glass. "You guys looked really cozy at The Odin last month."

"Did we? Oh! Well, there's nothing going on. We've never dated or anything. We're just long-time friends and work colleagues. After the scandal broke, Ash was the only one who saw me as something more than tabloid fodder. She's always had my back."

Evie still didn't approve of Ashley's judgmental take on the islands, but at least she was in Nick's corner—and not in his bed. "Loyalty's so important."

"More than ever, yep," said Nick. "I tell ya, the past few years have definitely tested my faith in people."

Her thumbs skated over the pitted curves of the glass. "Yeah, once trust is gone, what's left?"

Nick didn't answer.

Perhaps that was a little too close to home.

But Nick's mention of Bree and the scandal had poked old doubts as to whether he'd been honest with her when they were younger. Back then, he swore there was no romantic entanglement with Bree, so how did they get from "good mates" to a sex tape? Evie needed the truth if only to figure out where his deceit began.

"So, you and Bree *did* have a thing all these years."

His face creased. "No, never. Banff was a misguided, drunken one-off, the perfect storm of exhaustion, absinthe cocktails, and loneliness. Bree met a woman in the bar and brought her back to my room. The rest, in all its salacious glory, is online history. We both regretted it immediately. In fact, it ruined our friendship. We haven't really spoken since."

"That's tough. I guess some friendships aren't meant to last." Evie paused, her comment drifting on the breeze. "I heard you bumped into Sam a few weeks back."

"Yeah, but we were both in a hurry…"

And didn't talk. She slipped the sea glass in her pocket. *Of course they didn't.*

Nick and Sam hadn't spoken for years, the cracks in their bromance never really healing after the champagne incident on Inganess Beach.

"How is he?" asked Nick.

"Busy vet practice, loving boyfriend, cute house—Sam has it all. If he wasn't my brother, I'd probably hate him." She laughed.

"Well, good for him—and *you*, bossing it on Broad Street."

He noticed? She swept a piece of hair fallen free from her bun behind an ear. "Thanks. Winning the catering contract has meant a lot. I know we're a small island, but Marwick's isn't the only caterer in town."

"True. Competition was fierce. The Beeb even considered bringing in someone from Aberdeen."

"I'm glad I didn't know that before!"

"You've got nothing to worry about." Nick raised his voice over a high-pitched squeal in the distance. Seabirds were always telling off the seals. "Everyone's extremely pleased with the catering. Nothing but good feedback."

Gratitude bloomed inside her. "That's great to hear. I'll be sure to let Jamie and Sunita know—"

"YOU! Over there!"

Evie's attention flew down the beach following the panicked voice. What looked like a small whale was lying on its side in the low tide. Two people crouched beside it and a third stood on the sand waving their arms urgently. *Oh my god.* Adrenaline coursed through her veins as nausea roiled in her belly. "Nick!"

He spit out a brittle "Holy fuck!"

"Please!" A woman in a high-res jacket hollered and waved repeatedly. "Help us!"

She didn't need to ask twice. Evie and Nick took off, running as fast as they could across beach and seaweed, their heels digging in when the shifting sand slowed their progress.

As distance fell away, the creature's shiny black skin and iconic white markings near its eyes became clear. A savage chill ripped through Evie's chest. The small whale was an orca, her favorite since childhood. Being called into action to help rescue one was a serendipitous gift she had never expected to receive.

Trembling as they ran, she frantically fought through her shock, mining everything she had read about beached whales. "Nick, I think we should walk the last bit. Fast movements and loud splashing could startle it."

Nodding, he slowed his pace, and together they calmly entered the ankle-deep water in silent reverence.

"How can we help?" Evie asked quietly, her heart pounding in her throat as the young orca let out a shrill, heartbreaking cry, drawing tears to her eyes.

"We need to keep him upright so he can breathe," said the second woman, her blonde hair corralled in a neat braid. "If you could kneel down and help brace him with your body…"

Nick dropped first without hesitation. If he had concerns about his box-fresh hiking boots, the frigid water, or the ocean's number one predator by his side, he didn't show it. He promptly lent a shoulder, gently leaning into the whale. "It's okay," he half-whispered to the orca, "we've got you, buddy."

Ohh, Nick… Longing flooded Evie's chest as she sloshed over to the whale's right side. She lowered herself slowly into the water, copying Nick's stance. Leveraging all her weight, she glanced up as the blonde woman in front of her moved and the logo on her jacket became visible—UK Marine Rescue, an organization Evie had heard about through Sam. Made up of marine experts and volun-teers, the UKMR had teams situated around the British Isles, ready to help stranded whales and dolphins whenever the need arose.

"It's okay to touch him," said the woman. "Lay your palm flat on its skin. It's calming."

Is this a dream? Gingerly, Evie placed her hand on his rubbery back and caught Nick doing the same, his eyes wide and mouth open in wonder. "Can you believe we're doing this?" he murmured, clearly thrilled.

"Got the stretcher." A man in an indigo jacket carrying a large piece of vinyl joined the effort. "Clare, can you help?"

Together with the woman in the high-res jacket, he unfolded the long rectangle and positioned the stretcher near the upright whale. The rising tide, however, kept shifting sand and orca, making the process difficult and increasingly frustrating.

Try after try, minute after minute, they didn't give up, ignoring the escalating tides and their waterlogged clothes. What was once ankle-deep was now hitting their waists as they kneeled, but not a peep of complaint was uttered. Evie did learn more about the whale, though. Apparently, he was about five years old and healthy and from a pod known to frequent the area.

As the water rose and met their chests, their efforts were finally rewarded, maneuvering the stretcher beneath the whale. The crea-ture laid on top and bobbed his tail, which the UKMR team said was a good sign. With care, they moved as a group, turning the stretcher and the orca so it was facing the open sea.

Holding her stretcher handle, Evie peered over at Nick, who seemed to be suppressing a shiver as the sea swallowed his clothes. Still no grumbling, though, just full-on commitment from Mr. Fancy Pants Executive Producer.

"Hold positions," urged the blonde woman, and Evie braced as another wave threw itself into their huddle, but the orca flapped its pectoral fins and swished its tail, launching himself off the stretcher and back into the bay.

He's swimming! Evie couldn't believe her eyes. She wanted to shout a "Thank you!" to the heavens but held back as happy tears gathered. Obviously, she wasn't alone in her joyful relief because Clare and the man beside her began cheering and jumping up and down.

"We did it!" they bellowed, and Evie joined in, clapping and laughing and falling into their mini hug of three. As she let go, a strong wave rolled in and shoved her into another jubilant hug.

One with Nick.

Breathless, unease sliced through her as he clutched her close, their drenched bodies pressing, every curve, every hollow meeting from shoulder to thigh. She gasped upon feeling the familiar reassuring warmth of his body wrapped around hers.

Nick laughed playfully. "Oh my god! Evie, we saved an *orca*!"

Pushed and pulled by the surging tides as he held her tight, Evie's reluctant longing breached its banks, filling her heart with memory after memory of moments like this one when it was just the two of them against the world and everything felt possible.

Even love.

She hugged him back. "I still can't believe it!"

Nick laughed again. "Is there a better feeling?!"

Fighting back tears, she buried her face in his neck. "Not even close."

SEVENTEEN

EVIE

Then, Saturday, August 8, fourteen years ago

Insistent sun peeked through a smudge of gray clouds, its warm smile defying Bignold Park's sodden grass and squishy mud, unwelcome souvenirs of an early morning soaking. The storm, like most that blew into Orkney, was a disruptive guest, drenching forgotten laundry on clotheslines and sending sheep scurrying for cover. But once the winds picked up, the downpours were elbowed into the North Sea, leaving County Show organizers and attendees breathing a collective sigh of relief.

Except for Evie.

Where is he? As her daisy-patterned wellies squelched in the mud, she meandered past the kiddies' teacup ride for the second time. She pretended not to notice Fiona and Sunita's shared glances or "Lovefool" blasting through the funfair's speakers, and feigned interest in the untouched bacon roll going cold in her hand. Loaded with zesty brown sauce on a soft, home-baked bun, even her favorite sandwich couldn't rouse a grin. *Maybe I should text him again.* Her focus leapt to her phone in her other hand, her We're here! sent ninety minutes earlier still waiting, alone and unanswered. She shook her head mournfully as the Milk Bottles she'd brought for Nick waited unclaimed in her pocket. *Thursday night can't be a one-off.*

Soft and teasing—delightfully teasing—Nick's lips were everything and more. Hardly surprising, he didn't kiss like the guys from Orkney (sorry, not sorry, Stuart). Bold and hungry, then tender and slow…Evie wondered if Nick had mastered the art of kissing on the set of *Dalston Grove*. Regardless, it was safe to say: her long-unfulfilled fantasies leapt to sizzling life with every sweep of his tongue…

"Eves? *Evie?*"

She looked up as Sunita pulled down the cuffs of her oversized fisherman's sweater. "We've seen the craft tent, watched the Shetland ponies for, like, forever, *and* eaten our way through the food vans…"

Ugh, eating. Nerves twisting, Evie lobbed her lunch into the nearest bin.

"Or at least Fi and I have." Sunita tilted her head, concern lowering her voice. "You sure he's coming?"

And there it was, the unspeakable question of the hour—and the thirty minutes before that.

"Definitely." Evie forced a smile as she clung to her last slippery wisps of hope. She tugged her denim jacket closed over her white top, a recent online purchase. With its broderie anglaise embroidery and sweetheart neckline, it was trendy yet flattering, and hopefully something Nick would like.

"I'd text Rupert to see if he's heard from him, but his phone's off while he's showing his gran's baby bull," said Fiona, dipping her strawberry sucker into a packet of lemon-flavored powder.

"It's okay, Fi. He'll be here," said Evie. *I hope.*

"I bet he slept through his alarm." The tail of Fiona's oversized plaid shirt flapped in the wind. "Rupert said he was up late reading a script."

Evie blinked. "Really?"

"Nikolai Balfour"—Sunita tsked—"too good for the County Show."

Mid-candy dip, Fiona subtly elbowed Sunita. "I thought you were going to play nice," she scolded. "And apologize."

"I will—if he shows. And for our sake, I hope he does. My ears can't take any more."

"Any more what?" Evie halted beside the chair swing ride for little kids, forcing her friends to stop, too.

"You beating yourself up," said Sunita. "If Nick doesn't show, it's not because of what you wore or how you kissed or any of the other things you keep moaning about."

Due to Stuart dumping her twenty-four hours after they'd slept together, Evie's fears of sexual inadequacy were looming over her like a pesky gray cloud. For twelve months (and counting), she had agonized over every little thing she did (and didn't) do with Stu, ranging from *Should I have given him more blow jobs?* to *Is my body ugly?* The negative thoughts swirled and taunted, and now they risked tarnishing Thursday's kiss with Nick.

"But what if I gave him too much tongue?" she asked.

"Would you STOP!" demanded Sunita. "There's no such thing. Too much saliva, yes. Tongue, no."

"You say that, but he barely said goodbye." Unease fluttered through her. "He couldn't leap off the trampoline fast enough."

"Well, would you hang around if *his* parents caught you with your hand up his shirt?" asked Fiona.

Sunita smirked. "Shame Evie's wasn't down his pants."

"Sun!" Evie playfully swatted her. "Nick hopped the fence before they got out of the car. Then Mum gave me a lecture about boundaries and consent, and how to be safe the first time you have sex."

"Oh, Mrs. Sutherland!" Fiona laughed.

"Yesterday she left a box of condoms in my room."

"That horse has left the barn and is halfway across South Ronaldsay!" said Sunita.

"Mum would freak if she knew."

"But what does she expect? You're seventeen." Fiona dunked her sucker again. "Seriously, she never suspected you and Stu?"

"If she did, she's never said," Evie mused. "I think she knew I wasn't really into him. She probably thought I'd wait." Her attention strayed to the Outrage ride, a waltzer blaring old hits by Madonna.

"Oh, I meant to tell you!" Sunita leaned in. "Puggie said Rebecca got in shit for putting cannabis in her home bakes."

"Which Becca?" asked Evie. "Petrol station or octopush?"

"Octopush," said Sunita. "At her party. You know, the one you went to."

Shit! Evie reeled. *Nick ate her cupcakes!*

"Puggie said it was hilarious." Sunita broke into a laugh. "One girl stripped off half-naked and ran outside looking for faerie folk!"

Evie huffed into a slouch. "*Great.* That's why Nick kissed me. He was fucking high!"

The sucker popped from Fiona's lips. "Nooo! How many did he eat?"

"A few!" Evie paced. "I can't believe this—"

"*Eves!* Chill!" Sunita motioned toward the funfair ticket booth.

Exasperated, she followed Sunita's hand.

Scanning the crowd as he dashed through the obstacle course of slow walkers, Nick held a pink cloud of candy floss, which popped against his navy blue overcoat. Firecrackers of joyful relief exploded in Evie's chest, pushing out a buoyant "He's here!" from her throat. She waved fervently until Nick's harried gaze landed safely on hers.

"Just in time," Sunita mouthed to a smiling Fiona, her lips stained scarlet from her lolly.

Nick's chest rose and fell as he slowed his sprint. "Evie!" He swallowed thickly, his eyes hooded with remorse. "Thank god you're still here. I'm *so* sorry."

Admiring his chaotic hair and apologetic grin, not to mention the flossy sugar-bomb-on-a-stick color-clashing with his purple and white polka dotted shirt, Evie broke into a smile, her first of the day. "It's okay."

"No, it's really not"—he gasped, catching his breath—"I was running errands with Dad. We got stuck behind a tractor. Then his phone died during a call and he grabbed mine. Still has it, too."

"I'm glad you're all right," said Evie. "I was worried when you didn't text back."

Nick dragged a hand through his hair. "I would've, but Dad was yammering on. He didn't even shut up when he dropped me off down the road."

"You need your license," ordered Fiona, pointing her sucker.

How did I not know this? Evie's mouth fell open. "You can't drive?"

"Nope. Can you?"

"Yeah! Since I was fourteen." She'd also been driving by his grandmother's house and farm since she was fourteen, too, but some things were better left unsaid.

"We learn early here," said Fiona. "Lots of fields and country roads, no traffic jams—well, not counting sheep and cows."

"Makes sense." Nick's focus stalled on Sunita then slid toward Evie again. "You look so pretty."

Her heart fizzed with happiness. Fiona let out a lovestruck "Aww!"

"This is for you." He offered Evie the cotton candy bouquet. "An apology for being late."

"So cute!" Fiona elbow-bumped Sunita, who was busy fidgeting with her sweater.

Accepting the paper cone wound with strands of spun sugar, Evie's eyes shone. "This is *perfect*! Thank you!" She dug in her jacket pocket and produced a small bag of chewy Milk Bottles. "And these are for you."

His grin grew. "Nice! Cheers, Evie!"

She happily returned to her candy. "I'll take floss over flowers any day."

"Weird but true—unless it's daisies. Evie loves those." An apprehensive smile graced Sunita's face as she studied Nick. "Also weird...me being wrong for a change."

Is this what I think it is? Evie exchanged a hopeful look with Fiona.

"Nick"—Sunita nodded—"I owe you an overdue apology. I was an obnoxious know-it-all at the beach and treated you horribly. So, you know...I'm sorry."

The corners of his lips lifted.

"I'd like to be friends," Sunita added. "But if that ship's sailed, I totally understand."

"Nope, still in dry dock." Nick offered his hand. "Mates?"

Sunita grinned and shook on it. "Mates."

"Great!" Evie smiled as they let go. "Now, let's play some games and hit the rides."

"I can't—sorry." Pouting, Sunita pointed over her shoulder. "Meeting Mum for a mother-daughter manicure."

Fiona frowned. "Oh yeah. And I have to help my auntie at the young farmers booth."

Sunita hated manicures, and Fiona's elderly aunt, who she was boarding with over the summer, was on holiday several islands away in Papa Westray. Her best friends were making shit up, and Evie loved them for it.

Pulling her in for a hug, Sunita whispered, *"Never* enough tongue!" in her ear before stepping back.

Fiona leaned in carefully so she didn't crush Evie's candy floss. "Have fun!" Letting go with a smirk, she headed off with Sunita, their cheery chatter and over-the-shoulder glances raising Nick's brows and Evie's spirits.

Not subtle at all.

"Looks like you're stuck with me," said Nick, chewing a Milk Bottle.

"I can manage." Evie stared at his mouth. "I know the County Show inside out."

"Brilliant." He squinted toward the hot tub and trout fishing displays. "We won't miss any highlights, then."

Was he being sarcastic? Evie couldn't tell. She glanced down. Nick's pricey trainers and the bottom of his dark jeans were splattered with fresh mud. "I know it might seem twee compared to what you have down south." Looking up, she whisked a piece of hair away from her lip gloss.

"No, it's cool," said Nick. "Gran used to come every year. She's an Orkney gal, born and raised. Comes from Hoy originally."

"You serious? I love Hoy. It's beautiful."

"I've never been."

There was eager and then there was Evie. "I could take you!"

she blurted. "One of the ferries takes cars." Not even five minutes into their first date, and she was already angling for another. A flush heated her cheeks as Nick blinked quickly like he wasn't sure how to respond. *Yeah, way cool, Evie.* She retreated into her candy floss, wishing her mouth came with a rewind button.

"I'd love to go with you."

Love? Evie peered up, catching his boyish grin.

"I have some auditions booked soon, but we could go aft—"

"I *told* you, didn't I?!" Two rosy-cheeked teens, all braces and giggles, ambushed their conversation. The shorter of the pair bounced a wriggling infant on her hip.

Evie recognized the girls from school. "Hi." She smiled, under no illusion she was the one they were excited to see.

The young mother grinned, her eyes scooting to Nick. "Hope you don't mind. We had to say hi and tell you how much we loved the skinny-dipping scene!"

Evie and the *Dalston Grove* fandom knew that one by heart: Jake naked, having a sunrise frolic in a pond with Amanda after an adventurous London all-nighter. Evie had replayed (and paused) the scene over and over, but *dammit*, Nick's bare ass eluded detection every time.

"Could we get an autograph?" asked the second girl, hands shaking as she produced a pen and a scrap of paper from her jacket.

"Absolutely." Nick tucked his sweets in a coat pocket. "What are your names?"

Evie smiled over her candy floss, elated to witness this fangirl moment from the inside—beside Nick. She stared surreptitiously at his mouth again as he signed with his left hand. Butterflies teasing, she desperately craved a repeat of Thursday night, to press her lips against his, for him to open up so she could taste him with a sweep of her tongue—

"Oh! And a photo. Would you hold my bairn?"

The fan's little sprite blew saliva bubbles through her toothless smile and clung to a plush giraffe glistening with fresh goo. Eyeing Nick in his designer coat, Evie wondered how he would handle this.

He fiddled with its buttons for a beat then flashed a grin. "Sure."

Without hesitation, the teen unloaded her chubby-cheeked daughter into his arms. She gurgled and giggled, joyfully waving her toy as her mother snapped several photos on her digital camera.

After a flurry of ebullient thank-yous, the trio headed for the mini carousel, and Evie had Nick all to herself again.

She freed a few pink strands of cotton candy. "Just like Jake."

"Oh god no." Nick blotted a patch of drool on his sleeve with a tissue from his pocket. "That was me acting my balls off."

Evie popped the floss into her mouth, the spun sugar dissolving into crystalized beads on her tongue. "You don't like babies?" She tilted her cotton candy toward him.

Chucking the tissue in a trash bin, Nick made a face. "It's not that I don't *like* them. They're cute, but"—he tore off a tuft of pink fluff—"even when Rupert and Tarquin were born, I steered clear. Their wailing and smells, enthusiasm for gumming up my toys and clothes? No thanks."

"I thought you loved playing Jake."

"I did, but I didn't enjoy the teenage dad part. The little dude *hated* me." Nick slipped the floss into his mouth as they passed a pen of bleating goats. "What about you? Already choosing baby names?"

"For pets? Always. Humans? Never," said Evie. "The whole idea of giving birth freaks me out."

"I guess Amanda dying on the show didn't help."

"Nope."

"I got loads of fan mail about that saying the same."

"You're great with them by the way." Evie smiled proudly.

"Fans? I try. I don't get stopped as much as I used to. People forget you when you're no longer on telly."

True. Fiona's like that. Evie nibbled on a knot of floss, the roar of chainsaws growing louder. "Have you read any scripts lately?"

"I have! Most of what I'm sent these days is Jake 2.0, but the one I'm reading now is a whole other level. It's a musical!"

"Really?!"

"Yeah!" Eyes glued to the chainsaw sculpture demonstration on their left, he raised his voice. "And I also bagged a fifth callback for a high-budget, fantasy/drama series called *Plunder the Crown.*"

"A *fifth*?" She shouted. "Nick, that's fantastic! They really want you!"

"Hope so!"

They both upped their speed, leaving the noisy chainsaws behind.

"I'd sell a flippin' kidney to book it," said Nick. "Get this: filming's slated for Iceland, Northern Ireland, and Malta!"

"Wow! That's awesome!"

"Right? It could be a total gamechanger—my first adult role." Nick blinked, and a lash landed on his cheek.

Evie couldn't stop staring at it. "When's your callback?"

As he glanced at his muddy shoes, a frown trespassed across his face. "End of month."

"Sorry, I have to…" Leaning in, Evie stole his eyelash with a tap of her finger. "Timing couldn't be more perfect. Make a wish."

With a quick puff, Nick blew it away.

"I can picture you now." Evie smiled. "Wielding a sword, wearing leather, riding a horse! You'll be freakin' incredible."

His eyes gleamed. "Here's hoping the casting peeps think so. Filming is scheduled for next summer, which is perfect. I wouldn't miss uni."

"Best of both worlds. Your mum will be happy. And your dad."

"Gotta keep the parentals sweet." Nick stripped a curl of floss off the paper cone. "How 'bout you, how's school? What is it, two years of exams down, one to go?"

"Yep." Evie watched the pink fluff disappear between his lips. "I'm so close to finishing I can taste it."

"What universities are you considering?"

"Goldsmiths and the University of East London. Me, Sun, and our mums visited both last December."

"You escaped Scotland! Finally!"

"Yup!" *And was scared witless.* For most teenagers, traveling far from home and staying in a hotel would be thrilling, but it was terrifying for Evie. Sat far from the toilets on planes, eating unfamiliar food around London, and locating public washrooms were all substantial worries. The longer she was there, however, her fears calmed somewhat, only to ramp up again flying home. She didn't relax until she'd stepped through her door. "London was eye-opening. The people, the traffic!"

"Like another planet, eh?" said Nick.

"Yeah, but I liked it. Christmas decorations were up, and we saw *Hairspray*."

"Your first West End musical?"

She smiled like a lottery winner. "I KNOW! We also saw Big Ben and St. Paul's, shopped in Camden, ate a Big Mac—my first *ever*."

Nick did a double take. "And?"

My Crohn's wasn't happy. She shook her head. "No contest. Orkney burgers are way better."

"That's because the cattle are locals," said Nick. "You probably wave to them each morning."

Evie laughed. "There is that."

They swung past the queue for the ice cream van. "How were the schools?"

"Massive—but cool. Now I need the final grades to turn their conditional offers into guaranteed places."

"You got offers from both?!"

Evie nodded. "So, unless I screw up majorly, I'll be an English and creative writing undergrad next year."

"Holy shit!" His voice rose. "You're a writer?"

"Sorta. I have notebooks filled with stories, but"—she tore away a large plume of floss—"it's not like I've been published or anything."

"Published or not, you're still a writer. What's your genre?"

"Fiction." She lied through omission, worried Nick might re-evaluate his praise if he knew the truth. Romance owned her heart, but in Evie's experience people weren't always kind, calling it cheesy or lowbrow. She knew romance was neither of those things, but she also wasn't quite ready to have her soul crushed if Nick thought otherwise.

"That's so cool." Smiling, he licked his lips. "I think writers are super hot. Anyone with that passion and creative fire? *Huge* turn-on."

Evie bit back a grin. "Really?"

"I would love to read your stuff."

The horror. Evie waved him off. "Honestly, most of it is total rubbish."

"Says the girl with not one, but TWO conditional uni offers for creative writing."

"Key word: conditional."

"Semantics!" exclaimed Nick. "You'll be writing up a storm in London before you know it."

She laughed. "One day I'll be a famous author and you'll be asking *me* for an autograph!"

"Better believe it!" He smiled as they passed the craft tent. "And what about Sunita? What's she taking?"

"Journalism. We're planning on sharing her aunt's flat in New Cross."

"Smart," said Nick. "You'll be less homesick if you're together."

A hollow ache throbbed in Evie's chest. Amidst all the excitement of this grown-up adventure, the thought of leaving Orkney, of leaving her comfort zone kept her awake most nights. "It'll be weird without Fiona, though. It's been the three of us for so long."

"Rupert said she'll study here? Same school as him, right?"

"Yeah, she starts next month. The archeology program doesn't require Advanced Highers results, the lucky duck."

"At least you'll have one more year together before heading off to the Big Smoke," said Nick.

Evie watched his hand dive into his jacket pocket. How she wished she could hold it again. "Gotta make the most of it."

Finishing the cotton candy, they shared a waffle and strolled around the park, checking out various vendors and exhibits (the falconry attraction was a favorite). Evie challenged Nick to a spin on the bumper cars where they both plowed recklessly into one another over and over again. Then, Nick threw down his own dare at the bust-a-balloon game, bragging about his aptitude for darts until Evie burst two rows, capturing the grand prize (a googly-eyed elephant), which she happily pressed into his arms. But while they were having a laugh, the unspoken lingered between them—their kiss on the trampoline two days earlier.

Evie smoothed the tuft of black hair on the elephant's head.

"Horton *loves* that," said Nick.

"Horton?"

He nodded. "All my cuddly toys have names."

"All? How many do you have?"

"A few." He bounced the elephant in his arms. "See, I'm not as cool as people think I am, Tigger."

My nickname from the trampoline! A fire blazed in her belly.

"This one's special, though," said Nick, smiling. "I've never had a girl win me a prize before."

Evie couldn't avoid the elephant in the proverbial room—or on the island—any longer. Passing classmates, cousins, and neighbors with brief but cheerful greetings, she felt their hurried whispers and inquisitive glances. The Orkney rumor mill was whirling in full speculation mode and so was she. Were they *just* friends? Were they a couple? Or were they a couple of friends who'd crashed together, all feral lips and urgent tongues, only to realize they'd awkwardly crossed a line? Well, maybe Nick had checked that box, but Evie sure hadn't, and one thing was certain: she couldn't just pretend the trampoline kiss hadn't happened.

Sucking in a deep breath, she lifted her chin. "Nick—"

"Evie, I—"

Speaking at the same time, they both fell into nervous laughter.

Nick waved Horton's pudgy foot. "Ladies first."

His chivalry was adorable but dangerous. What if she offered her heart and he tossed it back? She couldn't risk it. Nick had to speak first. As much as it might hurt hearing *It was a mistake*, it would hurt more to spill her feelings and watch his sparkling eyes dull with pity and revulsion.

"Uh, no...*guests* go first." Dreading another public rejection, Evie sized up the row of funfair rides and their garish murals and backdrops. "Let's...head back here." She emotionally braced herself as they walked behind the rectangular hoarding. *It's best to know.*

"Oh wait..."

Evie's heart stuttered.

Nick reached up and pinched something off her upper cheek. "Eyelash." He held up his finger, showing off the little brown crescent. "You know what to do."

Her wish was a no-brainer, the same one she'd silently profess over birthday candles and shooting stars and seedy dandelion parachutes. *I wish Nick fancied me.* Evie blew the lash away, and with it her hopes for an angst-free conversation.

"Okay." Hugging the elephant, Nick let out a shaky breath. "I told myself earlier not to dick around and just...say it."

Evie gulped and tugged the hem of her jacket, curling it around her fingers.

"I'm sorry I left your place so quickly Thursday. I-I didn't want to meet your parents like that."

She nodded, recalling how he stumbled across their yard, blinded by the headlights of her dad's car.

"I had, uh"—Nick scratched the back of his neck—"a little *reaction.*"

"Panic?"

He winced. "Hard-on."

"Ohh!" Words catching in her throat, Evie felt a blush brewing but congratulated herself with a mental high five for getting Nick so hot and bothered. At the time, she'd felt *something* but didn't want to assume.

"Actually..." He bit his lip. "It wasn't so little."

Evie's blush became a full-on inferno inside and out. *He likes me!*

"I loved kissing you," said Nick. "It's all I can think about."

"Really?! So you weren't high?"

Nick snickered. "High?"

"Sun told me Rebecca put cannabis in her cupcakes—the ones you ate. Made me think you only kissed me 'cause you were off your tits."

"I might've been, but that doesn't change things." Nick edged closer. "Tigs, I really fancy you. Have done ever since that afternoon in your shop. You took my breath away..."

Is this really happening?

Trying to stay grounded, Evie nervously sought out the elephant's floppy ear, giving it a caress. "That wasn't me. You were mid-panic attack."

"No, *before* that, when I first saw you in the daisy dress. And then everything that followed—your concern, your kindness—made me like you even more." His eyes dipped to her lips. "I think you're amazing."

Her insides felt all hot and gooey like molten lava cake. If Nick was knee-deep in the honesty pool, maybe she should wade in, too? Letting go of the soft toy, she ducked her chin, unsuccessfully hiding her huge grin. "You're amazing, too. I've fancied you, like...*forever*."

"Forever? Christ, looks like I have some catching up to do." Smiling, Nick bent his neck to meet her gaze, his hair flopping forward. "So how 'bout it, eh? We'll give this a go? You and me?"

Evie beamed back. "You want to date me?"

"Well, date *and* snog you senseless—if that's all right?" He tucked the elephant under his arm.

"All right? Quickest wish granting EVER!"

Nick stroked her cheek with the back of his hand. "Fancy that. Mine, too."

Evie squealed inside as he leaned in and slid his lips over hers, kissing her slowly.

EIGHTEEN

EVIE

Now, Friday, July 21

"And then we hung around for another hour to make sure the orca didn't head back to shore." Evie looked across Fiona's farmhouse table at Sunita. "Sorry, I know you've heard this a thousand times over the past twenty-four hours."

"Yeah, but every time it makes me smile." Sunita finished her can of ale. After a long catering shift of breakfast wraps and lunchtime soups, the friends were kicking back with sourdough pizza and alcoholic refreshments, spare Evie, who was Sunita's designated driver.

"Any idea why it beached itself?" Fiona sipped her red Bordeaux, enjoying a rare child- and husband-free night after a day digging in the dirt at the Ness of Brodgar. Celebrating their love of all things stegosaurus, the girls (and Rupert) were at a 'Dinosnores' sleepover party at the Picky.

"It's anyone's guess," said Evie. "Sometimes they strand themselves when they're sick or by accident. And then there's other more sinister stuff like seismic exploration for offshore windfarms. Stuart used to talk about it all the time. When underwater pulses of sound are used to survey the seafloor, the noise can disorient and frighten sea life, pushing them off course or worse."

Fiona tore the mushrooms off her pizza slice. "And who's getting lots of offshore windfarms? Us." She sighed. "Great, now I've got the morbs."

"The *what*?" asked Sunita.

"The morbs," said Fiona. "It's a Victorian term I heard on set. Means feeling melancholy."

214

Evie did a double take. "Well, I hope the windfarms didn't cause the beaching, 'cause as wild as last night was, I don't think my heart could go through it again."

Sunita quirked a brow. "Whoa. Nick's hug must've been something!"

Fiona paused, mid-mushroom cull. "He hugged you?"

"We were celebrating. Everyone was."

"He almost kissed her." Sunita's cheeky declaration drew an audible gasp from Fiona.

"No, he didn't!" corrected Evie. "We pulled back from the hug and…kinda froze like our minds needed a minute to catch up to our bodies."

"Ooh, I bet." Sunita's smirk provoked a head shake from Evie.

"There was absolutely *nothing* sexual going on."

"Okay, but did you *want* there to be?" Optimism blooming in her eyes, Fiona leaned closer. "I think so."

"Fi!"

The corners of her mouth, tinted Bordeaux rouge, tipped upward. "What? Might as well come out and say what I'm thinking. You and Nick saved an *orca* together. If that's not a bonding moment, what is? It was life tri-humping over death!"

Sunita laughed. "Tri-humping? You mean *triumphing*, right?"

"Both!" Fiona squealed. "After a brush with death, there's nothing more primal or life-affirming than hot sex."

A blush heated Evie's face as she confiscated Fiona's wine bottle and teasingly checked the label. "What *are* you drinking? Thank god you have tomorrow off!"

"Joke all you want, but I *will not* bite my tongue." Fiona's voice grew uncharacteristically loud. "You and Nick were—*are*—great together. The whole whale tale proves it—again."

"You're biased." Evie returned the wine to the table.

"Fuck yeah I am! I'm a selfish cow who only wants her bestie and bro-in-law to kiss and makeup already!"

"I knew it! All the pained glances, all the 'You should talk to him, Evie.'" Lifting her hair, she examined the ends. "It's not that simple, Fi."

"Isn't it? *C'mon.* I saw how he looked at you in the café the other day. Don't tell me you didn't notice."

"He was being friendly."

"And flirty!"

"By discussing *quiche*?" asked Evie.

Sunita laughed. "Nothing screams 'fuck me' like an eggy tart."

"I *know* what I saw." Fiona pouted. "Evie, you can be honest with us, you know. Hell, you used to be."

"I still am!"

"No, you're not," snapped Fiona. "Not since Nick flew in."

Evie dropped her hair. "*I am!*"

"Then prove it." Sunita leaned in. "Go on. How do you *really* feel?"

She let out a big breath, remembering how Nick waited until she was safely inside the B&B before driving away and his text that arrived ten minutes later: Best evening with the best person. Sweet dreams, Evie

The warmth of his actions blazed through her, unraveling the negative stories she'd told herself again and again as a coping mechanism post-split. "Okay. *Yes*, I've been feeling…nostalgic."

"Nostalgic!" Sunita snickered. "You mean horny."

Rolling her eyes, Evie picked up a pretzel. "It's hardly the same thing!"

"You were staring at his ass!"

"When?"

"When Nick left, when the medic was wrapping your hand."

Sunita saw that? Evie scoffed. "I was saying thanks."

"Yeah." Sunita laughed. "Thanks for some tasty visuals for the wank bank later."

She lobbed her pretzel across the table, missing her friend. "You are *terrible*, Sun! Does Micah know you're such a perv? Actually, who are we kidding—he's probably thanking his lucky stars!"

"Ohh-kay, that's it." Sunita rolled up the sleeves of her blouse.

"Time to be honest. About *everything*."

"Such as?" Evie looked sidelong at Fiona, who shrugged. "Should we be worried?"

"I broke up with Micah."

"*What?!*" Evie and Fiona cried at the same time.

"It's fine. It was mutual. We both realized we're better as friends."

"You okay?" Evie clasped Sunita's hand.

"I'm great. It's just one of those things, you know? A bit of personal housekeeping like…quitting my job."

Her breezy delivery left Evie confused and Fiona demanding, "You didn't!"

"I did. Felt *incredible*."

Evie let go of Sunita's hand. "Why didn't you say something?"

"Everything was blowing up here. You didn't need to worry about me, too."

"I always worry about you."

"Eves, I'm okay! It's just that dishing gossip started to feel gross. *I* started to feel gross."

"Well, it's not the most"—Fiona paused, her tipsy brain searching—"*compassionate* of journo paths, is it?"

Sunita nodded woefully. "I damaged relationships. I destroyed lives." Fiddling with her pizza crust, she skirted Evie's gaze. "Actually, I…destroyed Nick's."

Fiona slumped back in her chair in stunned boozy silence as Evie sputtered, "You…*How?*"

"The sex tape exposé?" said Sunita. "I paid the source. I wrote the story."

Evie's jaw dropped. "But there was no by-line."

"On purpose."

"But…why'd you do it?" asked Fiona.

"For *Evie!*" Sunita turned to her oldest friend. "As payback for him hurting you."

Evie blinked. "Oh, Sun. He lost his career because of it."

"Well, I thought he deserved it at the time."

"And now?" asked Evie.

Sunita chewed her fingernail and shook her head. "Please don't hate me."

"I-I don't know what to feel. This is just...wow." Evie couldn't find the words. "If Nick finds out, he might think I goaded you into publishing it."

"Don't worry, I'm not gonna tell him," said Sunita. "He's off to London tonight anyway."

"What's he doing *there*?" asked Fiona.

"Some meeting, something in person. He'll be back late Monday," said Evie quickly, wanting to get back to what really mattered. "Sun, I can't let anything derail this catering gig—"

"Or their hot makeup sex," added Fiona, with a tipsy finger point.

I should be so lucky. Evie moved the wine bottle away. "Lady, I'm cutting you off!"

Sunita leaned on the table. "Look, I know you and Nick are getting along these days and I'm all for it—if that's what you want—but I don't know if you can rely on him for anything more. He's got bad form, Eves."

"And you're telling me something I don't know? Why do you think I'm so conflicted?"

"But he took the blame for the raisin thing," said Fiona. "And was a sweetheart when you burned your hand."

"Last night, too." Evie smiled fondly, ignoring a sinus headache that wouldn't quit. "He was talking to the orca, trying to keep it calm."

"See? Nick isn't a bad guy." Fiona popped a mushroom in her mouth. "And just 'cause it didn't work out when you were younger, doesn't mean it won't now."

"He does seem...remorseful."

"Then why not give him a second chance?" asked Fiona. "You gave Caleb one."

"That's completely different. Caleb didn't stomp on her heart. He didn't avoid her like a coward for years." Sunita looked at Evie, her gaze softening. "You were *devastated*."

Devastated, and yet, she still wondered where Nick was, what he was doing, who he was with. Evie tortured herself for months.

"I know." She nodded. "That's why all this is so fucked up. I'm having major déjà vu and feeling things I shouldn't be feeling." She picked at the label on the wine bottle. "Although, I *am* tempted to give up my grudge for good. It's not doing me any favors."

"Don't fight it," said Fiona. "That's your gut screaming, 'Give him a second chance!'"

No, my gut's telling me to avoid further drama. Her Crohn's was nagging more than usual. Her uncertainty around Nick, gobbling meals on the fly, and financial worries were fueling cramps and fatigue at the worst possible time.

"Fi, just because Nick rescued a whale doesn't mean he's here to rescue Evie, too," said Sunita.

She held up her hands. "I don't need rescuing…"

"But you need hot sex!" Fiona grinned devilishly. "And don't you dare deny it!"

Nineteen

EVIE

Then, Wednesday, August 12, fourteen years ago

Kicking off her shoes on her namesake beach, Evie whipped her t-shirt over her head and dropped it on her towels, the novelty of Nick's new *boyfriend* status (five days old and counting) setting off a ticker tape parade in her chest.

"Get 'em off, SaxyBoy!" She peeked coquettishly over her shoulder, the pink strap of her lacy bra matching the colorful tide rising across his cheeks.

"You sure about this?" Sidestepping tangles of kelp, Nick hugged his bowling shirt and peered out at Eynhallow Sound, its clear aquamarine waters relatively calm and deceptively inviting. "We could go for lunch and come back?"

"Or eat after? Gotta take advantage on such a beautiful day!" A rare heat wave had stalled over the Scottish isles, bringing breezy warmth in the high seventies, and Evie was determined to soak up every sunshiny second before school reeled her back in. She inhaled deeply, savoring the sea air as she popped the button on her jeans. "It hasn't been this hot in *ages*."

Nick swept his hair off his forehead, revealing a bewildered crease. "You call this hot?"

"Scorching!" Evie laughed. "Stay here if you want. I'm going in." She peeled off her denim and skipped across the gritty, silvery sand, leaving Nick scratching his head and gawking at her panty-covered butt.

Slosh! Splash! The water's prickling burn bit her toes. Stifling a yelp, she sucked in a sharp breath and sploshed joyfully through the freezing liquid like it was a toasty swimming pool. She didn't dare

220

shiver. Nick was already iffy about the whole Orkney swimming *thing* and didn't need another reason to balk. On the drive over, he'd fidgeted in the passenger seat, mentioning their lack of swimsuits and how tracking sand into her mum's car would be "messy and inconsiderate," but Evie couldn't be dissuaded. "Underwear is practically the same as a swimming costume, and sand can be cleaned up," she'd said. "Plus, wild swimming is invigorating and a great way to experience nature. We might even see selkies!" Nick stared through the bug-splattered windshield, clearly not sold on seals or anything else.

The tide hadn't reached its full height, but it was still high enough for a proper swim. Arms outstretched, Evie plunged forward, and the cold water whooshed over her shoulders and back, pebbling her skin with goosebumps as a pained squeal lodged in her throat. She glanced at the smaller islands of Rousay and Eynhallow across the Sound then held her breath and dove in, the frigid shock of her head going under for the first time catapulting her back up, breaking the surface all wide-eyed and sputtering. *Jeeez! That's c-c-cold!* As water seeped through her hair, tingling her scalp, she ducked under again where the serene, underwater beauty of the sandy sea floor and waving seaweed, all blurry golds and greens, welcomed her home. She took several long, leisurely strokes then popped up for air, finding it showered with salty expletives.

"Oh! My! Fucking! Christ!" Water edging his crotch, Nick let out clipped gasps with each stiff arm flap and leggy leap. Spoiled by yearly family retreats to Greece and Italy where the Mediterranean warmed to eighty heavenly degrees, Nick wasn't just out of his depth, he was mired in one f'ing belter of a freezing freakout. "Jesus!" He wobbled. "I'm losing feeling in my—FUCK!"

Belly-flopping the surface, Nick gawped, the searing sting stealing his ability to blink or speak.

Evie slicked back her hair. "That's it. Just fall in."

He hung in the water, lashes flittering and teeth chattering as a surprise wave slapped him in the face and his chin dipped below the surface.

"*Nick?!*" Evie's voice trembled. "You okay?!" Launching forward, she grasped his slippery shoulders and he came alive, his body unfolding like an awakening starfish. He wrapped himself around her and pressed his forearms into her back, drawing her closer in the most heavenly hug. They were hip to hip, chest against breast, the eager thump of Nick's heart mirroring Evie's.

"*Hi.*" Nick's mouth curled with a mischievous grin. "I'm more than all right—now!"

"You're kneeling on the bottom, aren't you?" Water droplets trickled down Evie's face, their saltiness teasing the rising corners of her lips. "You faker!" She laughed, splashing him.

Her playful response made Nick tighten his embrace. "Aren't you glad I'm okay?"

"Yes!" She looped her arms around his neck. "Want me to prove it?"

His sinful gaze flitted down to her mouth. "Go on, then."

And that means...what? Evie had yet to learn Nick's boyfriend shorthand—what turned him on, what didn't, when a sassy remark was really an invite for a cheeky fumble, a grind of her hips...or a full-on fuck. And time was ticking. As a twenty-year-old, Nick had years of experience on her, and unlike Stuart, he was popular and worldly and probably didn't wait a year for any of his girlfriends to sleep with him. Evie would have to move fast, be sexually available sooner rather than later to keep Nick happy.

She hooked her legs around his hips then pressed her lips to his neck, his skin ripe and salty for tender kisses and lingering sucks. Evie indulged blissfully, closing her eyes until Nick moaned and his mouth hungrily sought hers.

Meeting his tongue, she went deeper, teasing and taunting as Nick let out heated gasps and his fingers slipped under the waistband of her panties. His gentle squeeze of her ass unleashed a needy ache between her thighs followed by a whimper from her throat. *He's into this—so much!* Evie kissed him harder, their sumptuous dance coaxing her hand down his chest and stomach, between their hips, and over his boxer shorts where...

Huh?!

Nothing was happening.

Evie's stomach lurched. *I-I messed up.* When she withdrew her hand, Nick pulled back, breathless. *He's not into it!* She scrunched her eyes, dreading his rejection. "I'm sorry! I should've asked first."

"Oh, Tigs," he groaned. "Please don't think I'm not keen. I am! Really!"

She pried her lashes open, catching his downward glance.

"The water is *so* cold. Nothing's getting hard down there. Like, *ever!*" Looking up, Nick's mouth quirked into an apologetic grin. "It felt amazing, though. If we were on a couch or a bed..." He kissed Evie on the lips and rested his forehead against hers. "You would definitely have more to play with."

Was that a promise? Evie smiled. "Something to look forward to."

"But this is nice, right? Kissing and holding each other?"

Nick felt warm and slick, protective. "It's perfect." Evie's fingers flirted with the wet hair at the nape of his neck. She sighed dreamily over his shoulder. In the distance, a few seniors ambled across the sandy shore alongside a loping Labrador Retriever and a father and son brandishing a kite. The sun, now high in the sky, had a few feathery clouds keeping her glow company. Evie's heart felt full.

She nuzzled into him. "You've stopped shivering."

"Thanks to you. You make everything better."

And so did Nick. She loved who she'd become in his company: someone interesting and worthy, no longer the sick girl who was often forgotten and left behind.

The timing felt right. Time for Nick to know all her secrets, including the biggest one of all.

"Remember when I mentioned missing Sam's track meet in Inverness?" she murmured against his neck.

"Uh-huh." Nick removed a sprig of seaweed from her hair. "That's when your secret identity was revealed!"

She laughed and lifted her head. "Yeah." Taking in a deep

breath, Evie let her words escape with her exhale. "I missed it 'cause I was in hospital. I have an inflammatory bowel disease called Crohn's."

Nick's mouth fell open. "What?! How long have you had it?"

"Since I was twelve. Do you know what it is?"

"Isn't it like IBS? A bloke at Eton had it. Spent loads of time in the washroom."

"IBS shares some symptoms with IBD, but they're different," said Evie. "Crohn's is a chronic disease. Sometimes the pain's so bad I almost pass out."

Under the water, Nick's hand stroked her back. "Oh no. Oh, Evie, that's awful."

"Yeah, it sucks. I've had bleeding, anemia, skin rashes. Had a feeding tube in my nose for a while 'cause I wasn't absorbing nutrients. The doctor said I was dangerously close to becoming malnourished."

Concern darkened Nick's gape. "Holy fuck."

"Crohn's can permanently damage the GI tract, too."

"But it's curable, right?" he asked softly, his heart pounding against hers.

Evie slowly shook her head.

He looked shocked. Tears glistened in his eyes. "My god, Evie…"

She figured Nick would be empathetic, but his swell of emotion was a surprise.

"It's not, you know…fatal?"

Bless him. Evie caressed his cheek. "Don't worry. That's, like, super rare."

"*Ohh* good," Nick's voice shook with relief. Clasping her hand, he kissed her knuckles twice then held their entwined fingers against his chest.

"I take medication sometimes to help manage it, but honestly, it's not bad *all* the time. When I'm in remission, I barely notice it. I still have to watch what I eat and drink, but that's a small ask."

"Is it flaring now? I saw you rub your tummy in the car."

"Yeah, 'cause I'm hungry." Evie's reassuring grin seemed to relax Nick's shoulders. "Don't worry, things have been good lately." She playfully tapped her head with her fist. "Knock on wood."

"Thank god." His gaze strayed to a passing cluster of eider ducks riding the gentle waves. "The thought of you in pain or suffering…"

"Now you know how *I* feel when you have a panic attack."

Nick smiled. "Look at us. We are *so* broken!"

"But we're cute with it, right?!"

"So cute. You know, if you ever want to talk about it—" Nick jolted like he'd been zapped with an electric shock. "FUCK!" His whole body tensed, spare his heart, which drummed frantically against Evie's chest.

"What's wrong?!"

His fingers dug into her waist. "Something"—he scoured the water and shuffled sideways, pulling Evie with him—"something touched my leg!"

She relaxed. "Probably seaweed. Or a spoot."

Meeting her eyes, Nick gulped so hard Evie could hear it. "What the hell is *that*?"

"Razor clams. Totally harmless."

His knotted brow wasn't buying it. Was this the same actor who 'skinny-dipped' in a London pond?

"Their shells look like closed straight razors, but they won't hurt you," Evie explained amidst the squawk of swooping gulls overhead. "Spoots are terrified of people."

Nick smiled faintly. "I'm not the best with creepy crawlies." Unease lingered in his voice. "Or, you know…*nature*."

Better not mention the jellyfish, then.

His gaze fled over his shoulder back toward shore.

Remorse dragged in Evie's chest. *I forced him out here. I made him uncomfortable.* She kissed his cheek. "Let's head in. Get something to eat?"

"Sounds magic," said Nick.

As she walked silently through the receding water, Evie's skin tingled in the breeze. She hugged her middle, taking in the whirling blades of the windfarm high on Burgar Hill.

"Is anything totally off limits food-wise?" he asked.

"I can't drink coffee, eat red meat or spicy stuff, and certain veggies like beans and broccoli really do a number on me. Chocolate, fast food, and dairy can be tricky, too, which sucks."

"What can you eat during a flare?"

"Not much. Bland stuff mostly: marshmallows, bananas, rice, chicken broth. Sometimes I push the boat out and have a peanut butter and jelly sandwich or a baked tattie with applesauce."

"On the actual potato?"

"Yeah, I only eat the fluffy part, though, and leave the skin. It's yummy when you can't tolerate much else." Evie untangled her hair from her necklace. "That's the thing about Crohn's. When I feel good, I never take food for granted."

"Well, in that case, whatcha reckon? Sarnies, fish and"—as he glanced over, Nick's focus slipped and his words jammed—"and, I, uh…yeah." He swallowed. Hard.

Evie looked down. Glued to her chest, her drenched bra accentuated every curve, every swell, every cold, hardening peak. Everything was on jiggly display, and Nick seemed mesmerized by her tight nipples poking through the transparent lace. *He's a boob man!* Flashing a celebratory grin, she edged closer. "Cold water strikes again!"

Nick's eyes slowly skated up her neck then hovered over her lips. "You are so beautiful." He blinked up, meeting her gaze as he draped his arm around her shoulder, their wet thighs brushing as they walked. "You know that, right?"

She sucked in a breath.

All her life she'd been called cute Evie or smart Evie, but *beautiful* Evie? That person was definitely not someone she'd met in the mirror before. If Nick saw her that way, maybe she could, too? But some habits were hard to break, especially deep-rooted, seventeen-year-old habits tangled up with self-esteem and Crohn's disease.

How to respond? *Yes* would sound cocky (and so un-Evie), but *no* reeked of insecurity and neediness like she was clawing for compliments.

Nick smiled as the ruffle of the kite fighting the breeze filled her pause. She couldn't dawdle. An answer was needed now.

"Thank you." Evie veered left so they would dodge a large floating knot of kelp. "Depends on the day," she added. "And the boy."

"Well, this boy thinks you're hot."

Her cheeky stare vaulted south, but any excitement lurking within Nick's soaked boxers was sadly absent. Nick was right; cold water didn't do guys any favors. Shrinkage was real—real frustrating…at least for Evie.

Nick fussed with the band of his boxers as if he had read her mind. His sudden shyness about his body was unexpected and endearing.

"Sorry I'm such a wimp about everything." He grimaced, impatient waves lapping their ankles. "God, you have Crohn's, something scary for real, and I'm flipping out over a bloody clam."

"I get freaked out, too, especially about heights," said Evie. "You should've seen me on the steep escalators in the Tube." Her eyes strayed down to her left where a small 'spoot' of water shot upward from the sand. "Oh, speak of the devil!" Evie pointed. "*That* was a razor clam. When they sense vibrations, they spit water before burrowing into the sand."

Nick squinted. "Weird little fucker."

They hopped over a swathe of broken shells and some green sea foam kissing the shoreline. "Lots of people eat them," said Evie, her voice competing with the Lab barking along the beach. "I'm not fond, but my parents are." She bent down and collected a plastic six-pack ring entwined with seaweed.

"What about Sam? Does he like them?" Nick shivered.

"Why?" She dropped the plastic ring beside her backpack for disposal later and scooped up a towel, giving it a terse shake. "You wanna try 'em as some sort of male bonding exercise, Mr. Fake Shellfish Allergy?" Nick and Sam's friendship had drifted somewhat, and Evie leaned into the opportunity to pull them back together again. Grinning, she flung the blue terrycloth over his shoulder.

Nick wrapped the towel around his body and began blotting shiny beads of saltwater from his chest. "Not really. Just curious."

Evie kneeled down and claimed her towel, covering herself with the cozy material.

"Do you ever resent him?"

She wasn't expecting that. Rubbing her jaw, she stood. "Who, Sam? For what?"

"For going to school, becoming a vet," said Nick, slicking back his dripping mop of hair. "Why does he get to pursue his dream career, but you have to shelve yours for the shop? That hardly seems fair…"

"Who says I'm shelving mine?"

"You said you wanted to be an author at the County Show."

He remembers?! Evie tugged her necklace. Of course she fancied the idea—writing for a living, who wouldn't?—but Evie knew such pie-in-the-sky stuff didn't happen to girls like her. She flashed a smile and released her pendant. "Oh, *that*. Yeah, I was fooling around. I thought I wanted to be an astronaut, too, few years ago!" She bent sideways, her pulse pounding in her ears as she kneaded excess water from her hair.

"But working four part-time jobs and saving madly for a uni degree you don't actually *need* doesn't sound like fooling around, Tigs. That sounds like an escape, a path toward your dream. Not your mum's or your grandmother's—*yours*."

How can I explain this so he'll understand? Evie glanced at the orange buoys bobbing in the Sound, marking underwater lobster creels. "Yeah, but the women on my mum's side of my family run the shop. It's always been that way—for a hundred years." Giving her hair one last squeeze, she straightened up and pulled her towel tighter. "It's a Marwick tradition. I'm proud of it, actually."

"But traditions aren't set in stone, Evie," said Nick.

"Hello? Have you *been* to Orkney?" She laughed, hoping humor would soften his concerns and dampen his curiosity. Nick was such a sweetheart, but his pressing questions about university were circling a little too close for comfort. She didn't want to be the object of his pity.

"But if the shop's your future, why spend all that money to study at uni? It doesn't make sens—"

"So I don't feel left behind, okay?" she blurted, shutting him up. "Crohn's has stolen so much from me. Just *once* I'd like to be like everyone else!" Her ribs squeezed. *Nice one, idiot. Now he's gonna think you're pathetic.*

Nick's expression deflated. "Oh, Evie." His fingers brushed away a smattering of dried sea salt from her cheek. "I get it." He opened his arms.

She leaned in, welcoming his embrace. "I'll go for three years, experience life beyond the island, then come home and mind the shop."

"But what if you fall in love with that big wide world?"

Your world? The truth burned in Evie's throat. "I don't know."

The last days of August breezed by in a blur of romantic rendezvous, Nick's driving lessons (he only stalled her mum's car twice), and monologue practice (Evie helped Nick perfect his audition piece for *Plunder the Crown* inside the Broch of Gurness). The shortening summer days also signaled the start of Evie's final year of secondary school and exams, which, along with Nick's journey to London for his coveted fifth callback, delayed their trip to Hoy. With her boyfriend away temporarily, Evie had plenty of time for a gossip and a post-class takeaway with Sunita and newly minted university student, Fiona.

"I thought doing it at the beach would be sexy." Evie set her orange pop on the wooden bench and gazed across The Willows, a small parkette with a few trees and a babbling brook not far from Kirkwall Grammar.

Sunita's deep-fried mozzarella stick stalled between her mouth and its grease-stained polystyrene box on her lap. "Hell no! Where'd you get that from?"

"The Sexcapades column."

"In *Bella Faith*? Eves, those submissions are anonymous for a reason. It's people talking shit. The beach is the last place you wanna fuck." She leaned into Evie's right shoulder. "Seriously, all that sand shoved up your vag—"

"Sunita!" Seated on Evie's left, Fiona burped as she lowered her cherry cola. "We're eating!"

"Or trying to!" added Evie, plunging her plastic knife and fork into a pattie, the ultimate in Orcadian comfort foods. As she cut away the golden, deep-fried batter, the aromatic sweetness of onions mixed with potato and mincemeat made her mouth water—despite the questionable path their conversation was veering.

"All I'm saying is, it's a one-way ticket to UTI town," said Sunita. "Case in point, remember *wassername*? The fifteen-year-old who had the affair with our old PE teacher?" Evie and Fiona nodded. "She came in the pharmacy sobbing. Couldn't pee for an entire day!"

Fiona munched through a crispy onion ring. "God, how's that even possible?"

Sunita shrugged. "Why are you spending so much time at the beach anyway?"

"We're running out of places to snog." Evie yawned. "We got caught behind The Odin Hotel in Mum's car—"

"You didn't tell us that!" Fiona laughed.

"'Cause it was embarrassing! Gemma found us."

"The cook?" asked Sunita.

"Yeah, who used to babysit me and Sam. She said she wouldn't tell Mum if we promised never to come back. And now that school's in, we can't come here anymore. It's too busy." Evie glanced over her shoulder at the beloved fish and chip shop across the street, a lunch- and dinner-time staple for ravenous students.

"There's always Tankerness House gardens," said Fiona.

"No, go to Stromness." Sunita lowered her voice as a group of girls in the year below crossed the nearby footbridge. "It's super private."

Fiona leaned forward. "And a twenty-minute drive!"

"But worth every second," said Sunita. "All the tight alleys and closes? Puggie and I used to go there—well, until he hooked up with Rebecca."

Evie reached over and patted her forearm.

Sunita waved her off. "I'm over it. I'm all about blonds now."

"Why doesn't Nick come to yours?" asked Fiona, dunking the edge of her burger in a small pot of curry sauce. "Aren't your parents out at choir practice twice a week?"

"Bedroom it is, then!" Sunita chomped her mozzarella stick.

"Mum likes Nick. She's fine with him coming over. We just can't go to my room," said Evie.

"That's ridiculous." Fiona scoffed. "Like you can't get pregnant on your sofa!"

"Screw it, go up anyway!" Sunita mumbled through a mouthful of gooey cheese. "How would she know?"

"Sam for starters. He's been so weird about me dating Nick." Evie stabbed a chip. "I can't risk it. Mum said she'll take away my car privileges if we get 'carried away'!"

"His gran's then," said Sunita, her suggestion backed up by Fiona's exuberant nodding. "That house is HUGE."

"I wouldn't know," Evie murmured. "He hasn't asked me in."

Fiona's eyes bulged. "Still?! But you pick him up there."

Evie frowned. Rupert had been taking Fiona to his gran's since they started dating two summers ago.

"I thought you were having tea with his gran last night? Rupert said—"

"Last-minute change of plans. Nick's audition got moved up and he flew out yesterday. I was sitting my mock history exam and couldn't say goodbye." She blinked woefully, remembering their trips to the cinema and the exuberant singalongs to the *Jesus Christ Superstar* cast recording in the car afterward. "I miss summer."

"You worried about him going back to uni?" asked Sunita.

She nodded. "He's got loads of friends, many of 'em girls. They're all over his Facebook." Evie had spent far too much time on his profile, comparing herself to Bree and the others. All trendy and perfectly coiffed, some of Nick's female friends looked like they'd stepped out of the glossy pages of *Bella Faith*.

"But he's into *you*, Eves," said Fiona, swapping her half-eaten burger for her deep-fried Mars bar. "Even Rupert says so, and he rarely comments on Nick's love life."

She dropped her knife and fork. "Well then, shouldn't things be progressing quicker? Why hasn't he made a move on me? I can feel him against me when we're kissing. I know he's—"

"Up for it?" Sunita waggled her brows.

Fiona rolled her eyes. "Hello, Captain Obvious."

"His body might be, but who knows about his mind. He seems unsure, like he's trying to decide: do I take this further or not? Meanwhile, I'm *dying* to do way more than kiss." Evie chewed her lip. She'd stayed up till two a.m. the night before, her journal ablaze with erotic scribbles.

"You're obsessing over his fingers again, aren't you?" Sunita laughed. "And where they might go…"

"Well, they are *long*!" said Fiona.

A familiar warmth throbbed low in Evie's belly. "I wanna feel him *everywhere*."

"I think it's lovely, him not rushing," said Sunita. "Nick respects you, which is more than can be said for dickhead Stuart."

"You've changed your tune," said Fiona.

"A lot's happened in three years, Fi." Stealing two of Evie's chips, Sunita sighed wistfully then dunked them in her ketchup. "I'm older and I'm definitely wiser, 'kay?"

"Nick's a sweetheart. He doesn't want to push you into anything," said Fiona.

"And I *appreciate* it. Truly!" said Evie. "But Nick's *respect* is driving me to a whole lotta wanking. I'm gonna get carpal tunnel."

"Patience, dear Evie." Fiona fluttered her eyelashes knowingly. "If Nick's anything like Rupert, he's worth waiting for."

Two weeks later, September blew in bringing cooler temperatures, the fall harvest, and Nick. School and work ate up Evie's days, but on occasion, they'd watch DVDs (hello, *Grease 2*) and play games (Jenga and Mouse Trap) at hers or she'd beg off sick from her evening shifts at the laundromat and meet Nick in the secluded laneway beside the stationery shop in Stromness. Turned out, Sunita was right. The town's narrow alleys and claustrophobic closes were perfect for clandestine conversations and rapturous kisses.

That is, until someone told Nick's gran about these surreptitious trysts and Evie was promptly summoned to dinner.

Lily Balfour may have been Hoy born and raised, but her humble roots were nowhere on display, replaced by a wealthy husband, a lavish home surrounded by acres of farmland, and a familial legacy unmatched elsewhere in Orkney. She had also given birth to Nick's nasty father making Evie wonder—had *that* apple fallen far from the Balfour family tree?

The creaky hardwood in the chandelier-lit hallway suggested she was about to find out.

"So this is the Orkney lass who puts a smile on my grandson's face!" Lily flung open her arms and beckoned for a hug. "I'm so happy to finally meet you, Evie!"

Squashed within the seventy-two-year-old's formidable embrace, Evie found a sweet, unpretentious woman who cherished her grandson and the islands' traditional ways as much as she did. A mutual Orcadian admiration society was born.

That initial dinner became two, then three, which morphed into an open invitation to drop in "anytime to see Nick." Lily didn't just like Evie, she seemed to adore her—and happily encouraged their relationship.

If only they had more time.

In less than twenty-four hours, Nick would be back in Salford, stocking his apartment's fridge and preparing for his second year of university. Evie dreaded the thought of driving him to the airport the next day, but she slapped on a smile, bought an applesauce cake from the bakery in town, and headed to Lily's. Nick was out on a misty morning walk with Ross, so she settled in with his grandmother, enjoying cinnamon tea and a heartfelt chat.

"I love hearing your stories. I'm gonna miss these visits." Evie broke off a chunk of cake and spotted raisins inside. Her stomach clenched.

"Miss them?" asked Lily.

"When Nick's back at uni."

"Evie sweetheart, you're welcome here anytime, with or without my grandson. In fact, I think you, Fiona, and I should make dinner and a swadge afterward a regular thing. It's more fun to gossip when the lads aren't about."

"True!" Evie grinned.

"Can I let you in on a little secret?" asked Lily. "You're the first girlfriend of Nikolai's I've met."

Evie's heart did a sloppy cartwheel. "He's never brought them up here?"

"Nikolai isn't like his brothers," explained Lily. "They love coming up with their city friends, going on hikes and swimming in the sea. But Nick never has. I think he's always preferred to keep his London life separate, away from the rustic living we enjoy here."

Evie subtly studied the room with its antique chandeliers, Italian mosaic tile fireplace, and leather club chairs. Rustic wasn't the word she'd use.

"He's very much his mother's son in that way," said Lily. "I blame the acting. Always having things done for him, always being put on a pedestal—and from such a peedie age, too. Every year, though, I hope he'll fall in love with our bonny island. Now if it happens, you'll be the one I'll thank."

Evie sat up, the jingle of dog tags traveling down the hall. "Me?"

"Yes, Evie. You. I'm not one to meddle, but you're the type of girl Nikolai needs—a kind, smart Orcadian lass with her feet on the ground."

Lily's compliment felt warm and supportive like one of her epic hugs, but a ripple of worry gnawed, too. If Nick liked to keep his London life separate as Lily professed, did that mean *she* was a secret? That their relationship was a secret?

What happens in Orkney, stays in Orkney?

Ross scampered around the doorjamb and made a beeline toward Evie, bumping his small white snout against her knee. She scratched him behind his peaked ears as his curved tail whirled happily.

"See?" Lily lowered her teacup. "Even Ross approves."

"Approves of what?" Nick strolled into the room, his jogging attire (an expensive collaboration between Adidas and a designer Evie had never heard of) dappled with raindrops. He unzipped the jacket.

"Never you mind, Nikolai." Lily smiled, clearly her famous grandson's number one fan. "I've monopolized Evie for far too long. I know you don't have much time together before university calls." She quickly assembled two plates of strawberries, marshmallow biscuits, and slices of Evie's store-bought cake. "Take this upstairs. Should be enough to hold you over till lunch." She looked at Evie as Nick hung his jacket on the back of a chair. "You'll stay, I hope?"

After an enthusiastic yes, a chin covered in slobbery kisses from Ross, and a trek upstairs, Evie entered Nick's bedroom for the first time.

"The inner sanctum," she joked, peeking beneath the plates in her hands as she stepped over a TV remote and several splayed fashion magazines on the hardwood floor.

"Excuse the mess," said Nick, shifting a stack of clean socks and underwear off the unmade queen-size bed and onto a neighboring chair, already adorned with jeans and a wrinkled button-down. "Mum called this morning in crisis as per. I didn't have time to tidy." He pulled his phone from his pocket and tossed it on the crumpled duvet.

Evie gazed around the sizable but sparsely decorated room, the lack of personal possessions hinting at someone passing through. "Is she okay?" Glancing left, she was lured in by a messy hodgepodge of photos taped to the wall. *No way!* She gawped. *Nick met Kate Moss?!*

"Yeah, but I had to remind her for the millionth time…"

A rustle turned Evie's head.

Nick's t-shirt sailed over his damp hair. "…Mum, I am *not* your life coach." Balling it up, he stooped and tugged down his designer track pants.

Oh my god. Evie ogled him shamelessly as he stepped free. He adjusted the elastic waistband of his gray boxer briefs and strolled across the room, discarding his sweaty clothes in the closet's laundry basket. She'd seen Nick in his undies before at the beach, but they were baggy boxer shorts, the opposite of these gems, which hugged and displayed *ev-er-y-thing*. There was no shrinkage, no shielding hands this time. *Yep, Nick's definitely got a lot to work with!*

Want twisted in her stomach as she suppressed her delighted grin. She walked to his desk and set down the treat-filled plates, careful not to disturb an open script and a crochet project in progress. *He crochets?* As she peered over her shoulder, Nick pulled up his jeans by the fireplace. She pouted playfully. *Show's over—for now.*

"So you and Gran looked thick as thieves."

Evie smiled. "I like her. She gets me."

Nick dug through a hefty chest of drawers and removed a faded *Wicked* t-shirt. "I reckon she sees herself in you."

"Really? I'll take that as a compliment."

He stuffed his arms through the tee first, then his head. "You should!"

Evie studied his time capsule of a room, its vaulted ceiling crossed by exposed wooden beams. Toy cars crowded his bookshelves, parked alongside a stack of old board games, an ancient television, and Horton the Elephant. The childhood mementos carried over to the fireplace's mantle, too, where a crew of *Equinox Ten* action figures stood guard. She picked up a small boy dressed in a blue and silver space suit. "Look, it's peedie Nick! Do you play with yourself a lot—?"

His phone woke up, the instrumental Green Day hit replaced by an old school ring. He leapt toward his bed. "Ahh, it's Polly, my agent."

Evie sat at his desk as Nick breathlessly answered with "Hiya!" Privacy out of the question, she bowed her head and dissected Nick's cake slice with a fork, picking free all the hidden raisins.

He didn't say much. A serious "Yeah" and an "Okay" or two, then finally an all-business "Will do. Cheers."

Banishing the offending fruit into a pile, Evie swiveled to face him, but Nick was staring out the window. "All good?" she asked, setting down the fork.

"No, not really...*Plunder the Crown*," he murmured into a flurry of blinks. "Went to someone else." Dropping the phone on the bed, he let out a long exhale then shielded his mouth with his hand.

Someone who?! An ache panged in Evie's chest. *How? Why?* None of this made sense. She'd seen Nick's audition monologues. He'd slayed every line, every emotion, his borrowed Yorkshire accent was bang on—he would've been perfect. Evie rose from the chair, fury and sorrow tangling her tongue. "B-but this is bullshit! They brought you in *five* times!"

Shaking his head in disbelief, Nick closed his eyes and swallowed hard. "I-I thought I'd fucking nailed it. This was gonna be my comeback."

A "comeback" at the tender age of twenty? The notion made Evie crumble inside.

"I can't be a has-been." He sniffed, his tearful eyes looking imploringly into Evie's.

How awful to be so young and feel like your career is over. Her chin began to quiver. *No doubt, his mother will blame him, too.*

Evie gathered Nick in her arms, hugging him close. "I'm so sorry…" She could feel his heart thrashing through his t-shirt. "I know how much you wanted this."

Closing his eyes again, Nick buried his face in her neck. His jagged breaths puffed against her skin in short, quick bursts. "I can't catch a break. I-I don't know what to do—" A strangled sob broke through his lips.

His declaration wasn't a question, but there was only one answer.

"Breathe." Evie stroked the back of his head. "One breath, then another and another." She inhaled through her nose to the count of four, then let the exhale escape slowly as she counted to six in her head. "Like this. We'll do it together, okay?"

Nick lifted his head, tears spilling through his lashes. Evie had seen him cry twice before on *Dalston Grove*, when his TV baby was born and when Amanda died, but this pain wasn't for the cameras or ratings or lovestruck fangirls. It was authentic and deep. Vulnerable. The real Nick.

And like the afternoon behind Marwick's, Evie fell for him a little further.

"Okay." Nick took in a staggered breath then released it with a shudder. "I'm sorry I'm such…a loser." His bloodshot eyes skirted her gaze.

A sharp tickle throbbed in Evie's nose. She cupped his face in her hands, his tears dampening her fingers. "You're many things, Nick Balfour, but you're not a loser. Not even close."

"Yeah, but me crying is so—"

"Beautiful," Evie interjected as her eyes began to sting. "It's good to cry. It shows you care, shows things matter, *feelings* matter. Never be ashamed about that."

Nick's lips tweaked at the corners as he inhaled…and then

slowly exhaled…

"There's nothing weak about you, Nick. No matter what stupid shit your dad says, okay?" She swallowed hard. "The way you feel so deeply is one of the reasons why I like you so much."

Like.

As soon as that four-letter L-word slipped from her tongue, Evie knew it was a major copout. She *liked* French toast, daisies, and *The X Factor*, not Nick! Looking into his eyes, Evie's unspoken truth, warm and sweet like the first bloom of spring's snowdrops after a harsh winter, filled her chest. *I LOVE YOU. So much. Always have, always will.*

Saying it aloud, however, would have to wait. It was one gamble too many, and Evie wasn't ready to roll those dice. Not yet.

"You're too good for me, you know that?" He smiled through his tears.

She pressed the pad of her finger against his cheek and rescued a lost eyelash. "Hey, look. Make a wish?"

"Yeah. Go on, then." He sniffed then blew the lash free from her finger.

Evie was dying to know what Nick had hoped for—fewer panic attacks, another TV series, an easy year at university—but didn't ask. She leaned in and caressed his wet cheek. "It'll be okay. You're stronger than you know…"

"Because you're with me." Nick kissed her forehead, and Evie squeezed her eyes tight, wishing university and jobs and distance weren't conspiring to keep them apart. The next day, Nick would fly south to Manchester, and an agonizing countdown would commence. Christmas break felt like years away.

"I hate leaving you." He sniffed again. "Emails and calls aren't the same. I'm gonna miss you, Tigs."

A sob lodged in her throat as her tears escaped. "Me too. So much."

"Maybe I could fly up sometime, surprise you?"

"Really?!" She wiped her cheeks.

He nodded. "I want you with me always."

Then Evie had a thought.

She reached behind her neck and beneath her hair, unfastening her necklace. She held up her favorite piece of jewelry, its open chain a silver smile between them. "Wear this and a part of me will be with you…"

His watery eyes widened. "You want me to wear it?"

Embarrassment pooled in her gut. She fisted the chain and looked away. "I know. It's a stupid idea—"

"No!" Nick clutched her hand, prying her fingers open. "It's lovely." He rescued the silver *Evie* from her palm.

"You sure?"

"Yeah. I only asked because you never take it off!" Nick draped it around his neck and fastened it closed. His fingers slid down the chain and across the swirly script of her name. "But are *you* sure you trust me with it?"

Like she trusted him with her heart? Evie sniffed. "One hundred percent."

TWENTY

NICK

Now, Tuesday, July 25

Five days following the orca rescue, Nick's heart taunted and teased. Not even a quick jaunt down to London and back for several urgent meetings nor their pending job offer could compete with the soft warmth of Evie in his arms. Soaked and shivering, it reminded him of their first summer as a couple: swimming at Evie Beach, snogging in the shadows of Stromness, and making plans for a future together.

A future that never materialized.

And you only have yourself to blame.

Scolding himself as he left Kirkwall's Tesco with a bag of snacks, Nick slipped further into his Sanday reverie: how Evie softened in his embrace, how she ogled his lips as if they were something she craved. She seemed more relaxed, more open, the closest she'd been to the old Evie he knew and loved.

Well, at least that's what Nick perceived. Whether he was reading more into what had transpired on that remote beach was a worrisome question, one that stole sleep and fucked up budget calculations. Seeing Evie would hopefully dispel his fears.

Or confirm them.

Cutting across the parking lot, Nick spotted a familiar face exiting a small terraced house on West Tankerness Lane. Fondness swelling in his chest, he tucked his phone into his jacket and jogged toward her. "Hey! Just the person I was coming to see." His appreciative gaze pored over Evie's denim jacket and the daisy-patterned knee-length dress underneath. Recalling the flowery frock she wore when she comforted him during a panic attack as a teen, his heart

241

did a nostalgic somersault.

Evie slowed to a stop. "Don't tell me—three days in London and you wanna add a full English to tomorrow's breakfast options?" She cocked a brow, a grin rising.

"Ooh, now that you mention it…" His seriousness cracked with a laugh. "Actually, no. I was wondering if we could hang out." The production was taking a rare midweek day off before a laborious stretch of filming on the southern island of Hoy.

"I can't. I'm sorry." Evie adjusted the canvas tote on her shoulder, an oatmeal-hued carry-all emblazoned with an Orkney Library & Archive logo in purple. "I have errands to run before I relieve Fi and Jamie in the shop."

"Let me help, then. Many hands make light work."

Evie jutted out a hip. "It's nothing glam, Nick. You'll be bored within seconds."

"If I am, I'll buy you lunch."

She motioned toward Great Western Road. "Well, you better have deep pockets 'cause I skipped breakfast and could gobble up all of Kirkwall."

"Hold that thought…" Nick rooted around his shopping bag and pulled out a packet of Tunnock's Snowballs. "I saw these and thought of you."

A slow smile tugged the corners of her mouth. "You remember?"

"Of course. Hopefully, you still like them."

"I *love* them. Thank you." She accepted the treats and tore open the end. "I'd offer you one but…"

"Yep, still not a coconut fan."

Removing a single marshmallow, Evie tucked the package into her tote.

"Your dress is pretty."

"Oh! Thanks." Her grin reached her eyes. "Me and daisies…"

"Yeah. I remember that, too." Nick's gaze lingered, mingling with hers.

Until she glanced away.

"So…you sleeping better?" She took a substantial bite and chewed happily, flecks of coconut riding her lips.

"A bit, yeah. I blame the sea air." Nick smiled as her tongue flicked, licking away the coconut. *Christ, she's killing me.* He pointed over his shoulder. "So was that your place?"

"No, Gemma's. You probably don't remember her."

"Didn't she catch us snogging behind The Odin?"

"Yeah, that's her!" Evie looked away quickly, but Nick still caught a hint of her bashful grin as she finished the Snowball. "She was our catering cook until the puppet crash."

"How's she doing?"

"Much better. Just had a second surgery on her arm." She licked marshmallow off her fingers and pointed at the large building coming up on their right. "The library is my first stop."

Nick followed Evie under a metal arch and down a narrow laneway to the front entrance. She picked up a recipe book on hold and was about to leave when a passing librarian called out.

"Evie, I loved your book about that singer! I'm telling everyone to read it."

Your book? Nick turned, but Evie's smile was for the equally smiley librarian.

"Oh, thanks, Mrs. Kumari!"

"Anything for you, love!" Sunita's mother waved and resumed shelving books.

Evie led Nick outside. "Next two stops are on Albert Street." They rushed across a zebra crossing and continued down the road.

Nick's thoughts, however, were still lingering in the library. "What book was she talking about?"

"Oh. Just something I wrote."

Happiness bubbled in his chest. "*You?!*"

"I do some work on the side as a ghostwriter. Sunita introduced me to a publisher when I lived in London." They sauntered right onto a pedestrian-only lane leading to Marwick's and the cathedral.

"Evie, that's *brilliant*! What genre?"

"Biographies, mostly."

243

Nick beamed, taking her in. "Holy Christ! You're a published author!"

"I am, yeah." With his gaze unrelenting, Evie pointed at a broken chunk of pavement. "Uh, Nick? Be careful. Tripping hazard."

He reined in his stare with an "Oh, cheers" as he swerved the crater. "I am *so* chuffed for you! Wow. You writing anything now?"

"A few things."

"And this all started in London?"

She nodded.

"I knew you'd find it inspiring there." Following Evie's lead, Nick turned left onto Broad Street, skipping Marwick's altogether.

"It was for a while, but the noise, the crowding—got old really fast."

"How long have you been back?"

"It'll be four years in December." She adjusted the tote on her shoulder. "I came home after I was mugged."

Halting midstride, Nick reeled with shock. "Holy shit! Where?"

Evie stopped. "Ladbroke Grove. I was walking to work one Sunday morning and a guy grabbed me, held a lead pipe to my temple and demanded my phone."

"Bloody hell!" Nick covered his mouth as they set off again. "Did he hurt you?!"

"Just mentally. On the spot, I decided, *I'm done*. I quit my job and flew home a week later."

"That's terrible."

"Scariest moment of my life," said Evie. "In hindsight, though, it was the kick in the pants I needed. London was just another attempt to be someone I wasn't. I mean, seriously, cut me and I bleed salt water and groatie buckies, standing stones and the Ba'. Orkney is home and always will be. London was fun and somewhat inspiring, but in the end it wasn't for me. Not in the long run, anyway."

Evie's distaste for London post-mugging was hardly surprising, and yet, disappointment brewed in Nick's chest. London would always be *his* home, regardless of where he rested his head at night.

They crossed Castle Street and sauntered beneath the colorful bunting stretching from one side of narrow Albert Street to the other. Evie greeted almost everyone who passed by with a bubbly "Hi." For Nick, many of the storefronts were unfamiliar, owing to the changing tides of taste and commerce on a small island; however, two things set off his nostalgia: Kirkwall's much loved Big Tree, a two-hundred-year-old sycamore leaning precariously into the street, and a familiar model of blue SUV parked close by.

He gestured toward the vehicle. "Now that takes me back. Sitting behind the wheel, you giving me private lessons." His gaze locked with Evie's as their swaying hands almost touched. "And the driving tips were great, too."

As her lips parted, a blush reddened her cheeks. "We had some great adventures, that's for sure."

And some horrible misunderstandings. Fiddling with his bag of shopping, Nick flashed a tight smile then peered ahead. *The only way to move forward is to discuss them, but how? When?*

Out of the corner of his eye, Evie seemed restless, too, her fingers curling and uncurling along the strap of her tote.

Nick cleared his throat and chickened out, resorting to a safe topic. "I meant to ask, how are your parents?"

"Good. They're on a cruise right now, somewhere between Hawaii and Australia."

Australia. Nick's pulse ramped up.

Evie must've felt the tension in the air as soon as she said it because she quickly chirped, "Next stop," and darted through the bookshop's door.

Once inside, Nick lingered by the bestseller shelves, relieved for the respite. Evie walked up to the counter and greeted the blonde clerk with a smiley "Hi, Peggy" in exchange for a jovial "Take your time, love" and a towering stack of novels.

Picking up an acclaimed thriller, Nick spied Evie flipping open the cover of a Cordelia Ross romance novel. She wrote something inside with a Sharpie.

What the...? Breath catching, his jaw slowly dropped. He set down the thriller and meandered over as she signed another copy.

"Oh my god, you're—"

"Cordelia Ross." Evie closed the cover and moved on to the next book.

"Historical romance author." Nick blew out his lips. "I narrated your audiobook."

"I know, two years ago. My third novel."

"I had no idea Cordelia was you! The dedication and acknowledgments were pretty vague. Why don't you use your real name?"

"Kinda like you with acting," said Evie. "It's freeing being someone else, right? Being reborn with zero baggage."

"That's true."

Evie looked thoughtful. "Cordelia is sexy and well-traveled, loves sea bass and steak. She can wear jeans without them pinching and doesn't worry how exhausted she'll be after a night out on the razz." She signed a swirly *Cordelia Ross* in two more books.

"How'd you come up with the name?"

"I wanted something beautiful but meaningful: Cordelia was the role I played in *King Lear* when I was fifteen, and I think you know who Ross was." Her voice cracked.

My dog. She loved him like her own.

Taking a minute, she cleared her throat and autographed three more books. "As Cordelia, I can write and fly under the radar. I'm not as good with being recognized as you are." She closed the cover on the last book.

Nick promptly scooped it up and smiled at the clerk. "I'll buy this."

"*Nick.*" Putting away her marker, Evie shook her head. "You don't have to."

"I want to. You never used to let me read what you wrote."

"You read the third one. You narrated it, silly."

"And it was fantastic. I'm sure this one is even better." He tapped his card on the payment terminal.

"Ah, the pressure!"

With a nod of thanks, Nick collected the bag containing Evie's signed book from Peggy and they departed the shop.

"That was really sweet of you." Evie grinned as he held open the door. "Thanks."

"Hey, it's like a prophecy come true." Nick smiled back. "You always said I'd ask for your autograph one day."

After errands to the pharmacy and post office where Evie mailed off signed copies of her latest romance to contest winners, they strolled to Marwick's. Nothing monumental was discussed. Instead Nick and Evie's conversation stuck to the fringes, sidestepping anything hostile or quarrelsome. Orkney's (continued) lack of a bowling alley came up, as well as anecdotes about Tarquin and Rupert, and how much Evie was looking forward to filming around Hoy.

She stopped in front of her shop. "Well done, you! Not a single yawn."

"What can I say? You're still the only person I know who makes a trip to the pharmacy fun."

She impishly smacked his arm. "You're only saying that 'cause you didn't wanna buy me lunch!"

"No, I would—I will!"

"I'm kidding!" Evie patted her belly. "I'm thirty-one and still haven't learned that eating half a packet of Snowballs isn't the smartest idea."

"Jeez, sorry about that."

Her eyes popped wide. "Don't be. I enjoyed every second."

A flush of happiness roused his smile. "Me too." Nick licked his lips. *I don't want this to end.* His pulse quickened as he wound the handles of his shopping bags around his fingers, dying to spill his truth.

But a buzz sounded inside Evie's tote and the moment was lost. "Oh, that's probably…" She unearthed her phone and grinned. "*Yep.* Fi ordering my ass inside NOW!" She rubbernecked through the shop's window.

"Rain check for lunch?"

As she looked back, Nick swore Evie bounced lightly on the spot. "Sure." She flicked her head, tossing her bangs from her eyes. "Where you headed now?"

He lifted his bookshop bag. "Back to the hotel. If this is anything like your third novel, I know I'm in for some epic sexy times."

She leaned in. "Page ninety-nine, one hundred and forty-two, one hundred and eighty-six, and two hundred and forty."

"You memorized them?"

Evie held his gaze. "You'd be surprised what I've committed to memory."

You and me both, sweetheart. Nick's smile stiffened as he tried not to beam. "And on that bombshell…"

"Happy reading." Evie pushed open the door. "Oh…and Nick?"

He turned around. "Yeah?"

"You weren't my first choice."

Like a pin to a balloon, Evie's words deflated all the giddiness in Nick's chest. "For…?"

"Narrator. My publisher pushed for you. She thought your scandal might sell more books."

He scratched his temple. "And did it?"

She punched the air. "*Sunday Times* bestseller, baby!"

"Good girl. Making lemonade out of my lemons."

"Well, I am your *caterer*, right?"

"You are." Nick's heart panged. *And so much more.*

TWENTY-ONE

EVIE

Then, Friday, August 6, thirteen years ago

Evie knew long-distance relationships sucked; she just didn't know they could suck this much. Of the past three hundred and twenty-seven days, Nick had been in her orbit for a measly ninety-six hours. The culprits were unavoidable: Evie's studying and final exams, Nick's university course and production internship (dragging through June), and Kiki's last-minute 'mum and sons' getaway to Greece (swallowing up most of July), but Nick promised he'd make up for it. The rest of the summer would be just the two of them, and best of all, he'd be back in her arms the evening of August 6—the one-year anniversary of their first kiss on the trampoline. Evie had bought a new outfit, booked the weekend off work, and vowed to show Nick exactly what he'd been missing since their last desperate kiss during April's Easter break.

But Nick was missing out on more than kisses.

Thanks to a June Crohn's flare, Evie was taking prednisone, an inflammation-reducing steroid, notorious for side effects including bruising, acne, and facial swelling not-so-lovingly called moon face. Round and bloated, Evie's cheeks were chipmunk-esque. Cute on a baby; not so cute on a self-conscious eighteen-year-old reuniting with her sex-on-legs boyfriend. Nick knew Evie was at the tail end of the flare, but she'd carefully omitted the distressing change in her appearance, trusting her doctor's word that, as she tapered off the medication, the swelling would vanish completely. Unfortunately, after swallowing her final dose, she still felt puffy and still felt worrisome twinges in her belly.

Everything else, though, was picture perfect. The previous day,

Evie had received her final exam results and two firm offers for university, and tonight she was staying over at Sunita's—at least *that* was what she'd told her mum. DJ Klimaxx (otherwise known as Tarquin) was also throwing the biggest party of the year, if not the decade. Taking over his grandmother's largest pasture while she visited friends in Glasgow, Tarquin's dance party would provide Evie all the celebratory vibes, tunes, and fireworks she needed for a night to remember with Nick.

They had arranged to meet at nine-thirty so he could have a post-flight meal and enough time to give his baby brother a helping hand with his big show, but impatience whipped Evie's excitement into a bouncing-off-the-walls frenzy. Fiona and Sunita both agreed there was only one cure—arriving early so their best friend could dance her little heart out and burn off some pent-up, prednisone-fueled energy.

As the sunset's fiery kiss took its final bow, they picked up their day-glo wristbands from Nick's cousin Jonathan and strolled through the rusted gates of Lily's farm, passing food vans and porta potties and a table offering free bottles of water.

Evie gaped, soaking up the festive atmosphere, but it was the stage that demanded her attention. Dressed in black with a cigarette dangling between his lips, Tarquin danced and wore headphones as he spun his favorite tunes from a platform overlooking a sea of awestruck teens and young adults. Shimmering white lights coiled and climbed the temporary scaffolding, while blue strobes, pulsing in time with the music, sliced through a smoky haze. Behind Tarquin's turntables and speakers, an enormous backdrop reminiscent of the 'streaking stars' hyperdrive effect from *Star Wars* made the setup look like a speeding spaceship hurtling toward Earth.

"This is ah-may-zing!" Evie marveled.

Sunita unzipped her faux-leather bomber jacket, a hand-me-down from her sister. "Imagine having this kind of money…for a party?"

"Sam's gonna kick himself," said Evie. "He's totally missing out."

"Why'd he head back to uni early?" asked Fiona, squeezing through the crush, a bundle of unlit sparklers poking out from her mini backpack. "We've barely seen him this summer."

"I think he met someone there. Speaking of"—Evie bumped Sunita with her elbow—"check out that blond dude!" By Tarquin's side, a handsome guy in a white button-down, skinny jeans, and a rave-unfriendly blazer thumbed through a crate of 12" singles.

"That's Harry, Tarq's best friend," said Fiona. "Rupert said they're taking a gap year before uni."

"Where *is* Rupert?" Evie eyed his latest gift, a delicate gold chain circling Fiona's wrist.

"In the next field, calming the cows. I'll join him later."

"You and your boyfriends. Don't mind this third wheel!" Sunita laughed.

"Sun, you could have any guy here." Evie unbuttoned her jacket, and a simple camisole in aquamarine peeked through, skimming her stomach-torturing jeans. She reached inside, rescuing the scratchy bra strap slipping off her shoulder.

"Meh." Sunita shrugged. "I'm done with Orkney dudes."

"You should snog Harry. Or Tarquin!" Fiona smiled. "Then we'll all have a Balfour brother!"

"He *is* cute," Evie added as he began seamlessly mixing Paul Van Dyk's 'Nothing But You' into 'Children' by Robert Miles, his fist pumping the air.

"Nah. He's our age. I like 'em older like you do." Sunita grinned approvingly. "I hope you brought condoms, Eves."

"I did!" She ran her hand down the strap of her crossbody bag then not-so-stealthily yanked the itchy thong panties she'd ordered online out of her butt.

"Evie," Fiona murmured. "Stop."

Her stomach flip-flopped with nervous anticipation. "How do I look? Be honest—is my face tragic?"

"*Noo,*" both friends replied, with Fiona adding, "You look super cute."

"I don't want cute. I *want* sexy." Evie fidgeted, tugging her misbehaving bra strap back in place again. "Shit, what if I don't...*you know.*"

"Relax and it'll happen, I promise!" said Sunita.

"And if in doubt, follow Nick's lead. He'll get you there." Fiona winked. "I'm so excited for you!"

Sunita grasped Evie tight and rocked her back and forth. "You're gonna ride Nick's dick!"

Yeah, no pressure. Evie let out a shaky breath as their hug released.

Up on stage, two brunette go-go dancers joined the festivities, dancing the fuck out of their bedazzled boob tubes, ethereal angel wings, and metallic shorts so tiny their bum cheeks winked at the crowd when they twirled.

"They must be freezing their tits off," said Sunita, prompting an "I know!" from Evie as Nick and his latest pink shirt made an appearance.

Happiness bubbling up, she squealed and bounced on the balls of her feet, waving so enthusiastically she bonked Sunita in the head. Nick placed beers beside the turntables for Tarquin and Harry, but his gaze didn't wander, and Evie's greeting carved the air unseen.

"Ahhh, look at him." She leered as Tarquin spoke in Nick's ear, the desire to explore his body, for teasing kisses and toe-curling sucks sparking a dizzying heat between her thighs. "I wanna rip off his clothes and fuck him till he can't remember his name."

"That's more like it!" Fiona laughed, handing an unlit sparkler to Sunita.

Harry boosted the taller of the two angels onto a speaker while the other, all trendy pixie haircut and body glitter, grabbed hold of Nick's waist.

Evie's heart buckled along with her smile. "Looks like I'm not the only one."

Pixie girl's free hand snared a palmful of Nick's ass.

"What the hell?" Evie gasped, catching the dancer's salacious hip grind and an eyeful of blue strobe light. "Shit!" She blinked, fighting the swirly stars blinding her vision. "What's he doing?!"

"Looking embarrassed." Sunita huffed. "Jesus, she's unbuttoning his shirt!"

Peering up, Evie felt sick. "Why doesn't he push her away?"

"Those Balfour boys, polite to a fault," said Fiona.

Sunita's eyes narrowed. "That angel's gonna get a mouthful of my fist if she doesn't let go."

A former classmate, a frizzy-haired blonde accompanied by three whispering friends, strolled close, their hands busy with beer and burgers from the food vans parked in Lily's endless driveway. "All right, Noodle Nose?"

Evie bristled. "Piss off!"

Lifting her chin toward the stage, the girl smirked. "Looks like your so-called *boyfriend* is sending you a message, loud and cl—"

"FUCK. OFF!" Sunita lashed out with a rude hand gesture.

"Don't get too attached!" The interloper laughed and walked away.

Evie fiddled with her wristband as Nick danced in the woman's embrace. "What if she's right?"

"She's not!" Sunita and Fiona hollered simultaneously.

"But dirty dancing like that is so…public." Evie sputtered. "We don't even kiss in public."

"You do," said Fiona.

"Yeah, behind funfair rides and bushes. We're always hidden. Same with Stromness and the beach. We only go when it's quiet." She rubbed her cheek. "Maybe he's ashamed of me."

"Eves, he wouldn't text you at all hours and drop everything to call if he wasn't into you," said Sunita.

"Then why doesn't he have photos of me on Facebook?" A familiar ache pinched in the lower right side of her abdomen. Evie winced as Nick slid one arm around the woman's shoulders and the other beneath her knees, scooping her up. The dancer laughed and threw her head back, playfully kicking her chunky heels in gleeful protest.

Have I been kidding myself? Was he ever really mine?

Evie had certainly given it a go. All the money spent on clothes and cosmetics, copying Bree and Hayley and what was fashionable in films and *Bella Faith* magazine, chasing the need to be more girly, more pleasing, less Evie, less Orkney.

My face is so swollen and gross.

She left Nick and his twinkly angel and stared at the flattened grass beneath her knockoff Timberland boots.

I can't compete with girls like that.

Fiona whacked her arm. "He's coming." Her alert set off a boxing match in Evie's belly.

She glanced up. "Dance. Pretend everything's fine."

"Want us to say something?" asked Sunita.

"No. I'll do it," said Evie.

Neither woman budged, sticking close to Evie as Nick snaked around happy revelers, his fingers madly buttoning his shirt. Spotting his girlfriend, he gave up, leaving the top one undone.

"Evie! You're early!" Nick nodded to Fiona and Sunita then gathered her in for a tight hug. "Ohh, I've missed you!" Giving her a squeeze, he pulled back, a smattering of the dancer's body glitter shimmering high on his cheekbone. "Why didn't you text?" His gaze searched her face.

Evie ducked her head. "You looked…busy."

"Tarq saw you waving." Nick plowed a hand through his hair. "I'm glad he told me."

I bet. Evie broke their clench and resumed swaying to the music. Nick joined in with a body roll or two, his moves polished and oh so hot. He'd obviously ticked the dancing box on the performer's triple threat checklist.

I don't need no pity dance. Evie fought back a scowl.

Bending closer, his eyes narrowed. "You feeling okay? Want to head inside—"

"Who's that girl?" Evie interrupted, an edge tightening her voice.

Nick straightened up. "Uh, that's Rosamund. Olivia's best friend."

"And Olivia is?"

"Harry's girlfriend. The other—well, they're not *really* dancers. They're both up from London."

"Ahh, got it." Evie looked away. "I guess what happens in London, *doesn't* stay in London, then."

Nick's brows drew together. "Nothing's happened," he answered slowly, glancing at Sunita (arms crossed) and Fiona (eyes pleading), then back to Evie. "Tigs, I'm not into her if that's what you're—she's Tarq's friend."

"Who feels you up in public."

He edged closer. "Oh, *that*? Rozzy's off her tits on E. Makes her a bit handsy."

Rozzy? Make me puke! Glaring, Evie stopped dancing, and her bra strap slipped again.

"I couldn't push her away." Nick slowed his sway. "I wanted to, but everyone's got camera phones. If a photo of me manhandling her got out, it could hurt my career. I have to be careful."

Evie snorted, fighting with the rogue strap. "Right, so I guess that's why you refuse to hold my hand in public."

"I've never refused."

"You've never tried either."

"It's not that I don't want to. I do!" said Nick. "But you're not used to public scrutiny or being papped like I am. Did you see me in *The Mail* this week? Buying anti-fungal foot powder?"

"Eww." Sunita poked the tip of her unlit sparkler. "You have *foot fungus*?"

"*No!* My dad does. But that's my point. I want to spare Evie from all that invasive, humiliating bullshit"—he faced her again—"which is *so* stressful, and I've read that stress can flare Crohn's. I'd never do anything to hurt you."

She fought through her pout. "I'm not a holiday from your regular life, Nick."

"I know! Evie, you *are* my regular life. It's only being with you when I feel like I'm home."

The cotton wool wound tight around her heart began to unravel.

"So…you're *not* ashamed to be seen with me?"

"Does ashamed look like this…?" Nick twisted the second button on his shirt open. Hanging around his neck was her beloved necklace. "People ask me all the time, 'Who's Evie?' and I can't wait to tell them: 'She's my girlfriend, the kindest, most beautiful girl inside and out. She's a writer, helps run her family's business, and helps people research their roots.' And I couldn't be more proud." Lifting the silver pendant, Nick kissed it lovingly. "I never take it off. Tigs, you mean the world to me."

He didn't seem bothered by her swollen cheeks or fading acne either. Evie wanted to snog him into next week, but embarrassment weighed her down. "God, I feel so stupid."

"Don't. I can see how it must've looked. That's long distance, right? Toying with us." He bowed his head closer to hers, cupping her cheek. "I might not be the smartest bloke. I'm definitely not the best student on my course, but if I learned *one* thing while away at uni this year, it's this: I love you, Evie Sutherland."

She sucked in a breath as an effusive "Aww!" sprang from Fiona and Sunita.

"And no amount of distance or gropey girls will change that. I'm yours, Evie. Always."

Fizzy with joy, Evie's ongoing fight to self-censor her feelings surrendered. "I love you, too!"

Fiona shared a smile with Sunita, who removed a lighter from her jacket and set their sparklers ablaze.

"*Now* can I kiss you?" asked Nick.

Like he needed to ask. She flew at him, flinging her arms around his neck as he bent down to meet her.

Evie captured his mouth, her tongue flirting and slipping between his willing lips, eliciting a moan from Nick as he lifted her up, his hands cupping the swell of her ass. She wrapped her legs around his waist, savoring their first (truly) public kiss and let out a happy squeal, her jubilation going unheard amidst the whistle and crackle of thousands of shooting stars exploding above.

Fiona laughed naughtily and sliced the dark with her sizzling sparkler. "Tarquin's gonna be pissed! His fireworks went off at the wrong time!"

No, they didn't! Evie smiled, losing herself in another delirious kiss.

The trippy electronica of Paul Oakenfold's 'Ready Steady Go' swelled outside as Nick kicked his bedroom door closed, the song's urgent rhythm pulling a loud cheer from Tarquin's disciples.

Evie gasped between kisses, her feverish hands tearing at the buttons on Nick's shirt. "I want you so badly."

Nick's thumb stroked along her jaw. "You don't know how long I've waited for this."

"Oh, I think I might!" she answered breathlessly, ignoring the nervous jitters in her belly. *Is this really happening?* Yanking his button-down open, Evie claimed his mouth again with a hurried sweep of her tongue.

Nick kissed her deeper, harder as he stepped backward, his hand flirting with the downy hair at the nape of her neck. His tender touch aroused a shiver of pleasure and a ribbon of goosebumps along her skin.

My fantasy is FINALLY coming true! Eyes closing, she tasted and teased, staggering with him into the room until their legs collided with the bed. Suddenly, they were falling, toppling together in a gropey jumble of clashing teeth and tongues.

A burst of giggles bubbled up Evie's throat. She straddled Nick's thighs as he sat up.

"You okay?" Playfulness rippled in his voice. Tilting his head, he swept Evie's bangs from her lashes and pressed a kiss against her temple. His gaze burned with longing. "I'm sorry. I should've been here. The whole Greece thing with—"

Evie shut him up with another kiss. "It's okay," she whispered, her fingers happily in his hair. "You're here now. That's all that matters." Burying her nose in his neck, she inhaled deeply, the faint scent of body wash mingling with perspiration. *He smells amazing.* A loved-up sigh escaping, she trailed her tongue along his collarbone, the saltiness of his skin coaxing her into a long, wet suck.

Nick's head fell back with an open-mouthed groan. "Ahhh, Evie. That feels…" His throat bobbed hard. "Listen, we don't have to rush. If you're not feeling well or sure—"

"Oh, I'm sure! *SO* sure!" Evie resumed her amorous spree, peppering tiny kisses across his jaw. "It's all I think about. You"— she kissed him again—"deep inside me." Rolling her hips, she met the hot ridge straining against the zipper of Nick's jeans and drew in a sharp, celebratory breath as a swift "*Fuck*" bolted from his lips.

Smiling devilishly, Evie rested her forehead against Nick's. "I wanna watch you come."

"Yeah?" His grip loosened on her ass. "But could we, uh, discuss something first?"

"About protection?" She grazed his lower lip with her thumb. "I got us covered, SaxyBoy."

His grin tugged beneath her finger. "You're amazing, you know that?"

With a flirty response teasing on her tongue, Evie's gaze jumped upward, meeting Nick's, but instead of naughtiness staring back, a crease troubled his brow.

Her heart flipped. "What's wrong? Did I—" *Oh god!* She swept her cheek in a panic. "Is it my face?"

"*Face?* No." He dragged his hand through the front of his hair, unruly and ravished by her overeager fingers. "Evie, you—you're beautiful. You're perfect."

But…? A flutter of unease swooped in her belly.

"I'm, uh…" Nick winced and looked away. "I haven't actually…gone all the way."

Evie froze as his eye-popping confession careened, crashing into her brain's overflowing archive of Nick-centric sex fantasies. She blinked slowly, a croaky "Oh?" all she could muster.

A blush bloomed across his cheeks. "I *have* messed around, though. I've had oral, given it too. I know what the clitoris is—"

"Right!" Hoping he wouldn't divulge explicit anecdotes about his ex, Evie fell into a continuous nod as questions began exploding in her mind like heated popcorn kernels.

"But I haven't had full-on penetrative sex," he added quietly, his uneasy gaze slowly shifting, seeking hers. "I can imagine how that sounds after watching *Dalston*, but every kiss, every touch was choreographed by our director. Nothing was improvised or stolen from real life—well, not *my* life."

So Nick's a virgin—sorta. Evie's shock evaporated, surrendering to a sense of relief. He was less experienced than she was. "So…you're not like Jake at all."

"Nope. Not even close."

She smiled. "Well, I think the real Nick is way better."

He let out a held breath. "You sure?"

"Nick, who am I to judge? I'm not the most experienced either."

"You've had a long-term boyfriend."

"Who dumped me after the first time we did it."

"He *what*?"

She glanced over Nick's shoulder, a cluster of surprise gifts on his bedside table catching her eye: a notebook for writing, two plush otters holding hands with a heart that read 'You're My Otter Half', and a cellophane-wrapped bouquet of daisies, which crowded a new framed photo of…

Me.

Hair wind-tousled and eyes crinkled in giddy laughter. Nick must've snapped the picture the previous year during their first swim at Evie Beach.

She happily waved off his Stuart question. "Ancient history."

Nick softly skimmed his fingers along Evie's cheek. "Well, history won't be repeating on that score—unless you dump *me*."

"Never." She leaned in and kissed him then nuzzled into his neck. "Listen, your first time should be special. If you'd rather wait—"

"Evie, you're the one I've been waiting for."

Her heart nearly burst. She lifted her head, catching Nick's grin running wild. "Even with chipmunk cheeks?"

"*Especially* with chipmunk cheeks." He bit his bottom lip. "I have an idea. Fancy a shower?"

Evie couldn't believe her luck. *Bella Faith* magazine had listed shower sex as their Position of the Month and Nick was gagging for it—with her! An exuberant "YES!" flew from her tongue.

Within seconds, they were a storm of frantic hands and greedy mouths, leaving a path of hastily discarded clothing in their wake. Evie ached with anticipation, exploring his shoulders and chest.

Pulling back, she saw Nick's eyes were darker, needy, all traces of his earlier unease long gone. His fingers grazed her nipple through the coarse lace of her bra.

A self-conscious giggle edged past her enthusiasm. "Here, let me..." She unhooked the back clasp, shrugging the troublesome straps free, hoping Nick would still be turned on. Evie didn't have Hayley's desirable double Ds or her nipple piercing, which she boasted about in the comments on Nick's Facebook, but as her focus fell, all nagging fears of inadequacy nosedived too as she became distracted by the thick bulge straining against the thin cotton of his boxer briefs.

"Evie..." He filled his palms with her breasts, squeezing softly. She nodded and he bowed his head, taking her left nipple into his mouth, his hot tongue twirling and sucking, coaxing the hardening peak.

As she pulled in a breath, she dug into his hair, fisting the silky strands. "Harder," she whimpered, arching against his mouth. Nick complied, gently biting, licking, prodding, the insistent wickedness of his tongue around her swollen nipple intensifying the primal ache in her lower belly. If he kept this up, Evie would be liquid in seconds.

"Wait," she cried, and Nick paused, tipping his head back. "Not yet."

A smug smile awakened his dimples as he straightened up. His erection twitched, fighting its constraints. "Shower?"

Nick pushed open the shower's glass door and ran the taps, gifting her with an unobstructed view of his luscious ass sheathed in tight cotton. The thought of dragging the material down his hips and teasing his hardness with her tongue blazed a torrent of wet heat between her legs. Evie had waited seven years for her Nikolai fantasies to come true, and she couldn't wait another single throbbing second.

Let's speed things up. Shimmying free from her thong, she slid it down her legs, letting it pool in a wisp of lace on her pale pedicure. She stared at Nick's back, admiring the muscles tensing and relaxing as he tested the water's temperature with his hand, wishing she could wrap herself around him for eternity and tattoo his name across her heart. *My beautiful Nick.*

Turning, he dropped his gaze below her belly button. His quick grin and the intensity of his appraisal, ablaze with desire and delight, made Evie feel adored and bold. She rushed forward, hooking her fingers under the elastic of his boxer briefs, pulling them down.

She had never seen a more beautiful man. Granted, she'd only been naked with Stuart, but having Nick's impressive length standing to glorious attention was a panty-wetting journal entry come true.

She didn't have much time to gawk. Nick pulled her beneath the shower's warm, pulsating spray and closed the door.

Evie kissed him breathlessly. "I want your first time to be amazing."

Shifting closer, tighter, Nick's erection poked her stomach. "It already is."

He plucked a bottle of body wash from the shower's recessed shelf and squeezed a golden swirl into her hands. She mixed it with water, working the soap into a creamy lather across his shoulders and chest. Stopping for a sniff before rinsing her palms, she didn't recognize the potion's sexy scent.

"Musk and sandalwood," said Nick, his smouldering gaze

snagging on her taut nipples as he massaged her breasts. "Is this okay?"

The fact that he'd ask and put her first—unlike Stuart—made Evie love him even more.

His slick fingers circled and teased, arousing tingly shivers throughout her body. Lashes fluttering closed, she fell into a blissful nod. "Mmmhmm." She smiled and opened her eyes then met Nick's irresistible mouth, his tongue flirting and tasting as they staggered under the spray, rinsing away all traces of soap and bubbles.

Evie reached down and curled her fingers around him. *I can't believe I'm doing this.* Nick was hot, thick, and obscenely hard. She began stroking up and down.

He gasped against her lips. "Little harder. Faster…"

Evie fulfilled his wish, her grip tighter, growing more confident as Nick groaned, his lather-free fingers gliding between her legs.

Hand slowing on his erection, Evie drew in a quick breath as he slipped a finger inside her and another rubbed her clit, the sensation dizzying, more erotic than anything she'd ever experienced or imagined. Her thighs quivered and she looped her arms around his neck, the instinct to buck against his hand taking over.

Breaths ragged against her wet skin, Nick lifted her right knee, holding it by his hip. "Come, pretty Evie. Let me feel you come."

His surprise dirty talk and the deeper angle of his fingers prompted her to grind faster, chasing release, but her foot kept slipping and, along with it, her fantasy of wild first-time sex with Nick. *Why can't I do this? Concentrate!* She closed her eyes as his fingers teased and pressed, and felt her orgasm building, rising, all her senses heightened until she tightened around him and waves of throbbing pleasure ripped through her. Evie cried out, her body trembling as she clung to him, falling into breathless bliss. *My first orgasm with a guy—and it's Nick!*

"Was it okay?" he whispered, kissing her forehead.

"It was *everything*." Looking up, she caught his adorable grin and a slight shiver. Stood beyond the stream of water, Nick was sacrificing his warmth for hers. *He's freezing and I'm falling.*

Maybe this position was too ambitious, not to mention risky. "Nick?" she purred. "Wanna move to—"

"Bed?"

They didn't make it that far.

Amidst a sea of wet towels strewn across the floor, Evie dove into her bag and fished out a condom. Nick sat back and tore open the foil. Goosebumps riddled her skin as she helped him roll it on.

If this is a dream, don't let me wake up!

Nick settled between Evie's thighs, her silver name pendant swaying forward around his neck. "Okay."

Evie closed her hand around his hard, hot length. "Ready?"

He nodded, his focus intense, heavy with lust. Slowly, Evie guided him close until Nick took over, her breath hitching as inch by thick inch he pushed inside, filling her deep.

He blinked like the sensation was too much. "*Holy fuck*," he growled above her. "Evie, oh my *god*." His lips parted again in a moan of pure pleasure. "You all right?"

Letting out a low sigh, she dug her nails into his back. "So *goood*." Evie rolled her hips back and forth, the slippery friction pulling a groan from Nick's throat.

He began grinding against her, thrusting in and out slowly at first, but quickly need won out. Nick's gaze grew carnal and determined, only leaving Evie to look down where their bodies met again and again. "I don't think—I won't last…" he grunted.

Evie didn't expect a first-time marathon with Nick. She didn't expect another orgasm either. The deep feel of him, his weight moving above her, so intimate and vulnerable, was more than enough.

Mid-gasp, her fingers skated along his jaw as his hips unleashed a final frenetic thrust and a rushed "Fuuck!" fled his lips, followed by "I *love* you, Evie Sutherland!"

Fully spent, he collapsed on top of her, his weight ousting a satisfied giggle from her throat. *Now I know what all the fuss is about!*

263

TWENTY-TWO

EVIE

Now, Friday, July 28

"Our last day on Hoy," Evie murmured to herself as she parked the catering truck in the small lot in Rackwick. "The one where everyone gets to rough it."

Unlike the rest of archipelago with its green fields and extensive farmland, Orkney's second largest island was much more akin to the rugged, heather-covered Scottish Highlands with wetlands, glacial carved valleys, and mountainous hills. The production, whether intentional or not, had waded in slowly, spending its first two days on Hoy amidst the southern splendor of Melsetter House, a three-story mansion overlooking Longhope Bay where electricity and hospitality were readily available. The third and final day, however, couldn't have been more different. The northern township of Rackwick, while breathtakingly beautiful, came with little shelter, challenging terrain, and pesky midges—tiny flies with a big bite.

For the first time in a long time, Evie was hoping for unrelenting gusts. Midges hated them. She was also hoping for a problem-free day. Both Sunita and Jamie had come down with the stomach bug making the rounds and had stayed behind in Kirkwall, leaving Evie flying solo.

She hopped out of the truck feeling confident. *At least it's a small contingent to feed today.* Closing her eyes, she reached for the sky in a long overdue stretch, loosening the tightness in her muscles after an hour of travel via ferry and truck. The pop of gravel beneath tires signaled the arrival of the two SUVs carrying actors and crew, as well as the production truck loaded with cameras and equipment. Unlike Evie, who had to return to Kirkwall each night to restock, they'd been staying on the island in various hostels, B&Bs, and Hoy's lone hotel. She yawned, fighting through persistent exhaustion as she took in the dirt road leading to the curved bay and the day's shooting location, the stone croft of Burnmouth. Built in the early 19th century but now owned by the local trust, the one-room dwelling near the beach with its rare thatched heather roof, wood burning stove, and rudimentary toilet and sink in its adjacent shed was operated as a free, no-frills cottage, or 'bothy' as Orcadians called it, for campers. The lack of locks, electricity, and beds added to its rustic charm.

I hope they packed comfy shoes and bug spray. Evie yawned again. *No fancy people carriers will be driving down that path.*

The lead actors and several extras, some holding travel mugs, others wearing headphones, disembarked from one of the SUVs, their Victorian finery on display.

Evie smiled at the anachronism unfolding in front of her as Nick climbed out of the other vehicle, lavender shirt on point, jacket hung over his arm, and jeans hugging his butt to perfection.

Still hot. A giddy flutter frolicked through her chest. In the days following their catch-up during errands, their rapport had become more relaxed, and her feelings…less angry.

Their breakup had felt like the end of the world, but seeing him again and working side by side made Evie think maybe it wasn't. *Maybe I'm stronger than I thought.* She toyed with her truck's keys as Nick chatted with the production manager. *And people change, grow up. I have. So has Nick, I think.*

Spotting her, he lit up and headed her way. "Morning! It's official—Hoy is extraordinary!"

"Careful." Evie chuckled. "That sounds a little too much like you're enjoying it here."

"Well, Gran came from Hoy so can't be all bad, right? I took one of the SUVs yesterday and did a little tour, saw where she was born and lived as a young girl."

"Aw, that's great. Was it emotional?"

"Yeah. More than I expected. I wish I'd come here when she

was alive." He chewed the inside of his cheek. "I wish I'd come here with you."

Me too. Evie's ribs tightened like a vise, bottling her breath. So many times they'd planned to visit, but school, work, and family always stood in their way.

Nick glanced upward. "Hope the rain holds off."

She eyeballed the swollen clouds beyond the island's soaring red-sandstone cliffs. "You'll be okay. You're filming inside the bothy, right?"

"No, I meant for breakfast," said Nick.

"Oatmeal heats up quick. I'll have everyone fed and on their way before you know it."

"Perfect." His eyes loitered, traveling down the navy jumpsuit she had bought the previous year but was wearing for the first time. "Love the outfit by the way."

Evie's grin grew along with Nick's, the pleasure of being friends again lingering.

Today's gonna be great.

With the late lunch service completed by three p.m. and everyone down at the bothy for the last hours of filming, Evie cleaned her slow cookers, riding out each gusty lurch and tormented creak of the catering truck. Her windy wish was coming true, albeit more violently than she would've liked.

The alarm on her phone sounded, a reminder to pop an antibiotic for the sinus infection diagnosed a few days earlier. A compromised immune system was one of the side effects of her medication infusions, making her susceptible to all sorts of illnesses. When something nasty took hold, her next treatment—like the one scheduled in twenty-four hours' time—would be delayed, a situation that could trigger a flare. Evie had no choice but to cross her fingers and hope for the best.

Lowering her water bottle, she looked through the rain-beaten window. The tall grass along the path bowed as a hunched Nick, messenger bag clutched against his nylon jacket, ran on an angle, fighting to stay upright. Evie waved, ushering him in.

"Fuck me, that blew in quick." Nick slid the door closed behind him, his clothes mottled with fat raindrops. "I hope we get every-thing shot before this thing really hits."

"I thought it was going well," said Evie.

"No. It's been one crisis after another. Ashley and two actors called in sick then the generator wouldn't work. Now it's the winds playing silly buggers with the sound in the bothy." Nick removed his phone and lowered his bag to the floor as another gale rattled the truck. He braced himself against the wall. "Wow, this thing rocks—and not in a fun way!"

"This is nothing. The ferry ride will be even worse." Evie hung up a dish towel as the rain's ire grew more tenacious, lashing the window like a car wash. "You missed both meals. Are you hungry? I can make you a sandwich or"—she flipped open a large box on the counter and lifted a cupcake with blue icing—"I saved this one for you."

Nick's eyes shone as he set his phone down. "Smurfy blue!" He claimed the dessert, admiring it aloft. "You know me so well."

I used to. Evie smiled wistfully. "I guarantee it doesn't contain weed."

Nick snickered and pulled off the paper liner. "Been there, done that, have the trampolining scars to prove it."

Taking his discarded wrapper, Evie threw it in the bin as Nick tore away the cakey bottom and, like she remembered, pressed it on top of the blue cloud of frosting.

"I was hoping you'd do that."

"Why stop?" With a twinkle in his eye, he took a bite and hummed in playful pleasure.

"I can still make you that sandwich if you're—"

His phone vibrated on the counter, glowing with a text. Nick bent over and stopped chewing. "Bugger."

"What's wrong?"

"They're canceling the ferries due to adverse weather." He groaned. "We're stuck here."

After Nick's frantic phone calls with the production manager and her dinner-hour scramble to secure last-minute island accommodation for cast and crew, Evie evacuated to the bothy. Rooms elsewhere were in short supply, and she didn't relish venturing too far without her truck.

Warming up in front of the crackling fire, she looked sidelong at Nick, still dripping from their rain-whipped sprint down the path. "You should've gone with them."

He slicked back his sopping mop of hair. "And leave you here alone? No chance."

"I've stayed here before, Nick." Evie peeled off her raincoat and hood, having escaped the worst of the deluge apart from her bedraggled bangs (long and desperately needing a trim) and the legs of her jumpsuit, which were soggy and spattered with dirt. She studied the bothy's thick rubble walls and shallow pitched roof, her memories of weekend getaways with Fiona rousing a nostalgic grin. "It's safe and dry and"—the latest howl from the gales outside interrupted—"windproof. And no one else has shown up." She hung her coat on the back of a rickety chair, its seat holding a bulging trash bag from the truck. "I'll probably have it all to myself."

"Probably, but not guaranteed. Some hikers could barge in, party all night, and steal your stuff—or worse."

"That wouldn't happen."

"Spoken like a true Orcadian." Nick took off his waterlogged jacket. "Ever trusting."

Evie dipped inside her backpack, passing bottles of water and

Rice Krispie squares, and removed the thermos she had filled with hot, milky coffee before vacating the truck. "You say that like it's a bad thing." She set the thermos's cup on the small formica-topped table and pulled off the cap, pouring generously.

Nick turned, the angles of his face highlighted by the flickering tealights. "I just think you should've driven back to Lyness."

Evie handed him the coffee. His lavender button-down, like his jeans, was soaked through. "And get stuck? Storms like this can wash out the roads. And with the weight of my truck, I could hydroplane and tip over." She snapped the lid on the thermos, leaving it on the table beside a lighter and a roll of toilet paper.

"Jesus, I didn't think of that." Nick planted himself on a folding chair, which wobbled as he shifted. "Looks like you made the right decision then." He sipped his steaming coffee with care, closing his eyes.

Hauling her backpack with her, Evie sat on one of the raised stone platforms, which ran lengthwise along both sides of the structure. "But I guess you didn't?"

Nick's gaze fled toward the bare flagstone floor. "Don't I know it."

Her stomach clenched. "Cheers, grumpy pants. I'm thrilled to be stuck with you, too." Frowning, she leaned over and brushed the wet shins of her jumpsuit, but like her agitation, the muck wouldn't budge.

"*Evie.*" Nick jolted with a full-body shiver. "I didn't mean it like that." He set down his coffee. "You know I get grumpy when I'm cold and drenched. And I can't fucking believe I left my overnight bag in the crew's SUV."

There's only one solution. Evie pulled open the drawstrings on the damp garbage bag. "Take off your clothes."

"What?"

"Take off your shirt and jeans, and"—Evie plunged inside and lifted out the burgundy sleeping bag she kept in the truck for emergencies—"climb in here. Lie beside the fire and you'll be toasty in no time."

269

"Yeah, like I'm gonna hog your sleeping bag…"

"You can and you will." She lobbed the bundle onto his lap. "You're shivering."

"And what happens later? When the temperature falls and you're shivering?"

She motioned toward a folded camp bed. "I'll drag that closer to the fire."

"Without a blanket? Not on my watch." He blinked earnestly. "You'll share with me."

The idea *had* briefly popped into her head earlier when she grabbed the sleeping bag while exiting the truck. But thinking and doing were two different things, and as she appraised Nick's determined smile and the way his saturated shirt clung to the defined curves of his chest, all the reasons why sharing was such a colossally bad idea tapped her on the shoulder.

We've only just become friends again.

What if I get handsy in my sleep?!

Sunita will kill me.

Sam will kill Nick.

He's my CLIENT!

"Share?" Evie shook her head. "I don't think so!" *We'd be practically lying on top of one another, hot and sweaty. God, it's been ages since I've had sex!* Breath quickening, a yearning ache of want throbbed inside her.

Also not helping, Nick pouting his gorgeous kissable lips. "Share with me or I won't use it. I mean it, Evie. I'm not having you catch your death while I sleep all cozy."

Her shoulders drooped. "Fine, but we face away from each other."

"While we strip off? Or while sleeping?" asked Nick.

She examined her dirty jumpsuit. What was a chic, comfy choice that morning was now the bane of her existence. The whole thing had to come off. "Both!"

Getting undressed, however, was the easy part. Crammed back to back in their polyester and flannel burrito on top of the camp bed,

Evie was jostled every time Nick moved and fidgeted.

With anyone else, Evie would've been peeved. But bumping underwear-clad butts with Nick, feeling the flex of his back muscles against hers, and the familiar warmth of his body stirred up longing in her heart and an eager need between her thighs—feelings and urges she'd never thought could be resuscitated.

How can I crave the man who hurt me so badly?

Closing her eyes, Evie slipped a hand into her panties, her wetness a surprise even to her.

Stop lying to yourself. Bittersweet nostalgia weighed heavy and threatened to overshadow her growing desire. She withdrew her fingers from her underwear. *I* do *want him. To feel him, taste him, hear the sounds he makes.*

None of this was logical, but when had she and Nick ever made sense? Different worlds, different dreams, lives spent separately for most of their time as a couple. Truth be told, they never really had been on the same page, but despite that, their relationship *was* beautiful for a while.

Until it wasn't.

But now older, wiser, carrying knowledge from a hard lesson learned, maybe she could fulfill her carnal needs *and* protect her heart if she approached a potential dalliance like she had in London? An itch to be scratched and nothing more?

We're both consenting adults. I can definitely separate love from sex. I didn't love Stuart or the three guys I've slept with since Nick.

Pulling her eyes away from a stack of old board games on the floor—Risk, Trouble, Sorry!—she glanced over her shoulder. Nick was propping his bent arm under his head in lieu of a pillow.

We could hook up for fun. On the down low, of course. Can't be feeding the island gossips. That is, if Nick's keen.

But the former actor couldn't have sounded less keen if he tried.

"*Sorry,*" he mumbled for the tenth time, settling into stillness. But then he jerked violently and elbowed her in the back, a breathy "BOLLOCKS!" hurtling toward the wall.

"What's wrong now?" She lifted her head, blinking wearily as the amber glow of tealights danced along the stone.

"Ss-spider!" The rattle from the wind-beaten windows was no match for his loud stammer.

Nick and creepy crawlies. Evie suppressed a giggle. "Hate to break it to you, but this ain't The Four Seasons."

"Fuuuccck!" His body stilled. "It's *moving.*"

"Ignore it."

"I can't! It's HUGE! I'm serious, Evie." Nick fumbled with something on the floor. "Look!"

Humoring him, she flipped over and shifted onto her elbow, peering at the spotlight cast by his phone. Sure enough, a massive, meaty spider hung from one of the wall's large boulders. "She's probably frightened of *you.*" Evie lay down again.

"But spiders can detect fear. I read it online somewhere! I won't be able to sleep with that fucking thing near me."

"Fine, I'll get rid." Evie peeled back the sleeping bag, her skin pebbling with goosebumps as she withdrew from its snuggly warmth. She threw her raincoat over her champagne-colored bra and matching underpants and collected a cup and a piece of paper from her backpack.

It took many tries, but eventually she trapped the eight-legged nightmare and set her free outside.

Shivering, Evie dropped her wet coat on the chair and dashed toward the sleeping bag. Nick held it open, welcoming her back.

"C'mere, quick!" He promptly cocooned the material around her, its warmth melting the chill from her journey outdoors. "My hero—saving me again!"

"It was nothing." Evie looked away, knowing her fervent thirst for sex wouldn't be mirrored in his eyes.

"Talented cook this morning, spider wrangler this evening." He inched back, creating space between them. "You're amazing, Evie."

His words were familiar, a loving compliment repeated long ago, and yet her pounding heart sank as their recent conversation on Sanday rolled like a storm cloud through her memory: *I no longer mix business with pleasure, no matter how tempting.*

She bit back her disappointment and nudged his shoulder playfully. "Stop it. You'll make me big-headed." Glancing up with a resigned half-grin, she found a rueful look in his eyes.

"If anyone deserves all the flattery, it's you."

She held her breath, reveling in Nick's kindness as hopeful yearning surged through her again, a rapturous yet bittersweet buzz.

"Wake me if you need anything, okay? Sweet dreams."

Nick turned toward the wall, leaving Evie in the howling darkness with her bruised ego.

Twenty-Three

NICK

Then, Saturday, August 7, thirteen years ago

Sex was something Nick thought about *a lot*. How to do it. Who to do it with. And now all he could think about was when he and Evie would do it again.

As he lay curled around his sleeping girlfriend in a tangle of legs and rumpled bedsheets, his heart swelled with joy. He left a loving kiss on her temple. "You were incredible," he whispered, the needy ache between his thighs growing hard and eager again. "Sorry I didn't last. I'll be better next time. Promise." He caressed her shoulder with a barely there touch, silently counting out one, two…six, seven tiny freckles in a familiar pattern—like Ursa Minor, the constellation known as the Little Bear or Little Dipper. Nick grinned dreamily, pondering her cheeks and parted lips. "You'll always be my North Star."

Evie's swollen appearance and recent acne weren't a surprise, not after the countless web articles Nick had read in Greece about prednisone and Crohn's. However, her self-doubt *was*. Watching her at the rave, hearing the worry in her voice regarding Rosamund, Nick wasn't sure if their lengthy time apart or the side effects of her treatment were the cause. But whatever the reason, he would do everything possible moving forward—more kisses, more time together—to ensure Evie felt safe, supported, and loved. He would never let her feel *less than* ever again.

A familiar laugh, followed by a stampede of footfall, erupted on the other side of the bedroom door.

Cheers, Tarq. Nick winced. *You and your inconsiderate mates are gonna wake her.*

274

Evie's lashes fluttered into a flurry of hard blinks.

Nick smiled. "Hey! Good morning, gorgeous."

Her sleepy eyes meandered, finding him. "*Hi.*" A grin roused her lips. "You're here."

"Where else would I be?"

She succumbed to a yawn. "Last night was…spectacular."

Relief filled his chest. "*Really?* Thank god. I was worried."

"Don't be." Wriggling closer, Evie snuggled into Nick's hair. "Anything we don't know, we'll learn together."

"I'll need loads of hands-on tutoring."

She eased back, matching his smile. "And surprise quizzes."

"Like a drop trou now, show me what you know situ?" asked Nick.

"Yep. Could happen anywhere, anytime."

His heated gaze plunged to her breasts. "Like now?" He placed soft, open-mouthed kisses along her neck as his erection throbbed and pressed against her hip.

Evie let out a silky gasp. "Can I ask you something?"

"Anything," he murmured across her skin, kissing her again.

"Why'd you wait? I mean, it's not like you haven't had plenty of opportunity, or offers. You could've been with anyone."

Pausing his passionate wake-up call, Nick looked up. "I didn't want to be with just anyone."

A hint of a grin curved Evie's lips as her fingers skated over his collarbone and twirled the chain of her necklace adorning his neck.

"I also didn't want to be someone's trophy fuck either."

"What's that?" she asked as Nick's phone buzzed on his bedside table.

He didn't budge, ignoring the incoming text. "What you become when someone sleeps with you and sells their story. It happened to this bloke I know, another actor. It made me second-guess every girl, every snog, every potential relationship."

Letting go of her necklace, Evie froze. "Me?"

"God, no! You're my best friend. I don't second guess anything with you, Evie."

"Same." She smiled. "I'm happy, Nick."

He beamed back and traced his finger along her jaw. "What took us so long, eh? One thing's for certain, you were *definitely* worth the wait."

"I wish I'd waited for you." She took in a deep breath and let it go. "My first time was *not* good."

Stuart.

The tight ache between Nick's inner thighs began to fade. He despised her ex for a whole litany of Evie-related offenses and the mere suggestion of Stuart being with her *like this*—well, if there ever was a boner killer…

But something in her voice sounded off, troubled. If Evie needed to talk, he'd listen. Even if it involved shithead Stuart.

"What happened?" Nick rubbed her arm. "You can tell me if you want."

"You sure? I know it's weird, talking exes."

"Everyone has a past. I can handle it." He kissed her on the forehead. When he pulled back, a ghost of a grin flexed her lips.

"Well, we were at the pub for Stuart's birthday. I wasn't drinking. I was feeling fine, but alcohol and Crohn's don't always mix for me."

Nick nodded.

"The more Stu drank, the more frustrated he got because I wasn't joining in. He'd always been pushy about booze but was extra aggressive that night, forcing shots on me. Then he demanded sex in his disgusting car. I said no and he accused me of ruining his birthday and being a prick tease."

Nick's jaw dropped. "Whoa! He didn't?"

"But it sorta felt like I'd brought it on myself. What did I expect? Making him wait while I figured out how I felt, ignoring his needs—"

"*His* needs?" Nick's pulse quickened.

"His words, not mine," corrected Evie. "The first time he said it was on our second date. Apparently, my hesitance to do anything beyond kissing was giving him blue balls and causing long-term physical harm."

"What?! That's complete bollocks—no pun intended." He seethed. "What a lying, manipulative asshole!"

"But how was I supposed to know? I asked Sunita and Fi afterward, but they had no idea. And I couldn't look it up on the internet in case Sam or my parents opened the search history."

"You could…delete it."

Evie half-laughed. "I know that now!"

"I'm teasing."

"I know *a lot* of things now." She scratched her chin. "Anyway, I worried non-stop. What if he told his mates I was frigid? Or dumped me? I didn't want to be *the* girl everyone gossiped about, so gave in on our third date. Gave him a quickie hand job."

My assumption outside the stockroom was right. Nick felt sick.

"A few dates and lots of pestering later, I gave him my first blow job—or at least I tried to. I had no idea what I was doing. I didn't enjoy it…"

The asshole bullied her. Nick brushed her bangs from her eyes. "Evie, trust me on this. Stuart had no right to pressure you when you weren't ready. You owed him *nothing.* You were young and vulnerable. He was older and took advantage. That's never okay, no matter the circumstances." His phone buzzed again.

Evie's eyes darted over Nick's shoulder toward the noise. "I guess, but I can't pretend I'm totally innocent. Most of the time I was a willing participant. I wanted to have sex."

"And why shouldn't you? It's completely normal and natural to want it."

"I know, it's just…" She bowed her head. "I wanted to wait till I was sure how I felt about him. I only did it 'cause I didn't want him to dump me—*which* he did anyway."

Nick stroked her temple. "Regardless of whether or not you wanted it, that still didn't give him license to bully or force you. You have nothing to feel guilty about."

Her expression brightened. "One good thing came of it, though—I now realize sex is amazing with someone you love."

"It is!" Nick kissed her nose.

"Have you ever felt pressured?" she asked.

"Yeah. Playing Jake certainly didn't help. Everyone thought I was at it. Even my brothers."

"They didn't know?"

"Hell no. Tarquin lost his virginity at fourteen. Rupert's been with Fi since, well, forever. I'm the oldest—I should've been giving them advice, not the other way around.

"And my PR made things a helluva lot worse. She booked me for late-night talk shows and lad-mag interviews, all of which cater to an older, male demographic, so you can imagine their questions: Where did you lose your virginity? What's your favorite position? Ever had a threesome? I had to lie or get caught out."

"That's awful."

Nick nodded. "I hated every unbearable second. Suddenly, all the bad stuff about being famous started canceling out the good."

"You mentioned that at music camp but didn't get into specifics."

Did I? Nick fought to remember but nothing materialized. "I would've been in the thick of it back then. But like you said last night about Angry Eyes, it's ancient history. Live, learn, and move on."

"I like moving on with you," said Evie.

"Yeah, me too. You're so lovely and gorgeous—have the cutest innie belly button." She giggled as Nick leaned in for a kiss. "So, there's something I've been thinking about. Next September when I'm done uni and you're preparing to head back for year two, how 'bout we move in together?"

"What? In London?"

"The very same!"

Evie gasped.

"I know I'm *kinda* jumping the gun. I still have to graduate from Salford and you just accepted your place at Goldsmiths yesterday, but waddaya say? Wanna get a flat and play house in a year's time?"

Evie subtly bit her bottom lip mid-smile. "But it'll just be while I'm at uni, right? We'll come back for summer? I need to help out in the shop."

"Yeah. *Sure.*"

"Okay!"

"Great! My family's always lived in Chelsea, north of the Thames, but"—he grinned cheekily—"I guess I *could* live south of the river close to your uni."

Evie's left brow peaked. "What's wrong with south London? Seemed nice when I visited."

"Oh, it's a silly London thing—the north-south divide. It runs *deep*." He narrowed his gaze. "So…care to convince me?"

A naughty twinkle shone in Evie's eyes as she sat up and tucked two fingers in her mouth, giving them a prolonged suck.

Holy mother of... Nick felt her visual tease between his thighs, a throbbing hot ache as his semi grew thicker, harder. Breaths quickened and all thoughts of flat-finding and bickering Londoners evaporated, replaced by an all-consuming need for Evie and whatever she had planned next.

Yanking away the sheets, she drifted downward, popping her wet fingers from her mouth and boldly wrapping her hand around his scorching heat.

"Will this help…?" She slid up to the softness of the head and back down, then up again, her thumb lingering, pressing the tip. "Persuade you, I mean." Squeezing tighter, she moved her hand down again, pulling a groan-imbrued "I *love* persuasive Evie" through Nick's buzzy, blissed-out smile.

"Convinced yet?" she purred mid-stroke.

"Uhh…" His legs twitched with feral pleasure, the ability to formulate an answer…

What was the question?

Giggling naughtily, she nudged her hair out of the way with her free hand and bowed her head, closing her lips around him.

"Holy shi—" Nick's breath caught as the tip of her tongue danced around the head. "Oh…!" Reaching down, he threaded his hands through her hair and gently pulled, and Evie took him deeper, sucking and stroking, the slippery heat of her mouth bringing stars to his eyes.

She looked up through her bangs and grinned, the shift of her lips and jaw increasing the tingling and pressure, whisking him closer and closer to—

His phone buzzed again. Then again.

"Go away!" he grumbled toward the ceiling.

Evie stilled and sat up. "That's the fourth time. Maybe something's wrong?"

Nick closed his eyes and let out a staggered breath. "Fuck! Brilliant timing. Okay, I'll have a quick peek." As Evie released him, he rolled over. "If it's bloody Tarquin looking for guinea pigs, I'm gonna kill him."

"Guinea pigs? Here?" A strange excitement rippled through her voice. "That takes me back. We used to own five: Scary, Baby, Posh, Sporty, and Ginger."

Ignoring the ache between his thighs, Nick laughed and glanced over his shoulder. Combing her fingers through her bedhead, Evie looked like she was prepping to join the search party. "Well, I hate to disappoint, but Tarq's guinea pigs are of the taste-testing variety. His new thing is making waffles from scratch."

"Your favorite! Aw, that's sweet of him."

"Nah, I know my baby brother." Nick lunged past Evie's plush otters, marshmallow Snowballs, and still-wrapped daisies on his bedside table and scooped up his phone. "This is all about upping his morning-after game. He reckons if he makes a hot breakfast for his hookups, they'll come back for a second helping of *him*."

"You gotta admit, that's pretty clever for an eighteen-year-old guy!" Evie crawled toward the pillows.

Nick tapped in his passcode. "Like I said, Tarq doesn't need sex advice from me." He opened his texts, and a stack of messages hogged the screen.

Mum: Darling, you awake? I'm at the Sandpiper Hotel.

Fuck, why is she here? Annoyance burned in Nick's throat as he skipped to the next texts.

Mum: Need to see you.

Mum: Breakfast is waiting.

Mum: Sending my car. Be ready in fifteen.

He dragged his hand over his face. *What the hell does she want?*

Evie's arms hugged his middle. "Is it waffle o'clock?" She placed a kiss below his ear then rested her chin on his shoulder. "Or time for more *persuading*?"

Nick looked back, catching an anticipative glint in her eyes. He suppressed a frown for her benefit. "I wish. It's my mum. She wants to meet in Stromness for breakfast."

Lifting her head, Evie frantically swiped at her smudged eye makeup. "Ooh, she's here?! Can I come?"

"She's not like your mum, Tigs. She can be…difficult."

"I know. But I have to meet her sometime, right?"

Nick didn't have the heart to say no.

"This series is attracting the crème de la crème of young British talent." Kiki Balfour tapped the thick script with an impatient finger. "All your contemporaries are tripping over themselves, begging to get attached to this project, so the sooner you start reading, the better. We'll run lines on the flight home, get you prepped for Tuesday's audition. Polly's already booked you a slot." The forty-something actress tossed back the sunny dregs of her second mimosa then straightened the collar of her burgundy sheath dress.

Bloody typical. Sat across the table, Nick fumed over his Kiki-ordered bowl of porridge. *She barely said hello to Evie and now this?* The pungent smell of hairspray prickled his nose as his mother patted her jet-black tresses, twisted tight into a headache-inducing top knot. No doubt, the industrial-strength lacquer had been applied generously by her ever-present stylist in the hopes of combating Orkney's relentless winds. His gaze followed the sweep of her hand. An escaped tendril defiantly dangled beyond her French manicure.

Nick bit back a smile and said, "I'm not flying to London."

Kiki shoved aside her untouched egg white omelet. "Well, you're not staying *here*." She sneered, her eyes homing in on the silver *Evie* dangling from Nick's neck. His mother's hatred of the islands was legendary. While her boys visited their grandmother each summer, she'd remain in London for polo season (which bored her senseless), citing an "aversion to salty air, small minds, and silly accents."

Nick glanced sidelong at Evie. Wearing his beloved bowling shirt, she hid behind her bangs and chewed a small bite of maple syrup-drenched French toast. "I'm twenty-one, Mum, not twelve." He dragged his spoon through the gloopy oats. "I *am* staying—till uni resumes next month. I've already arranged it with Gran. And Dad said—"

"DON'T!"

Nick's gaze flitted up.

"Don't you DARE mention that louse, not after he paraded his latest tryst all over social media! She's YOUR age for heaven's sake." Kiki's outburst drew curious looks from a neighboring table of guidebook-flipping tourists. "Of all people, Nikolai…" She pouted her plumped-up lips and discarded her empty glass on the table. "I thought you'd be on my side."

Mid-swallow, Evie silently avoided the passive-aggressive circus across the table and drifted toward her boyfriend.

"No, I'm on *my* side, Mum," Nick batted back confidently. "I haven't worked this damn hard for two years just to blow off my final year on some half-baked film. For fuck's sake, it's based on a stupid theme park ride!"

Lips knotting, his mother looked like she was chewing a wasp. "Nikolai, language!"

"I shouldn't be surprised." He rejected her admonishment. "It's not like you ever ask about uni, but for the record, I'm *thriving*! My grades are good, I'm learning loads, and my mental health has never been better. I'm even seeing a therapist."

Kiki flinched.

"So, yeah, next month, I'll head back to Salford, finish my degree, then come next August"—with a smile, Nick gathered Evie's hand proudly—"we'll get a flat in London near Evie's uni and I'll see what's on offer acting-wise. I'm not making any promises, though. I might work behind the scenes for a bit instead, put my degree to good use."

"*Oh.* I see." Kiki dropped her napkin on the table. "Twenty-one years young and you've got it *all* figured out. I knew that university would put all sorts of rubbish in your head." A skittish server leaned in and swapped a fresh mimosa for Kiki's used glass, its rim tattooed with scarlet lipstick. "Should I assume there's no changing your mind?"

"Correct." Nick gave Evie's hand a squeeze and let go.

"Principle photography doesn't start in London till next summer," added Kiki.

He shook his head.

"Polly could negotiate a sizable signing bonus."

"Nice try, but I can't be bought," said Nick.

"And I can't support this decision." Blinking her feathery false lashes, Kiki snatched the full drink. "It's reckless and catastrophic. You better be prepared for the fallout." She stared above Evie's head and took a lengthy sip.

"What fallout?" Nick shoveled a spoonful of lumpy porridge between his lips.

"What do you think? You haven't acted in four years."

This tastes like paste. Cringing, he maffled through the gluey gruel. "Not for a lack of trying."

Kiki scoffed. "I wouldn't call ignoring all the scripts Polly sent your way the past eleven months *trying*, Nikolai. You haven't returned any of her calls or emails, let alone stepped foot inside an audition room."

His concern flew to Evie. Eyes questioning, she poked her barely eaten breakfast with her fork. *Shit, I wish she wasn't hearing this.*

"Polly's been breaking her back for you *for years* and THIS is how you repay her, being flighty and unprofessional, scurrying off to uni?" Kiki tilted her head. "Do you realize how badly this reflects on us?"

Us? Nick scrunched his face.

"I could let you burn all the bridges your pretty little heart desires, but I refuse to stand by and watch you do irreparable harm to our Balfour name."

"*Me* causing harm?" Nick bit his tongue, holding back a verbal onslaught about her numerous affairs and the hush money paid (under the table) to London's unscrupulous tabloid editors.

"Yes, you! Agents talk, you know. I cannot imagine why you haven't called Polly back."

"I needed a break!"

"From what?" his mother spit back.

"From non-stop rejection. It's doing my head in!" Abandoning his spoon, Nick whisked his hand through his hair. "Every audition it's something ridiculous: my brows are too arched or they don't like my chin or I remind them of their brother. Christ, one of them said I looked 'too Londony' to be riding a horse!"

"This is about *Plunder the Crown*, isn't it?" Kiki huffed. "Nikolai, it's been a year. Grow up, get over it, and get back to work!"

A loud clank arose from Evie's plate. Nick glanced over. Knife and fork splayed across her French toast, his girlfriend scowled at her breakfast, silently fuming.

He picked up a slice of five-grain toast (plain, no butter), another inedible breakfast request by food cop Kiki. "She said the same thing after my first panic attack."

"Allergic reaction," Kiki corrected, frantically eyeing the room.

"Told ya." Turning away from Evie, Nick bit into the rock-hard toast.

"Well, maybe *you* don't care about being called a has-been, but I do!"

Has-been? Nick choked on his breakfast.

Rushing to his aid, Evie rubbed his back as he sputtered. "You okay?" She grasped her water. "Drink this."

"Who called me a—?" Nick croaked, unable to say the belittling word aloud. He accepted Evie's glass with a heavy heart and took a slow sip, his eyes watering.

"Producers, casting agents. At this point, though, you're not even part of the conversation."

Nick swallowed hard. *Is she lying?*

"I *know*. It's an outrageous cheek!" said Kiki. "But you and me, we can FIX it with this film. Marty and Frances at Pinewood think it could be as successful as *Pirates of the Caribbean*—you know, that *other* film based on, oh, what did you call it? A stupid theme park ride?"

Lost in the water glass, Nick refused to give his mum the satisfaction of an emotional reaction, but his pulse was so frenzied, pounding in his chest and ears, he was surprised no one could hear it.

"And on the off chance you don't book it, the audition should put you top of mind for this fall," said Kiki.

"What's this fall?" blurted Evie.

Nick was amazed she'd jumped in. He glared at his mother. *Don't you dare bite her head off.*

"A veritable casting *bonanza*, my dear." Kiki sipped her mimosa.

"Oh, don't lie to her, Mum." Nick swallowed again, his throat rough. "We both know pilot season doesn't kick off till January."

"That's where you're wrong. The major players are getting an early jump, casting their leads now. There are some incredible projects coming up." Kiki licked her pillow lips. "You *should* be in the thick of it, but if you want to finish university and throw away sixteen years of hard-earned success, well, that's *your* call, not mine. Don't come crying to me or Polly when you're bagging groceries at Tesco, wondering where it all went so horribly wrong."

I'm not listening to this. She has no fucking clue! Looking away, Nick sank down in his chair. *I've worked my arse off at uni. People there actually think I'm pretty great, and it's not because I'm famous. Who'd have thought, eh? Obviously, not my mother.*

He glanced back, skimming Evie and her abandoned breakfast before landing on his mother polishing off yet another drink. *I love acting, but I'm not tough like her. The rejections, the industry gossip—she feeds off it. But it eats away at me. Not that she cares.* He downed another gulp of water. *If only I didn't miss it so much.*

"Moments like this always remind me of that quote..." His mother stared off dramatically into space. "Excuses will always be there for you. Opportunities won't."

Ditto mothers. Rolling his eyes, Nick sat up. "You're right."

Nodding smugly, Kiki raised her empty glass. "I always am, darling!"

"It *is* my call...and I'm finishing uni," said Nick. "End of discussion."

Kiki's unflinching glower flittered to Evie in her son's bowling shirt and refused to budge.

TWENTY-FOUR

EVIE

Now, Saturday, July 29

"But what if someone wanders in?" Easing back onto a small 19th-century sofa embroidered with roses, Evie tugged down the hem of her daisy dress and peered across Balfour Castle's drawing room. A slightly ajar door, the secret passageway back to the library, furrowed her brow.

"Not a chance. The shooting party will be gone for hours." Nick whipped off his black single-breasted frock coat, flinging it onto the nearby piano.

Evie eyeballed his starchy white shirt, short waistcoat, and wool trousers as he fought with the elaborate knot of his black bowtie. *Why is he dressed like a* Tomlinson *actor?*

His collar finally open, he fell to his knees. "I want to ravish you at least twice before they're back!" Nick made quick work of the buttons on her dress, exposing her lacy bra, which roused a naughty grin. "And we *cannot* forget the spider."

Her gaze climbed the walls. "Spider? You're scared of creepy crawlies."

"Not this one!" His hand slid inside her bra, cupping her breast. "It's a sexual position. It's challenging, but *so* worth—"

Awaking with a snorty jolt, Evie's eyes popped open. Gone were the ornate wallpaper, oil paintings, and relief plaster-gilded ceilings of the castle, and her hands, not Nick's, were palming her breast and stuffed down her undies.

Shit! Stomach dropping like a freefalling elevator, her toes curled with embarrassment. *Sex dreaming about Nick while touching myself beside Nick?! This is SO wrong on SO many levels!* She froze. *Did he notice?*

Behind her, his gentle mid-slumber inhales and exhales pricked her ears, joining the sporadic crackle of the dying fire and the screech of seabirds, their flapping wings flickering the daylight spilling through the bothy's streaky windows. Thankfully, the cacophony of driving rain and snarling winds from earlier was long gone, tormenting another isle perhaps.

She let out a breath.

Then she felt it.

Hard, unrelenting, digging into her lower back.

Oh! Evie bit her bottom lip, hemming in a smile. *Hello, Nico!* Fingers scrunching the sleeping bag, she rolled slowly to her right, the shift jostling Nick awake.

Hair wild and an imprint from the sleeping bag denting his left cheek, he lazily blinked his long dark lashes. "Evie? *Hi…*"

"Sleep well?" she whispered back.

"Uh-huh." The curve of a grin stretched his lips as his eyes peeled open, his initial bliss suddenly scuttled with a gaze-widening, body-stiffening "Fuck! Sorry!" He fisted the sleeping bag. "I-I must've turned over during the—" Halting, he lifted the covering and peeked downward, his frozen expression melting into a mortified wince. "*Oh shit!* I'm beyond sorry."

I'm not. Waking up with Nick's erection drilling into her back? The most action Evie had felt in years.

Hugging the sleeping bag against his bare chest, he scrambled as far back as its constraints would allow. "Wasn't on purpose!"

"I know."

"I fell asleep facing the wall."

"I know." She smiled softly, but Nick still looked horrified.

"I would never intentionally—" His hunched shoulders collapsed with remorse. "Forgive me."

Evie felt a blush rising and glanced away. "It was kinda nice. I haven't had a boner wakeup call in ages, let alone…" She shrugged and found him again, his gaze growing heavy, settling on her lips.

Oh?! Her heart tripped.

Nick swept her bangs slowly away from her lashes like he was seeing her for the first time. Either that or he thought she was long overdue for a trim.

There was only one way to find out.

With his fingers still in her hair, Evie pitched forward, meeting his mouth with a determined kiss, fully expecting him to pull back.

Which he did.

A flash of desire lit up his eyes. "Wow, Evie." Licking his lips, the glimmer vanished, displaced by narrowing uncertainty. "I'm more than willing, but are *you* sure about this?"

Am I? The spark of doubt flamed again. *What if this is a mistake? What if I'm opening myself up to more hurt?* For thirteen years, she had tormented herself, replaying their sizzling kisses and hurried fumbles, how Nick had pledged his love "for always" and spoken of a shared future together. She had believed him, trusted him, allowed herself to be vulnerable only to have his actions shatter her completely, heart and soul.

Clutching to past wrongs and avoiding Nick had become a deep-rooted habit, but was she happier because of it? More fulfilled?

A mournful ache throbbed in her chest.

Not even close. It's preventing me from living fully now. I can't keep dragging old baggage into new situations. The thought of climbing back into her self-imposed cage of what-ifs and might've-beens pinched in the worst way, and Evie was sick of it, sick of blaming her disastrous love life on Crohn's, sick of holding herself back with unproven assumptions and cruel labels—labels she wore by choice.

Like calling myself a burden.

The epiphany hit her hard.

I'm not a burden. I'm strong and resilient. A survivor.

A sense of hope and empowerment bloomed in Evie's chest.

And it's up to me—not Nick or anyone else—to set myself free.

Sometimes the greatest act of kindness is the kindness you grant yourself.

Evie nodded. "Couldn't be more sure." She kissed him hungrily and he responded in kind, his hands cradling her face, holding her still, making her his.

Pausing momentarily, he smiled against her mouth, his tenderness feeling like home. "I've missed you, Tigs."

Tigs. Parting her lips, she welcomed him in, his tongue deliciously flirty as she tasted him, going deeper, harder. A familiar groan escaped his throat, and paired with the mention of her old nickname, it was all the encouragement Evie needed. She trapped his thigh with hers, tugging him closer as her fingers trespassed in his hair, thick and soft—*god* how she'd missed it. Making the most of the moment, she grasped fistfuls, reviving cherished teenage memories of snogging on the beach, in her mum's car, in Nick's bedroom.

He must've been feeling the pull of nostalgia, too. Breaking their kiss, he took his fingers on a detour, tracing the constellation of freckles on her shoulder as the hard heat stretching his boxer briefs prodded her stomach. "I want you," he whispered. "More than anything."

Evie opened the front clasp on her bra and he closed his mouth around her peaked nipple. With a hard suck, a rush of pleasure tingled between her thighs. She bucked, bewitched by his wicked tongue as she dug her nails into his shoulders and arched her back, pressing harder, wanting more while her other hand explored Nick's body.

Familiar but different, a fine sweep of hair now darkened his chest, which was wider, more toned than it was at twenty-one, and his arms were ripped, but not *too* ripped, proving he had a life outside the gym. Gasping as Nick teased her breasts, Evie slid into his tented underwear. She cupped his balls for a cheeky squeeze, earning a low growl from his throat, then closed her hand around his eager length, her confident strokes drawing a strained "*Faster*" against her skin. The thought of him—larger, thicker—deep inside her made Evie obscenely wet and obnoxiously impatient. Her skin pebbled with goosebumps. Nick's physique had left her breathless before, but *this*...this Nick, thirty-four years in the making, was a whole other work of art.

As his breaths quickened, he stilled her hand. "*Fuck*, Tigs. You're incredible." His lips curved into a cheeky grin. "But I don't want to rush or come yet. I'd like to make this last—for both of us."

Delight danced in Evie's chest as she released her grip. Nick was generous and caring, dedicated as much (if not more) to her pleasure as his own. She smiled. "We were always in such a hurry. Do you remember?"

"Oh god, yeah. The joys of having sex in our childhood bedrooms, hoping we wouldn't get caught."

Evie smirked at the lock-free door. "Kinda like tonight."

"Makes me feel right at home." Nick pressed his lips, warm and wet and deliciously naughty, against her neck.

Closing her eyes, Evie ran her hands up his arms and along his back, feeling his muscles flex as his kisses and adoring moans feathered her breasts then her stomach where they abruptly stopped.

Nick Balfour—once a tease, always a tease! With a sassy response on her tongue, she opened her eyes and found him looking at her six-inch scar. The faded vertical line extended from just above her belly button—now slightly deformed post-surgery—to the top of her pelvic bone.

Her heart leapt into her throat. *Shit. I didn't even think...*

For Evie, her scar symbolized survival and resilience, but what would it represent for Nick? Their shattered past? A red flag?

"Evie..."

Here come the excuses. She stared at the ceiling, furrowing her brows. "I *know*," she sighed.

"Well, I'd hope so." Low with a hint of a playfulness, his reply sounded...keen?

Evie dropped her gaze back down to Nick.

A lascivious smile curved his lips. "You're so beautiful and sexy. I am one lucky bloke." His eyes darkening, he continued where he left off, kissing her scar and belly tenderly.

Evie tingled, giddy with relief as he kept heading south, his mouth and tongue flirting over her underwear and down the softness of her inner thighs. Licking, biting, sucking—he left her whimpering and writhing, fisting his hair, gasping for more.

She tore at the silky fabric of her panties, helping Nick yank them away. But her frenzy was overtaken by the feel of his fingers gently parting her and the ragged warmth of his rapid breaths against her skin.

He glanced up, locking eyes with her. "You're so wet for me."

She trembled with anticipation as he buried his tongue inside her, his hands squeezing her ass, holding her still. Gasp by gasp, Evie unraveled into a moaning puddle of molten want as he teased and sucked, only pausing to say how amazing she tasted and how much he had missed her, had missed this. Every lick of her clit, every finger slipped inside made her wetter, more desperate.

But it still wasn't enough. Evie wanted more. She wanted all of him.

"Nick..." she purred.

He paused, retreating with a grin like he recognized her tone from years past. Pulling back the sleeping bag, Evie worked his underwear down his legs, and his erection sprang free. She straddled his thighs, beholding the sight laid bare in front of her: the slight curve of his hard length, his subtle six-pack and glorious chest, and his smile—mischievous and beckoning—setting off a cavalcade of dimples. *Still so fucking sexy.* She had never thought she'd find herself here again, curling her fingers around him, teasing him with her tongue, taking him in her mouth...

"Yesss." Nick's head fell back, his eyes fluttering closed. "Oh babe, that's—" His fingers slid into her hair as he moaned. "God, I've missed *you*." His breaths quickened.

If he thinks that's good... Taking him deeper, Evie sucked harder and swirled her tongue, loving every second of his salty taste, of being in control, of driving him wild. He bucked his hips and she groaned softly, the vibrations pulling a torrent of sweary appreciation through his lips.

Moving her hand faster, she sucked and licked, her confident rhythm twitching Nick's thighs.

He let out a low growl. "Fuuck. This—you, you're amazing," he gasped. "But I'd rather be inside you."

Mid-suck, she blinked up, meeting his eyes.

"I think about it all the time. You and me." Disappointment dampened his wicked stare. "But I don't have any condoms here. I never thought we'd…"

Evie popped off. "I didn't either." She berated herself for a lack of lustful planning. "But I have an IUD. And no history of STIs."

The corners of his mouth rose. "Same. Got tested after my last relationship. I haven't been with anyone since."

The word *relationship* surprisingly pricked, but Evie held her ground. *No baggage, remember?* She stroked her hand up and down his length again. "So…"

Nick grinned naughtily. "*So!*"

"Me on top then?" she asked. "If that's okay?"

"Yeah! Why wouldn't it be?"

"Well, it *used* to be your favorite." She scratched her brow. "Maybe that's changed."

"Nope! Probably because I had an awesome teacher."

Evie's heart skipped, but she knew the past was best left behind. All that mattered was what she was feeling right now…

Lifting her thighs, she guided Nick inside her and sank down slowly. His exquisite girth stretching her tightness felt rapturous, eliciting a feral groan as she sucked in a measured breath.

Nick gasped gruffly and gripped her ass. "Thatta girl." His eyes seemed to roll back in ecstasy and Evie took full advantage, hell-bent on experiencing a morning worth remembering.

Grinding against him then rocking forward and back, Evie fell into an intoxicating rhythm matched by Nick, his upward thrusts building in urgency, hitting where she needed him most. She rode him hard, thrilled by his control and stamina, skills he had lacked at twenty-one.

Much had changed, but much had remained the same, too, like Nick remembering that Evie wouldn't orgasm without a little help.

Sliding his fingers between their sweat-drenched bodies, he circled her swollen clit as she bucked and bounced, arching her back.

"Fucking hell, Tigs." His heady, half-lidded gaze locked on her. "I'm gonna come just by watching you—"

"I'm close," Evie panted, rolling her hips as the dizzying sensation spiraled, lifting her higher and higher, stealing her breaths till her frenzied chase crashed into an explosion of sensual pleasure and an expletive-laden cry. She froze, mind and body surrendering to every throb, every thrum of their clandestine reunion.

She whimpered into a huge grin. *Who says second chances are a terrible idea?*

Not Nick. With her name owning his lips, he thrust one last time and came hard, jerking with each pulsating release.

TWENTY-FIVE

EVIE

Then, Saturday, August 14, thirteen years ago

Evie cracked open a box of puffin pillows and peered past a shelf stacked with glassware. Head popping through the neck of a blue lambswool sweater, her temporary 'helper' promptly neatened his unruly hair, straightened the Fair Isle pattern skimming his abs, and resumed the demolition of a packet of locally baked beremeal shortbread.

"Nom, nom, nom! Me love Orkney coo-keee!" Nick crunched cartoonishly through his seventh treat, doing his best Cookie Monster impression.

Evie dragged the opened box behind her. "Nick, you're supposed to be *counting* inventory, not eating it."

"But they're dead good. I've been hooked ever since our night on your trampoline."

Yeah, me too. Evie smiled.

"Want some?" He bobbed his head to the Beatles' "Strawberry Fields Forever" on the stockroom's crackly radio. The island's only station preferred oldies to the day's current hits.

"Tempting, but no, I'm good. I had a sandwich earlier." The lie curdled in her stomach. She hadn't eaten anything since dinner the night before.

"I promise, I'll pay for everything I eat." Nick budged up the sweater's cuffs. "I'll take this, too. I need a toasty jumper. Winters in Salford are terribly damp." Lunging forward through his open legs, he rescued his fallen inventory sheet from the floor and resumed his count of lemongrass-scented candles, tapping each tin with his pencil's Highland cow eraser.

He hasn't complained once. Evie sat on an unopened crate of gin, delighted by his newfound appreciation for the shop and its merchandise.

Since his mother's surprise visit a week ago, Nick hadn't grumbled about Orkney at all. He had even offered to visit Evie's favorite places—the Brough of Birsay, Happy Valley, Hoy—but when her work prevented their escape, he happily hung out in the café, playing games on his laptop and sampling her mother's menu until Evie was his again. It was like he was doubling down against Kiki and her demands, digging his heels into the island's earth while waiting for university to resume. Evie couldn't have been more thrilled. Having Nick by her side—even if he was leaving shortbread crumbs all over the shop's merchandise—kept her heart happy and her mind somewhat distracted from the troublesome twinges multiplying in her belly.

But still, Evie couldn't shake the cruel comments made by his mother: calling him unprofessional, a has-been, yelling at him to "grow up, get over it, and get back to work." Where was her love for her son? The concern for his mental health and the toll years of rejection had taken on his spirit? Years back when Nick first opened up about Kiki, Evie thought—no, *hoped* he was exaggerating, but witnessing the nasty put-downs in the flesh made her heart ache for him. Parents were supposed to love and protect their kids, not view them as a commodity.

Silently mouthing his count, Nick caught Evie's gawk. "Gotta keep the boss happy!" He laughed and wrote down his candle tally then shifted toward a box of rune-pattered socks, wedging a finger of sugar-dusted shortbread between his lips.

"And she is! You're helping me so much." Evie smiled as he dug through the hosiery. *His mother doesn't deserve such a sweet, considerate son.*

After Kiki's maelstrom, Nick apologized to Evie in private—twice. First, for keeping her out of the skipping-auditions loop, citing the stress it might cause her, and second, for his mother's snobbish dig about bagging groceries at Tesco. Nick stated, "It's a tough

job that's not so different from yours." Both involved public inter-
action, standing on your feet all day, and occasionally, a lack of
respect from customers. While it was thoughtful of Nick to speak
up, his apology, along with Kiki's dismissive squints, gave Evie no
doubt as to how she was perceived: unambitious, unimportant, a no-
hoper—and that didn't even take into account her lowly Orcadian
roots.

She pulled her gaze away from Nick and removed the protective plastic layer from the box of pillows, her snap-happy fingers
decimating bubble after bubble with gleeful satisfaction.

"Won't you reuse that?" asked Nick.

"Yeah, for stress relief. Works wonders." Evie giggled as his
phone buzzed once, twice. Leaning away from bundles of socks, he
lazily glanced at its screen.

"Is it Rupert?" Evie paused her bubble torture. The middle Balfour brother was competing again at the County Show, this time
with an adorable ewe lamb, but Nick's sneer told her all she needed
to know. "What's your mum want *this* time?"

"Her pound of flesh. She's banging on about the audition
again."

"Why? It was days ago."

"They're holding another casting call." Nick left his phone on a
neighboring box of glassware. "They haven't found their male lead
yet."

Really? Evie burst another bubble. All week she'd been watching him closely, wondering if he was having second thoughts. One
lunchtime, she passed his table in the café and he was gnawing on
the end of his pen, immersed in an article about the film on his laptop.

Nick's eyes flew over her shoulder. "Ooh, chocolate seagull
eggs! Can I?"

Evie swiveled and spotted the sweets behind her. "Nick, maybe
you should go…"

"Awww, really?! But if I stop eating, *then* can I stay?"

"No, I didn't mean"—she plucked the packet of the sugar-coated 'eggs' from the shelf—"I mean the audition." She tossed the sachet his way.

Nick caught the candy with one hand. "Evie, it's a lame project. Werewolves are *not* my vibe."

"Neither was playing a baby daddy and you smashed that."

"*That* was different." Mouth drawing tight, he bowed his head and twisted the top corner of the package one way then the other, but the plastic wouldn't tear.

A sharp ache ripped through Evie's side. *No! Not in front of Nick.* Body tensing, she bit back a yelp as her fingers bunched a cluster of bubbles, snapping them loudly. Thankfully, the pain didn't linger and Nick didn't notice, his hunger and the ongoing fight with the stubborn bag of sweets commanding his attention.

Evie let out a staggered, silent exhale and pressed for answers. "Different how? Why won't you even consider it?"

Ditching the seagull eggs on the inventory sheet in his lap, his gaze turned flinty. "'Cause Mum will think she's won. You saw what she's like." His nostrils flared. "She'll be fucking unbearable."

"Is she always like that? Baiting you? Not listening?"

"Yep. And if I don't do what she wants, she makes my life a living hell—Polly's, too." Nick's scowl softened. "I need to send Pol a groveling apology with a massive bouquet of flowers. She's always been supportive and encouraging. Regardless of what's going on"—he pointed at his head—"in here. I shouldn't have ignored her."

"I bet she'll be thrilled to hear from you."

"We'll see. I know she'd be ecstatic if I went to this audition."

"It might get your mum off your back, too," added Evie.

"For now. Then next week it would be something else." Nick chewed his top lip. "That's the thing. If I do this one, Mum will have me making the rounds, talking to anyone and everyone with a pulse."

"So, you *are* thinking of going?"

"*No.* Fuck, I don't know." His left knee began to bounce. The candy packet, pencil, and inventory sheet shimmied in his lap. "The desire's strong to stick to my guns and *not* go to spite her. But I can hear my therapist saying, 'That's not a healthy way to deal with this, Nikolai.'"

"Well, if you did go…"

Nick looked away. "They won't want me—"

"You might get it." They spoke at the same time. Evie grinned as Nick faced her.

"Do *you* want me to go?"

She reached over the box of socks and held his hand. "I want you to be happy, whatever you decide."

His knee slowing, he squeezed her fingers. "Tigs, I *am* happy."

"You didn't look happy the other day, reading articles about the film on your laptop."

Releasing her hand, Nick's head dipped in a slow rueful nod. "Busted."

"It's okay to be sad. I know how much you miss acting. You've said it yourself, when we sat behind the shop that day—you're lost without it."

Nick drew back. "Christ! So dramatic! I sound like a complete tosser."

"You *sound* like someone who misses their true calling," said Evie. You love acting, right?"

"Yeah…but it doesn't always love me back."

"But I do. I'll love you regardless of what happens—good or bad. And if things don't go as planned, I'll be here for you. I'll listen, take you for a meal. We'll tape those stupid casting agents' faces to dartboards and punching bags and—"

"Bowling pins?" A toothy smile broke through his lips.

"*Well*, I would, but…"

Nick sighed. "Still no bowling alley on the island."

"I could watch *Grease 2* with you again?"

"I'll hold you to that!"

"I know you will." She grinned empathetically. "I don't want you having regrets about staying here with me and missing out on these auditions. And I think you might…"

He paused for a few seconds then scrubbed both hands over his face like he was carefully considering his options. "Okay…if I *did* go, I might be gone a week."

"That's fine. We'll still have the rest of August *and* half of September. You're not due back at Salford till the twenty-first, right?"

He nodded and picked up the packet of candy eggs again. "What if you came to London with me?"

"Oh, your mum would love that!" Evie smiled sarcastically. "I would too—for different reasons, obviously! But I have to work. Next week will be busy with cruise ships, and Mum's relying on me. Besides, you don't need me distracting you with geeky questions about the West End and all the musicals playing there."

"I guess." He fidgeted, the cellophane candy wrapper crackling in his hands. "You know, this film's scheduled to shoot in London next summer." Nick looked Evie in the eye, his gaze gentle, hopeful. "If by some fluke I do get it, we could still get the flat like we planned."

"Well, there you go!" Evie spoke quickly, clasping his hand again. "Auditioning is a win-win."

"Kinda feels that way, yeah." He matched her grin. "Okay, fuck it—let's give this acting lark one more shot."

Four days into Nick's spree of London auditions, severe cramping and frequent vomiting sent Evie to hospital. Blood tests, ultrasounds, and an endoscopy followed, but their investigative limitations, along with a lack of gastrointestinal expertise in Kirkwall, left many questions unanswered and Evie and her mother on a tiny, tartan-tailed plane to Inverness.

"I wish we didn't have to travel for this MRI thing." Pale and tired, Evie loosened her seatbelt and leaned into Marianne. "I'm scared, Mum."

She lowered the latest issue of *Cheer* magazine. "Honey, it's gonna be okay."

"I don't want to drink some weird gunk." Evie spoke loudly, fighting the loud drone of the plane's propellers. "The nurse said it tastes awful."

"If you pinch your nose while you drink, it'll dull the taste."

"Where'd you hear that?" asked Evie.

"Your auntie. She had an MRI years back, said the worst part was the drink beforehand. The actual test is painless. You lie still and let the machine take pictures."

Evie had been so freaked out over the prospect of flying south for the test, much of what the medical team explained that morning hadn't registered. "Why'd the nurse mention earplugs?"

"The machine thumps and bangs while it works, but it won't hurt you." Marianne returned to her magazine and its 'at-home exclusive' with a legendary British soap star.

Evie squirmed in her seat, unable to find a comfortable position. She awoke her phone and re-read Nick's most recent texts.

Nick: One more audition then dumplings with Kyle and Zach. My boys say hi! x

Nick: Love you, Tigger. Can't wait to hold you in a few days. We can do all the things including that Brough of Birsay place if you'd like x

A tiny tidal island with no restroom that's only accessible by foot during low tide? Evie peeked out the window of the plane. The brief glimpses of Scotland's Highlands between cottony tufts of cloud did little to calm her fears. *I wish.* She leaned into her mum. "What if it's bad news?"

Marianne held her hand. "If it is, we'll deal with it, love."

Every flare, every new treatment, her parents said the same thing, and every time, Evie was frightened yet hopeful, but here on the thirty-three-seater plane a new emotion was along for the ride—

guilt.

"Mum, sorry I didn't tell you earlier. I thought the pain would go away. I didn't want to worry you." *Or ruin my reunion with Nick.*

"I'll always worry about you and Sam. It's part of my job description." Marianne glanced at the phone resting in Evie's lap. "Did you text Nick before takeoff?"

"No. I don't want to distract him. He's got a big audition today. He thinks everything's okay and…maybe it is. I don't see the point in worrying him if I don't have to, you know?"

Her mum nodded.

"I told Sam to keep quiet, too—in case they text. Nick needs to focus on his career right now. I can't be why he doesn't get this role."

"Nick wouldn't blame you, sweetheart."

"Yeah, but his *mum* would," said Evie.

"It's a shame she's so…difficult. But Nick"—Marianne smiled and let go of her daughter's hand—"he's a lovely lad, Evie. So thoughtful and kind. I get the feeling he'd do anything for you."

"Yeah." She giggled. "I hope we didn't mess up the inventory count too much. He got a little carried away, trying on all the jumpers. That boy *loves* clothes." *And shortbread. Hope Mum didn't notice.*

"He did a grand job. Stock take isn't the most glamorous of tasks, it was sweet of him to help." Marianne leaned closer as the flight attendant strolled down the narrow aisle, offering shortbread and complimentary non-alcoholic refreshments. "Ooh, that reminds me—we sold *a ton* of shortbread that week. I had to double our usual reorder!"

Evie bit back a laugh.

TWENTY-SIX

"A second chance is what we wish for
A second life is what we seek"
'Smile When We Whisper', Torquil Campbell

EVIE

Now, Monday, July 31

Finished with the breakfast service and cleanup, Evie and Sunita took a breather on a seaside bench looking out toward the Brough of Birsay. With Nick departing their smouldering embrace forty-eight hours earlier for a week of emergency meetings in London, Evie was riddled with uncertainty about their future.

What *were* they, exactly?

Together again? Friends with benefits? A one-time hookup? A cringeworthy mistake?

Evie's heart wrenched with a pang. For thirteen years, sex without love had been her forte post-split—in London, in Orkney—but not any longer. Not with Nick, bothy sleeping bag vow be damned. On Saturday morning, the long-neglected embers in Evie's heart had reignited.

For better or for worse.

For Nick.

She tightened her grip on her phone and stared out to sea, finally admitting what she'd been fighting all summer. *It's always been Nick.*

An incoming message buzzed her hand and quickened her pulse.

But will it be different this time?

"Eves!" Sunita urged, "you're missing it!" Glued to the kiss being filmed on the beach below, she elbowed her arm. "What could be more riveting than this?"

Evie's eyes dipped to her phone:

Nick: London's sweltering. Missing those Orkney breezes. And you x

I'm missing you, too. Evie bit her lip, remembering how safe and warm she'd felt in his arms, her head on his chest, and the *thump, thump, thump* of his heart soothing her asleep. "This." She shared his text.

Sunita craned her neck, reading the screen. "Nick's missing Orkney? Well, that's a first. Must've been *some* orgasm on Saturday." She sat back as Evie lowered her phone.

"It was! His, mine…"

"So that answers my next question."

"Which is?"

"Any regrets?"

"Sun, you've asked me that *five* times since Saturday."

"You might've changed your mind."

Cocking her head, Evie squinted into the morning sunshine.

"I know that smug look. You'd do it again, wouldn't you?"

The smile Evie had been holding back burst out into a cheek-plumping beam. "Would *you* say no to the best sex of your life? And we cuddled for ages till we fell asleep. He helped me clean up, too."

"The bothy?"

"No!" Evie motioned with her eyes toward her apron and the lap of her yoga pants. "*Me.*"

Sunita snorted. "And people say romance is dead."

"Don't mock! Sharing responsibility afterward felt respectful and mature…and kinda sexy."

"Well, it was the least he could do, not bringing condoms," said Sunita.

"But I didn't either." Down on the beach, the director's shout of

"Action!" stole Evie's attention briefly. "Strange to think it was my first time having sex without, but…I trust him."

"You do?"

"He hasn't shown me a reason not to. And anyway, it's not like we're getting married or anything. It was just sex."

"But was it?"

Evie nodded despite the uncertainty whirling in her chest. "I think? We didn't have a chance to discuss it. The production manager banged on the door, waking us up, and"—she giggled—"I've never dressed so quickly *in my life*. Nick's been texting a lot, though." She scrolled back to their messages since Saturday, showing Sunita:

Nick: Hated rushing off and leaving you. Must be important if London can't wait till Mon. Text me when you're safely back on Mainland, k? x

Evie: Hope your flights are comfy. I'm home now, missing you. Gonna have a LONG bubble bath

Nick: Ahh, you're killing me! Will be thinking about THAT sexy visual all day. Good thing I'll be sat behind a big table. LOL. What else you up to? Btw landed in London x

Evie: NICK! Your daisies arrived. There are SO MANY! Thank YOU!

Evie: I plan to write, have a baked tattie for dinner then watch *Xanadu* for the zillionth time. Bet you're glad to be in London after hearing that, eh?

Nick: Rather be there with you. Glad flowers arrived. First long meeting done. Off to meet Zach for dinner. Wanna FaceTime after? x

Evie: So tired. Don't think I'm awake enough for a virtual booty call.

Nick: As lovely as that would be, I was only asking so I could see my gorgeous girl and wish her sweet dreams x

Evie: What am I like?! Mind = gutter. Yes! Call in 5? x

Sunita pulled back. "That's not just sex, Eves. That's Nick wanting a second chance."

"You think? I didn't want to assume. Assuming has landed me in trouble before."

"Do *you* want him back?"

The question from Sunita she'd been dreading. Evie tucked her phone in her apron. "Am I an idiot if I say yes?"

"No. I think he's changed...or maybe I have?" said Sunita. "It's funny how time and age can make you see things differently. I know I've had my issues with Nick over the years, but I feel like he's redeemed himself this summer. When you burned your hand, I thought his quick response was down to health and safety 'cause ultimately it's his responsibility. But then there was the raisin thing and the orca and him buying your book—"

"Sending me daisies." She grinned softly. *Kissing my scar.*

"The guy can't do enough for you," said Sunita. "It's like he's groveling through actions, not words."

"I *know*. And I love it!"

"But if he hurts you again"—Sunita balled her hand into a fist—"he'll be leaving Orkney with one less testicle."

Evie snickered.

"Seriously though, it doesn't matter what I think," said Sunita. "If you're happy, I'm happy."

"Well, I don't know if he wants to get back together—and even if he does, I have to be realistic about what a relationship with Nick might look like." She watched the actors kiss again. "And then there's the split. That needs to be discussed, too, obviously. Everything needs to be out in the open if we're gonna stand a fighting chance."

"What if he doesn't reveal anything new?" asked Sunita. "What if the severity of your Crohn's really *was* the reason?"

Gazing beyond the actors, Evie's eyes settled on the jutting layers of ancient sedimentary rock exposed during low tide. "Then I have to hope he's learned from his mistake. I might not understand why he did what he did back then, but I'm done with feeling hurt and angry all the time. It's exhausting, Sun. I can't be that bitter person anymore, letting it eat away at me. It's time to pull on my big girl pants and accept that *I'm* the only one who can give myself closure.

"And I have to stop seeing myself as a burden. I've successfully managed the shop *and* cooked meals for a major TV production—all without calling my mum or begging off sick. That's hardly the behavior of a burden."

"Nope!" Sunita smiled.

"I can't control what other people think or say…or if they want to date me, but I can control how I react and what I believe," said Evie. "From now on, I'm gonna be less self-critical and practice more self-compassion."

"Hear, hear!"

She looked away, trading the four-million-year-old rock formations for her best friend. "Thanks. It's early days, though. I might slip up and tumble back into bad habits…"

"If you do, I'll prop you up." Sunita leaned in for a side hug. "So…will you forgive him?"

"Maybe. I'd like to. In a way, forgiving him feels like forgiving myself for my part in all this. And for being stubborn and stuck. I know I wasn't much fun to be around."

Sunita nodded slowly like she was measuring what to say next. "Yeah, but who isn't after a breakup. It's like they say: you can't heal or move on if you suppress the ugly stuff. You gotta live through it."

"And I did—for thirteen unlucky years," said Evie. "It might sound odd, but Saturday morning I felt…lighter, more content."

"And that's down to Nick?" asked Sunita.

"A bit. But mostly me."

Raised voices pulled their attention to the beach where the lead couple were exchanging barbed insults between takes.

"Fiona thought those two were fucking like rabbits." Sunita chuckled. "I bet she was thrilled about you and Nick."

"So thrilled she squealed and woke up Rupes. But I told her what I told you: no one can know. Not yet, anyway. At least not until I know what we are—if anything."

"How's your Crohn's through all this?"

"A few aches, the usual tiredness," said Evie. "Nothing worrisome. I finish my antibiotics in four days and should be able to reschedule my missed infusion for next week."

"And be clear to have a glass of wine this Saturday!"

"Yeah! Rebecca's wedding is going to be epic. And Nick is best man!" Evie swooned, picturing him in a morning suit in the church.

"I still can't believe Becca's marrying his cousin after a month of dating," said Sunita.

Evie pulled a face. "Neither can poor Puggie!"

After seven long days apart and countless flirty messages, Evie couldn't wait to join Nick at Rebecca and Jonathan's weekend wedding. Fate, however, had other plans. A leaky freezer in the café and a tardy repairman unexpectedly delayed their reunion, and Evie missed the entire church ceremony and half the evening reception.

Approaching The Odin Hotel, Nick's **At head table, missing you like mad x** text quickened her pace, her heels' purposeful *click-click-click* on the pavement parting the swarm of smokers loitering outside.

Incandescent in her fanciest frock—a sleeveless symphony of sea green sparkle with a plunging neckline and a swishy, ankle-length skirt—she rushed into the dining room and chanced upon Sunita and Fiona, their azure blue and buttery yellow dresses a bright respite in a sea of black and pastel.

"Evie!" Fiona waved as Ava munched chocolate wedding favors and a pouting Poppy tugged at her dress.

"Mummy! *Mum...*" The pink-cheeked cherub bounced desperately on the spot.

"One moment, sweetie." Smoothing Poppy's auburn ringlets, Fiona glanced up. "Eves, I bet the kitchen still has meals."

Food was the last thing on her mind. "Oh, it's fine. I ate already," she fibbed, looking for Nick. To her left, the bride and groom plied guests with the Bride's Cog, a drinking vessel resembling a mini wooden barrel cut horizontally in half. Boasting two handles and a warm, brain-numbing concoction of whiskey, brandy, rum, gin, port, beer, stout, spices, and brown sugar, the long-celebrated Orcadian wedding tradition was passed from reveler to reveler until the potent mixture was finished (but even then, it was usually replenished). Recipes varied from family to family and were a sworn secret.

"Evie Sutherland!" Rebecca held out the tub-shaped cog, inviting her to partake.

"Congratulations, Becca! I'm so happy for you!" Evie stuffed her clutch under her arm and took the smallest of sips. Sweet and spicy, the flavor was as familiar as the winds on an Orkney beach. Lowering the cog, she leaned in to hug the bride, spotting Nick over her shoulder.

Hollywood handsome, wearing the morning suit he'd teased her with in an earlier text, his shoulders were stiff and eyes cold as he engaged in what looked like a heated conversation in the corner with her brother.

Shit. Evie snapped the clasp on her silver clutch. *Sam knows already?*

Distracted by a blond toddler careening past, her friends were oblivious to her unease. Diaper bag dangling from his shoulder and a plush baby Yoda in his hand, Tarquin nodded hello tightly and darted through the crush of guests in hot pursuit of his offspring.

"Peedie"—Fiona crouched down to Ava while Poppy yanked her dress again—"why don't you help Uncle Tarq with Luke?"

The corners of Ava's chocolate-speckled lips dipped. "But Mum, Luke bites!"

Sunita held her hand. "Let's teach him how to be a gentleman, yeah?" With a wink, she whisked Ava away.

Lifting Poppy, Fiona turned to Evie. "This one needs the loo. Be back in a sec."

"'Kay." Evie smiled, her cheeks blazing. *Wow.* She fanned herself. *That cog was something else!* Revisiting the corner, she saw Nick and Sam were gone, but she spied Gemma, rosy-cheeked and arm in a tie-dyed sling chatting with Rupert. She scanned the other side of the room. Caleb held hands with the school's sprite of a science teacher while Puggie, the bride's (and Sunita's) ex, slumped against the wall beside a moustached Stuart and his pregnant wife, an eco-lawyer from Glasgow. The trio clinked their pints in celebration and—

"*Evie.*"

Goosebumps pricked her bare arms as she spun around, fighting the angst knotted in her belly. "*Nikolai.*"

"You look lovely." His expression remained all business, but his voice crackled with smouldering want. And that suit! Nick rocked a bespoke suit like 007, but this traditional attire—the fitted black jacket (with tails), crisp white shirt, charcoal-striped trousers, and cream waist coat—made him look like he'd stepped off the world's most delicious, raisin-free wedding cake.

Ignoring the thrum in her chest, Evie kept a respectful distance, determined not to reward the rubbernecking guests mingling nearby with a lusty grab of his lapels. "We need to talk," she said calmly with a blink-and-you'll-miss-it glance around the room.

He nodded once, his focus skimming her simple updo. "Meet

me upstairs in five. Room twelve."

It felt like the longest five minutes of Evie's life.

Door flying open, Nick pulled her close, his heavy gaze locked on her mouth. "God, you look stunning! I've missed you."

"Me, too." Breathless, Evie met his lips and let him in, tasting the cog's heated spice on his swirling tongue. She pushed him back against the closed door, her hands roaming through his hair while Nick pressed into her, his thigh wedged between her slightly parted legs. He moaned into her mouth and Evie pulled back. "*Nick…*"

He peppered a curve of open-mouthed kisses along her jaw. "Yeah?"

"We really need to talk."

Nick's lips stilled on Evie's neck. "Right." He straightened up and motioned into his messy hotel room. "Want a drink first? Some water—?"

"Does Sam know?" she blurted. "About…*you know*?"

"No! I haven't told anyone."

"He looked angry."

Scratching his brow, Nick glanced away. "Yeah, because he hates my guts and I stupidly asked how he was."

"And that's it?" Evie searched his face. "You're sure?"

"Yes." He plowed his hands into the pockets of his trousers. "But he's going to find out sometime."

"Find out what exactly?"

Nick tilted his head. "I'm *sorry*?"

"What are we doing, Nick?" She licked her faded lipstick. "What IS this?"

"Whatever you want it to be."

So dismissive, so bloody non-committal. *Fuck!* Evie's stomach dropped. "You serious?!"

Nick swiped a hand over his closing eyes and shook his head. "*Sorry.* That was a misguided and obviously failed attempt at self-preservation."

"What does that even mean?"

He dropped his hand, his gaze finding hers again. "For the past week I've been on tenterhooks wondering if what I want and what you want are the same thing."

His words sucked all the air from the room. Evie picked at the waist of her dress. "Which is?"

"I'd never pressure you," he answered quietly.

"Just tell me!" she urged, her eyes bulging.

His posture stiffened as he swallowed. Hard. "To get back together."

Giddiness exploded through Evie's veins, releasing her breath and a radiant grin. "I want that, too."

Nick's shoulders dropped. "Oh, thank *god*!" Sweeping her into his arms, he kissed her with reverence, the haste of earlier gone.

Not that Evie was alarmed or disappointed. She took her own sweet time, too. Mouth-crushing snogs and teasing tongues, while sexy as hell, could wait. Nick wanted a relationship with her, and she no longer had to rush every kiss like their bubble was about to burst. They had all the time in the world to discuss their past, to figure things out...to tell Sam.

She smiled against Nick's mouth. "As much as I want more of this, you've got a job to do, Mr. Best Man." She brushed the pad of her thumb along his mouth, removing a smudge of lipstick. "We should head back down. If we're both missing, Sam might put two and two together."

"Well, let's give him and everyone else something worthy of a good gossip." Nick's eyes gleamed. "Let's walk in holding hands."

There had been a time when young Evie would've handed over her pink flip phone and glittery-wheeled roller skates in exchange for Nick suggesting such a thing. Thirtysomething Evie, however, knew there was more to gain if they stayed under the radar a little longer. "I'd love to, but we can't steal the newlyweds' thunder."

Nick played with a loose tendril of hair by her ear. "Another reason why I adore you—always thinking of others."

"And thinking of how sexy it'll be...watching you across a crowded room like a stranger I'm dying to get into bed."

"Look, but don't touch?" He briefly bit his bottom lip. "Foreplay dialed up to eleven equals explosive orgasms later."

She nodded naughtily. "Great minds…"

Nick gazed into her eyes. "I love you, Evie Sutherland."

His easy declaration soothed her battered heart, and yet a bolt of panic fizzed through her. Not about Nick—sliding back into Nick's embrace was easy.

But love?

Selfless, all-encompassing, I'd-walk-barefoot-across-shards-of-glass-for-you love couldn't be rushed after a single night in a sweaty sleeping bag. Present Nick seemed to be everything she had hoped for and more: caring, considerate to a fault, self-deprecating, extremely skilled in bed, but until they unspooled their messy past, a real future and true love (at least for Evie) would remain tightly wound beyond reach.

Her hesitance didn't slip away undetected.

Nick caressed her raised brow. "It's okay if you're not ready to say it back."

Evie smiled ruefully, hoping with everything in her heart she could speak those three beautiful words soon.

TWENTY-SEVEN

EVIE

Then, Monday, August 23, thirteen years ago

"Surprise!" Bounding into Evie's bedroom like an excitable Labrador puppy, Nick dropped his backpack and swept her off her feet, his spinning embrace flinging the sweater she was folding to the floor. "I freakin' love you!"

I love you, too—but ow! Snatching two fistfuls of the back of his track jacket, Evie winced over his shoulder, the fluttery giddiness in her chest no match for the barbed wire uncoiling in her abdomen. "You're a day early!" Her voice was raspy, struggling through clipped breaths.

"Changed my flight and came straight here. Your mum let me in."

"Upstairs, too." His twirl slowing, Evie's bare feet happily reunited with the carpet.

"My inventory skills must've really impressed to get the green light today."

Evie knew the real reason for her mother's clemency but didn't spill. "I'm glad you went, but I'm even happier you're back." She adjusted the fallen strap of her tank top and looped her arms around his neck, kissing him slowly, tenderly until Nick's lips curved into a smile.

"You always make everything better."

Evie had been dreading this moment. She blinked up at him. "I'm sorry about London."

"Ahh, it's okay. Actually, it's a blessing in disguise." Kissing Evie's nose, he let her go and glanced around the room, giving her shelves of romance novels, sea glass, and jelly bean-bright My Little Ponies a non-judgmental once-over. "The thought of sitting in makeup for four freakin' hours a day put me off the project *pretty* quick." He strolled past the window, framing the sunset's sherbet glow, and picked up the stuffed Loch Ness Monster from Evie's desk, a recent acquisition from Inverness—so recent its hospital gift shop price tag still dangled from a plush flipper.

Her eyes widened, hoping he wouldn't notice where Nessie came from. She planned to tell him everything—about her flying visit, all the tests, and her upcoming surgery—but not until he had a moment to decompress.

Nick ran his finger over the sea monster's back humps. "The final nail in the coffin was the new scene they added—the werewolf smothered in live centipedes. Can you imagine, Tigs?! ME with all those tickly, wriggly legs crawling across my skin?!"

Hugging her belly, Evie squirmed. "That's a panic attack waiting to happen."

"God yeah. I told Polly, 'I don't give a toss how large the payday is, I don't *do* creepy crawlies—ever!'"

"Was your mum disappointed, though?"

"Does Rupert love cows?"

"Well, it's still good you went," said Evie.

Nick gave Nessie an affectionate pat and returned her to the desk. Evie breathed easier as he moved on, passing her cork bulletin board and the treasure-trove of postcards from his travels over the years: Corfu, Saint-Tropez, Positano, and many more. Written in Nick's messy boy scribble, the messages celebrated sun-drenched pools, packed nightclubs, and drool-worthy meals, and always ended with "Wish you were here, Evie!" and the much treasured "x". He might've been thousands of miles away, hobnobbing with his family's famous friends, but Evie always felt connected to him.

"Oh, I brought you something from London." Lowering himself onto one knee, Nick tore into his backpack, pulling out tangled earbuds and balled-up Milk Bottle wrappers. "I know you said not to, but…"

As he plowed through his belongings, Evie surreptitiously loosened the tie on her flannel pajama bottoms and climbed onto her bed. With a careful scoot of her bum, she reclined into the welcoming mountain of pillows leaning against the headboard and hugged her cherished orca.

"This"—Nick's hands reappeared with something white and made of fabric, rolled up tight—"is SO you." Rising to his feet, he gave the bundle a firm shake and unfurled a t-shirt, its front adorned with a sparkly blue, roller-skating Starman.

Evie fell into a jaw-dropping stare. "Noooo!" she squealed as Nick draped it across her bent knees. "*Starlight Express*? How'd you—?"

"One of Andrew Lloyd Webber's people. I told her how much you love the musical and she sent this to Polly the next day."

Trading her orca for his thoughtful gift, Evie skimmed her finger across the glittery artwork. "Oh my god, Nick! I *love* it!" She hugged the t-shirt against her chest. "Thank you!"

"She also gave me sheet music. Got Andrew to sign it, too."

"WHAT?! You do realize my mum's gonna love you forever, right?"

Nick laughed. "Hey, gotta stay in her good books somehow."

"Like you have to worry."

"Maybe you and I can try to play it together on your dad's piano later?"

"Definitely—!" A stitch stole her breath.

Nick did a double take, his brow knotting. "Tigs, you okay?"

"Oh. *Yeah.* I'm just, you know, tired and a bit crampy." Skirting his gaze, Evie folded the *Starlight Express* t-shirt as Nick joined her on the bed. "I ate something I shouldn't have yesterday. Stupid, really…" The lie didn't sit well, and another cramp twisted in her abdomen. Gritting her teeth, she relinquished the t-shirt to her bedside table.

Nick gently stroked her leg. "It's hurting a lot, isn't it?"

"It'll fade. Always does."

Lifting her bare feet, he placed them in his lap then began massaging the arch of the left one firmly with his thumbs. "Is there anything I can do?"

His tender touch, kneading and caressing, unlocked the knotted tension in her lower back and shoulders. "Ahhh! More—more of *that*! Your hands"—Evie's eyes flitted closed—"pure magic." She sighed, her body blissfully liquifying into the pillows. "Stay with me for a bit?"

"You got it." His doting hands swept along her foot, working their way around her left ankle and back again. "So, I have some news."

"Me too," she murmured lazily, catching his sly grin.

"Go on, then." Nick broke into song, "What's the buzz? Tell me what's a-happenin'!" He winked. "Ladies first."

"*No.* You know the drill, Balfour. Guests go first."

"Right." Rubbing and pressing, Nick's fingers circled her foot. "Well, I don't know if you'll remember, but before my fifth callback for *Plunder*, I was reading a script for a new musical."

Evie nodded. "That didn't go anywhere."

"Yeah, the writer and director had creative differences. Didn't even reach the audition stage."

"Such a shame," she said. "All that work…for nothing."

"But here's something…the director called me in last week." Hands stilling, Nick's mouth quivered into a full-on, eye-shining smile. "Evie, he offered me a job!"

HELL YES! Adrenaline zipped through her veins faster than a sugary energy drink. "NICK! OHMYGOD—this is AMAZING!" She flailed with glee. "So, what *IS* it?!"

"*ONLY* Judas in *Jesus Christ Superstar*!"

As if her heart couldn't race any faster. "What?! That's a dream role! Oh my GOD! NICK!"

"I know! I-I still can't believe it. I figured I had no hope in hell, but then he offered it to me on the spot."

Evie waved him closer. "Come here!"

Nick shifted her feet off his legs and crawled up the duvet. His embrace was eager yet cautious like he didn't want to cause her further discomfort. Evie, however, was having none of it and nuzzled into him, tugging him tight.

"I *knew* someone would snap you up!" She inhaled deeply, losing herself in his scent. "Didn't I say?"

"You did!"

"This is the biggest news EVER! Nick, you deserve this *so* much."

"Thanks. Yeah, it's huge—so huge I'll have to defer my final year of uni and pick it up *next* September."

She lifted her head. "Oh! Opening night is soon, then?"

"September 21st." Nick laced his fingers through hers. "Four weeks away."

"That *is* soon."

"And the run extends over several months."

"Wow! You know what this means?" Evie grinned. "I'll have *lots* of chances to see you sing on stage!"

"I was hoping you'd say that." Lifting her hand, Nick gave her knuckles a gentle kiss. "I'll send you orchestra seats and plane tickets."

She snickered. "Plane tickets? I'll *be* in London, silly. You know, for uni?"

"Yeah"—Nick's throat bobbed as he lowered her hand—"but *I* won't be."

"Won't?" Her stomach twinged. "*Why?*"

"It's a touring production. We're performing in Japan and Australia, then we move on to Europe."

Touring? Evie deflated into the pillows. "We'll be apart for months."

Nick budged closer, his thumb stroking back and forth over her hand. "But we don't need to be! Like I said, I'll fly you out regularly. I can even book a weekend off and fly home. I just have to give them a bit of notice so my understudy is ready and my travel can be sorted."

Nice in theory, but... Evie dragged her orca onto her lap. "You'd fly all the way back from Australia for a weekend? Isn't that, like, a twenty-four-hour flight?"

"Well, maybe *not* Australia, but I could from Europe."

That's months away. She let go of his hand. "Right."

"Tigs, this doesn't change anything. We'll still see each other, but instead of you coming up to Salford or me traveling down to London, we'll hang out in Osaka or Sydney. How cool is that?"

The thought of a long-haul flight left Evie nauseated. How would her Crohn's hold up, flying across multiple time zones? What if it flared so far from home? How would her illness impact Nick or his performances?

How would I even do this?

"When do you leave for London?" she asked quietly, stroking what was left of her orca's loved-off black plush.

"Tomorrow morning."

Her heart fell along with her face.

"I know, baby, I'm sorry." He spoke quickly. "But there's no way around it. Rehearsals started last week and I have SO much to learn and—"

"Nick"—Evie clutched his hand—"it's okay. *Really.* I'm just surprised by how fast everything's happening. It's all...it's a lot to take in."

"I know."

As they slipped into silence, Evie's mind raced as the laugh track from her father's favorite sitcom drifted upstairs. *So much is changing, too fast, too soon.* She chewed the inside of her cheek, fretting over their carefully constructed plans now scattered like toppled Jenga pieces. "I guess the flat in London next summer won't be happening? Not if you're returning to uni after the tour."

"No, but we can get it the year *after* that."

Evie looked down, averting his gaze again. "So two years from now."

"Better late than never, right?"

Two years. Two years was an eternity. Evie ran a finger over a repaired hole on her whale, her throat feeling sharp and tight like she had swallowed a seashell. *Don't cry.* She blinked back the rising sting in her eyes. *DON'T CRY.*

The reality of him leaving and being absent for months on end was doubly troublesome. What if the person she'd become by his side ended up disappearing too?

Nick tilted his head. "Evie?" Placing a finger under her chin, he lifted her face up to meet his. "*Hey*, it'll still happen. I promise." Leaning in, he kissed her. "I'm going to take care of you. For always. You and me, right?"

Suppressing her tears, she felt her chest tighten. She nodded, letting out a breathy "Right."

"We might even see each other *more*, you know? I'll buy plane tickets to every city on the tour, we'll have an amazing time exploring them together, yeah?"

She glanced down, digging deep, desperate to elbow aside her fears and be present. She refused to let her own worries overtake her happiness for him. "I'm beyond chuffed for you. I'm thrilled and proud—*so* proud."

"I hope I can carry it off."

"Of course you will! I have zero doubts. Honestly, it feels like my heart's about to burst."

Nick winced playfully. "In a good way?"

"The best way," she half-lied, hugging her stuffed orca.

"Would it be all right if I kept this for luck?" He lifted her *Evie* necklace, still adorning his neck.

"Yeah, provided you both come back."

"Like a boomerang, baby!" Nick grinned and leaned in for another lingering kiss. "Hey! Enough about my stuff. What's your news?"

Evie's secret weighed heavily. She wanted to tell him about the looming surgery, but what if it caused a panic attack? Or made him stay? *Staying would ruin everything he's worked so hard for.* Pulse pounding, she collected her water from the bedside table. *I can't risk it. Think of something else. Quick.* She flashed a smile over the rim. "Mine's nowhere near as exciting as yours." She took a leisurely sip, playing for time.

"Come on, I'll be the judge."

"No, really"—leaning away, Evie cleared her throat—"it's *not*." She set down the glass beside a recent letter from Goldsmiths University of London. Her eyes snagged on the jagged tear scarring the envelope. *That'll do. It's not definite, but it's better than mentioning my surgery.*

Shifting back, she faced Nick again. "Me and Sun will be sharing our uni flat with her cousin from Nottingham. It'll be a tight squeeze, but he—"

"*He?*"

"Yeah. Vikram's a fine art student. Has a live-in boyfriend, too, so I'll have an instant London clan."

"Aw, Tigs, that's brilliant! Honestly, your new friends will *make* uni. I'm so excited for you!" Nick gathered her in a hug. "So much good stuff coming up." His hand threaded through her hair. "You at uni, writing up a storm; me playing Judas, singing in Australia—talk about living the dream!"

Over his shoulder, Evie bit her bottom lip, fighting a surge of tears. *So far apart...*

TWENTY-EIGHT

NICK

Now, Tuesday, August 8

Ever since he was a kid, the last days of filming always gave Nick a buzzy brain and a stomach ache. The exhilarating sprint to the finish was a natural high like no other, but the tearful hugs and agonizing farewells with castmates (found family, really), often left him sad.

Luckily this time he had a cherished souvenir from set—Evie.

Nick relished the freedom they'd be gifted once the shoot wrapped, but it wouldn't be all moonlight beach strolls and lazy mornings tangled in bed. Hard work loomed. Building a solid, loving relationship from the ashes of their split would take patience and persistence.

So much had gone unsaid for years, and Nick worried Evie wouldn't feel the same about him once everything was laid bare, including his latest news from London. The fear of her possible rejection roused a panic attack while there as well as a review of his medication by his long-time therapist. The psychologist also advised Nick to keep an open mind, telling him that obsessively ruminating over something that might never happen was unhelpful and unproductive. Ultimately, though, Nick knew if Evie chose to walk away, he couldn't blame her.

Looking up from a thirteen-year-old text, the last sent by teenage Evie, Nick shoved his phone in his jacket pocket and closed his laptop, joining his staff in the *Tomlinson* production trailer calling it a day.

"Nick, you coming with?" asked Ashley, tapping pink gloss on her lips with her finger.

He peeked outside at the boats nestled in Kirkwall Harbor,

checking the weather: slight breeze with another hour or two of day-light. "No, I'm meeting Evie for a drive. I think we both need some air, sea views, and a good ol' singalong in the car. Today was…" He blew out his lips.

"Frustrating, grueling, disappointing?" Ashley snickered. "Why do you think we're all headed to the hotel bar?" She tossed the makeup inside her studded leather purse. "Well, enjoy. Meet us later if you get bored of fields and sky."

"With Evie?" He grinned. "No chance."

"I'm having major déjà vu." Nick squeezed Evie's left hand as she continued singing along to 'Take What You Got' from *Kinky Boots*. "Passing through Stromness, seeing beautiful Birsay…" He watched the ruins of Earl's Palace, a 16th-century castle, surf past the windows as Evie lowered the music's volume. "I feel like I'm twenty and you're seventeen, and we're driving around on the sly again."

Smiling, Evie parked her forest green Ford Fiesta outside a two-story house with a sunny yellow door. "In a way we are, but snogging will have to wait." She shut off the engine and unfastened her seatbelt. "First, we dine."

"Eat? Here?" Freeing himself from his seatbelt, Nick peered beyond the mini orca dangling from the rear-view mirror. "Is this a dinner party?"

Evie swung open her door with nary a word.

Walking past a sign on the ground announcing HONESTY BOX, she led Nick through an opening in a waist-high dry stone dyke and into a small, grassy yard where an unattended yellow cupboard with a gray, peaked roof waited.

"Ahh! I've heard about these," said Nick, spying the black heart hanging above the hut's double doors with 'open' written in chalk.

"Never visited one, though."

"Get your wallet ready! Prepare to have your mind blown." Evie promptly tugged the handles, revealing a multitude of home-made jam, chutney, and baked goods inside.

Nick leaned in with a gobsmacked grin. "Look at all this!" He perused the chalkboards affixed on the inside of both doors listing the day's fresh offerings and their prices.

The premise was simple: treat yourself to rhubarb jam or brownie stars and leave money in the tin provided. The honesty boxes dotted around Orkney offered everything from eggs and home-grown produce to flowers and even handknit toy pigs. Most donated a portion of their proceeds to island charities.

Nick skipped over packages of tiffin as well as fatty cutties, both Orcadian home bakes that contained raisins or currants. Instead, he helped himself to a large loaf of lemon drizzle cake. He dug inside his jacket pocket and deposited the requested £7 in the tin.

"All these years..." She glanced up from his cake. "You've been missing out."

"Too right. Time to make amends and apologize for being such an absent twat."

Her eyes left his in haste, roaming over the jars and baked goods.

Oh shit. Does she think I'm being flippant about US?

Honesty might have been the day's best policy, but Nick wasn't ready to unpack everything just yet, not after the arduous twelve hours they'd both endured. This excursion was supposed to be a fun, stress-free breather. He cleared his throat, keen to lighten the mood again. "I should buy up the entire cupboard! So, whatcha fancy, then? Cake lollipops, maybe a scone? Pick a few things, Tigs. My treat."

A smile warmed Evie's face and a murmured "Thank you" flew from her lips. She selected a packet of vanilla tablet. Similar to fudge, the coarse, sugary confection came sliced into bite-sized cubes. Nick left an additional £5 note as payment and closed the cupboard's doors. However, the sweet exchange didn't temper their short walk back to the car, which fell silent with awkward unease.

Nick pulled his seatbelt across his chest as Evie clicked hers closed. "Where to next?" she asked, turning on the engine.

Yeah, where do *we go from here?* Whether Nick liked it or not, his glib remark had pried open the Pandora's box of their relationship. He owed it to Evie and himself to salvage their evening. Snapping his seatbelt in place, he rescued his cake from the dash. "I meant it, you know."

Fingers curling around the steering wheel, Evie stared ahead.

"I want to be honest and make amends for everything."

Her chin dipped in a tentative nod. "Me too."

"I have so many regrets…"

"Nick, please…can we wait until the shoot's over before we bring up the past?" She threw him a quick sidelong glance. "Things have been good and…"

"I know."

Evie chewed the inside of her cheek. "Just *fun* till then, 'kay?"

Nick smiled. "Yeah, absolutely. Whatever you want, Tigs."

Evie leaned over to kiss him then checked her rear-view mirror and began reversing the car.

Till then.

The thought of what they now shared ending scuttled Nick's appetite for lemon cake or anything else.

TWENTY-NINE

EVIE

Then, Tuesday, September 14, thirteen years ago

Shivering in her hospital gown, Evie hugged the pair of otters from Nick as the nurse checked the beeping monitor beside her bed. The machine's squiggly lines and flashing lights were a veritable fright of cardiac, blood pressure, and oxygen readings.

I can't feel my legs. Her heart hammered. *Or anything below my ribs!*

"Everything looks normal," said the nurse, her soft Inverness accent doing little to soothe Evie's spiraling worry. She jotted numbers on her clipboard and bent down, examining the urine output in the catheter bag. "If you have any questions—"

"I'm a bit freaked out," Evie blurted, staring down at the nurse's bleached blonde bun. "I can't feel my tummy or my toes."

The nurse returned with an empathetic smile. "I know it's scary, but that means the epidural's doing its job, blocking your pain. The numbness is temporary. Everything will return to normal after your operation." She wrote on her chart again. "I'll tell your parents they can come back in." With a flit of her pale manicure, she flung open the privacy curtain and left, leaving Evie alone with her otters, phone, and anxiety. She resumed texting, hitting send on a reply to Fiona.

Evie: Nurse says feeling will come back. It better! PLEASE don't mention ANYTHING to Rupert. He'll tell Nick.

Three dots pranced below her message for a minute or two, then…

Fiona: Don't worry. Rupes is in North Ronaldsay for his course.

Thank god. Evie scratched the crooked surgical cap on her head. No doubt, Rupert was studying the rare seaweed-eating sheep, an ancient breed found only on Orkney's most northern island, one she'd always hoped to visit someday.

More bouncing dots yielded to a second text.

Fiona: Love you, Eves. Keeping everything crossed. Get your mum to text me later? x

Before she could type a response, a flurry of messages landed.

Sunita: I wish I could be there w/you.

I wish I could be traveling to London with you. Evie sulked. Missing all the university excitement sucked.

Sunita: You SURE you don't wanna tell N? I think he'd wanna know. x

And as if his ears were burning…

Nick: I'm such an over-packer, LOL! If my case doesn't burst on the way to Japan, it will be a miracle.

You and your clothes. Evie's heart dipped as she typed. She hated lying to Nick, but it was for his own good.

Evie: You know, they DO have washing machines in Japan! Leave space for stuff you bring back!

Nick answered within seconds.

Nick: Better idea: teleport here now, help me pack & give me a proper farewell? I KNOW you want to, you saucy minx!

Looking up, she swooped her jittery gaze across two drooping bags of clear liquid hanging from the IV pole then slid it downward, riding their rubber tubes. One line (the epidural) disappeared behind her back while the other (saline) was secured with crisscrossing medical tape on the back of her right hand.

Sorry, Nick, but I'm a bit tied up.

Evie flexed her fingers and a nerve-shredding pain shot up her arm. "Ou—ch!" she sucked in a staggered breath.

And not in a sexy way.

As the searing burn subsided, she typed carefully.

Evie: Would if I could! I have a longgg day of travel myself! Can't wait to drop my stuff at the flat then head to the West End with Sun!

Evie: Oh, flight attendant's scowling. Will say bye now.

She paused, her heart leaping into her throat.

Evie: I miss + love you, SaxyBoy xo

Eyes stinging, she sent the final message and kissed her otters.

Marianne pulled the privacy curtain open just enough for her and Graham to enter.

"Look what we found in the gift shop!" His brown eyes crinkling behind his glasses, Evie's father held up a thick book of word search puzzles. "Should keep you busy while you're recovering."

"Aw, thanks, Dad." Evie swallowed, but her mouth remained dryer than the pastry on her mum's homemade Scotch pies. "Has Sam arrived?"

Graham tucked the puzzle book under his chubby arm. "Not yet. His flight was delayed. Stopped in Edinburgh for some reason."

"He's gonna be so pissed, missing school."

"Don't be silly. He'll only be off for a few days," said her dad.

Evie's shoulders slumped. "Unlike me."

Marianne leaned over the bed's rail and stroked her daughter's IV-free hand. "Honey, it'll just be a month."

"Yeah, the *first* month—when everyone makes friends." Pungent lemon disinfectant infiltrated her nostrils as a ragged, wet mop licked the tiles below the hem of the curtain. Evie scrunched her nose.

"Sunita and Vikram will help you get caught up," said her mum.

"But they're not on my course—" Evie's phone buzzed in her palm.

Nick: Safe journey to London. Enjoy *Sweet Charity* with Sun tonight! Will text when we get to Japan. LOVE YA, TIGS! x

God, I wish you were here. Evie sighed ruefully.

"Is that Nick?" asked her mother. "Evie, why don't you call him?"

"I'm not that good an actor. Plus, he'll hear the machines beeping and know something's wrong."

Marianne shared a concerned look with Graham. "Keeping this from him, though…"

"He'll worry, Mum." Evie left her phone on the blanket. "I don't want him stressing before his flight. I'll tell him after, once I'm all patched up."

"But if he calls during his stopover while you're—"

"He won't. I told him this morning I was going to a musical with Sunita tonight, and like a good theater nerd, my phone will be off."

The metal curtain hooks screeched as a stocky, swarthy man in blue scrubs yanked aside the material and stepped inside, accompanied by the anesthesiologist she'd met earlier. Marianne and Graham stepped back, allowing the medical team access to their daughter.

"Good morning, Miss Sutherland," said Dr. Marcus. "How are you feeling? Any pain?"

"No. I can't feel *anything*." *Except nerves. Those suckers won't quit.*

Pulling on a pair of blue medical gloves, the anesthesiologist rounded the foot of the bed. "That's what we like to hear." She smiled and her large eyeglasses collided with her cheeks. "I'm gonna take a look at your epidural. Could you roll a bit further onto your side, please?"

Hugging Nick's otters, Evie complied as the physician examined the catheter taped to her back.

"All good." The anesthesiologist patted Evie's upper arm. "You can relax now."

Easy for you to say. She shifted backward.

"So, to recap what we discussed last week..." Dr. Marcus clasped his hands together as the anesthesiologist stood by his side. "Today we'll be performing a resection, which involves the removal of a damaged section of your small intestine. We won't know how much we'll need to take out until we go in and can properly assess the narrowing and inflammation."

Evie nodded. "It'll take a few hours?"

"Two to four usually."

She glanced at her parents. "I hope you bought magazines and snacks."

"Don't worry about us, love," reassured Marianne.

"Most patients who undergo this surgery will have a good number of years remission, but future reoccurrence *does* tend to happen at the site of the resection," said Dr. Marcus.

"I hope this buys me lots of time..."

"Well, if it does reoccur, the treatment may differ. That's the thing with Crohn's, every instance is a little different. Do you have any questions?"

"No." She aimlessly fussed with her otters' tails. "Mum? Dad?"

Graham looked at Marianne, her grin wavering. "You'll come

see us straight after? Tell us how she's doing?"

"I will. Before she leaves recovery."

"Great." Graham tenderly rubbed his wife's back. "Thank you, doctor."

With a confident nod, the surgeon and anesthesiologist departed, their exit prompting a flurry of renewed activity. The nurse returned with a hospital aide Evie hadn't seen before. He offered no introduction, only a sharp tug of the privacy curtain along its track, which exposed her family's huddle for all to see. Evie's attention vaulted across the pale peach room, leaving behind the flying swallow tattoo on the aide's meaty bicep and landing on her fellow surgical-patients-in-waiting, their expressions weary and glassy, resigned as if awaiting their doom.

Is that what I look like? Evie's heart lurched, pounding frantically as the nurse moved the IV bags. "Mum, I'm scared." The otters slipped free from her grip, tumbling to the floor beyond the curtain.

Marianne caressed her daughter's hand. "Everything's going to be all right, sweetheart."

"We'll be here the entire time," added Graham, rescuing the otters.

The nurse re-hung the IV medications onto the pole attached to the head of Evie's bed then unplugged the vital signs monitor, unleashing a chorus of annoyed electronic bleeps. "It's the battery. Nothing to worry about." She fastened the machine to the pole with the dangling IVs. The aide, meanwhile, reached below and unlocked the brakes with a bed-rattling screech.

"Shit. This is really happening." Squeezing her mother's hand, Evie gulped as the aide stepped behind the head of the bed, ready to steer.

"When you wake up, it'll all be over and done with." Leaning in, Marianne collected her daughter's phone and kissed her cheek. She held her hand one more time. "We love you, darling girl."

Graham's chin quivered as he rubbed her arm. "So much."

"I love you, too." Evie's voice trembled. She fought the rise of prickly tears as her parents stepped away and the bed began moving, curving toward the hall and the short journey to the operating room. *Please bring me back to them.* Craning her neck, she locked eyes with her parents until their loving faces vanished and she was alone, passing scuffed walls, locked custodial rooms, and tall metal shelving jammed with bedpans.

God, please let me get through this. Let me see Nick soon.

"But she's my sister—!"

"Sam?!" Evie's heart leapt into her throat. "Wait!" Waving her hand, she threw a pleading look over her shoulder. "Please, can we stop?"

"You'll have to be quick," said the aide.

She nodded as the bed slowed. "I will! Thank you."

"Sprout!" Perspiration glinting on his forehead, Sam broke into a relieved grin. "Oh god." He bent over the bed's railing. "I thought I'd missed you."

Evie burst into tears, the emotion of the last twenty-four hours catching up to her. "I'm SO glad you're here!" She threw her IV-free arm around his neck and hugged him.

Sam let out a shaky breath into her shoulder, holding her tightly. "Where else would I be, silly…" When he pulled back, his watery eyes met Evie's with a caring smile. "Come on—no more tears. You're gonna be fine. And when you wake up, my ugly mug will be the first thing you'll see, okay?"

Evie laughed, blinking through her tears. "Promise?"

"Cross my heart. I've got your back, Sprout."

THIRTY

EVIE

Now, Friday, August 11

With the thirty-nine filming days in Orkney complete and added to the four months spent earlier in the year on a London soundstage, the *Tomlinson* shoot was finally in the can. To celebrate, extras, cast, and crew convened in a renovated 19th-century herring store-house for the production's wrap party. After cooking and catering seventy-eight servings over seven weeks, Evie was more than ready to tear off her net and let her hair down, both literally and figuratively.

Shame her health issues were crashing the party.

A mild fever combined with abdominal discomfort, a dwindling appetite, and the odd dash to the washroom meant she didn't need a doctor's appointment to know she was flaring. Her specialist recommended she stay home and rest, but Evie was having none of it. She had earned this night out, and no amount of fatigue or cramps would steal the occasion away.

Stood in front of a gold sequin curtain in her daisy dress, she adjusted the plastic Viking helmet on her head and foisted a stick topped with red lips in front of her mouth as a passing Rupert hollered, "Say *Orkney cheddar!*"

"Orkney cheddar!" Evie parroted along with Sunita and Jamie, their silly poses in the open-air photo booth inciting another round of belly-busting laughter.

She looked at her catering team: her double-denim-wearing cousin hidden beneath his ever-present Yankees cap and a pair of star-shaped sunglasses (which kept slipping down his nose), and Sunita, shoulders back and chest out in her electric blue bodycon dress, rocking a pair of rabbit ears and holding some sort of sign. Pride swelled in Evie's heart. *For three amateurs, we catered the hell out of this shoot.*

"NEXT!" The photo concierge waved them away as Tarquin, dressed all in black and reliving his teenage dream as DJ Klimaxx on the far side of the restaurant, mixed into a pounding dance track. The music vibrated inside Evie's chest and assaulted her ears.

"God, it's so LOUD." She returned the lips and Viking helmet to the props table.

"I was gonna say!" Sunita squinted mid-shout. "Who *are* we? And when did we become so boring?!"

Evie laughed, unaware that behind her, Jamie was sneakily sliding the starry sunglasses into his knapsack. Within seconds though, he must've thought better of it and left them beside the Viking helmet.

"I feel old." Evie groaned as her smirking cousin claimed his strip of photos from the collection tray and set off to meet his friends. "And tired."

Sunita parted with the bunny ears. "Wanna go somewhere quieter, grandma?"

"Cheeky!" Evie watched Sunita place the sign face down on the table. "Hey, what's that say? Hot Mess?"

Sunita flipped it over.

Evie's brows jumped. "Best Boss?"

"What? I'd say it's pretty accurate! You gave us clear roles and instructions, were encouraging yet firm—when you needed to be— and never skimped on praise. I know it made a difference to Jamie, having you trust him."

"Well…I tried my best. It wasn't always easy."

"Or pretty." Sunita faux-coughed into her hand. "*Raisins!*"

Wincing, Evie claimed the two remaining photo strips from the tray and handed one to her friend.

"*But* despite everything, you nailed it. Your mum will be ecstatic."

"I'll find out soon enough. They're back in two weeks." Traipsing past the lead actors snogging each other's faces off, Evie elbowed Sunita and shared a smile. They veered toward the party's soft play area where the production's peedie extras, including Ava and Poppy, enjoyed clootie dumpling and ice cream.

"Just watch, she'll go on holiday a lot more now," said Sunita.

Evie laughed. "Yeah! With my luck, I've rebooted her pre-kids love of travel—"

"OH!" Sunita's eyes popped wide. "Speaking of reboots, you must be thrilled about *Dalston Grove* coming back, eh?"

Evie's train of thought derailed. "*Dalston?*" She slowed to a stop. "Where'd you hear that?"

"My mate at *The Mail* caught wind of it," said Sunita. "Why? Hasn't Nick told you?"

"No. He said his London meetings were film-related."

"Maybe the reboot's a movie? My friend did say Nick's involved, though. Someone close to the showrunner confirmed it."

Why's he keeping secrets?

Evie rubbed her pinchy stomach. "I'm all for it if he wants to act again, but at least *tell* me. He used to tell me everything when we were younger, before—" Her gaze strayed beyond Sunita, catching Nick in his silky black shirt with the white polka dots bopping past a pocket of dancing extras that included Fiona. "He's coming," she whispered, straightening up and dropping her hand from her abdomen. "If we want a future together, we can't be hiding things."

Sunita nodded reassuringly as Nick danced around her, his palms full with two small paper boats piled high with beer-battered fish and chunky chips.

"I thought you both might like some appetizers."

"Ooh, yes please!" Accepting Nick's offer, Sunita dove into her tray and promptly munched a golden chip. "Mmm! Now to score one of those beer slushies." She winked at Evie and set off. "See ya in a bit."

Evie waved.

Nick waited a beat. "Why are you hanging back here by the kids' party?"

"The music isn't as loud. And you know…ice cream."

Grinning, he held out the chips again. "Hungry?"

Yeah, for the truth. Troubled by Sunita's news and the growing discomfort in her abdomen, Evie's appetite had frittered away. "Not really, but that looks yummy."

"So do you." He leaned closer so little ears couldn't hear. "Not kissing you right now is fucking killing me." With a brief but lustful stare, he popped a chip in his mouth then straightened up, resuming their 'we're only work colleagues' ruse. "I can't wait for tomorrow when everything's done and dusted. We should take a wee holiday, get away…just you and me?"

"Maybe." Evie licked her lips. "Nick, can I ask you something?"

He nodded mid-chew.

"Your meetings in London, were they about a *Dalston* reboot?"

Swallowing quickly, he laughed. "Wow. Where'd you hear that?"

"Sunita. A friend at *The Mail* told her."

His light-hearted smile faltered, giving way to a terse exhale. "Of course. The bloody *Mail*." A server strolled past, and Nick discarded his barely touched fish 'n' chips on her empty tray.

"So it's true then?"

Nick nodded somewhat reluctantly. "What did they say?"

"That it's happening and you're involved." Weaving slightly, Evie frowned as Nick's focus strayed over her head, his eyes widening. "Why didn't you tell m—?"

"Careful!" he barked, tugging her close, but his reaction wasn't quick enough and someone slammed full pelt into her back.

"Oww!" Evie exclaimed into his chest, her ears filled with the perpetrator's "Sorry!" and a child's shrill wail.

"It's okay, sweetheart." The woman sniffed. "I've got you."

Leia? Looking over her shoulder, Evie saw little Luke's tear-streaked cheeks and then, as she turned around, Leia's panicked blue eyes.

"*Oh, Evie!* I'm sorry!" She clutched her son tight, her hand shaking as she cradled his blond curls. "Some drunk guy crashed into us."

Evie spotted a staggering Stuart, the contents of his pint glass saturating the children's play area. A pair of quick-thinking staff members rushed over, calmly ushering him toward the exit while a server distracted the kids.

Asshole! Evie touched Leia's arm. "Are you two all right?"

"I'm a bit freaked out." Her voice wobbled. "It happened so fast and with Luke's health issues…" The previous summer, Leia and Tarquin's two-year-old had undergone surgery for a heart defect. She kissed her son on his forehead. "I should tell Tarq I'm heading home, call a cab."

"I'll drive you," said Nick. "And I'll stay till Tarquin's done DJing."

"You sure?" Brushing her red hair away from her eyes, Leia glanced at Evie. "I don't want to pull you away if…"

She shook her head. "We're fine. It's nothing that can't wait."

With the ache in her abdomen stealing her fun, Evie decided to trade Sunita and Fiona's drunken dance-off for her Paddington Bear hot water bottle at home. She did a loop of the restaurant, hugging goodnight to her friends and saying goodbye to all the wonderful *Tomlinson* folk she had served over the summer, her memories fond and plentiful. Once outside in the quiet briskness, she rang Sam asking if he could pick up a few things for her from the late-night grocery near his house. She also texted Nick during the five-minute walk to her apartment.

Evie: Left the party early. Have overdue accounting to tackle before Mum's back. Hope Leia and Luke are okay. Talk tomorrow morning x

Evie needed to know Nick's reason for keeping the *Dalston* news from her as soon as possible, and even more worrisome, if he harbored any additional secrets he had conveniently forgotten to share.

Within the hour, her brother and her Crohn's-friendly groceries had arrived on her doorstep. Sam busied himself in the kitchen while Evie turned off her phone and snuggled up on the sofa, co-cooned in her old *Starlight Express* t-shirt, baggy track pants, and purple hoodie. She held her Paddington hot water bottle against her belly and began to doze off as a repeat of *Lost* played on the TV.

"Here you go."

Blinking awake, Evie spied Sam walking toward her, a steam-ing bowl in his hands. She gladly accepted the chicken broth with a heartfelt "Thanks" but received a judgmental glower in return.

Honestly? After all these years?! Let it go! She stirred her soup. "Don't say it."

"Someone has to—"

"Sammy!"

"What's up with you and Nick?"

Oh—didn't expect that. Evie looked up from her bowl. "I thought you were gonna scold me for going out—for old time's sake."

His silent stare signaled that her attempt at levity fell flat.

"Nick and I are bound to be in the same place, Sam. I am— well, *was*—working for him." Evie blew on a spoonful of broth and took a careful sip.

"I know about Rackwick."

She dunked her spoon again. "So? I got stranded. The whole crew did."

"But the whole crew didn't bunker down in the bothy with Nick, did they?"

She refused to take Sam's bait, which seemed to redden his cheeks and piss him off even more.

"You were spotted the next morning, Evie. The caretaker saw

you kiss Nick goodbye on the doorstep." Clenching his jaw, Sam threw his hands in the air. "I can't *believe* you're seeing him again."

Evie lowered her spoon. "And what if I am? Sam, it's *my* business, not yours."

"Oh, I think it is! Remember, it was *me* who picked up the pieces last time."

Her heart warmed with gratitude. "I know. You were my rock. I couldn't have gotten through it without you. But I'm older now and...smarter, I hope, and I'm *done* with hating him for something that happened ages ago. It's too exhausting. We were kids and bad decisions were made on both sides. I think we both know that now."

"So you've discussed it?"

Evie retreated into her soup again. "No, not entirely."

Sam shook his head. "Yeah, I didn't think so."

"But we will. And I wish you would mend things with him, too, Sammy. Sometimes it feels like you're unwilling to move on."

"And that's what *you're* doing?" asked Sam. "Moving on. With Nick."

"Maybe—"

A triple knock on the door cut her off. Evie sat up. "Ooh, might be my elderly neighbor. Her cat's always wandering off. I help her search."

"Eat your soup," said Sam. "I'll help her."

As her brother headed around the corner and down the almost non-existent hall, Evie rested her bowl beside her open laptop on the coffee table. Pieces of paper towel, unused tissues, and crumpled receipts littered its surface, each scrap bearing scribbled-on-the-fly notes for her current Cordelia Ross romance in progress.

A draft from outdoors invaded the room. Evie tugged her hoodie's cuffs over her palms and craned her neck as muffled snippets of conversation teased her curiosity. "Sammy, who is it?"

"Evie, it's me."

Surprise tingled in her chest. "Nick? Uh..." She hid her hot water bottle under a throw pillow and grabbed her laptop. "Come in!" The floorboards creaked as she hastily opened a Marwick's spreadsheet. Nick appeared first, not waiting for Sam.

"Hey!" She smiled, taking in his posh overcoat and dark trousers. "To what do I owe the pleasure?"

As Sam joined them, Nick glanced uneasily around the room. "Tarquin called Leia and mentioned that you didn't look well. I texted, but you didn't answer."

"Sorry 'bout that. I turned it off and fell asleep." Evie closed her laptop and slid it onto the table, her coming-home-to-work ploy busted.

As he sat down beside her, Nick's eyes narrowed. "Tigs, be honest. Are you in a flare right now?"

She nodded. "I had a sinus infection and missed an infusion. I can't reschedule until my fever subsides."

"A fever can mean active Crohn's," said Sam, jumping in. "The doctor's ordering tests."

Nick gathered her hand in his. "You have to *tell* me when you're unwell. I want to be here for you, help take care of you."

Crossing his arms in front of his flannel shirt, Sam scoffed. "You can't do that from London, Nick."

Holding Evie's gaze, he raised her hand, kissing it. "Things are different now."

"Are they, though?" Sam glared. If looks were lethal, the former child star would've been bleeding out on the sofa. "'Cause it doesn't take a vet to know a leopard can't change its spots."

Evie stiffened. "Sam, *really*...?"

Nick's jaw tensed as he peered over his shoulder. "*Maaaate*." He stretched the word into three syllables. "Aren't you a little *old* to be dragging around some ludicrous teenage vendetta?"

That's enough. Evie rippled with annoyance. "Would you guys *quit* it?" She met Sam's angry gape. "If you're gonna argue, go outside. I feel like shit and don't need this."

"I know. I'm sorry." Nick caressed her hand, and she met his eyes again. "For so much."

He's apologizing for...? Her heart tripped. She sucked in a staggered breath.

"Evie, you need to know the truth. About our split. About the night of your surgery."

"The night of—?" Evie glanced between him and Sam, who slumped into the neighboring arm chair. "Why? What happened?" she murmured, letting go of Nick's hand.

THIRTY-ONE

NICK

Then, Tuesday, September 14, thirteen years ago

"Come on, *COME ON*!"

His foot frantically tapping as he gnawed his bottom lip, Nick cursed the slow blink of the elevator's floor numbers. Ticking upward, they took their own…sweet…time. "It'll be bloody Christmas by the time I get there!" His pulse, fueled by caffeine and worry, pummeled beneath a cellophane-wrapped bouquet of daisies pressed against his car coat. "Hurry—the fuck—*UP*!" he growled.

DING!

He yanked his hefty suitcase forward. "Finally!" Squeezing impatiently around the sliding door, he bolted down the hall, past a bank of telephones and an empty vending machine, his overstuffed knapsack bouncing against his back.

"Tigs, where ARE you?" Looking frantically left then right, he tossed his hair from his eyes and scoured the hospital's signs. *Ward 4A? 4—oh! Down here.* He took the corner sharply and his trailing luggage clobbered something, creating a clatter.

"What. Now?!" Nick grumbled under his breath and threw a harried glance over his shoulder. A tray from a diagnostic cart laid on its side, its ear thermometer and blood pressure equipment scattered on the worn vinyl floor.

Turning back with a quick crouch and a determined swoop, Nick set the cart back on its wheels and safely returned the medical gear to its basket as the squeak of running shoes drew closer.

"Nick? What the hell are you doing here?"

I know that sing-songy accent. The tightness in Nick's chest gave way as he spun around, clocking Sam in a rumpled plaid button-down and faded jeans, a tea-stained paper cup in his right hand. "Mate, I'm *so* glad to see you! I've been all over trying to find Evie. I couldn't call you because my bloody phone ran out of juice." He sucked in a much-needed breath and exhaled forcefully. "How's she doing? Is she awake?"

Exhaustion creased Sam's brow as he scratched his auburn stubble. "Shouldn't you be on a plane to Japan?"

"I *would've* been if Sunita hadn't called. Just in time, too. I was literally handing over my passport at check-in and—"

"You shouldn't be here, Nick."

"Oh…yeah, I know all about that *now*, thanks to Sun." The daisy bouquet crinkled in his hands. "Typical Tigs, not wanting ME to worry. But once Sunita told me, I dropped everything, jumped on the first flight up here."

"What about your tour?"

"I'll catch 'em up. Opening night is in a week's time. As long as I'm in Japan a few days prior, I'll be good." Nick eagerly gripped the handle of his suitcase and craned his neck, surveying the hallway. "So, what room's she in? I can't wait to see her."

"She's sleeping." Sam tore the paper lip of his empty cup. "Mum and Dad went for some dinner—finally. I was taking a walk, stretching my legs. It's been a long, nerve-racking day."

"I was going to say, you look *knackered*. Why don't you go, get some rest? I can take over. Do the night shift."

"And what about tomorrow and the day after that?"

Nick smiled. "I'll be here."

"But you'll be gone by the weekend."

"Well, yeah…I kinda have to be. I signed a contract, Sam."

He jutted out his chin. "You could break it."

"Uh, *yeah*"—Nick pawed the back of his neck, his gaze skating over the nurses' station down the hall—"but that wouldn't look good."

"Neither does bailing on your sick girlfriend."

Head snapping back, Nick's hand stilled. "Bailing?!" He slowly lowered his arm.

"Well, what would *you* call it? You come and go from Orkney more often than the flippin' ferry. How's that for being reliable, being present? It doesn't take a medical genius to see how being with you hasn't been good for my sister."

"Based on what?"

Face reddening, Sam pointed down the hall. "Well, she's *here*, isn't she?!"

Nick's pulse stuttered. He blinked slowly, fiercely. "Mate, I didn't cause *this*."

"But the stress of dating you sure as hell did."

What the actual fuck?! Dropping eye contact, he looked off into space. "Now you're making shit up."

"Oh, so I'm lying when I say Evie falls ill when she doesn't hear from you?"

The muscles in Nick's shoulders stiffened as he glanced back. "What do you mean?"

Sam nodded. "Evie *pines* for you, Nick. For your calls, your texts. She'll even ditch Sunita and Fiona and stay home on the off chance you might fly in unexpectedly. When you don't, she gets stressed, and within hours, her Crohn's flares."

Shit. Nick's throat thickened.

"Why she'd wait like that for you, I have no clue," said Sam.

I do. The first Marwick's visit, the bonfire, Rebecca's party—all unannounced drop-ins, not to mention what he tearfully blurted on the heels of his *Plunder the Crown* rejection. *Bollocks, what have I done?* Raking his hair off his forehead, Nick swallowed, but the wave of nausea in his belly wouldn't abate. "I…might've said something about flying in and surprising her sometime. But things have been so *nuts* lately…" He trailed off, dreading Sam's reaction.

"So you gave her false hope, something else to fret over? Like she doesn't have enough with school and Crohn's and worrying about other girls—"

"Hey, I'd *never* cheat on Tigs. I love her, Sam. I'd do anything for her."

"Anything, eh? Nice. Like moving to Orkney?"

Except...that. Fleeing Sam's judgmental stare, Nick curled both hands around Evie's bouquet, escaping into the sunny blooms.

Sam snorted. "Nah, didn't think so. Now I know why you suggested the London flat—to take her away."

"That's not fair." Nick lifted his chin. "I suggested it because I want to be with her."

"But not enough to live where she feels safe. I know my sister better than *anyone*, Nick. London might be fun for a while, but it's not home. It's not Orkney. She'll always come back. Unlike *some* people, Evie doesn't see the island as a dead end."

"I never sai—I have to live near London for my career."

"And Evie needs to live in Orkney for hers," retorted Sam.

"But does she?" Nick fired back. "Have you ever asked what *she'd* like to do? Why is it a given that she'll take over the shop? Why her? Why not you? And don't give me that *tradition* bollocks. That's just a reason to hold her back."

"If you think she's being forced into it, you couldn't be more wrong, mate."

"Says the bloke with the most to lose," said Nick. "If Evie moves away, the responsibility might fall on *your* shoulders."

"Maybe, but the truth is, Evie *wants* Marwick's. Always has." Sam let out a quiet chuckle. "When we were peedie, she loved playing shop. She'd steal my toys, Mum's handbags, and ring up pretend sales on our granny's typewriter. When stuff went missing, we'd always find it in her room. Drove us bonkers."

I can actually picture her doing that. Nick couldn't help but smile...but only a little.

"I know your dad bullied you to take on Sports Now and maybe that's why you're suspicious, but Evie isn't you, Nick. You've seen her, how engaged she is with customers, how she takes pride in the merchandise and the shop's legacy. Marwick's isn't *settling*. Not for Evie."

As much as Nick hated to admit it, she did seem perfectly happy there—at home—like he was on a soundstage in front of cameras and crew. He pulled back slightly. "I want what's best for her,

Sam."

"I know you do. We *all* do. Especially now. She's been through so much, and today was…grim."

Nick stilled. "Why? What happened?"

"There were complications."

Oh god, no. His heart dropped into his stomach.

"The tissue damage was worse than they'd thought, and Evie lost a lot of blood. She needed a transfusion."

"Will she be okay?"

"Hopefully, but the surgeon said her recovery could be tough. University will have to wait. Evie needs to put all her energy into getting better."

"Fuck." Nick winced. "Poor Tigs. She'll be gutted about uni."

"Yeah, well, that's not the only thing that has to take a back seat." Sam rubbed his forehead. "Look Nick, with everything you've got going on, it's…A LOT. I honestly think it's too much for Evie. I know your heart's in the right place, but maybe it's time to…" Pressing his lips, Sam shrugged like he hoped Nick would fill in the blanks.

He narrowed his eyes. "To what?"

"Let Evie focus on Evie. She can't be wrapped up in all your drama," said Sam. "The next few weeks and months will determine whether she goes into remission. If she doesn't, she could be in for years of pain and additional surgeries—life-*changing* surgeries. Is that what you want for her?"

A lump swelled in Nick's throat. "Of course not."

"Then fly to Japan, do your acting thing, and think hard about whether all *this* is really what's best for her…and you, too."

Wait—is he implying I should dump her?! Nausea rolled in Nick's belly again. He tugged at his hair. "I-I can't believe this. You want me to break up with her?!"

"I *want* what's best for her."

Nick shook his head. "Evie loves me…a-and she'd be fucking furious if she knew what you were suggesting."

"I thought you said you'd do *anything* for her," said Sam.

346

Nick glared, the sting of impending tears tormenting the back of his nose. "I *would*!" he snapped, his mind careening through memories of Evie laughing till she couldn't breathe, playing with Ross at his gran's, and singing loudly in the car.

Ultimately, he wanted good health and happiness for her—even if it meant they'd be apart. He swallowed, but the knot in his throat wouldn't budge. *I will do anything for her.* He nodded sullenly. "I'll leave tonight. I'll give her more space, but only until she's better."

"You can't tell her you were here," said Sam. "Evie didn't want you to know about today, and we should respect that. This drop-in will be our secret, okay?"

"What about Sunita?" Nick sniffed.

"Tell her"—Sam glanced into the empty cup in his hand—"I don't know, you couldn't get a last-minute flight up or something."

"She'll rip me a new one."

"Better that than Evie thinking we betrayed her trust," reasoned Sam.

Nick blinked back tears. "I guess…"

"So, we're good?"

"Yeah, but on one condition." Nick sniffed again. "Let me see her."

"Nick—"

"*Please*, Sam," he begged, his voice cracking. "I promise. I won't wake her."

As monitors beeped around the corner, punctuating the ward's eerie calm, Evie's nurse gave Nick and Sam a subtle nod. "Visiting hours end in less than five minutes."

"Okay. Thanks." Nick hesitated in the hall, preparing himself for what he was about to see…and say.

Sam held out his hand. "Flowers?"

"Oh right." He passed Evie's brother the verboten bouquet of daisies and hugged his middle.

"First bed on the left," said Sam.

Legs suddenly weak, Nick slowly wandered around the doorjamb.

Eyes closed and skin pale, Evie looked so tiny, so vulnerable. Tubes and wires seemed to come from everywhere: her nose, wrists, chest, and under the blankets.

Oh, Evie baby... The ache in Nick's chest stole his breath as he crumpled on the chair beside her bed. "I wish you'd told me," he whispered through tears. "I love you, Tigs. For always." He gently stroked her hair. "And I'm *so* sorry."

THIRTY-TWO

EVIE

Now, Friday, August 11

"Oh my god." Evie wiped her eyes and runny nose. "You were *there?*"

Nick nodded.

"I dreamt it. I dreamt you were holding my hand, stroking my hair." His face blurred through a watery veil of tears. "It was real. *You* were real." Evie scowled at her brother. "I can't believe you sent him away and then lied about it all these years."

Sam held up his palms. "Sprout, I *only* suggested he go—no one put a gun to his head. Frankly, I was surprised he actually left."

Nick scoffed over his shoulder. "That's bollocks, mate. You *knew* I would. I would've done anything to help Evie recover." Turning back, his expression softened with tender sincerity. "Even walk away."

Evie blew out her cheeks, her gaze hardening as she side-eyed Sam. "You said you wanted what was best for me, but...why didn't you think that was Nick?"

"Because he was a bad influence! You were *constantly* twisting your life to fit his!"

Evie huffed. "That's not true."

"Dressing differently"—Sam counted on his fingers—"champagne on the beach, raving at his gran's, moving to London permanently—"

"But I didn't move permanently, did I? I realized London wasn't for me—*myself*. And despite that, years later you still hate him for something that never happened."

"I don't *hate* him," replied Sam. "I just think you'd be better off

349

with someone local and responsible."

Nick rolled his eyes. "Cheers, mate."

"C'mon, Nick. You've said it yourself: your life is a circus."

"*Was* a circus," he corrected. "It isn't now."

Sam's attention slid to Evie. "You didn't need outside distractions. You needed to get better. I needed you to get better!" He leaned closer and she noticed tears glinting in his eyes. "The day of your surgery was the worst of my life. The complications and blood loss...we were so scared we might lose you."

Stomach churning, Evie wiped her nose.

"I was furious at the world, thinking how could this happen to my baby sister? Then Nick showed up out of the blue and...I saw red. I needed someone to blame, and there he was: the cause, the reason you'd gotten so sick..."

Evie closed her watery eyes. "So, I've been living all these years thinking Nick didn't love me the way I loved him. All because you hatched up a stupid plan—"

"Evie, you were *only* eighteen," said Sam. "That's far too young for a serious relationship, especially long distance. I figured time apart might help you see sense."

"And break us up."

"If I'm honest, yeah. But you have to see I did it out of love," said Sam. "I thought it would be best for everyone."

Evie pushed her lips out. "Not your call to make, Sam."

"I know that now." Scratching his scruff, he stared downward. "I've been dreading this day. You finding out...you hating me."

"Yeah, well"—she swiped her cheeks—"it sucks getting caught out, doesn't it? You know, I can't even look at you, let alone talk to you right now, so—"

"Evie, I'm sorry—"

"Please Sam, just *go*."

Glancing at Nick, he hoisted himself out of the chair and grabbed his windbreaker. He left the living room without further protest.

Evie waited for the front door to snap closed then spoke. "The day after my surgery, Sunita told me she'd texted you. She didn't approve of me keeping you in the dark."

"You didn't want me to be there?" asked Nick.

"I did, but not at the expense of you playing Judas."

"Can I ask…did you know you needed surgery when I first told you?"

Evie nodded.

"I would've delayed my flight, joined the tour later."

"That's why I didn't say anything. I was worried you'd find out and quit. I even googled 'actor breaking contract' and read that it usually ruins their reputation. That sealed it for me: I'd tell you after the surgery, once you were in Japan."

"You were protecting me and I was protecting you." Nick looked down then met Evie's eyes again. "Leaving you was the hardest thing I've ever done, but I knew I couldn't live with myself if I delayed your recovery or made your Crohn's worse."

"I don't think you would have. If anything, you would've helped. Do you remember our first phone call after my surgery?"

Nick grinned faintly. "Two days after—the longest forty-eight hours of my life. You apologized for keeping it secret like ten times before rattling off a list of questions: how was my hotel room? Did it have a view? What was sushi like?"

The memory warmed her heart. "Just hearing your voice, I swear my smile could've powered the whole hospital. I even managed two slow laps of the ward with my nurse after. She was amazed. I wasn't. I knew you would spur me on. You did for weeks."

"I hated being separated from you." Nick blinked away. "Hated the tour…"

Evie tilted her head. "You never said."

"Because you'd worry."

True. "What went wrong?"

"What didn't," said Nick. "It was a disaster from start to finish. I was homesick and missing you. Didn't want to socialize with my castmates, who mistook my reticence for snobbishness. Then the one time I did go out with them, I caught mononucleosis from a shared glass and ended up out of the show more than I was in it."

She blinked rapidly. "You told me it was laryngitis."

"Yeah. Another wee fib so you wouldn't stress. The mono co-incided with panic attacks and a bout of depression. I could barely get out of bed let alone message you about it. I felt like such a twat, feeling sorry for myself when you'd had major surgery and barely said a peep about it. I asked you, but you wouldn't—"

"I know." Evie tugged at the hem of her hoodie. "I didn't want to be a bummer."

"You told me only good things. How bad was it—really?"

"It was *hard*," her voice softened. "The surgery cut through my stomach muscles. I lost all my core strength. I had trouble lying flat, walking and standing. And coughing and sneezing hurt like hell."

His eyes widened.

"I had to slowly reintroduce food, do breathing exercises, phys-io. And I went through this weird mourning period, grieving every-thing I'd lost, things like my place at uni, my social life—talking regularly to you." Sniffing, she paused. "You didn't always answer my texts. I thought I'd done something wrong."

"No, never. It was me—*all* me."

"But I didn't know that. I'd message anyway, not knowing where to begin, if I was saying the right things. And when you *did* reply, you seemed…distant."

"So much was happening, but it felt like I had nothing to share," said Nick.

Evie nodded. "Except 'I miss you, I love you' over and over, but sometimes even that felt strained. I started to think my Crohn's was spooking you."

He leaned forward. "No, honestly, it didn't. Hearing how you were doing was inspiring—even if I didn't know the whole story."

Guilt panged in her chest.

"You were so strong and resilient, Evie. The opposite of me, really."

"Nick…"

"No, it was." He slouched. "I fell completely apart on tour. I had to drop out for health reasons six months in."

Evie's heart plummeted. "Really?"

He ducked his chin. "So, you see, Sam wasn't too far off about me. I failed. I fucked up my dream job."

"You didn't fail, Nick. You weren't *well*. That's hardly your fault."

"But it felt like it. I kept hearing my mother's voice in my head—'Grow up, get over it, get back to work.'"

Hateful woman. Evie curled her lip. "Well, she was wrong."

"Two months later, I parted ways with my agent and...waited for you to dump me, too. I was such a shit boyfriend, not responding, hiding the truth, so when you didn't..."

"You ghosted me."

He looked up with tears in his eyes. "I didn't end us because I fell out of love with you. I did it because you didn't need a loser like me dragging you down or making you sick again. I knew if I broke up with you properly over the phone you'd cry and fight me on it. I couldn't handle that." He fidgeted with his watch. "I took the fucking coward's way out..."

So it wasn't about me or my Crohn's...well, at least not how I thought it was.

Evie stared across the room. "I held on. I thought you might call or appear at my door, apologize. If you had, we could've worked things through, could've gone back to the way things were. But I waited and you didn't call, you didn't come back..."

"So you texted me." Nick pulled his phone from his jacket. He tapped and scrolled and held up the screen.

Swallowing hard, she read the message:

Evie: I thought you were my forever. I was wrong.

Her breathing slowed as she ached for her younger self. Mere days before her nineteenth birthday, riding out the side effects of her new, post-operative treatment, Evie had hit send on that final message while sobbing inconsolably into her stuffed otters, her once hopeful heart torn at the seams. "I changed my number after that." She sniffed as Nick lowered his phone. "And deleted yours."

"I know saying sorry doesn't feel like enough, but I am Evie, I'm *so* sorry," he pleaded. "For leaving you, for hurting you so badly. For everything."

"You made me feel seen and beautiful, and not like some freak with a nasty disease." She picked at her nails. "I thought you were the one person who would never hurt me. And then you did."

He nodded dolefully. "It's my biggest regret."

Evie glanced away.

Nick rubbed the back of his neck. "I cried for weeks. Couldn't eat. Didn't know what to do with myself. The only thing that helped was getting wasted. I'd be that prat at parties running about with no shoes on, urging everyone onward to the next boozy stop. Then I'd greet the morning with a banging headache and a Bloody Mary for breakfast. Calling it a night was a struggle. I couldn't let the party end because if it did, my mind would snap back to you. In a weird way, my sales exec job actually helped with that. They paid me to schmooze clients in London and abroad. That's when I met Olympia."

Pia with her honey blonde highlights and skinny nose.

Evie sniffed, the all-too-familiar sting of tears burning the back of her throat, of spotting Nick and his new girlfriend at Rupert and Fiona's wedding. Eight months after that, around the time of Ava's baptism, she'd heard they'd broken up.

Her glare sprang back. "Do you know how I found out about you eloping?"

Nick wouldn't hold her gaze.

"In the cathedral. Holding baby Ava in front of *everyone*. Can you even imagine how heartbreaking that was? Hearing it from your mother in front of my parents and friends that the boy I still loved four years on had married someone else? And on a whim, too!"

His throat bobbed.

"I was excited to see you, hoping to smooth things between us.

Fuck, I even naively thought *maybe* we could find a way to get back together. But it was like Fi and Rupert's wedding all over again except Pia the surprise girlfriend was now Pia the surprise wife. I was so humiliated." Evie shook her head. "Everywhere I turned, every street, every corner of Orkney held painful memories—*our* memories. Mum suggested I visit Sunita in London for a bit, use the money I never spent on uni to make a fresh start. But I knew you lived there—somewhere—so I just had to hope our paths wouldn't cross. All I wanted was to forget you."

"I couldn't forget you." Nick touched her bent knee. "I missed you. I *loved* you."

"Yeah, so much that you married someone else," she snarled.

"I didn't think you'd take me back. I was trying to heal my heart—"

"Oh, spare me."

He pulled his hand away. "I know it sounds ridiculous, but I was so messed up, trying to numb the pain of losing you. I don't even remember my wedding. And I kept on making the *worst* decisions. If I could go back, I would do *everything* differently."

Crossing her arms, she looked away with a disgusted huff.

"I would've," he repeated. "I wouldn't have listened to Sam. I would've stayed at your bedside, holding your hand, and when they sent you home, I would've brought marshmallow Snowballs and Ross and made sure you didn't want for anything. And obviously, I would never have met Pia, let alone married her."

Evie always wondered: when did he realize he'd made a mistake? The morning after? A week, two months? Or was it Pia who pulled the plug?

"But you *did* marry her."

"We lasted seven months," said Nick. "I mean, shit, if that doesn't tell you everything you need to know."

Well, there was one other thing.

"Did you love her?" she asked.

"No. I loved *you*."

Evie wiped tears from her cheeks. "Well, I hated you."

Nick closed his eyes for a beat then slowly opened them. "The split with Pia was mutual. I planned to tell you at Gran's funeral, but…"

I stayed in London and didn't fly home. Shame softened Evie's anger. "Lily was always wonderful to me." An ache thickened in her throat. "I can't believe she's been gone eight years now."

Nick nodded into a sad fleeting smile. "Gran was always rooting for the two of us."

Fighting against an undertow of melancholy, Evie gave in, drifting off into regret and remorse. "I still feel awful about missing her funeral. I wanted to come, but I didn't think I could keep it together if—seeing you with Pia…" She swallowed. "Fi told me later that you'd divorced. I adored Lily. I *should've* been there."

"And she adored you. I used to ask Gran if she'd seen you, how you were. She wouldn't tell me a thing."

"You can't blame her, Nick. You were married. You had a *wife.*"

"A wife she hardly said a word to. Then again, that wasn't a surprise. Gran knew I wasn't in love with her. She wasn't *you.*"

Evie's heart ached as she looked away.

And none of the men I met were you…

Nick dipped his chin and continued. "You always made me feel less alone. You always believed in me and lifted me up." His lips curved slightly. "You even helped me clean my disaster of a bedroom…"

Yeah, so we had somewhere tidy to snog. Evie glanced back, fondly remembering the endless summer days up in his room.

"…No one understands my love of Jenga like you do or lets me sing to *Grease 2* in the car. Looking back, you star in all my favorite memories. You remind me of what's *good* in this world, and I was *so* stupid to let you go." He blinked up at her. "Evie, I'm so sorry. I know I have no right to ask, but I'll do *anything* to get you back. Whatever it takes, I just want to be with you. For always."

She toyed with her hoodie's strings as silence settled between them.

For years she had kept Nick at arm's length. Avoiding, hiding, changing plans so they wouldn't be in the same place at the same time, fearful his presence would tear open old wounds and unleash more hurt.

But now? If the past two months had taught her anything, it was that regardless of what life threw at her—a damaged shop, an injured cook, a Crohn's flare—she would be okay. None of these unforeseen hiccups had broken her spirit or her resolve.

And neither would the unexpected return of her first love, or the truth about how and why their relationship had come to a painful end.

The Nick sat beside her was different, too. He was more self-aware and emotionally mature, and he took full responsibility for his actions. While the prospect of being vulnerable again was scary for Evie, it was also invigorating. But with his sincere apology melting her heart and her gut screaming, *Just kiss him already!*, there was still one final puzzle piece to slide into place.

"Why didn't you say anything about the *Dalston* reboot?"

"Oh, I wanted to so badly, but I signed an NDA. We all did."

The tension in Evie's shoulders eased.

"*Well*, I say that. Obviously, someone broke confidentiality and contacted *The Mail*." Nick sighed. "But I can see how my lack of transparency might've looked like I was being secretive or, you know, lying by omission."

"No, I get it," said Evie.

"But now that the cat's out of the bag, I can tell you I'll be executive producing the film."

Her brows rose behind her bangs. "You're not acting?"

"Well, I'm penciled in for a Jake cameo"—his lips parted in a bemused grin—"with his now fourteen-year-old son."

Evie fell back into the couch. "No way!"

"*I know*, right?! I feel so bloody old." Nick laughed with charming self-deprecation. "This reboot is a next-generation thing. Jake's kid will be the heartthrob, not me."

"It'll be amazing," she replied genuinely then paused for a beat.

"Thank you for telling me. I won't tell anyone."

"I know. You've always kept my secrets."

She nodded slowly with a slight grin. "NDAs aside, if we're trying again, we have to be honest about everything."

His face lit up. "So you still want to be with me?"

"Yes," said Evie. "We were both so young back then, trying our best, making mistakes, but like Fi said to me, just because it didn't work out for us before, doesn't mean it won't now."

Nick wrapped his arms around her. "My Tigs, I *never* stopped loving you." His brown eyes sparkled. "It's always been you." The smile in his whisper brought happy tears to Evie's eyes.

She let out an elated laugh. "It's always been *you*." The heartfelt words tumbled off her tongue. "I love you, Nick." Hesitation gone, Evie pressed her mouth against his, the tenderness of his kiss drawing a grateful sigh from her throat.

THIRTY-THREE

EVIE

Now, Wednesday, August 22

The sweaty break of Evie's fever the morning after their heart-to-heart meant her missed biologic infusion could go ahead at the hospital several days later.

For two hours, Nick sat by her side, watching the drip, drip, drip of the medication as it trickled into the IV line and swept through the clear plastic tubing into Evie's bloodstream. She dozed on and off with her pillow and blanket, completed word search puzzles with Nick, and nibbled on a bland menu of salted crackers and flat ginger ale. Afterward, Nick drove her home and lavished her with foot massages, a baked tattie with applesauce, and a cuddle on the sofa while watching her new favorite (roller skate-free) musical, *tick, tick... BOOM!*

True to his word, Nick doted on her around the clock and only left to pick up groceries or medication. Cleaning, cooking, washing clothes—he took to caretaking with aplomb, erasing any lingering doubts as to whether he'd stick around when life got messy.

Eight days on, Evie's infusion had started to work its magic. Her Crohn's flare had diminished considerably, and the stabbing pains and urgent trips to the washroom were no longer keeping her in pajamas or tied to home. A celebration was in order. She threw on a t-shirt, track pants, and hoodie, and joined Nick on a relaxing stroll through the dappled shade of Happy Valley, a hidden gem of flowers, rare woodland, and quiet paths along the Burn of Russadale, one of her favorite spots.

Evie swung Nick's hand as they meandered in front of a small, abandoned stone cottage called Bankburn. Her cheeks ached from grinning. "I still can't believe it." She claimed a seat on the bench below one of the cottage's windows.

"Got a great price, too." Nick followed her lead and sat down.

"*You*...the new owner of my beloved Sinclair house! I bet it has lots of space for clothes. No more cramming your designer duds in the hotel's peedie closet."

"Yeah, but here's an idea..." Nick kissed her hand. "Why don't we change that 'you' to 'we'?"

Is he suggesting what I think he is? Her heart skipped.

"I know we've just reunited, but thirteen years is an awfully long time to be apart. I don't want to miss another second. So how 'bout it, Tigs? Move in with me?"

Evie would've moved into a cardboard box with Nick, but the fact that he was asking about *the* church-turned-house she'd admired since childhood? Her enthusiasm got the best of her.

"YES, PLEASE!" Eyes wide, she bounced, the sudden movement tweaking her side slightly. "And let's get a dog—a Japanese Spitz like Ross!"

"Just the one?"

"Well, I'd welcome an entire kennel, but it's your call. You'll be the one working from home, taking them out all the time."

"When we're not hanging out in the shop's café," said Nick. "That's still cool, right?"

"Dog-friendly *is* Marwick's middle name, Crispin!"

Nick laughed and let go of her hand. He pulled a bag of Milk Bottles from his jacket pocket and offered his stash.

Evie crinkled her nose. "Oh, no thanks. I've never really been that fond."

Lips parting, Nick let out a laugh. "Eighteen years since we met and I'm *still* learning things about you. I thought you liked them!"

"I liked *you*. Back then I would've done anything to make you like me—even forcing down those rubbery monstrosities."

"And hate-watching *Grease 2*," Nick added with a wink.

"I actually enjoy it now."

"C'mon. *Really?*"

"I kept it, didn't I?" She grinned slowly.

"And my bowling shirt," he smiled. "It always did look better on you."

Evie leaned in. "Keeping them made me feel closer to you somehow."

"Yeah, I can understand that." Nick lowered the bag of candy and fussed with the neck of his white Henley. He pulled out something silver and shiny, something Evie had thought was a long-lost casualty of their shattered past.

She froze. "My necklace?! You still have it!"

"It's my most prized possession. I had to tuck it away for a while, but it's been to London and Tokyo, Greece and New York City. It was always with me, and in a way, so were you."

Smile iridescent, Evie reached up, her fingers caressing each cursive letter. "You did say you'd both come back to me." She blinked up, finding his loving gaze waiting.

"Some promises just take a little longer."

Letting go of her necklace, she stroked his cheek, the shadow of stubble tickling her fingers. "I really want us to make this work."

Nick nodded. "We will. We've both lived through enough heartache to know relationships aren't like fairy tales. They require care and attention. You can plant the seed, but if you don't water it, nothing will bloom." As Evie eased back, he wound his arm around her shoulders.

"Nothing except miscommunication." She sighed, happy. "Keeping secrets, even when you think you're doing it for the right reasons…never ends well."

"Amen to that." Nick looked up as the canopy of leaves whispered in the wind. "This…*this* is what I needed after this morning's conference call." His focus traveled downward, skimming the clusters of tiny flowers. "Serenity amidst the bluebells with my girl."

Evie studied the nearest tree, one of nearly seven hundred planted by a nature-loving gentleman named Edwin Harrold who once called Bankburn his home. Beech, oak, elm, and sycamore—common elsewhere, these trees struggled to prosper in Orkney but flourished here. *Just goes to show you.* She grinned, a joyful melody of birdsong greeting her ears as Nick's fingers weaved into the hair at the nape of her neck. *A little patience, some hard work, and a lot of love can grow into something beautiful and everlasting.*

"Your gran always hoped you'd fall for Orkney."

Nick nodded. "She knew what was best for me before I did, that's for sure. She loved these islands fiercely. Always said the open sea and sky would soothe whatever ailed me—*if* I gave it half a chance. And like always, she was right. I didn't appreciate this place when I was younger, but boy, do I now."

"Do you think you'll miss London?"

"I might a little, but I'll get my fix, popping down occasionally for work. That's what I love about technology these days. I can exec produce from almost anywhere, really. What matters most is waking up next to you each morning." He kissed her temple. "But the big question is, have *you* made a decision?"

"Yes. I think my days as an event caterer are over. I enjoyed the challenge of cooking on location, but Gemma's raring to go now and I've missed the shop."

"Your heart's desire," said Nick.

She nodded. "It really is."

"Lucky for me and my shortbread addiction."

Evie patted his stomach. "The perks of sleeping with the manager...who will be resting much easier going forward."

"Why is that?" asked Nick.

"The quote finally came in to fix the roof."

"And?"

"The *Tomlinson* fee will cover it and then some. They'll start next week before Mum's back." She nudged her hair away from her mouth. "I also spoke to Sam this morning."

"Oh really? Good! That's a start."

"He groveled a lot, and I *get it*, I do, so...I'm gonna forgive him."

A wry grin curved Nick's mouth. "The ol' Sutherland family's slow-to-forgive trait, gone forever. I'm proud of you, Evie."

"Have you forgiven him?"

"Yeah. At the end of the day, I can't blame Sam for loving you and protecting you. He was doing his job as your big brother. I wouldn't expect anything less."

"You're amazing, you know that?" She rested her head on his shoulder. "I can't wait to live with you."

Nick pulled back slightly, his expression playful. "So, I guess this means we're together-together?"

He remembers that? Blissful memories fluttered through Evie's mind of the night that changed everything: Nick's beer-stained shirt, stargazing on her backyard trampoline, and their first kiss...the first of so many. Her smile stretched with unbridled joy. "Yes-yes, Saxy Boy. Together-together, and this time it's for keeps."

EPILOGUE

EVIE

Saturday, August 10, a little less than a year in the future

Unzipping her raincoat as a welcome burst of sunshine blanketed a squelchy Bignold Park, Evie retrieved her phone from its front pocket. She leaned away from the railing and tilted the screen, fitting Nick into frame.

"Nice one, Rupes!" Her boyfriend applauded, celebrating Rupert's heifer calf capturing the top prize in its County Show category. Nick's backward ball cap, quilted plaid jacket, faded denim, and wellies were a far cry from his usual polka dots and designer labels.

Evie snapped several photos, capturing his enthusiasm for posterity. "Nikolai Balfour, I never thought I'd see the day!"

"Ye of little faith, Tigs!" Nick held his hand up in a wave as his grinning brother, dressed in a white lab coat and jeans, paraded his freckly grin and winning calf out of the ring. "Rupe's heifer was head and shoulders above the rest."

"No, I meant *you*, being totally into this." She looped her arms around his neck. "I love seeing you embracing your Orkney roots. It's so hot!"

"Yeah?" Hands slipping beneath Evie's coat and around her waist, Nick gathered her close, his fingers dipping into the top of her leggings. "Well, if you're up for it later, we could roleplay a scene from that film we watched last night. You know the one in the dairy house? I'll be the lonely, sex-starved farmer"—his darkening stare teased more than her mind—"and you'll be the feisty milk maid in the barn wearing nothing but a smile—"

"That'll scare the cows!" A just-arrived Fiona laughed cheerily, her two-month-old daughter, Lily—named after the Balfour's late

364

matriarch—snoozing in a BabyBjörn against her chest.

As Nick shifted backward, Evie dropped her hands from his shoulders and gazed lovingly at her newest goddaughter. "You would know, Fi!"

She smoothed Lily's wisps of light brown hair. "And I have *zero* regrets."

"We didn't think you were coming," said Nick.

"My friends from the Ness of Brodgar decided to come last minute. Excavation ends for good soon, so I wanted to see them before they leave."

He stuffed his hands in his jacket's pockets. "I bet they miss you at the dig."

"Yeah, but not as much as I miss them and all the cool discoveries we made last summer." Fiona peered down at Lily. "This is where I wanna be, though. Well, at least today I do." Glancing up, she fought back a yawn. "I just wish I could get her down for a full night."

"I can swing by tomorrow after the lunch rush?" offered Evie. "Bring you soup or take the girls for a bit, give you a break?"

"Oh, that would be *amazing*. Rupert's got meetings with the agricultural society, and I'd love a long soak with your latest book, which you still need to sign, lady."

"That's me told." Evie snickered. "I'll bring the candles we just got in, too. Their scent is super relaxing and not stinky. I know how much you hate that."

"Sounds heavenly!" Fiona kissed her baby's head. "Well, I should be getting back. It's almost time for Lily's feed. Have you seen Ava and Poppy about?"

"They're probably in the funfair with Sunita," said Nick.

Fiona's eyes widened. "Sun came? I thought she'd be busy packing."

"She was, but she wanted to see the girls one last time," said Evie. "Want to head that way?"

"Yeah." Fiona grinned as they started walking. "How are you guys? Have you heard from Jamie?"

"Not a peep," said Evie. "He's been super motivated since his promotion."

"Full-time shop assistant today, general manager tomorrow," said Nick, the funfair's music and laughter drifting closer on the breeze. "I reckon he knows a good thing might be on the horizon— maybe even the chance to be the first male in your family to run Marwick's."

"Yeah, if he plays his cards right, but he's in for a long wait! I'm not going anywhere and neither is Mum." Evie spied her waving mother with her dad in tow, lined up for the waltzer. "*Well*, except up and down on a rickety, old ride!"

"I didn't know they liked amusement park rides," said Fiona.

"They never used to," replied Evie. "Dreamworld in Australia has *a lot* to answer for."

Nick leaned in. "I hope we'll be like that." He raised his voice, fighting Taylor Swift's 'August' blaring from the ride's speakers. "Finding new hobbies to share when we're older."

Evie shared a smile with him as they sidled up to the queue. "Hey!"

"Having fun, kids?" Evie's dad tilted his head and let out an "Aww" as Fiona brought Lily closer, her hands protectively covering her baby's ears.

"Not as much as you two teenagers!" said Evie.

Marianne's grin morphed into a look of concern. "Actually, love, do you think we should head back soon? Make sure Jamie is on top of everything?"

Sometimes Evie thought her mother worried more about Marwick's than anything else. "Mum, don't worry. The shop's fine! If Jamie needs help, Gemma's in the kitchen, and I'm on speed dial."

"I know, but—" Marianne's shoulders dropped. "I'm doing it again, aren't I?"

"Yup!" said Graham, squeezing his wife's arm as the teenagers ahead of them claimed seats on the waltzer. "Let it go, love. Evie was fine working solo. Jamie will be, too."

"Old habits." Marianne stepped forward in line and turned suddenly. "Oh, Nick?"

"Yeah?" He rubbed Evie's back.

"Don't overdo it on the treats here. I baked two dozen cupcakes for dessert later."

Nick grinned. "Aw, cheers, Marianne. Can't wait."

Leaving behind the loud music blasting from the adult midway, Fiona removed her hands from Lily's tiny ears. "I love all this: Marianne baking for Nick, you two happily together with your dogs and gorgeous house. You know, I'm totally taking credit…"

"Here we go." Evie smiled and rolled her eyes.

"…'cause it was me who told you both to get over yourselves and *talk* already!"

Evie's brows rose. "*Both?*" She glanced at Nick. "She was harassing you, too?"

"Oh god yeah. In the makeup trailer, in line for the portaloos…"

Fiona looked pleased with herself. "Worked, though, didn't it."

"Mummy!" Darting through the crowd with a bright grin, Poppy clutched her mother's right leg, her fingers tinted fluorescent pink.

Sunita followed in her footsteps. "Eves, look! Pops bought you candy floss…" She handed over a paper cone, bare except for a sad wisp of pink fluff.

Fiona tsked as her middle daughter released her knee. "*Poppy!*"

"It was *yummy!*" She hopped on one leg, her latest quirk.

"It is! Thank you, sweetie." Evie pulled the sticky strand free and slipped it in her mouth as Poppy stomped in a muddy puddle, splashing Nick's wellies.

He didn't seem bothered, though. "Helicopter ride, Pops?"

"Pleeese, Nee-coh!"

Scooping Poppy up under her arms, Nick spun around and began humming "Gonna Fly Now", the theme from *Rocky*.

"Ava's with her friends." Sunita's announcement was soundtracked by Poppy's adorable airborne giggles. "Apparently, hanging with me is totally uncool now."

"Don't take it personally, Sun. Happens to the best of us," said Fiona. "What time's your flight?"

"Half five. I can't believe I'm leaving already. Feels like I just got here."

"Well, if you're missing us that much, you *could* skip sunny Spain in December and spend Christmas here instead…" Evie pouted for effect as Nick lowered a laughing Poppy to the ground. She wobbled and staggered like a pint-sized drunk.

"It's a deal—but *only* if Nick plays in the Ba'." Sunita pursed her lips in a dare as Evie collected dizzy Poppy's sticky hand.

"And let you miss out on all that delish turrón and sangria?" Nick countered with a nonchalant shrug. "I couldn't possibly!"

Evie laughed. "Did you get your first editor's letter finished?"

"Nearly," said Sunita. "I'll finish on the plane."

"My girl! Editor-in-chief of *Bella Faith* magazine—"

"Who's bringing back the Sexcapades column!" Fiona added. "How ironic is that?"

Sunita bobbed her head back and forth. "I know, I know! I used to make fun of it, but I'm hoping the revamped version will get teens talking about sex in a healthy manner."

"What? Like we did?" Fiona laughed, and Evie joined in. "Beach sex—*bad*!"

Nick's eyes narrowed. "Is it?"

Evie patted his arm. "I'll tell you later."

She did a double take, eyeing her bronzed brother in a white hoodie and faded jeans walking past the bouncy castle. Her grin reached her eyes. "Sammy!" She waved the floss-free cone until he headed her way. "Welcome back!" Still holding Poppy's hand, Evie leaned in for a one-armed hug.

"Nice tan!" said Sunita. "Majorca looks good on you."

After squeezing Evie, Sam let her go. "Does now." He grimaced. "Angus was calling me lobster legs for most of our trip."

"Where *is* Angus?" asked Nick. "He texted last night saying he'd check out the vintage cars with me. Haven't heard from him since."

"He got called out on a rescue," explained Sam. "It's nothing serious, someone stranded halfway to Rousay. What time you headed to Mum and Dad's?"

"Half four." Evie looked down as Poppy's wee fingers slid free from her palm. She hopped toward her mother. "After Nick drops Sun at the airport and I pick up Pretzel and Popcorn from home."

"I brought them back a few toys," said Sam.

Evie grinned. "Always spoiling your floofy niece and nephew."

"Of course! Work before play, though. I need to show my face at our booth, see how our doggie dental care promo is going. Catch you later, 'kay?" Sam waved in farewell.

"I'll bring bottles of Skull Splitter," hollered Nick, oblivious to Tarquin's arrival behind him with a squiggly Luke in his arms.

"I'd kill for one of those, the day I've had."

"Fatherhood not agreeing, Tarq?" Fiona held Poppy's hand.

"Luke stuck gummy bears up his nose this morning. Then at the walk-in clinic, he just starts stripping off, right in the waiting room."

Nick laughed. "Sounds like you at that age."

Tarquin snorted, not impressed. "Now he wants Leia and *only* Leia. She has a wedding dress to finish, so we're having a boys' day out, giving Mummy some space..."

Ruffling Luke's blond hair, Nick lulled his nephew into stillness, but as he withdrew his hand, the child roared like a tiger and kicked his feet, one of which barely missed Tarquin's nether regions.

Nick clenched his jaw. "*That* was close."

"If Luke remains an only child, now you know why." Tarquin tried to kiss his forehead, but his son's squirming ruined that idea. "He calms with you, Nico. You want to hold him?"

He narrowed his eyes. "Cheers, but I'll pass. I value my testicles too much."

Evie bit back a laugh.

Poppy pulled her gaze away from the ladybug carousel and blinked up at Fiona. "Mummy, what's test-gulls?"

"They're a type of seabird, sweetheart," Fiona chirped, unruffled. "Hey, why don't you go for one last ride on the *ladybugs*?"

"YEAHH!" Poppy squealed and tugged her forward.

"You coming, Eves?" asked Sunita.

"I'd love to, but I should circle back to the shop." Leaning in, she hugged her oldest friend. "I wish you weren't leaving."

Sunita kissed her on the cheek. "Why don't you fly down with Nico next month? We could catch a musical, hit up some bookshops while he films his *Dalston* cameo. Maybe you could even arrange a signing or two."

"Maybe, yeah."

"Think about it and let me know." Sunita withdrew from their embrace.

"See you tomorrow, Eves." Fiona waved. "Bye bye, Balfour bros!" Joining Sunita, she ushered Poppy toward the spinning tea-cups.

"This one needs some food." Tarquin adjusted Luke in his arms. "Text later, bro?"

"Sure. Say hi to Leia for us." Holding Evie's hand, Nick led her around a pack of meandering teens glued to their phones.

"It was great seeing everyone," said Evie. "Weather cleared, too."

"You know the best part?" asked Nick.

"My candy floss gift?" She smirked and dropped the empty cone into a trash can.

"We can love our nieces and nephew, spoil 'em rotten *then* go home—to our dogs!"

She swerved closer, planting a kiss on his clean-shaven cheek. "I wouldn't trade our life for anything."

"It's the best," smiled Nick. "I love our home. I love Pretzel and Popcorn. I love watching you write…"

"Really? Why?"

"I love that cute thing you do, pulling up the hood on your hoodie when you're on a roll."

She chuckled. "How else will I trap in all my creative ideas?"

"Like I said—too cute!" His gaze didn't waver as they walked. "How about something that'll make today even sweeter?"

Evie balked. "Ooh, no we shouldn't. Remember, Mum made cupcakes!"

"No, this is even better."

"Coming from the cupcake connoisseur himself?" She smirked. "Then this *must* be good."

Nick licked his lips. "My production company is optioning your novels for streaming."

Evie swore her heart stopped. Her feet definitely did. "*What the—?*" Their hands still tethered, her sudden halt snapped Nick back. Her jaw dropped. "But my agent hasn't—"

"I asked her not to. I begged her to let me share the news. I *had* to see your face when you heard." He brushed her bangs away from her widening eyes.

With the sting of tears rising, Evie clasped his arm tightly. "My god! *Nick!* I never dreamed my books would—" She laughed and hunched forward, giddy.

"Well, they are! The first three episodes of *Tomlinson* have netted huge ratings and the streaming services are falling all over themselves, desperate for the next big historical romance, and your books are *it*, babe. My partner will handle the financial negotiations, so expect a call soon."

"Wow. This is just…" Evie covered her mouth with her hand.

"The cherry on top?"

She nodded, lost for words.

Nick grinned smugly. "I told ya it was sweet."

Evie cradled his face in her hands. "*Thank you!*" She leaned in, kissing him tenderly on the lips. "For doing this for me."

"Hey, I did nothing. This is all you, Tigs. Your novels are so well researched and written they sold themselves."

How would he know? She cocked an eyebrow and looped her arms around his neck.

"What? I *have* read them, you know."

"When?!"

"Last year during the shoot, after I bought your signed book," said Nick. "But I didn't read that one straight away. I started with your debut and went from there. I love how they're all interconnected."

"God, I had no clue, you crafty bugger!" Evie playfully punched his arm. "I love *you* so much!"

"You know, I never get tired of hearing that." He smiled.

"I feel SO lucky!"

"Yeah, well, luck always plays a part in which books get adapted," said Nick. "And even when the rights are purchased, there's no guarantee they'll—"

"No, I'm not talking about that, Nick. I'm talking about *you*." Evie gazed into his eyes. "I don't know what might've happened if we weren't separated all those years ago, but I no longer think it matters. All that counts is we got *here*. The wrong turns, the detours…marauding Viking puppets—they all brought us here. Now."

"I couldn't agree more." Nick leaned in for a kiss, but his focus jumped up. "Oh, Tigs, you've got…"

She hastily rubbed her cheek. "Argh, do I have melted cheddar on my face again? I swear I wear more mac 'n' cheese than little Luke."

"No, it's an eyelash. May I?"

Evie nodded, and Nick tapped his index finger against the side of her nose. He presented the dark lash for perusal. "Go on, Sutherland, you know what to do." His dark eyebrow arched with anticipation.

"I would, but…" Evie's heart fizzed with joy. "It's already come true."

ACKNOWLEDGEMENTS

Thank you for reading *A Smile in a Whisper*! Like my other novels, this story was a true labor of love. Part of my family hails from the Orkney Islands, so after spending years researching my grandmother's Orcadian ancestors, visiting for the first time in 2018, and then writing *Say Hello, Kiss Goodbye* (with its Orkney chapters), I made a vow to write an entire love story set there—and now I have!

This novel was also another opportunity to portray mental health in a realistic and empathetic fashion. As an own voices author living with anxiety, panic attacks, and depression, I hope others like me will see themselves within these pages and know they are not alone or a burden.

I equally wanted to shine the spotlight on Crohn's disease. My husband has lived with it since he was a kid, has gone through multiple surgeries and treatments, and has always amazed me with his resilience and strength. I don't watch superheroes on the big screen because I live with one. I love you, Darren, and thank you so much for creating yet another stunning book cover!

My dear friend Maria MacKay was also a major help with the IBD representation in this book. No two IBD situations are the same and Maria graciously provided a female perspective on dealing with the disease. Thank you for being so forthright and informative, and for being such an awesome friend. I love you & miss you.

Sending massive thank-yous and squishy hugs to…

Kendra Towns: The beautiful Orkney photos on this book's cover and in many of my teasers are Kendra's work. She also patiently answered my endless questions, took me on the ferry to

Shapinsay, and made sure I ate lots of yummy home bakes. View her gorgeous photos on Instagram @CanadianGirl_Abroad.

Marlene Thomson: Last year, I experienced the best of Orkney with the best company, and left the islands with a tummy full of cake, a heart brimming with memories, and a friend for life. She answers all my island queries with knowledge and humor—she's awesome! If you're planning a visit to Orkney, book Marlene online at MyOrkneyTours.co.uk.

Jenna Rubaii: While writing, I finally saw my favorite musical, *Jesus Christ Superstar*, live on stage—a dream come true! —and met Jenna Rubaii who played Mary Magdalene so brilliantly. Jenna gave me loads of insight into the workings of a *JCS* tour. She's lovely and talented and I adore her. Follow Jenna on Instagram @jrubaii.

Love and many thanks to photographer Phil Chester for the wonderful couple image on the cover, the always incredible Caitlin (Editing by C. Marie) for her eagle-eyed editing, the teams at Grey's Promotion and Tandem Collective for book buzz, my beta and sensitivity readers, and lovely Melena who manages the Keeganites United romance book club in my Facebook group.

Cheers to Torquil Campbell from the one of the best bands on the planet—Stars—who wrote and recorded "We Smile When We Whisper" to celebrate Evie and Nikolai in song. Listen on my website (www.JacquelynMiddleton.com).

Much love to my family and friends and my floofy boy Charlie. You are *everything*.

Last but never least…to the members of my Facebook group, Keeganites United and all my faithful readers, as well as the librarians, bloggers, reviewers, bookstagrammers, and booktokkers who love books like I do—THANK YOU! You make the book community sing! This indie author will always be grateful for your support of my love stories for hopeful romantics. You rock! xoxo

GLOSSARY

Some people, places, and things mentioned in *A Smile in a Whisper* might not be familiar to all readers. Here are a few helpful explanations.

Bairn: Scottish word for child

Beuy: Orcadian greeting when a male addresses another male

Bigsy: Orcadian word for conceited

Blethering: Scottish word for talking a load of nonsense

Blowin' a hoolie: A strong gale/wind

Broch: Conical stone towers built in the Iron Age and unique to Scotland, pronounced "brock". What they were used for is still up for debate.

Clootie dumpling: A Scottish dessert of spices, dried fruit, oatmeal, and flour, boiled in a 'cloot', which means cloth.

Croft: Unique to Scotland, a croft is a small area of agricultural land situated on a much larger estate. The people who work this land—crofters—are usually tenants who grow vegetables and raise animals. Some crofts also have a small stone dwelling on the land.

Curly doddies: Orcadian word for clover blooms, both the red and white varieties

Doonies: One of the two teams who battle in the Ba'. Traditionally, males would be designated as a Doonie (short for doon the gates) if they were born north of the Mercat Cross, which stands in front of St. Magnus Cathedral. The arrival of the new hospital in the 1950s, however, gave the Uppies an unfair advantage, so allegiance is now based on which team your father and grandfather played for.

Dry stone dykes: Stone walls constructed without cement, a technique dating back to the Neolithic Age.

Equity card: The membership card Nick would have as a member of Equity, the British union for the performing arts and entertainment industries.

Kiss-chase: A British schoolyard 'game' where children chase each other and kiss

Octopush: UK name for underwater hockey

Old Kirk: An old church

Otters holding hands: It's true! Sea otters (of which Orkney has plenty) do hold hands while sleeping, so they don't float away from their group.

Puggie/Puggy: Orcadian word for stomach

Second unit: An additional, usually reduced crew filming a TV series or film at another location

Selkies: Gray seals

Swadge: I love this Orcadian word! Can be a verb (swadging: to kick back and relax after a yummy meal) or a noun (a swadge: a rest after eating).

Tattie: Potato

Uppies: One of the two teams who battle in the Ba'. Traditionally, males would be designated as an Uppie (short for up the gates) if they were born south of the Mercat Cross, which stands in front of St. Magnus Cathedral. The arrival of the new hospital in the 1950s, however, gave the Uppies an unfair advantage, so allegiance is now based on which team your father and grandfather played for.

MENTAL HEALTH RESOURCES

**If you or someone you know suffers from
anxiety, panic attacks, or depression, help is available.**

United States
Anxiety and Depression Association of America
www.adaa.org

Canada
The Canadian Mental Health Association (CMHA)
www.cmha.ca

United Kingdom
Mind
www.mind.org.uk

IBD SUPPORT AND RESOURCES

United States
Crohn's and Colitis Foundation
www.crohnsandcolitisfoundation.org

Canada
Crohn's and Colitis Canada
https://crohnsandcolitiscanada.ca

United Kingdom
Crohn's and Colitis UK
https://crohnsandcolitis.org.uk

MEET MY OTHER BOOKS!

My novels are written as standalones.
However, they're all interconnected
and take place in the same 'Middleton Universe',
so characters from one book often appear in another.

LONDON BELONGS TO ME
Contemporary coming-of-age story with a touch of romance

LONDON, CAN YOU WAIT?
Contemporary romance and the sequel to *London Belongs to Me*;
however, it can be read as a standalone.

UNTIL THE LAST STAR FADES
Blurs the line between contemporary romance and women's fiction

SAY HELLO, KISS GOODBYE
Contemporary romance
Sex positive and (you've been warned) *very* steamy!

THE CERTAINTY OF CHANCE
Christmas in London contemporary romance
One of *Entertainment Weekly*'s best holiday romances of 2021

All titles available in paperback and ebook from all major retailers.
London Belongs to Me is also available as an audiobook.
Content notes (language, heat levels, etc.)
can be found on my website under the 'Books' tab.

.

A Smile in a Whisper

Enjoyed Evie and Nikolai's story?
Please consider leaving a review on the retailer's website.

Stay in touch!
Follow Jacquelyn:

Instagram: @JaxMiddleton_Author
Facebook: JacquelynMiddletonAuthor
Twitter: @JaxMiddleton
and join her private Facebook readers group
to hear book news first, participate in her book club,
and have the chance to enter exclusive giveaways.

Visit Jacquelyn's website
for book playlists, behind-the-scenes exclusives,
and to sign up to her newsletter.
www.JacquelynMiddleton.com